RICHARD UPRISING
PATRICK SILKEN

Copyright

Dedication

This novel is dedicated to my family. This is what I was doing in the basement during COVID.

Table of Contents

First Amendment

"Congress shall make no law respecting an establishment of religion, or prohibiting the free exercise thereof; or abridging the freedom of speech, or of the press; or of the right of the people peaceably to assemble, and to petition the Government for a redress of grievances."

**United States Constitution - Original Version Circa September 2024

Chapter One

The house lights cut off sharply.

Some in the crowd twitched at the sudden change in light. In normal times, darkening house lights would have simply signaled to the audience that the show was about to start. Yet this gathering was anything but normal. These spectators were on edge. Most nervously milled around and occasionally glanced up from their phones or their conversations in order to survey the dimensions of the warehouse that was recently converted into a makeshift concert hall. Before the makeover, it was a stereotypical industrial building. It even had soot stain streaks on the walls. Whoever designed it didn't expect a large gathering of concert goers. In fact, the only functional entrance and exit point was a large bay door in the warehouse's front. The door was too small for everyone to escape during a stampede. Other potential escape routes were narrow doors in the corners of the room. Most of the windows had cracks running through them, which caused the imbedded steel octagonal grids to appear angular and uneven. The most anxious among the audience imagined how those windows could double as escape hatches if the worst happened. Smart ones planned their escape route in advance.

The sudden change in light dilated the audience's pupils. After a few seconds, their eyes adjusted, allowing them to focus on the semi-transparent sheet that enveloped the stage. There was a soft amber light behind the curtain. The back light barely illuminated the shadow of a tall human figure who stood behind a blurred microphone stand.

A momentary burst of feedback pierced out from the speakers, causing the audience to recoil as the figure spoke.

"Hello New York City!"

Mentioning the hometown always was a crowd pleaser.

"Thank you so much for coming tonight and, on behalf of everyone in this warehouse, we welcome and thank you for coming. It truly means everything to us. Despite it all, you keep coming to our shows. And by the way, it's great to be back in our hometown. Believe me, I know it's getting more and more dangerous to do this, so thank you, from my heart, thank you."

The congregation reacted with a smattering of applause and whistles of appreciation as they settled in. They hoped the concert would meet the hype and justify the potential danger of attending one of these shows. Anyone who attended understood that it might cost them dearly. Some came for the thrill of an unauthorized show. Some came as an act of defiance. All had one thing in common. They were tired of being afraid.

"In case you didn't know who you were coming to see tonight, I'm Richard Uprising and I'm part of a band called MicroAggression and we are here to do three things."

Richard paused after that statement to give any new fans a chance to wonder what was coming next.

"First, we're here to entertain you, and second, we are here to blow the fucking doors off of the Speech Codes. All you snowflakes can get your candy assess out the door now since this is your one and only trigger warning." The audience chuckled and applauded, but no one left.

"Be warned, some might find our words offensive. Some might find the same words funny. But in the end, they are just words. No one will leave this place with an actual injury from us. For my money, those damn speech laws aren't worth the toilet paper they're printed on, and I guarantee you that if you keep coming, we'll keep playing."

Laughter, hoots, and hollers echoed back to Richard, and he absorbed them all.

He smiled and said, "Oh, I forgot to tell you the third thing we're here to do tonight..."

Now louder applause and even a few screams emanated from the audience. Things were starting off well as the crowd seemed pumped, so he gave them one of his signature opening lines.

"The third thing we're here to do is ROCK AND KICK ASS!"

That line signaled to the band that it was showtime. A pale blue light pierced through the warehouse and Simon, the drummer, started the show.

Thump tha tha thump thump,

Thump tha tha thump thump.

It started as a slow, cold, lonely beat that evoked a sonic vision of a series of icicles hanging off of a long-abandoned house as they slowly dripped themselves out of existence. Simon paused for a moment and resumed with a slightly quickened tempo. He repeated the taps until they grew louder into a demanding rhythm.

A white spotlight joined the pale blue one, and both beams glared from the back of the stage. Together, they formed a perfect visual complement to the drum rhythm. The blaze of light illuminated a distorted shadow of the drum kit that splashed across the sheet. Simon's outline hovered over it as he struck the snare and the cymbals in perfect time. The coordinated movements of his arms and the natural wavering of the sheet blurred the line between instrument and musician, causing the images to consume each other until they formed a pulsing, amorphous silhouette.

Listeners swayed and moved in lockstep with the beat. The sheet rippled a bit more. This caused a shimmering effect on the shroud covering the stage. The shadow of the drum kit started to undulate and flow. The viewers' movements caused air to flow against the sheet and as it waved harder, the flickering effect became more prominent.

Another spotlight shot through the back left side of the stage. This time, the light cast a shadow of Trent, the bass player, as he picked at his four strings.

Bum bum bummm bummm bum bum.

The low octave notes hummed in perfect harmony with the rat-a-tat of the drums. The two outlines spoke to both the crowd and each other through their strings and their sticks.

Thump tha tha thump thump.

Bum bum bummm bummm bum bum.

Thump tha tha thump thump.

Bum bum bummmm bummm bum bum.

Simon and Trent continued their musical conversation until Cat Chaotic, the guitarist, scratched his guitar pick up and down his fret board. The resulting caterwaul of sound drowned the drums and bass out for a measure.

Sccccreeeeccccchhhh.

Cat then angrily jabbed his pick at his strings and caused high-pitched, angular sounds to shriek from his amplifier. He hit some notes hard, so they reverberated through the venue.

The three-part dialog between the drums, bass, and guitar grew louder as Richard stood motionless behind the microphone stand. The angle of the backlighting caused his outline to grow. His shadow loomed large over the rest of the band. He slowly spread his arms out and moved his hands toward himself, urging the crowd to give him more of a reaction. Some obliged by knocking into each other as their bodies writhed to the beat. Some collisions were intentional, some were not. None of the participants seemed to notice or care that they invaded each other's personal space. Instead, they forgot their fears and lost themselves in the music. They only cared about the moment.

Richard pointed at the audience as if he was giving them his approval of their adulation and slowly raised the mic back up to his mouth. He cocked his head down, closed his eyes, and cast his head downward toward his boots.

"These were the scrolls that bore his name," he sang, but his voice was barely audible.

"He was a minor pawn in the game."

Waves of chaotic, sharp notes from the guitar rolled through the crowd. The room filled with echoing, intense music. Some in the crowd stood still, fixated on the stage. Some danced slowly, some violently. The moment consumed everyone.

"With the stroke of a scribe, he's now erased." Richard's voice was only slightly louder than his opening lines.

"His name and face are now debased."

Richard paused and pointed with his left hand, and an eight-foot-wide section of the sheet fell to the floor. The rest of the covering of the stage remained intact, but the spotlight now pierced directly into the crowd through the gap. The opening in the sheet was wide enough that Trent was visible to the audience, but the rest of the band remained obscured.

"They wiped his page out of the book." Richard yelled.

"And splayed his carcass on a hook,"

Thump tha tha thump thump.

Bum bum bummmm bummm bum bum.

Scccccreeeeecccccchhhh.

Once the guitarist finished his last riff, the rest of the sheet dropped, exposing MicroAggression to the crowd.

Richard was now fully visible to his fans. His head remained tilted downward, and his eyes stayed shut. It was as if he was in a trance. His black hair was messy, teased out in all directions, with strands falling into his eyes. It was hot in the warehouse and the black leather jacket he wore caused his body temperature to skyrocket. Sweat dripped down his face, his dark eyeliner ran. The openings in his ripped jeans did little to ease the heat. He also wore a long sleeve shirt. This top layer partially obscured a black tee shirt, revealing only a jumbled set of jagged white lines.

"Damnatio Memoriae,"
"Ends a problem that could persist."
"Damnatio Memoriae,"
"Wrongs rights without fists,"
Richard crouched down. One black boot was slightly in front of the other. The microphone remained in his right hand, nearly touching the floor. He raised the mic again to his lips.
"Damnatio Memoriae,"
"Ends a problem that could persist."
"Damnatio Memoriae,"
"Wrongs rights without fists,"
The spectators kept moving to the beat, hypnotized by Richard's voice and the booming sounds of the drums and bass and the piercing wails of the guitar.

Unfortunately, they didn't notice a series of lasers that penetrated through the broken windows and formed red dots on various points on the stage.

"Thank you, thank you, thank you very much."

Richard smiled nervously as he thanked his supporters. He quickly surveyed the show for any anomalies. These days he couldn't be too careful. The band had run into trouble in the past with protests, bomb threats, hurled bottles, and even lawsuits. He kept his guard up every time he performed. Richard figured that those types of problems came with the territory when you challenged intolerant individuals. After all, they wouldn't take his provocation lying down. What he couldn't handle was someone getting hurt. Nothing would stop him from performing, but it only took one idiot to do catastrophic damage.

"You guys know we would never, ever get a normal venue to host our shows. None of the ticketing agencies will even touch us, but just remember that whenever you see our stickers posted at the usual clubs, it means we've scheduled a show or have something else for you. We gave you guys the codes so only fans can find the venue. It sucks for our ticket sales, but it's the only way we can keep the brown shirts out. We're still in deep trouble..."

Richard didn't need to remind the audience that MicroAggression concerts violated the Speech Codes. He warned his fans of the danger they were in at every show he put on. He couldn't be too careful. Just showing up at a MicroAggression concert was an enormous risk.

This was because a small but vocal group started a movement to change the First Amendment's protection of all speech. Congress obliged and, with the help of a weak president, they changed the First Amendment to only protect "non-offensive" speech, whatever the fuck that meant. Everyone knew that the "non-offensive" qualifier meant whatever the powerful people wanted it to mean. The elites distorted the line between offensive and non-offensive and guess whose interpretation always won out? At least there were no criminal sanctions on unprotected speech. Well, not yet anyway.

"So, since we are clearly on the wrong side of the fascist regime anyway, let's kick it up a notch and turn it over to my boy Cat Chaotic for the next one. What do you think?"

The crowd responded with a mix of cheers and nervous laughter. Longtime fans knew Cat sang some of the band's most offensive songs. He stepped up to his microphone and strummed a few notes on his black Schecter Platinum Series guitar. Physically, he had a similar look to Richard. He was slightly taller, more muscular, and probably outweighed Richard by 50 pounds. Cat wore a long-sleeved collared shirt over a retro concert tee shirt. He didn't have his leather jacket on. Richard had a much better heat tolerance. Cat's hair was light brown and spiky, but he kept the sides short, so it was less of a rat's nest. Shorter hair usually prevented the spikes from flopping into his eyes when he played. Not this time. Some hair drooped into his eyes. It was boiling on stage and the warehouse had awful ventilation. He brushed the hair away. He was glad it didn't flop while he was playing. Cat was also glad he ditched the eyeliner. Had he painted his face, he would have had black streaks running down to his jaw by now. He checked his cuffs to make sure his hands were clear. He needed to play fast and hit every note cleanly in the next song. The sound effect he used caused the guitar to sound like a sitar, which gave the melody a distinctive middle eastern feel. Once he played his warmup notes, a good chunk of the audience knew exactly what was coming, and they cheered.

Richard signaled to Cat that he needed one more minute to tune his guitar, so Cat engaged the crowd.

"I think I can handle the next one Richard." Cat responded, knowing that some of their biggest fans were getting primed for an old favorite and that their new converts were about to hear a big "fuck you" to the Speech Codes.

"While Richard gets his shit together, I'll introduce the rest of us MicroAggressions. On bass, we've got my friend Trent. He's been with Richard and me since the beginning, so if any of you remaining snowflakes need to blame anyone for your hurt feelings, you can include Trent in your sorry ass pity party."

"Gee, thanks Cat." Trent didn't miss a beat in perfect deadpan.

The crowd chuckled at that line. Even Cat laughed.

He continued. "And keeping time on the drums is our good friend Simon. He just joined the band, so make sure you go on your phones now to find him on social media and cancel him."

Cat strummed a totally unnecessary power chord. He was playing lead guitar on this song, so he plucked a few notes to make sure his mind wouldn't wander and play the wrong riff.

"Richard, I just hit a personal record. Correct me if I'm wrong, but did I speak for thirty seconds without offending anyone? Is that right? Can't be."

Cat then corrected himself.

"Oh, come on, of course I offended someone. No one can speak that long in this day and age without someone posting online how unhappy they are."

"Richard, are you done with your guitar yet? I'm out of jokes. They don't want to hear me talking anymore, so what do you think they want to hear? I've got one that's going to blow the roof off this place. What do you think?"

Richard smirked and deadpanned to the crowd, "I'm ready Cat, but don't tell me you're going to play *that* one. Our dictator in chief Ramirez will not like it. I mean, she might get upset..." He was setting Cat up for the perfect intro line.

"Yeah, well fuck Ramirez, fuck her and her fucking band of Nazis, gimme a count, Richard."

"One, Two, Three, Four."

Once Richard finished the count, Cat unleashed a guitar jam that transported listeners to a Byzantine Bazaar. After the noisy intro, Cat began singing.

"I spent a lifetime running on a day in Algiers,"

"I tried to flee my mind, but couldn't dismiss my fears,"

"The slaughter I committed and the Muslim I remitted."

"Burned an image in my eye that I justified,"

"With a homicide."

"One day in Algiers."

The song had a fast beat and a bass line that pumped a raucous underlying tone that meshed perfectly with the quick pacing of the drums. Simon kept perfect time by punctuating every fourth measure with a huge double crash of the cymbals. After a brief guitar solo overwhelmed the other instruments, Cat continued,

"I live far away from my time in Algiers,"

"My body may be here, but my mind is in tears."

"I've wasted time repenting, and the Muslim now is nothing."

"Now I'm petrified."

"I want to be purified."

"Of a day in Algiers."

As the song wound down, there was some feedback coming from Cat's amplifier. He gestured to Richard, signaling that he needed a moment to tune his guitar. Richard spoke to the audience again.

"Well, we've got plenty more for you tonight and I know you all must really want to be here ..." Richard trailed off, struck by someone in the crowd. It was a girl in the front row. She had to be in her early twenties. She had jet black and pink hair teased up similar to Richard's, and she had drawn out her eye makeup to make her face appear as if she could pose in an Egyptian hieroglyphic. As striking as her appearance was, what caught his eye was the tee shirt she wore. It was a black one from MicroAggression's first tour. The old shirt depicted Richard's face in a comic book style. His eyes filled with tears, and he fought to control himself.

"Sorry, I didn't mean to stop there. I just, well, I just saw that lady in the front, and she's got a shirt on. There's a much younger me on that shirt. I just can't believe that I am still doing this. I mean, we are, despite it all, playing music all these years later and you guys keep coming. It's just so surreal. If I could say something to that earlier me, I would tell him that, man, shit is going to get crazy, but you know what? It's all going to be worth it. You people are worth it. The guys in the band are worth it, and this country is worth it. I can't thank you enough for showing up despite the Speech Codes."

Cheers filled the room as Richard paused and absorbed the moment. He treated every concert he played as if it was his last, and this one was no exception. However, he had a nagging feeling that he had spoken excessively. Time to sing.

"Cat, Trent, Simon ... enough talking ... IT'S TIME TO WAIL."

With a power chord slide, Cat sent a heavy metal rock explosion through his guitar. It was loud, but the crowd could still hear Richard as he screamed through his microphone:

"Weeeee've got an invading problem, and it just won't stop."

"Wave after wave up from the south."

"There's no more room or money to pay the freight."

"The drugs come up in titanic weight."

"The cartels get rich, and the children get pimped."

"But the rich don't care as long as that lettuce gets picked."

"BUILD THE WALL, BUILD THE WALL."

"BUILD BUILD BUILD BUILD BUILD THE BORDER WALL."

The crowd pulsed. They created a mosh pit where participants collided. A large part of the audience shifted to escape the violence. One person wasn't paying attention and got knocked over. Thankfully, three of the combatants stopped to pick him up.

Build the Wall was a fan favorite. It captivated everyone in the audience.

Unfortunately, no one noticed a silver sphere fly through the window and land in the mosh pit.

It was a grenade.

It spun on its side before someone kicked it. Then it exploded in the middle of the crowd.

The flash caught almost everyone's attention. The mosh pit distracted others. Unfortunately, some fans thought it was part of the show.

They were wrong.

Upon hearing the blast, Richard quickly turned and observed the smoke. Out of the corner of his eye, he saw a red spurt spew out from Simon's head. Simon twitched and then fell forward and slumped over his drum set.

Richard's eyes widened in terror as he realized what was about to happen. He'd received threats. The band took precautions. He never thought that this would happen.

Black-clad figures invaded the warehouse like ants swarming a dead frog.

Bullets ripped through the crowd. The rounds cut the audience into pieces, and blood splattered everywhere. Those who could run raced in a panic toward any exit they could find. Their footsteps smeared the wet blood as they skidded across the floor. Others stumbled over bullet-riddled bodies, leaving themselves vulnerable to becoming the invaders' next victim.

Richard hopped off the stage and steadied himself as he hit the floor. He first looked at the corner doors. Bodies piled in front of those exits, so none of them were an option. Then he looked at the front door. It was wider and only partially blocked. That was his best chance to escape. He took off running into the scrum of bodies.

Two intruders saw him and ran to cut him off in the middle of the room. The lead one got within five feet of Richard. He lowered his shoulder and tried to tackle him at the waist. Just as he lunged at Richard, his foot skidded through a pool of blood, and he fell on his side. He wasn't the only one on the ground. Several bodies had piled up, preventing Richard from getting out. He realized he had no chance of getting to the large bay door. Richard faked to his left before running diagonally toward an exit on the right side. He stopped to make sure his path was clear and suddenly felt something thump against his head.

At first, he was more shocked than hurt, but then he stumbled.

The other black-clad figure had bashed him with the butt of his rifle, hitting him squarely in the temple. He pounced on Richard, tackling him to the floor, and used his full body weight to hold him down. As the effects of the blow faded, Richard tried to orient himself, only to find his hands restrained by handcuffs. He tried to wriggle his body, but someone had a knee on the back of his neck so he couldn't move. He felt breath pulsate on his left ear and heard a whisper, "Hey Richie." The deepness of the voice surprised him, as he had only experienced female voices whispering in his ear.

All Richard could utter was a bewildered, "What the fuck?"

The attacker grabbed onto the handcuffs and pulled on them to make sure they were secure. He rose and yanked Richard's arms, forcing him to stand.

Richard was alone with his attackers in the slaughterhouse. The only other ones left were the dead and the dying.

Someone shoved him from behind. A voice said, "Go get the camera". Then he felt someone grab his other arm and push him toward the stage, causing him to stumble. As he righted himself, he looked directly at the stage and fixed his eyes on a mangled female figure with black and pink hair crumpled over in a heap. He could only shake his head.

"Got it, boss," a high-pitched voice spoke from behind him. The second voice was definitely male but higher in pitch, almost cartoon like. He also had a subservient tone. High pitch was definitely not in charge.

"Good, set up over there. I want to get the stage in the shot."

The lower pitch voice asked, "You got the camera set up, right? Are we rolling?"

"Yes, we're ready."

Two captors spun him around toward the camera. The leader stood in front of Richard with his back toward him. Without turning around, he took off his black mask and helmet, which caused a mess of sweaty blond hair to pour out from the top of his head. He faced the camera and spoke:

"Okay, well, ladies, gentleman, oops, sorry, I mean good evening to all genders and identifications. Have we got a treat for you?" He sounded like a ringmaster at the circus as he urged his audience to plunk down a nickel to see a freak show.

"You've seen the footage of the 'concert' that Richard Uprising and MicroAggression played just a few moments ago, and now he's going to pay for his offensive conduct."

Silence filled the room, interrupted only by the ringmaster's voice and the occasional cries of pain from dying spectators.

"Richard Uprising has no regard for the feelings of others and how his behavior triggers severe psychological reactions in the oppressed, the taken advantage of, and the discriminated against. You heard him. He thinks it's funny to kill Muslims and make fun of asylum seekers and other dreamers. We've had enough of his vile brand of hate and anyone like me who has ever had the misfortune of witnessing any of his other concerts knows that he's a racist white supremacist."

He gestured to the men who were holding Richard, and they removed his leather jacket and his shirts so that they could fully expose his chest.

"This is the height of white male privilege and now we're striking back against him, and others like him." A hand appeared and covered Richard's mouth with a gag. "Little Richie is about to get loud for the very last time."

The ringmaster pulled a medical scalpel from his pocket and disengaged it from the protective sheath. He walked over to Richard and stopped about a foot in front of him. He moved aside slightly so the camera could fully capture what was about to unfold.

"This will not end well for you, Richie boy..."

Richard tried to speak. He fought the bandanna gag with his teeth, but all that came out was a spattering of drool and a muffled sound that vaguely resembled something like, "go fuck yourself."

"What's that Richie?" the ringmaster asked.

"I believe he just told me to commit an unnatural act on myself and I think he wants to say something else, but, really, hasn't he said enough?"

"There will be no encore tonight." The ringmaster laughed and pushed the scalpel into the upper left side of Richard's abdomen and cut diagonally across his stomach. Blood spilled out of the wound, and Richard screamed in agony. He tensed up and his body spasmed like he was trying to twist himself away from the ringmaster's cutting, but his executioners held him in place.

After he cut the first diagonal slash, the ringmaster once more stabbed Richard's torso, specifically aiming for the upper right part of his stomach. Richard continued squirming and contorted his body as the blade dragged through his body, completing the letter X.

The blood spill became a gush. Richard's intestines and other organs were now visible to the camera, just as his executioners intended.

The ringmaster turned back to the camera and brandished the scalpel like a laser pointer at a lecture before he aimed it back at Richard.

"Make no mistake, the blood is on *his* hands and *he's* getting what he deserves. He is the one who likes to offend. He is the oppressor. We tolerated this man's behavior way too long and now Richard Uprising must pay the price. Let this be a lesson to anyone else out there that chooses such a path."

The camera panned back and focused on Richard. He was pale. Blood trickled from his stomach and the life disappeared from his eyes.

The shot lingered on Richard's lifeless body for several moments, much longer than necessary, belaboring the point. A few moments later, the image of Richard's corpse faded into darkness, but the audio continued. The ringmaster chuckled and uttered one last remark.

"Ladies, gentlemen, and everyone else, Richard Uprising, has left the building."

Chapter Two

Cat rounded a corner and leaned up against a wall and wheezed. He had been running for at least a half hour and congratulated himself. He had just run thirty minutes longer than he had ever run in the last ten years. Running was never his thing. He was, however, scared shitless. And fear helped him run really, really fast.

"Why ... am I ... going there... again?" The question crossed his mind in a cadence that mirrored his labored breaths.

Cat was one of the first ones to notice the terrorists entering the warehouse. This gave him an advantage because his pathway out of the massacre was relatively clear. While the smoke, explosions, and gunfire shocked and disoriented others in the building, he ran to one of the corner doors. Just as he was about to get away, an attacker blocked his path. As luck would have it, Cat had taken his guitar with him, and he used it to club the assassin over the head. He cut his arm on something as he escaped, but he was otherwise fine physically. He had some doubts about his mental state.

"Oh, yeah..." he answered himself. "Need to get that."

He was having a hard time focusing on the task at hand. In fact, his mind drifted into some strange areas while he made his mad dash away from the concert. In fact, Cat thought about his grocery list, a vacation he was planning, and a flashback to a fight he had with his ex-wife. He thought about anything and everything except the concert. He worried that his lack of concentration could cause him to make a mistake. One wrong move could cost him his life.

Thoughts raced, adrenaline waned, exhaustion crept in. He was going home to get his money, gun, and other necessary items to escape from the city. Most importantly, he needed to get his fake passport and his hacked travel token so that he could become 'Kevin Reilly' and disappear on the first train out of the city. His plan was risky, but he really didn't have any other options. He never thought to bring his "travel bag" to the show. If he had, he would already be in New Jersey.

With his escape plan settled, his thoughts shifted and his mind took him to an even stranger place than his grocery list. He flashed back to a long dead and buried memory that seemed to serve no purpose. Why wasn't he focused on the details of his plan to get away? Wasn't that more important than his grocery list or reminiscing about his past? Unfortunately, his brain had other ideas.

Oddly, the event his mind replayed for him occurred a long time ago. Back when things made sense. There was a certain order to events, symmetry of cause and effect. Unlike now, as his life currently seemed like a series of random events. Moments followed each other in no discernible order. Well, no order that was apparent to him, anyway.

His mind recalled a day in the past, a typical morning, when he headed to the office. Cat never expected that this day would hold anything extraordinary. Turned out he was wrong.

Cat sat down at his desk, booted up his computer, and waited for his email to start up. He finished the last drops of his coffee and mentally reviewed his "to do" list. Cat, being a creature of habit, always began his day in the same way. He glanced at his unread emails, searching for any west coast fire drills that flared the night before. Nothing urgent, so he reviewed this morning's emails. Most were junk. Except this one.

CARL - COME SEE ME ASAP.

Cat noticed it was from his boss, Bryan. He sent it fifteen minutes ago. Cat wasn't late for work, so this was really odd.

He re-read the subject line:

CARL - COME SEE ME ASAP.

It was in all caps. He also noticed that there was only one word in the email. "Thanks."

Uh oh.

Immediately, his mind raced through the potential reasons his boss would send such a message first thing in the morning. There couldn't be a performance issue. All of his projects were under control. In fact, he had completed or was ahead of schedule on most of them. Could it be his numbers? Highly unlikely as he exceeded his target this quarter and outperformed the rest of the year. He didn't have any shit storms raging, so an empty email with that subject line was unusual.

Uh oh.

Then, he had a conflicting idea. Could it be the long-awaited promotion to Assistant Vice President? If that was the case, then a cryptic email was a strange way to inform him of the good news. An empty email in all caps was the best way to give him a heart attack, not promote him. It was also poor corporate etiquette, even for a schmuck like Bryan.

Either way, this was something big. He got up and walked down the aisle of cubicles to the corner office where his boss sat.

As usual, his nerves caused a mild flush to creep into his face. He recognized the familiar sensation of chills running down his spine. Those feelings usually occurred before a "you're fired" discussion. This time was different, though. If they were firing him, then this was a total blindside hit. Couldn't be that. He would have seen it coming. He brushed away all those happy thoughts of a promotion and replaced them with feelings of dread. His intuition warned him that this one would be worse. In retrospect, he would have preferred that they had just fired him.

"Hey Bryan, you wanted to see me?" he declared to his boss in his best falsely confident voice.

"Yes, come in and sit down and close the door."

"Close the door?" He thought to himself. This wasn't good.

"Hold on one second." His boss clicked his video link app, and, after a few rings, he heard a female voice come through the computer's speakers.

"Hey Allison, it's Bryan. Carl McKnight is here in my office."

"Hey Bryan, Hi Carl." It was Allison in Human Resources, and her video feed appeared on his screen.

Shit.

"Hi Allison" Carl croaked. His false confidence façade had cracked. This was no promotion.

Bryan turned his chair to face him and pulled out a paper from beneath a notepad. Carl noticed the document contained double-spaced text across a few pages. It looked like a script.

As Bryan started reading from the page, any doubt Carl had that it was a script vanished.

"Carl, thank you for coming in today. We have made the difficult decision to end your employment with the company. As you know, you are an 'at-will' employee, and the company can fire you for any reason as long as it is not a reason that is prohibited by applicable law. And this is not a prohibited reason."

Carl's mind swirled. Where the hell did this come from? He noticed a dull ringing in his ears that only happened when something strange occurred. It sounded like a low hum at the moment. But it was about to get louder.

"Allison, I'm about to show Carl the video, so make sure you keep your camera on and that we are recording."

"Okay, will do." Allison responded flatly.

"Carl, we recently received a video where you displayed conduct that does not meet the standards of this company. It's highly offensive, and we have decided that we need to part ways."

Bryan swiveled back to his computer and made a few clicks on his mouse. A flash popped, and the screen turned to white noise before an image of what looked like a college student's apartment appeared. Junk filled the room. In the background, there was an old, worn-out couch. Beer signs hung on the walls. The video quality was poor. So bad that it looked like someone had uploaded it from a VHS tape or some other outdated form of media.

Carl's heart sank as soon as he saw the apartment. Now it all made sense.

The video camera shifted its focus to a chair, revealing a younger Carl slouched in a recliner. He wore ripped jeans and a paisley dress shirt over a black concert tee shirt. His hair was long, teased out to look like his favorite rock star. He enjoyed channeling the eighties new wave rock era while he was in college. It was a good look for him. But that was before he had to grow up, cut his hair, and change his clothes. He changed everything just so he could get a job and get fired.

Cat had his feet up on an ottoman and the tongue of his white high tops was sticking out of his shoe. He was reaching down to remove his sneaker when he looked up directly at the camera. His eyes were glassy, and it was abundantly clear he had consumed plenty of alcohol and took some hits from the community bong.

"Turn it off." Carl whispered to his boss. He didn't mean to, but his throat was dry, and his voice cracked.

Bryan ignored him.

"Turn it off." He repeated. Now his voice was louder and filled with desperation. There was no need for the video. He knew what was on it.

"I can't turn it off," Bryan responded. "I'm required to show the video to you in its entirety before I go over the remaining terms of your termination. This is company policy, and if you are looking for any kind of severance, you'll need to comply." Carl was pretty sure Bryan was bullshitting about "company policy." It was more likely that Bryan just enjoyed humiliating him.

Carl looked away from the video. Occasionally, when sleep evaded him, thoughts of a day like this crossed his mind. And here it was.

The video continued to play, serving as a perfect description of the end of his tenure at the company.

"Hey Cat," the man behind the camera lens said to Carl. Cat was Carl's fraternity name. Like many fraternity nicknames, it was a mix of compliment and humiliation for him. Sometimes his friends used it to call him a pussy when they were making fun of him. They also used it to praise him for the number of women he bedded during college. Cat had moderate success with women, but he couldn't match the expertise of the fraternity's professionals. He was also dating someone, and that made him feel guilty when he picked up a woman at last call. Going home alone was the only other option, but that was no fun. Hell, the guilt only lasted a little while.

"Hey" Cat muttered. He had come back home from the bar before last call. A rarity, but he was in a bad mood. The night was an epic failure, as he couldn't pick up anyone he was interested in. His girlfriend was home with her family, so he was alone and pissed. Perfect time to have a recorded conversation.

"What the hell are you doing home tonight?"

"Eh, no luck at Northbound and I'm exhausted. Anyway, I was about to go kill it and go to bed. Long day." Cat rose from his chair and staggered toward the bathroom.

The voice behind the camera stopped him.

"Hold on Carl, I need a favor. I have to finish something for my communications class project. It's due Monday, and I need a few more minutes. It'll just take a second."

"Really?" Cat was skeptical. Nothing ever took a few minutes. "What is it?"

"Well, I'm supposed to record spontaneous, 'man on the street' types of conversations with people so I can improve my interviewing skills. I've got to edit it all tomorrow, and it's going to take me all day, so can't you help me out?"

"This is an actual class?" Carl asked. It was a genuine question. Most fraternity brothers considered screwing with each other to be a skill. In fact, the more they embarrassed someone, the prouder they were.

"Why the fuck did you wait until two A.M. to finish it?"

"Man, I totally forgot." Now, this was a legitimate response. School work was low on the priority list for most of his fraternity brothers.

Cat wasn't pleased.

"You know what? I've got nothing to say. I'm totally just looking to go into my bedroom and pass out. And you know what else? I'm almost feeling like I'm going to pass on jerking off too and I've never lost interest in that." Cat was definitely exhausted.

"Just a few minutes. That's all I need."

"Okay, fine." Cat really didn't like being recorded. These were the days before everyone had a camera in their pocket. Still, he didn't like it. "What do you want to talk about?"

"Well, I hadn't thought that far ahead, but just give me a sec."

"For fuck's sake!" Now Cat was getting really annoyed. He wanted to go to bed, but he also wanted to help his friend.

"Okay, okay, I got it. I was reading for my World Politics class about how back in the Cold War, the Soviet Union was having all kinds of problems and people were worried that it was going to fall. If it did, then East and West Germany would have to unify, and it could have ruined the German economy for generations and potentially given rise to another Nazi-like government. A lot of the same issues are presenting themselves these days. What do you think? Could that ever happen again?"

Carl stared at the camera, stunned. He loved history and politics, but this was the last conversation he wanted to have tonight.

"Where the hell did that come from? It's two in the fucking morning and you want me to discuss world history and politics? What the fuck, dude?" All Cat wanted to do was sleep. Actually, he wanted to pleasure himself and then sleep. Now he was losing his interest in both.

"It has to be topical and not about sports, and you know about all this kind of stuff. I seriously doubt they want us to discuss you flogging it and going to bed."

"Goddamn it, okay, you want to know my opinion about that? I think it could happen. Remember, Hitler was just a politician and really did some positive things to help the German economy rise out of the ashes after the reparations that the Allies imposed on them after World War I. I'm not saying that anything having to do with the murder of the Jews, Catholics, Gypsies, and everyone else they hated as 'useless eaters' was anything but evil. But history is complex. In some respects, he was charismatic and led the Germans in a way that was necessary in the beginning. He was a great man in some respects."

At that point, Bryan stopped the video. It was more than enough.

"I can explain some things, Bryan. Can't you at least give me that? HR is recording this conversation, so I'm sure you want the arbitrator to hear that you at least gave me a chance to speak before you fired me."

"Well sure, why not?" Bryan said but what he really meant was "let's get this over with and move on."

"Listen, I said all of those things and I own them. But I said them before I educated myself. I even thought back later in my life, in my private moments, and asked myself whether the things I said and thought when I was younger were fair or right. It started after I watched some really horrific movies about the Holocaust, and I questioned my old self. Did I know what I was talking about? Did I really understand anything about that time period?"

"It bothered me, and I decided I needed to look deeper into it. I needed to educate myself. I read a few books on the subject, including *The Rise and Fall of the Third Reich,* and I realized that what I said when I was a kid was misleading.

Hitler was pure evil. There was nothing redeeming about him, and what I said was a simplistic take on a very complicated situation. I know better now, but I never thought that anything that I said as a teenager would come back to haunt me. And believe me, I said worse when I was younger."

Bryan smiled dryly. He looked forward to the part where Carl groveled and begged for his job. The highlight of the dance for Bryan was knowing Carl was gone and there was nothing he could do about it.

"You understand that none of that matters now. Someone tagged the video to your social media. We've received multiple complaints online about associating ourselves with a racist. It's affecting our ESG credit score. You understand that if we allowed you to work here, it would negatively affect our standing in the community, don't you?"

Despite his tone, Bryan really didn't think that any of that was true. The online mob was usually just a few disgruntled people who tried to show how big they were by threatening boycotts, doxing, etc. The actual problem emerged when the mainstream media took control of a narrative and decided what speech was permissible in society. Besides, Bryan was no big fan of Carl. He thought he was after his job, and this gave him the perfect opportunity to get rid of a rival.

"Bryan, you know I'm not a racist and you know I've never once treated anyone any differently than anyone else. I believe in respect and dignity for every person and the fact that I spouted off some shit about something when I was a kid has nothing to do with the person I am today. I was high and drunk, and you know that. You're better than this." Carl believed everything he had just said except the last sentence. Bryan wasn't better than this. This is who he was.

"Yeah, well, all that said, you'll just need to clean out your desk now. We'll pay you until we process the final cancelation. Sorry, I mean termination of your employment. We can then work out a severance package. Of course, we'll insist on a non-disparagement clause. If you want any money at all, you'll just have to agree to our terms."

Carl glared at Bryan and his mind went blank. He had seen cancel culture in action. It spared no one, and he knew his day would come. Anyone who didn't toe the line for the powerful was a target. Bryan was in control. He used that authority to cancel Carl because he could. Bryan could barely hide the joy he had in ending Carl's career.

A surge of anger welled up inside Carl as he observed the smirk on Bryan's face. Two competing sets of thoughts raced through his head. Thought one: tell Bryan his honest opinion of him. He wanted to scream that Bryan was a sycophantic asshole who only knew how to use corporate language and deliver meaningless PowerPoint presentations. Cat thought Bryan was no smarter than a parrot that squawked phrases like "throughput" and "synergies" with authority. Dupes bought his nonsense and thought that he actually knew something about the underlying work. Bryan's background in consulting made him a master of vacuous corporate-speak vocabulary, necessary for industry survival. Nothing would have made Carl happier than to shout thought number one at him.

Thought number two was just to shut his mouth. Many people cautioned him about the repercussions of expressing anger in a corporate setting, especially in a familiar industry. Once Bryan released the video, his career was effectively over. So, why not express his true thoughts to the fuckhead? Might as well go out with a bang.

Just as Carl was about to unleash hell on Bryan, something inside stopped him. The two voices argued and implored him from opposite sides. One told him to release his raw emotion. The other begged him to calm down and avoid further problems. He didn't listen to either of them. Instead, he uttered what would be his last sentence as a corporate drone.

"Bryan, if you think for one minute this can't happen to you, you are sorely mistaken."

After remembering that line, Cat jolted back to his present reality, and he realized he was still in the alleyway.

He wished he had spent the last few minutes focused on getting out of New York City, but on one level, this flashback made sense. Having confronted death at the concert, he would grapple with this trauma for years. The connection between these two cataclysmic events bonded them together. Cat realized he had just cheated actual death instead of just merely corporate execution. There was a big difference.

But he needed to calm himself down so he could think. First, he needed to figure out how long that flashback took. He was still wheezing, so it probably only lasted a few minutes. Cat couldn't trust his perception of time. He hadn't bothered to check his location either. That could have been a fatal error.

After scanning the area, he realized he was at least a mile from the concert. He was still in the warehouse district, so there were plenty of hiding places. The river was still in sight, so he had run parallel to it rather than inland. Once he exited the industrial area, he wouldn't have as much cover.

He estimated he was also roughly a mile away from his apartment and could reach it within half an hour by walking. Cat didn't want to take the subway. He had no desire for a chase through the disgusting tunnels. He didn't want to call a car or a cab, since he didn't want to use his credit card in case they were tracking his spending. Of course, they could also track his phone.

Ultimately, he walked home but took an indirect route. Best way to avoid an ambush.

It took him an hour to arrive at his apartment. It was a three-story walkup, and his place was on the top floor. Peering down the alley between his building and the neighboring one, Cat noticed nothing out of the ordinary. He pulled out his phone and checked the video from his security cameras. The feed showed multiple camera angles. He could see the inside of his apartment, the hallway in his building, and the outer perimeter. Everything looked fine. He programmed his cameras to record any motion in the apartment, yet there had been no activity since he departed for the concert earlier in the afternoon. He switched his security cameras to infrared. There were no human-like heat signatures in his apartment. Cat had another place to clear before going inside. He circled to the backside of his building and checked the fire escape. No one was on it, so he went inside.

He made it into his apartment without incident and did another sweep. Nothing seemed amiss, so he poured himself a glass of scotch. He liked it on ice, which was heresy in some circles, but it worked for him. He took a long pull from the glass and found the burning liquid soothing as it slid down his throat. That was the stuff. He needed it tonight, badly.

Cat put his glass down on the kitchen counter and made his way into his bedroom. He had no intention of staying one second longer than he had to. He would get his escape kit and get the hell out of New York. As he stepped into his closet, he bent down and raised the carpet square that perfectly blended into the floor. He chucked it aside and put his palm on the top of the steel lid of the safe below. The lockbox emitted a glowing green light that scanned Cat's hand. It turned blue as soon as the scanner confirmed his palm print. He heard the lock click. It was ready to open.

The first thing that appeared was his 9mm Beretta. It was highly illegal to possess any kind of firearm in New York City, but he wasn't in the business of taking chances with the heat he and the band were under. He had two clips of hollow point rounds already loaded in magazines and several boxes of ammo buried at the bottom of the safe. Just underneath his weapon was Kevin Reilly's passport, which he stuck in his pocket. Cat opened a large envelope, counted $10,000 in cash, and moved it to the side.

Finally, and most importantly, he picked up the brown satchel that concealed his fake travel token. Speaking of illegal objects, this was a big one. Getting caught with the gun would be bad enough. It was a mandatory five-year sentence.

But getting caught with a counterfeit travel token? Well, that five-year stretch would be the least of his worries.

He had bought the token from one of Richard's friends, who he understood was sympathetic to the band's cause. Richard told him the guy was ex-military or maybe former police. Either way, he was no fan of the government. In fact, Richard mentioned the guy was training with a militia. These were scary times.

He opened the satchel and pulled out the token. It looked like a large thumb drive, and he needed it to use any form of interstate public transportation. The transit police would do a facial scan and compare the picture to the information in their database. They would arrest him on the spot if the information on the token didn't match. If he used his real token and passport, then the government could track his movements. Should this token perform as promised, he could disappear as Kevin Reilly. Much better than traveling as Carl McKnight or Cat Chaotic.

He pushed the button on the bottom of the token, and the port gradually slid out the front. It stopped before it fully elongated. That wasn't right. It was supposed to eject out quickly and lock into place. Also, there should have been a glowing blue LED light indicator showing that it was powering up. Instead, there was nothing.

"Son of a bitch." He sighed.

The token was dead. He had to charge it.

"Of all the fucking luck, right now, really?" he yelled at himself.

He inserted the token into its charger and waited for the light to turn on. A faint white light flickered. Uh oh. That only happened when it was totally out of power. Really, *really* dead. It would take him several hours to charge it, leaving Cat with no option but to wait in his apartment. Not an ideal start.

He picked up the Beretta and pushed the clip into the weapon until it clicked. Cat slid the barrel back and engaged a round in the chamber. Then he flicked off the safety. At least he would have a fighting chance against the goon squad.

He walked back to his living room, planning to turn on the television and watch the news. He hoped there would be stories about the massacre. On his way, he noticed something on the kitchen counter.

His scotch on ice.

"Well, hello there," he thought to himself, "I can't let you go to waste. That would be a sin. Maybe I'll just finish what's left in this glass and then try to get some sleep. Yeah, that's a good idea."

Naturally, one glass led to two. Two let to four. The booze calmed his nerves, which he hoped would help him sleep. Or pass out really, which he did sometime later. He slept like a nervous drunk, which meant that he crashed for four hours and then tossed and turned for most of the rest of the morning. He alternated between boiling hot and freezing cold. It felt like he slept for minutes at a time and then woke up. But he didn't fall into a deep sleep until a couple of hours later. He must have finally sweated out most of the booze. That allowed him to sleep peacefully for a little while.

Until he heard a knock at the door.

Chapter Three

Boom... Boom... Boom... Boom

"Oh God, what did I do?" Cat mumbled to himself as he slowly awoke from his drunken sleep. He even slurred his thoughts as he slowly brought himself to a state of semiconsciousness. The ear-splitting noise was so intense that he could feel it through his eyes. And then it happened again.

Boom... Boom... BOOM... BOOM

He knew he was in for a severe hangover. Sound piercing his eyes was an all-time worst. Never felt something like that before. Sure, he had had bad ones. Thrown up on some carpets. Woke up in some strange places. But. Nothing. Like. This.

BOOM... BOOM... BOOM... BOOM

"Wait, that noise is outside? It's not in my head?"

Cat asked himself. He really wasn't sure.

His inner voice continued. "Look around the room. You had yourself quite a night, didn't you?"

Cat did as he was told. There was an open bottle of vodka and empty beer cans everywhere. Apparently, his internal voice was suggesting to him that mixing vodka, beer, and scotch may have been a poor choice. Thankfully, the voice was just whispering. But he was quite an asshole.

As he scanned his bedroom, a ray of sunlight pierced through the blinds, causing his eyes to pulse with pain. Normally, Cat woke up early in the morning while it was dark out. The sudden brightness signaled a problem. He needed to get up. Well, it wasn't just the blinding light. There was also that pounding sound.

BOOM... BOOM... BOOM.

"Okay, okay," he yelled through the corner of the pillow that was stuck to his face.

As he pushed himself up, the pillow peeled off his face. He was trying to get off the bed, but his body was having none of it. His shoulder dipped, and he rolled over onto his other side. His hangover told him not to move. It also told him to go back to sleep. He needed more hours. Or maybe he needed a few days. He drifted off again.

BOOM... BOOM... BOOOM.

There was that pounding again. Is it getting louder?

His body jerked, and now his whispering voice screamed at him. "End the pounding by any means necessary." Cat forced himself up and started toward the door. As he lumbered over, his hangover-induced anger caused him to fling it open without thinking and yell, "WHAT THE HELL DO YOU ..."

As he bellowed, a fist emerged from outside of the door and hit him square in the face. It felt like a sledgehammer.

Cat had forgotten to check his security camera, and he paid a price. Having a blood alcohol level comparable to the national deficit naturally clouded one's judgment.

The sucker punch completely caught him off guard. And it was a good one. He fell down onto his right side and laid there for a moment. Cat's day was off to a rough start.

"Fuck, that really hurt."

No one responded to Cat's complaint. Not that he expected an answer.

He looked up from the floor and the first thing he noticed was a Black guy standing over him. Cat was still shocked and wasn't exactly thinking clearly, but he noticed a couple of things about him. Black dude was tall and thin, and he had a concerned look on his face. He leaned down and asked Cat, "Are you alright?"

What kind of question was that from someone who just walloped you?

"No, not really." Cat responded.

Black dude smirked. Cat couldn't think of anything funny about the situation and yelled, "Well, what the fuck did you think I would say? That really hurt!"

"I know, and I'm sorry about that." The Black dude chuckled. "Well, kind of sorry."

From the look on Black dude's face and his snickering, Cat didn't quite believe that he was sorry. He seemed much too proud of himself. Black dude turned around and motioned to someone behind him. The sound of footsteps followed. From his angle, all Cat could see was a pair of black women's shoes. They were slingback style high-heeled pumps, with a pointed toe and small silver chains around the ankles. Cat knew nothing about women's shoes, but he knew that these were high end. He looked up farther and noticed that the shoes accompanied a tall, slender woman with long, dark brown hair.

"Well, hello there..." Suddenly, Cat's day was getting better.

Tall woman had an athletic build and soft features that were altered by the angular way she wore her makeup. Heavy black eyeliner highlighted her dark brown eyes. Tall woman had clearly adopted an eighties style but without the shoulder pads and ugly leg warmers. While her look had elements of the "Goth" style, she didn't go all out with white face paint or anything too extreme. He found her beauty striking and needed a witty opening.

"Hello?" was all that came out of his mouth.

"Hi," she replied. Her eyes narrowed. She left little doubt that she wasn't pleased.

Cat attempted to get up, propping himself up with one elbow. Glancing at both intruders, a rush of questions flooded his mind. Who the hell were these people? Why were they here? He didn't ask either of those questions. Instead, he asked the Black dude,

"What the hell did you punch me for?"

"Why did I punch you?" Black dude rhetorically responded to Cat's legitimate question.

"I punched you because I'm Black. It's what us folks do."

The effects of the booze, the punch, and that knockout of a woman still distracted him, but Cat's brain slowly processed Black dude's response and all he managed was, "Huh?"

The Black dude smirked again. He was having trouble with his deadpan. Black dude and Tall woman exchanged glances and struggled to keep straight faces. Neither one could keep it up much longer, so Black dude finally laughed as he spoke:

"No, you idiot, that's not why I punched you. I punched you because you were about to say something, and we all know that we are being watched. I needed to get you inside so we could talk privately. Honestly, I really think I got you with a good one."

"Oh, yeah?" Cat retorted with his best playground response.

"And by the way, my name is Robert. I've got no idea what name you referred to me in your head when I belted you, but just so you know, for future reference, my name is Robert."

"Well, I wouldn't really say it's nice to meet you Robert and, if you must know, I was referring to you as Black dude in my head."

All three of them laughed at that one.

On to more pressing business, Cat looked at Tall woman and asked, "and you are?"

She half smiled and said, "Kendra".

Cat noticed the understated frostiness in her response. She must be hiding how attracted she was to him.

"Hi Kendra, I think it's nice to meet you. My name is Cat. I mean Carl, well, Cat, I guess."

"Yes, I know, we both know," Kendra responded again in an even tone.

"Okay, well, now that we've formally introduced ourselves, I've got some more questions, like who the hell are you and what are you doing here? I don't seem to recall meeting either of you, but if we have, then I'm sorry. I really tied one on last night and I wouldn't exactly put any stock in anything I say right now."

"We're here because you are in a lot of danger," Kendra said in the same expressionless tone. "We were at the concert last night."

"Oh, boy," Cat responded. He had completely forgotten about the concert. "Yeah, that was something else. I got out through a corner door. I had to knock out a guard. That was insane. How did you guys get out?"

"We were toward the back when it all went crazy. Robert went to the bar for drinks, and I was walking up to the side of the stage when the shooting started. We made it out the back by sticking close to the walls. The smoke helped, but it was mayhem. We are very sorry for your loss."

"My loss?" Cat asked. The night remained a blur. It was now just dawning on him that shooting could cause deaths. "Who got shot?"

Kendra and Robert just looked at him.

"Plenty of people," Robert responded.

Cat said nothing. He just stared at his two new acquaintances. The three of them sat in an awkward silence until Kendra broke it.

"You mean you don't know?"

Adrenaline raced through Cat, causing his stomach to churn. He knew things were about to get worse. Much. Much. Worse. The uncomfortable silence continued. Cat didn't respond to Kendra's question. Robert refused to speak as well. Kendra swallowed hard and shattered the stillness.

"Richard is dead," she murmured, but this time her tone was anything but even. Her voice cracked as she told Cat his friend had died. Robert looked down into his chest, clearly shaken by Kendra's words.

Cat opened his mouth, but he couldn't say anything. He had no clue how to respond. Richard was like a brother to him and the idea that he could have died during the attack never occurred to him. He assumed everyone he knew had escaped, but clearly that was not the case.

"As bad as that is, there's more to it. I'm not sure how to tell you the rest, but you need to know." Kendra almost spat the words out. She met Cat only a few moments ago but still felt horrible telling him about his friend.

The blood drained from Cat's face. He prepared himself as best he could, but couldn't fathom what else she had to tell him. A fleeting thought of "what the hell, he's dead anyway" raced through his head. It caused him to ball his fist and release it quickly. This was an involuntary spasm that sometimes occurred when unwanted thoughts ran through his mind.

"Okay," Cat said.

He looked at Robert and noticed a tear streaming down his cheek. He tried to prepare himself to hear something horrific. Easier said than done.

"They killed him, but they didn't just kill him with a gunshot or anything like that. They targeted him like they were trying to make an example of him."

"How do *you* know?" Cat asked Kendra a pointed question. He was clearly entering the denial stage of grief.

"I tried to make my way to the bar to find Robert. I stuck close to the wall as I tried to get there. The smoke was thick, but I noticed someone walking past me with a video camera. A big one. It was strange and I couldn't help myself. I needed to know what was happening. Looking back, it was a stupid thing to do, but I hid behind a column so I could see what was happening."

Cat didn't know either of these people, but intuitively, he trusted both of them. Of course, Kendra's looks helped ease any skepticism he might have had about whether she had an ulterior motive. That was a common but dangerous assumption among males. Yet, both Robert and Kendra seemed genuine. Which was surprising, considering Robert had knocked him out just a few minutes ago.

"I didn't see the whole thing, but what I saw was disgusting, and I'm guessing that the rest of the world will see it soon." Kendra couldn't look at Cat anymore. She turned her head, unconsciously hoping that not seeing him would give her strength to finish telling him the rest.

It didn't work.

"Do you want to hear the rest of this now? We can stop here since you know most of what you need to, but in all honesty, I don't think it's going to matter soon." She asked Cat and hoped he would say no. Unfortunately, he nodded his head yes.

"Well, they didn't just shoot him and run like you would if you were worried about getting caught. They wanted to humiliate him and cause him as much pain as possible. They..." Kendra's defense mechanisms faltered, allowing her emotions to break through.

"What did they do?" Cat asked, even though he didn't want to know the answer. Kendra couldn't finish, so Robert told him the rest.

"Well, they cut him. They, they, they didn't just cut him, they disemboweled him."

"Oh, my God." Cat shook his head. He couldn't believe what he was hearing.

"Yeah, and they filmed it. The fucking bastards filmed it." Robert whispered.

Cat tried to hold his feelings in and keep his emotions from overwhelming him. He could only hold them back for so long. In less than a minute, his mind unleashed nonsensical and contradictory thoughts against him.

"That could have been me."

"Why on earth would they film that?"

"Why weren't they afraid?"

"I want to kill them."

"I want to go to sleep."

The only thought he verbalized was, "Why on earth would they film that?"

"I've been thinking about that, Cat, and that's part of the reason we're here." It was clear from Kendra's tone that her sadness was giving way to anger.

Cat cut her off, "Yeah actually, that's a good fucking question. Just why *are* you here?"

Kendra ignored Cat's sarcasm and continued, "I'll get to that in a moment, but the 'why' of all of this is the most important thing. Whoever did this wanted to make Richard an example, but it's also really brazen right? I mean, if you're going to film yourself killing someone, then you want everyone to know that you are not afraid of anyone or anything. And they didn't take a quick video on their phones. They brought a camera, a large one. In all honesty, that last part is the scariest. I mean, what if they weren't afraid of getting caught? What does that say about them?"

Cat was still wrapping his mind around everything and didn't have an answer to Kendra's question. His thoughts were swirling and blocking his ability to analyze what Kendra and Robert were saying.

Abruptly, Cat shifted back into attack mode. "I'll ask again, why are you two here at my house?"

Cat surprised them by how quickly he focused on the more pragmatic aspects of this situation. Clearly, Cat hadn't yet started grieving for this friend. Robert guessed Cat was still in denial, but time was short. He had to tell him the whole story.

"We've been watching your band for a long time. And we're not the only ones. We're here on behalf of a powerful friend, and Richard agreed to meet with us tonight after the show. The four of us were going to explore working together. Now everything has changed, and we're here because we want to help you. You are in grave danger. If you haven't noticed, it was really easy for us to find you and it's going to be really easy for whoever did this to track you down. You need to think about your safety, Cat, and what you are going to do next."

"What I'm going to do next?" Cat repeated the question. "What the fuck? How on earth could you ask me that?" He added a sarcastic chuckle to stress the point.

Kendra interjected before Robert answered. "Maybe we need to back up a bit and again ask ourselves why they did this to Richard? Why did this happen? The best answer I have is that I believe you guys pissed off some powerful people who want to silence you. MicroAggression railed against the Speech Codes and there are an awful lot of people that use those restrictions as a weapon. As strange as this is going to sound right now, I think whoever did this feels threatened by you. You don't disembowel someone as revenge for some bad words. You do it because you're afraid."

Kendra detested the Speech Codes and despised the governmental-media-technology cabal that conspired together to get the law passed. Murdering Richard had upped the ante, and she really needed to convince Cat that he couldn't let this stop him. She fully realized that she was hitting him with a haymaker after telling him about the gruesome murder of his friend. Unfortunately, she didn't have time for the delicate approach.

"Whoa, whoa, whoa, hold up." Cat shot back at Kendra. "What makes you think I want to do anything but disappear?"

Neither of them answered, so Cat pressed the point.

"Look, I don't know you from anyone, and you come into my house, cold cock me, tell me someone cut my best friend to pieces. Then you tell me that his murder is on video and that I could be next. On top of that, you want me to get back up on stage and play? Are you insane?"

"Well, when you put it that way, it kind of, sort of, sounds crazy." Robert responded, trying to lighten the mood a bit.

Even Kendra smiled and laughed at that one.

Cat noticed a soft expression on her face for the first time.

"Hello there, beautiful." A second voice chimed in, but this one didn't originate from Cat's head.

It arose from a separate area of his body that was nowhere near his brain. Never the most logical, but always the most powerful. He had listened to this voice many times, with mixed results. Maybe he needed to think before outright rejecting Kendra? Despite lacking intelligence, this voice possessed an astonishing ability to persuade, even amidst murder, chaos, and carnage.

Still, that voice opposed his "flight" voice and despite both voices beginning with the same letter, the "flight" voice was losing. Neither his "fight" nor "flight" voice had any real chance against his anatomical voice. Instead, he punted. "Look, I need to think about this."

Kendra was relieved that she had gotten through to him a bit. "I get it, but we don't have a lot of time right now. If you're not being watched now, you will be soon. But there's someone who can help."

"Okay, I'm listening." Cat's anatomical voice had a pretty high batting average.

"Do you know who Swamp Simmons is?"

Cat recognized the name, but wasn't exactly sure who he was. Richard mentioned him as someone that they may need to contact in the future, but Cat hadn't really given it much thought. It was never a top priority on his "to do" list.

"Kind of, well maybe, okay, no, not really." Cat's response was nothing more than a stream-of-consciousness word salad.

"You really don't know? You're involved in unsanctioned concerts, and you really don't know?" Yes, that was true. He really didn't know. Anatomical voice had failed him. He should have known to tell him to lie.

"Swamp is the guy Robert was talking about. He's one of the last unapproved online journalists who is trying to expose this government for what it is. He's figured out some way to break through the 'Patriot' or 'Freedom' Firewall or whatever the fuck they are calling it these days. The one that blocks us from putting non-offensive stuff on the internet. The government installed it after they imposed the Speech Codes. You mean you really don't know?"

"Look, Richard mentioned him to me a few times, but I'm just not that good with computers, so I wasn't able to find him online." It was the best half lie his anatomical voice could think of on such short notice.

"Okay, well, I'll show you how to do that when we have a few minutes, but Swamp sent us because Robert and I are in the music industry. He asked us to contact Richard. I called Swamp after the concert and told him what happened. He gave me your address and asked me to come here. He wants to help us." Cat zeroed in on Kendra's choice of the word "us." This was a good sign. Anatomical voice was pleased.

She was winning him over, but he wasn't ready to commit. "Like I said, I need to think about this, but one more thing. When you were at the concert, did you see what happened to Trent?"

"I think he escaped." Robert chimed in. He remained silent as Kendra and Cat bantered, recognizing that Kendra had the best chance of convincing him, and he didn't want to interrupt. He could tell that Cat was listening to his anatomical voice. Robert knew that voice very well.

"And Simon?"

"I don't know for sure," Robert responded, "But I saw someone slumped over on the drums. I wouldn't get your hopes up."

Once again, Cat's heart sank as the full weight of the situation became more apparent. Things had changed forever and for a moment Cat let himself grieve. "How could this happen?" he asked himself. "This is all my fault." But almost immediately, his mind triggered a defense mechanism, and he switched his focus to the task at hand.

"I need to find Trent."

Trent, Richard, and Cat had been inseparable when they first began performing. Trent recognized the necessity of transforming MicroAggression into a rebellion. Richard and

Cat had discussed the idea of playing offensive music to entertain, but Trent saw the Speech Codes as a wedge to splinter society into tribes. He predicted the government would weaponize these laws, and the Speech Codes were a slippery slope. Although Simon was a friend, he joined the band later and functioned as more of a session player. He had replaced their first drummer, John, who didn't share their vision. John had no interest in delivering a political statement. He was perfectly happy playing for an audience. He just liked the band for the music and nothing else. Given the current state of his situation, Cat realized he may have been onto something.

"Look, I meant it when I said that I wanted to think about this, but if you can help me find Trent, then we can talk about it more, okay? If I'm in danger, then so is he. I'm making no promises about doing anything, but I promise you I will honestly think about it. Is that fair? Do we have a deal?"

Kendra and Robert looked at one another, and then both said in unison, "Deal."

"Good. I need to clean up and get some things around here, and then we need to go. I also need some aspirin. None of this is doing my hangover any good."

"One other thing." Kendra continued after Cat had thought the negotiations were done. "You said you needed to clean up, right? And by that, you mean you need to take a shower, brush your teeth and stuff, right?" She looked at Cat directly in the eyes as she spoke.

"Yeah..."

"Okay, thanks, just making sure."

Cat caught the subtle barb she threw at him and thought to himself, *she* woke *me* up. She has no right to complain that I stink. She was hot, though. Deciding some things were better left unsaid, Cat left the room to shower.

Chapter Four

"One word, my little darlings," President Annabelle Ramirez screamed at the crowd.

"We only needed one word to undo the damage those rich, entitled, White men did to this country back when they stole it from the Indigenous people."

She held up her outstretched hand and raised her index finger to the crowd and beamed a smile that was gleaming with pride.

"And what was that one word?" she extolled the crowd to respond, opened her arms out wide and waved her hands toward herself, inviting adulation.

"NON-OFFENSIVE!" they screamed in unison.

"What is it?" Ramirez playfully questioned her fans.

"NON-OFFENSIVE!" the crowd shrieked even louder than the first time.

"I can't hear you!"

Lost in the captivating rhetoric of their leader, they frenetically chanted "NON-OFFENSIVE, NON-OFFENSIVE, NON-OFFENSIVE."

"That's right, non-offensive." Annabelle spoke quietly, almost in a whisper. "That's the one word that changed the narrative. Changed the course of history. Changed this land, our land, from the land for the few to an America for the many."

The crowd that was raging a mere five seconds ago calmed down to match Ramirez's hushed tone.

"The word that changed the world and ushered in a new future, a tomorrow brighter than we ever could have imagined before."

Ramirez dropped the fake street accent long ago. She deployed it during the early days of the revolution, but not anymore. In fact, Annabelle from the block was really Annabelle from the suburbs. She was well-educated and grew up in an upper middle-class family. Street cred was important back then and she could drop her g's with the best of them when she needed to. Those days were gone, and now she could use her own voice and be herself. Well, whatever was left of herself.

"But before we changed the world with that one word, we failed. You remember our failures. Remember when we tried crunchy granola liberalism? That failed. Remember when we believed slick politicians and their craven wives? That failed because we bought their lies as long as they were right on abortion. They were Democrats in name only and may as well have been Republicans, and none of them were the solution."

"That's when we said, 'no more failures.' We realized we needed to change tactics and play the long game. Politics, voting for that matter, was for losers. We needed a more permanent solution. We needed to make sure that America would eventually implode from within so that we could rebuild it in our image. No more singing protest songs. No more bargaining and compromising. To get our permanent solution, we needed to expose and exploit America's fatal flaw."

"And what was that flaw?" Ramirez thundered. Her congregation instinctively knew her next proclamation would provide that purpose that they were all seeking.

"It was guilt," she whispered.

"Guilt would cause a slow leak in the boat so it could not lift with the tide."

"Guilt ensured that anyone who succeeded would never be happy." She nodded her head in a rhythmic cadence while chanting like a preacher.

"Guilt made them see the truth, and that truth is that no matter what your circumstances were, good or bad, your fate was undeserved."

"Guilt, for once and for all, solved the problem that our spineless politicians couldn't fix."

"But what good would guilt be if we didn't make them feel it?"

She paused a moment to calm the crowd down so she could redirect them.

"Indeed, how could you make those that benefited from 'liberty,' 'wealth,' and 'prosperity' resent it so?" She surrounded those founding principle terms with air quotes to further denigrate the American experiment.

"We had to make sure that Americans opened their eyes to the country's flaws. We needed to cut through the bullshit and show once and for all what America really is and what it is not. America is not at its heart an eternal struggle to achieve higher levels of greatness. That was just the nonsense they used to teach in grade school before our teachers finally told kids the truth."

"Once we got our teachers into the schools, they taught kids that America's founding was, in fact, a lie, and everything it was ever about was a sham. It's all a sick joke."

"But it wasn't easy to undo America's brainwashing. We needed a plan to win the battle for the heart and soul of this country."

"And how did we do it? Well, it was actually pretty simple. We armed ourselves with the truth and we got in their faces, and we wouldn't back down. Let me give you a couple of examples."

"One time, a straight-White-privileged-male tried to tell me that Americans accepted that slavery was wrong. He also tried to convince me that the country paid an enormous price and atoned for its sins by fighting the Civil War."

Annabelle paused, allowing the crowd the time to envision an image of the straw man she created.

"Yeah, I know. Can you believe it? A straight White male telling *me* that. You know what I told him? I told him that all the Civil War did was change the way America enforced its racism. Now, America keeps its White privilege alive, not with chains, but with its very institutions."

The crowd burst into applause, showing their approval of Ramirez's fictional encounter.

"And then some blonde-haired Karen said to me that America has come a long way since Jim Crow."

"You know what I said to her? I said Jim Crow is still here since *you* have an unconscious bias. You can't help it. Your very thoughts and microaggressions perpetuate the suppression of all minorities."

"That's right, we had an answer for everything. In fact, I even told a guy who clearly ain't Black that he was a Xenophobe because he wanted to close the border. I mean, who was he to tell anyone they weren't welcome here? Good people don't need borders. I asked him why. Why did he actually think America is only for privileged White folks? We are no better than anyone else in the world!"

"Are you seeing the theme here? The most important thing is to make sure you expose the lie. Reveal the true character and impurity of anyone who would dare oppose us. We have an answer for everything, my little darlings, and we also have our, dare I say, trump card."

The crowd booed as soon as Annabelle uttered that last phrase.

"Yes, I'm sorry, I'm sorry. I hate to bring up such a triggering expression." With a half-smirk, she cunningly convinced the crowd that she had unintentionally used that offensive idiom.

"What was our last card, our ace in the hole, if you will? Come on, you know what it is..." She motioned to the crowd with an outstretched hand, waving it toward herself. The crowd mimicked her motion and screamed its approval. Annabelle paused and gave the crowd a moment to whip itself into a frenzy. Finally, she gave them what they wanted. "We told them that if you didn't agree with us, you are a racist."

"That's right, we played the race card early and often. Throwing that down ensured that the only acceptable response to the question of what America is, was, and ever will be is that it is rotten to the core. America is a lie, my little darlings, and they either needed to see it for what it is or just shut the hell up."

"And if they didn't, we would hit back hard. We had one major weapon in our arsenal to help us fight our existential war. No, it wasn't a tank, a plane, a gun, or even a neutron bomb. We had something far more powerful. We had social media."

"That's right. With a few strategic posts, we convinced a generation that their wealth was undeserved and stolen. We used 'likes' to convince them they had friends. Of course, those friends would abandon them if they stepped out of line. We helped them see that no matter what they had, someone else had it better. Tribes replaced churches. Chat rooms replaced Little League. Type a few keywords and boom, you've got instant friends that agree with you. Type another few words and you will find someone to hate. The fuse was lit. Society was about to explode. And once the inevitable empty feeling arose, government was right there to fill the void."

"The plan was in place, but we needed one more tool. After all, you couldn't just hope that America's guilt and envy would tear it apart. We also needed to prevent a revolt. We needed to keep everyone in line. And just what was that ultimate tool?"

"Cancelation!" a lone voice screamed before anyone else could.

"Yes, cancelation!" Ramirez repeated in response to her drone.

"Cancelation was the vehicle, the mechanism, and dare I say again, the 'TRUMP' card to be played in response to all threats to our movement."

"Think about it, my little darlings. We could still maintain the appearance of free speech, but we could make the consequences of dissent so horrible that no one in their right mind would openly oppose our movement."

"Complain about us tearing down statues? We'll humiliate you online and blast you to everyone in your life."

"Don't approve of rioting? Lose your job."

"Support the police? Well, now, it seems like you didn't learn your lesson. Maybe we won't just go after you? I guess we'll just have to ruin the lives of your children, friends, and family."

"Unfortunately, a small group of deplorables just didn't get it. They elected that bad orange man as a middle finger to the rest of us."

"So, we did some soul searching and realized we made a mistake. We had skipped a step. No one identified the root cause of the problem. Everyone knew what it was, but no one had named it and shamed it. And just what was the root cause? The biggest obstacle to achieving our goal?"

"Why, it was that dusty old document called the Constitution. An anachronism that was written *by* old White men slave holders *for* old White men slave holders. A document that counted slaves as three-fifths of a person. A document which only allowed White land-owning men to vote. How could such a document exist for as long as it did? The Constitution needed to be canceled!"

"And we canceled it alright. After all, the Constitution was a living document, right? All we had to do was change it. All it said was that Congress shall make no law respecting an establishment of religion or prohibiting the free exercise thereof or abridging the freedom of speech. Couldn't we make those words disappear? Better yet, couldn't we change it by adding one paltry word? Why couldn't we make one teensy weensy change? Yes, we could, so we did the hard work and unleashed America's collective guilt in order to change the First Amendment. Now, that moldy old document says Congress shall make no law abridging the freedom of *non*-offensive speech. Isn't that much better? Isn't that more equitable?"

"And now here we are..."

Annabelle paused again, and the audience erupted. Her last line always had that effect. She reveled in the attention and admiration. Feeling power and purpose never got old.

"But of course, even though the Constitution now only protects non-offensive speech, we have so much more to do. This country still stinks of the rot and stench of its illegitimate founding. Really, it needs cleansing. Yes, I'm willing to give America that cleaning. I'm here to cleanse America's soul!"

That was one of her favorite closing lines. Time to take them home.

"But I can't do it alone." She almost whispered.

"So, join with me my little darlings, on the rest of our journey, while we fight to finish the job. We cannot tolerate offense. Our movement cannot tolerate dissent. We must all move in the same direction. The privileged among us have lost the right to complain since they only got there as a benefit of their skin color and their money. Onward and upward toward a more just and fair society. I can't do it without you. You are the real bosses here. I am only a vehicle. But if you'll ride with me, we will get there, my little darlings, we will achieve utopia!"

"A utopia where no one offends anyone. A utopia where everyone respects each other's feelings and focuses on the collective rather than the individual. We will achieve equity with no one left behind. The rich White privileged among us will not be the only ones to enjoy the fruits of our labors. But for all, the exploited, the oppressed, the masses. Let us unite and rebuild a perfect union from the ruins of inequality. This is now the land for all!"

*   *   *

Ramirez finished her speech, then walked through the vestibule and into the back offices, surrounded by a phalanx of armed guards. She strode past her secretary, who knew better than to look directly at her. As Ramirez walked by, she kept her eyes fixed ahead, while her assistant remained focused on typing the latest series of orders, directives, and letters.

Ramirez waited for one of her guards to open the door to her office. As he pulled the doorknob, her secretary said, "Oh, Madam President?"

Annabelle stopped for a second. She was not expecting anyone to talk to her, much less her admin. This never happened. No one dared ask for her time or even looked directly at her. Best not to make eye contact either unless you absolutely had to. Self-preservation was a survival skill that most of her administration had mastered. Apparently, her secretary didn't value her job.

Ramirez wheeled around and glared at her without saying a word.

Her assistant was no fool and would have preferred to email her question to Ramirez rather than speak to her and risk her wrath. Unfortunately, this couldn't wait.

"Max called. You told me you wanted me to let you know when he did. He didn't say what it was about, but he asked me to let you know."

Ramirez's face softened, and she smiled.

"Oh, okay. Thanks, I'll call him."

"Do you want me to set up the call through the security link? You have some time this afternoon and I can let him know when you'll be calling him."

"No, I'll call him. I'll let you know if I need to block off some time, but I'll probably just wait until the end of the day. I doubt I need to move anything."

Ramirez turned to go into the back office. The security officer had been waiting with the office door open and closed it behind her.

She walked over to her chair and stared out the window behind it, gazing out into the golden rays of the Washington, D.C. late afternoon sun. The architecture of the buildings and monuments captivated her, despite her disdain for those responsible for building them. She wondered how people with such misguided views could construct such a grand city. It really was awe-inspiring to her and taking a few moments to bask in the outright power the city landscape projected gave her a sense of her place in the world. This was her city. This was her country. It was her world, and she intended to do everything in her enormous power to keep it that way.

Annabelle leaned back, propped her feet up on the desk. This wasn't the Oval Office. No chance for an unflattering photo by a photographer. They all knew better anyway. She pulled her second cell phone out of her jacket and scrolled down to find Max's number. This was a private cell phone that came directly from the CEO of a defense contractor. She had awarded him a lucrative no-bid contract. In return, he encrypted it with the same technology that intelligence agencies used, so no one could listen in on her calls. It was unregistered, so she didn't have to worry about foolish Freedom of Information Act requests. It was highly unlikely that the CEO would step out of line. He fully supported the movement and was more than happy to help. There was also little risk of blackmail. He had a penchant for little girls and, well, that type of information could be useful to both of them. After all, one hand washed the other.

She found Max's contact information and pressed the call button. His cell was also unregistered and encrypted with the same technology and invisible to anyone but her.

The line rang a few times, and then Max picked up.

"Hello Sandy." This was Max's codename for Ramirez. He used it just in case anyone was within earshot.

"Hi Max, how are you doing?"

"Doing fine. How are you?"

"Great, Max, Great. Is this a good time?"

"Yes, it is, but just give me a second. I'm pretty sure I'm alone, but I'll take a quick look around."

"Sure, no problem."

The line was quiet for less than a minute when Max rejoined the call.

"Looks good. It's just me. Thanks for calling. I know you're busy, so I'll get right to it. I wanted to..." Max was about to give her an update when Ramirez cut him off.

"Thanks, Max, I appreciate that, but before you fill me in, I wanted to just say thank you."

Annabelle's compliment caught Max off guard. She wasn't the type to thank anyone. Something was wrong.

"Well... thank you?" Max uttered the last word in a slightly higher pitch, as if his statement were a question. He also stuttered slightly as he processed her praise.

"Yes, I really mean it. Our movement wouldn't be here if it wasn't for you and your team. It's rare to find someone who believes in the cause like you do and will do the dirty work. I mean, think about it, we've been through a lot, since we met at the Portland protests. And how can I forget what you did for me during the Free Palestine movement? I couldn't have imagined in my wildest dreams that we would have gotten here without you and your dedication."

Now, Max's curiosity peaked as he wondered where she was heading. Max had never witnessed this side of Annabelle before. He listened closely, sensing the importance of the upcoming conversation.

"Think about it, we grew from a small, so-called 'fringe' group into a national movement, and it was no accident. It was because we were all pulling in the same direction. We all had our role to play and without yours, I don't think we would have gotten to where we are. You should really be proud."

"Well, thanks Sandy, I really appreciate that, but I owe you a lot of the credit. You helped me realize we needed to do more. I mean, the protests were fine, but we really needed action. The brawls were fun, and all and had their place, but without the grassroots effort, we would have just fought without purpose. The fight would have been useless without your vision."

"Yes, we did." Annabelle trailed off as a flood of memories flowed through her mind. She caught herself and realized this was no time to reminisce. She needed to focus on the here and now.

"You got it done, right?" She was vague about what she was referring to, even though this was a secure line. Annabelle knew better than to take unnecessary chances. Even she could go to prison if the wrong person heard this conversation.

"Yes, it's done." Max was also smart enough not to admit that he had committed a murder.

"And you got the footage, right? Have you cleaned it yet? Is it ready for upload?" Annabelle asked him to shoot a video of Richard's murder, but she never specified the reason.

Now he knew.

"What?" Max responded. She wanted to post the video now? He agreed with the plan to kill Richard as a warning to other subversives. He thought word of mouth and any news coverage would be enough. Max wasn't concerned about the police; they could bury any investigation, even a murder. But uploading the video so soon was an unnecessary risk. Still, Max had to choose his next words carefully. No one fucked with Annabelle Ramirez and lived to tell about it.

"Do you really think that's a good idea?"

"Well, why did you think I wanted the video?" It was a logical yet rhetorical question. She really didn't care what Max thought, but why would he say something so stupid? Anyone listening could easily connect her to the murder through that question.

"I wasn't really sure, but I thought you would eventually post it. But why now?"

"Deterrence." Annabelle let the word hang out in the air. Max knew she played for keeps, but this was reckless.

"The time is now Max. We need to squash all the Richard Uprisings in the world as quickly as we can. If their movement gets any stronger, it could ruin everything we've done, everything we've worked for. We need to scare the shit out of them before they get any traction."

"Okay." Max was extremely uncomfortable with these developments. Murder was one thing, the asshole deserved it. But this was a totally different animal. Once they uploaded it, there was no taking it back. Things could get ugly if this backfired.

Knowing her decision was final, Max moved on to logistics. The video camera they used had intelligence grade technology but had intentional limitations. For one, the camera's video feed did not connect to the internet. In fact, it almost resembled an old-fashioned VHS tape system, except that it was digital. The Department of Defense developed this camera to be used by the psychological operations department. "Psy-Ops" needed video to study the efficacy of their torture techniques during the War on Terror. For obvious reasons, this camera was one of the most secure devices in the government's toolbox. Only a highly sophisticated hacker that had access to significant governmental resources could decrypt the video. Max didn't have the codes, so that led him to his next question:

"How am I going to do that?"

"Bring the chip to the guy who gave you your phone. He will take it from there."

"Wait!" Max responded as his self-preservation instinct kicked into high gear. "You want me to bring in a civilian? I'm all over that footage. I even gave the speech you wanted. That's my voice on there!" His voice rose steadily as his blood pressure spiked.

"Come on, Max, you know me better than that." Her tone was dismissive, driven mainly by her disappointment in him. Did he really think she was going to risk losing one of her most useful assets? She still needed him, so he was safe.

"You don't think that I would let any harm come to you over this, do you? I still need you." She laughed as she scolded him so he would know she supported him. He was a critical part of what she had planned.

"We'll doctor the video. You have nothing to worry about. The deep fake AI technology we have has really gotten better and we can make you and your men look and sound like people that don't exist. We splice the features of random faces and voices together. You and your crew will be unrecognizable. We've used this technology to control the narrative for some time now. Don't you know that?"

Yes, Max knew that, but it didn't bring him much comfort. But it really didn't matter, anyway. He didn't have a choice in the matter.

"Okay, I'll bring the chip to him. What's the next step?"

"We'll discuss that later. I've thought of the perfect way to use these developments to our advantage and if all goes well, we might very well be in the endgame now. I've already put together an outline of my next speech that will put this all together. Max, we are almost at the end of this, and it's going to be amazing."

Chapter Five

"And then what happened?" Swamp asked Jack, and prepared himself for the inevitable unhappy ending.

"Well, well, well, well..." Jack stuttered. His nerves were much worse than he thought they would be. He took a deep breath, slowly let it out, and then paused.

"It's okay Jack, take your time." Swamp tried to ease Jack's mind, but he had every right to be terrified. After all, he was publicly exposing police corruption on the Swamp Simmons Show.

While Jack was undoubtedly taking a risk, Swamp took precautions. He disguised all non-public figures with an AI generated face and an unrecognizable voice. In real life, Jack was tall and muscular, with a short beard and long, slightly graying hair. He looked very different on the show. In fact, the audience saw Jack as a composite of facial features scraped off of random pictures from the internet. Swamp also cloaked himself in an AI disguise. He appeared to the audience as a male model, complete with a flawless face, perfect hair, and a killer physique. In reality, he was slightly taller than six feet, wore glasses, had completely gray hair, and a slight "dad" bod.

Jack composed himself and continued. "The captain told me to check my privilege or some other bullshit. He told me if I didn't like the 'reimagined' police, then there was the fucking door. He also warned me that if I wanted my full pension, I should walk through it quietly."

"Back up for a second," Swamp stopped him. "Full pension? He was threatening your retirement?"

"Yeah, he was. Funny enough, he said he wanted to keep me on because I could be useful, but when I pressed him on details, he wouldn't say. He just told me there was a 'right way' and a 'wrong way' to do things and if I was part of the team, then my life would be really easy. My other choice was to leave. And if I 'chose' to leave, I could either leave with everything I worked for, including my full pension, or I could leave the other way. He was smart enough not to specify just what the 'other way' was, but he conveniently omitted the words 'full pension.' Pretty clever for a sick son of a bitch."

Swamp had to be cautious with what he allowed Jack to disclose. He wanted Jack to give enough details so that he could expose police corruption. He didn't want him to disclose any identifying information. It was a fine line to walk. He could clean up any slip ups in postproduction, but better to prevent the problem during taping. One screwup could bring severe consequences.

"Well, what were they asking you to do?"

"They were asking me to join the 'special investigative unit.' I knew the guys on that squad. Most of them were genuine pieces of shit. They would tear someone's life apart, investigate anything and everything they ever did. It was like the old Soviet-style of policing: show me the person and I'll show you the crime."

"At first, they recruited the pricks that they knew couldn't care less about actual police work. Those assholes just enjoyed busting heads for the fun of it. One guy I knew who retired early just to get out of the unit told me it was disgusting. The top brass gave them a target, usually someone who pissed somebody important off and they would rip his life apart. Start with something easy, like taxes. Get any hook you can into him and then use every investigative tool and every government database to find anything and everything the guy ever did in his life. If they couldn't find much and the guy absolutely had to go down, then they would either plant something on him or turn everything they found over to a civil division of the government. They would sue him for everything he had. They could bankrupt him with legal fees alone. The negative publicity could also cost him his job or his business. He told me if they wanted the guy bad enough, they would manufacture something horrible like finding 'evidence' that his computer accessed child porn. That type of blackmail was the nuclear option, but it usually worked."

"And if you refused to leave the force?"

"Well, usually they would open or reopen an internal investigation from your past. Do a conduct review of an old Civilian Review Board complaint. Those complaints happened to everyone and the administrative board usually dismissed them unless the cop really fucked up. You almost always got the benefit of the doubt unless you did something terrible, like putting a suspect in the hospital for no reason. People used to understand that this was a hard job and most of us did our best, so we had some latitude. Well, that was the old way. And then..."

Swamp cut Jack off before he could finish his thought. "Did your union do anything? Sorry, didn't mean to interrupt, but your story scares the hell out of me."

"Yeah, no problem." Jack chuckled as he spoke. "To answer your question, no, they didn't do jack shit. I think they were in the club, too. But what I was going to say was they would use those prior civilian complaints as leverage. If you did what they said, no harm, no foul, and they dismissed the complaint. If you didn't, well, then they would find fresh evidence in one of those old cases and change the finding from 'unfounded' to 'founded'. That was a big deal. Guys lost their pension when that happened. Worse, the plaintiff's lawyer had all the ammunition he needed to sue you back into the stone age. That's what happened when they got rid of qualified immunity."

"If I'm hearing you right, Jack, it sounds like you had three pretty terrible options. First, you could make nice, look the other way, harass who they told you to harass, and enjoy the benefits. Second, you could say no, refuse to leave the job, lose all your money and maybe go to jail. Third, you could leave quietly and keep your pension. No choice anyone wants to make."

"No, it's not." Jack looked down sheepishly.

"No, it's not," Swamp repeated to validate Jack's statement. "You were a good cop, and you were being asked to violate your principles under the threat of financial ruin or worse."

"Yeah, that about sums it up. I absolutely refused to do any of that. No way I could live with myself. It's just not who I am. I really tried to do the right thing while I was on the job. You had to eat a lot of shit on the force. You got smeared as a racist. Some people really thought we killed unarmed minorities for sport. District Attorneys turned horrible people loose because they wanted to protect the criminals rather than the citizens. It sucked most of the time, but there were those moments that I helped people in need. There were a lot of good cops. There were bad ones too, that one percent. Everyone else wanted to do the right thing. That was what those defund the police assholes ignored. It was easy for them, they had private security. They didn't live in the areas that suffered because of their idiotic policies."

"So, Jack, we need to wrap this up. But before we go, thank you for sharing your story on my show. It means a lot to me and my audience. We all know that there are still good cops out there. I know this wasn't easy for you and we, of course, shielded your identity. You paid an enormous price for doing the right thing."

"Thanks for having me, Swamp. I really mean that, but can I say one last thing?"

"Absolutely, it's my show and how many other people can say that?" Swamp laughed. There were plenty of other shows where government stooges spewed official propaganda. They all followed the same script and Swamp could write it for them. Swamp's a subversive and Jack's a traitor. They would call both of them white supremacists, racists, bigots, etc. The same tired old tropes. Wash, rinse, repeat.

"I just want to say that I left the force quietly because my family came first. It would have been great to go out with guns blazing, but I couldn't because I needed to keep them safe. I'm ashamed, but I really didn't have a choice. That was horrible, but what really sucked the most was that was the end of my brotherhood with other cops. Twenty-five years of service on the job, sacrificed for what? For my career to end like that? What a waste. And if you don't mind, I have one more thing to say."

"Of course, Jack." Swamp's respect for the risk Jack was taking was immeasurable.

"Despite it all, I am proud of what I did. I know I made a difference in a lot of lives. I helped many people. The job meant something to me, and I really didn't do it for the money. Hell, I would be lying if I said I didn't like car chases and getting into it when I had to, but that wasn't why I did it. I did it because I wanted to help and thought I could do some good. And that's why I'm here today. To tell you my story, to give you a perspective that people might not know. It sickens me they've corrupted the police department. Once that goes, we all go. We have to get it back. We'll never survive if we don't."

Jack bowed his head, and Swamp could feel Jack's shattered soul. He wasn't acting or exaggerating just to make a point. The corruption of an institution he loved deeply hurt him to his core.

"I don't think I can add anything, so let's just leave it here. As always, I thank all of you out there for watching the Swamp Simmons Show, one of the last dissenting voices in America. I'll continue to bring you stories like Jack's for as long as I'm breathing as a free man, which might not be much longer. I'll keep up the fight for however long it lasts so that maybe we can reclaim free speech as a birthright for our children and grandchildren. They didn't make this mess and they don't deserve the future we are giving them. This is Swamp Simmons, signing off as one of the last voices of the voiceless."

Swamp hit the button to stop the recording.

"Whoa," Jack exhaled, "what did I just do?"

Swamp noticed a very familiar look on Jack's face. It was a mix of fear, angst, and exhilaration. Most guests exhibited similar emotions. They all realized they had just put everything on the line by appearing on his show.

"I know. It's scary, isn't it?" Swamp didn't exactly have the most reassuring way about him.

"You know they can stop my fucking pension payments or do worse, right?"

"I know, and you need to be really careful, or you'll get us both killed. You can't tell anyone, and I mean anyone, that you were on this show. I can protect you from being exposed if you keep quiet. You did a great job. I don't think you gave any detailed information, and I will make absolutely sure that my guys scrub it for anything that could come back to bite you. The one thing I can't control is who you tell about this."

Jack nodded his head slowly. He understood the danger. Jack was no amateur, and he was good at keeping secrets. He wouldn't have lasted a month on the force if he didn't know when to shut his mouth.

"Can I ask you something?" Swamp sensed Jack was nervous about the upcoming question.

"Sure."

Jack hesitated but asked anyway, "How did you get into this? I mean, I think you are the only one on the internet who can get away with posting this stuff and you've been doing it for a few years now, even after they imposed the Speech Codes." Jack's voice faded, but he pressed on.

"And I guess the better question is, how the hell do you get away with it?"

Swamp normally answered this question with one of his stock truisms like "we are both better off the less we know about each other" but decided against it. His people confirmed Jack's story with their best sources in the police department. All agreed that Jack was a straight up guy that Swamp could trust. He also wanted Jack on his side. Jack had a lot of knowledge and contacts. They could really help each other out. Also, Swamp had taken a liking to him, and that was important to him.

"Well, that's an interesting question. I can't tell you everything and I don't think you want me to, but my background is in tech. I did time at the conglomerate that built the government's firewall. Some of us had no intention of unleashing Frankenstein's monster, but that's exactly what we did. So, part of my story is a little like yours. Except, I was a much bigger part of the problem than you ever were, and now I'm trying to become part of the solution."

Jack nodded again. "No doubt I've got debts to pay." The conversation resembled daytime TV, but in truth, they saw each other as kindred spirits.

"Yeah, we both do, but you know what? I really like all of this, talking to people and having them tell their stories." Now it was Swamp's turn to reminisce. "It was hard in the beginning. I was worried about losing everything: the wife, the house, the money. All that scared the shit out of me. Funny enough, I was still working in the industry at the time I started this show. I hated my job, and, rather than drowning myself in Scotch, I started making the videos as a kind of release. Losing myself in producing some kind of rant or story that flipped the middle finger to the government was cathartic. I loved that part, but I would get so nervous about getting caught that I would hyperventilate every time I uploaded a show to the internet."

Jack laughed and agreed. "I had the same experience when I first joined the police force, especially when I wrote up the paperwork after making an arrest. I was afraid I would write something wrong, and some lawyer was going to tear me apart on the stand. Worse, someone would beat a charge just because I made a mistake."

Swamp nodded. "Same here, but you know what? After a while, I got over that fear. I've been able to conceal my identity, and the wife left me and she had no clue that I film these videos. I'm able to manage that anxiety since it's only my ass on the line. It's still scary though. You can never eliminate it, but you can deal with it. It's always there, though."

Surprisingly, Jack immediately felt connected to Swamp, and that didn't happen very often. He usually needed time to warm up to someone since his days as a cop had ingrained distrust in him. Only other time he could think of when he instantly bonded with another male was with his first training officer. Jack fell for his wife immediately, though. She passed away several years ago because of complications from the virus. He missed her dearly. Since then, he mostly kept to himself, but this was a pleasant change. He might have found a friend.

Swamp continued. "It's strange, but I don't fear getting caught anymore, but you know what keeps me up at night? Putting out shitty content. And you know why? Because if I bore them, I'll lose them. No one will listen to me if all I do is complain. I can't just be an angry muckraker anymore. I have to entertain them." Swamp was giving Jack some inside baseball and Jack seemed to enjoy it.

"Now don't get me wrong, the anger helps and some days it drives me so much that I just want to beat people over the head and scream 'can't you people see what's going on here? Aren't you all scared shitless?' No one would listen to me if all I did was yell at them. Instead, I want them to feel like they enjoyed spending their time with me while I'm terrifying them."

Jack laughed, and Swamp smiled. Yet another satisfied viewer.

"But to answer your question a bit more directly, I've made peace with what I'm up against. Hell, what are we all facing today? I know I'm a dead man if they ever find me and it won't be enough just to kill me. They'll want to find out how I get through their firewall and make an example of me. I have no illusions that they will start by ripping off my fingernails, and then they'll get really nasty."

"No shit," Jack stated the obvious.

"Yeah, no shit." Swamp giggled in response. "I've got one more thing to tell you today. Only reason I'm telling you this is that my people vetted you and I know you're a straight up guy. When I realized what my company had in mind for the 'Patriot Firewall,' I built a minor flaw in the program that runs the damn thing and I have the codes you need to open it up. It's stored in a safe place and I'm the only one that knows the codes to use it. Even the best military intelligence guys don't have the technology to break it. Well, not yet. I know it won't last forever, but for now, they can't stop me."

Jack was not much of a technical guy, but he followed Swamp's story. He was also a superb listener, and that came in handy when he was questioning suspects. Jack could also pretend to be someone's friend, even if that person was a vile sub-human being who had just murdered an innocent victim. He wasn't pretending today. In fact, he wanted to help Swamp, but something he mentioned triggered his cop's instincts.

"You built it, right? And you're the only one who knows the flaw? Why didn't they drag everyone one who ever worked on the damn thing into some off the grid apartment and beat the shit out of them? I would have been at your house in five minutes."

"Wow," Swamp thought to himself. Jack's investigative skills were truly amazing. Swamp was glad Jack didn't join the special investigative unit. He would have been in big trouble.

"I'm glad you weren't after me, but my cyber security masks my location. In fact, my guys told me the government thinks that the hacks are coming from Russia and all I am is foreign disinformation. Can you believe that? It was all a farce the last time they blamed the Russians. Now, it's really not Russian disinformation, but they actually believe it is. They are telling as close to the truth as they ever have. Even though it's false."

"You used about three contradictory statements in that explanation, but believe it or not, I followed you. They knew the last Russian disinformation story was false, but they told it anyway. This time, they actually think it's the Russians, but it's not. Yeah, that is pretty funny."

Swamp snickered as he realized Jack had given a far more coherent explanation than he offered. "Look, I need to go, but I don't think that this is the last time we'll meet. I would love to have you on the show again if you want to come back. Also, please let me know if you have any trusted friends that might want to tell their story. Regardless, let's keep in touch."

Jack responded, "Yeah, I would like that. I might know someone..." Just as Jack was about to give him another name, a bell rang on Swamp's computer.

"Hold on just one second." Swamp looked down at his screen and clicked on the pop up. After a quick glance, he re-directed his eyes to Jack and then fixed his gaze back on his computer. He sat silent for a long moment. Afterward, he quietly muttered something under his breath.

"Murder, what? What the hell?" Swamp gazed directly at Jack as he spoke, but Jack didn't respond because he wasn't sure if Swamp was talking to him.

"Really?" Swamp's face scrunched up. It was a sign that he was struggling to understand something nonsensical.

"They just murdered him?" Swamp hadn't really asked Jack or anyone else the question, and he didn't expect an answer.

"Huh?" was all Jack could muster.

Swamp simply replied, "This is some sick shit. I've got to make a call."

*   *   *

More heavy knocks on a door.

This time, Cat was the one making the noise. He pounded on the entryway to their rehearsal studio and hoped he would give Trent a headache comparable to the one Robert and Kendra gave him. Cat had his key with him, but he didn't use it. He really didn't want to walk in and startle Trent since he was probably armed. A round of friendly fire would have been an ironic ending to his time on earth.

"Trent, it's me, Cat. Open the door, okay?"

Cat wasn't certain, but he thought he heard faint rustling noises behind the door. He hoped for a verbal response, but nothing came. The rustling could have been anyone or anything.

Cat kept pounding, "come on Trent, it's me, open the door. I have my key."

A soft voice finally emerged from behind the door.

"Cat?"

It was Trent.

"Yes, it's me, I'm coming in."

"Wait, wait," Trent pleaded. "I've barred the door. Are you alone?"

Now Cat had a problem. How would he persuade Trent to allow Kendra and Robert inside? And if he had a weapon...

"No, I'm not. I've got some friends with me. We can trust them." Cat winced, as he knew Trent wouldn't believe him.

There was a brief silence until Trent broke it.

"What the fuck were you thinking, Cat?" Trent's tone was a mix of anger and exasperation. Cat had brought people Trent didn't know to the studio after the massacre at the concert. Not the smartest thing Cat ever did.

"No, no, it's not like that, I swear. These are good people. I just met them, but they want to help us." Cat immediately regretted saying something so stupid.

"Are you out of your fucking mind?" Trent screamed. He had every right to.

"No, really, I mean it. It's not like that." Cat paused for a moment. He had an idea.

"Look, I'll come in myself, just me, and we can talk for a few minutes and after that, these guys can join us if you are okay. How about that?"

Silence again. Cat knew Trent wanted to see him, but he just told him he brought strangers to the studio. Who could blame him for not trusting him?

"Trent, I have another idea," Cat tried again. "I'm going to put my gun on the floor with the clip out. You open the door and pick it up, so you'll have it. I'll come in. Just me, and then we can just talk. Here, listen, I'm doing it now." Cat pulled his Beretta from his waistband, dropped the magazine, and placed the weapon on the concrete.

Kendra glared at Cat. "You had *that*, and you didn't tell me?"

Cat shrugged his shoulders and gave her a dismissive look. He asked himself why she wasn't packing heat?

His gesture with his gun seemed to help Trent relax as he just let out a "Hmmm." But he didn't open the door.

"Okay, Cat, one more thing before I let you in. I need to make sure you aren't being forced to do this. I'm going to ask a question and you need to answer it correctly. You'll know it, but I doubt they will. If you get it wrong, then I'll know that you are signaling to me I need to get the hell out of here."

Trent posed it before Cat agreed to a security question.

"Where was the very first gig MicroAggression played? What was the name of the place?"

"Whew." Cat thanked his lucky stars that he knew the answer. That was a close one. What if Trent had asked him something he didn't know? This could have easily gone off the rails. Cat smiled, but just as he spoke Kendra shouted, "Pete's Candy Store in Brooklyn, I was there."

There was that silence again.

Cat looked at Kendra in stunned disbelief. She actually knew that.

"What?" she rhetorically asked Cat. "I saw that one, and I figured we could cut through all of this super password bullshit."

They heard the lock and the deadbolt disengage. The door slowly swung open, and Trent stood motionless in the opening. He grabbed Cat's gun and the clip, handing both back to him. "Here," he said with a grin, "I have no clue how she knew that."

The three of them followed Trent into the rehearsal space, formerly known as a garage. Cat had leased it for five years and recently renewed it for another five. The rent was cheap because the prior tenant had used the space to cook meth. Some days, the smell of the prior tenant's chemicals gave Cat a headache. Apparently, five years wasn't enough to get rid of that stench. The meth lab/garage/rehearsal studio was in an awful area, but it had plenty of square footage for the band's instruments and gear. Best of all, it was cheap. Trent holed up there after escaping from the concert. Cat wasn't sure what he was doing the whole time, except he knew for certain he didn't spend any time cleaning up after himself. There were beer cans, pizza boxes, and empty fast-food wrappers strewn about.

"Looks like all of you guys enjoy fine dining with your booze," Kendra noted dryly.

"Yeah, why else would you be in a band?" Robert chimed in. Trent and Cat nodded in agreement.

Trent had calmed down somewhat after Kendra cut through the nonsense. In terms of height, Trent was a little shorter than Cat. Cat was approximately six feet two inches, but Trent had a slightly more muscular build. Trent was wearing a hooded sweatshirt but the same jeans he wore at the concert. Cat could tell because his pants still had the powder burns from the grenade.

They all gathered around the large table in the center of the room. This was where MicroAggression sat when they needed to have a discussion. No one said anything as they instead exchanged glances. A few moments passed before Trent broke the ice. He needed answers, and he needed them now.

"Well, now that we've gotten through all the pleasantries, I've got a lot of questions for the three of you." Trent punctuated his statement with nervous laughter.

"Cat, I've got two reasonable questions for you. First, just what the fuck went down at that concert? And second, who the hell are these people?"

Cat nodded his head. Trent was right. Those were two reasonable questions, and Cat had sarcastic answers for both.

"Okay, let's start by answering the second one. As for introductions, this is Robert. He sucker-punched me earlier. And this lady on my left is Kendra. She told me I smelled bad. As for what's going on, it's really pretty simple. They showed up at my door and told me that both Simon and Richard were dead. They also mentioned that the sick pieces of shit who shot up the show disemboweled Richard. And you know what else they did? They fucking videotaped themselves while they were cutting Richard's guts out. Did I miss anything guys? How is your day going, Trent?"

Cat continued his diatribe: "And now, my new friends want the four of us to form a band together and continue playing our songs. How does that sound to you, Trent? Make sense? Good, let's go out for a few beers."

Cat saw the look on Trent's face and immediately realized that his anger had gotten the best of him. He had just let Trent know that two of his best friends were dead. At least Kendra had braced him for it. Cat just let him have it.

"Trent, I'm so sorry. I shouldn't have told you that. Well, I should have prepared you for it. God, I'm so, so sorry."

Trent said nothing. He just stared at Cat, who closed his eyes and shook his head.

"They videoed it?" Trent asked sheepishly. "Why?"

"We don't know," Kendra added. "We are trying to figure that out. I'm so sorry Trent."

Trent's eyes welled up, and he halted with a sob.

Cat felt awful, but he continued.

"Trent again, that was terrible of me. I really shouldn't have done that. I know I haven't come to terms with this yet, but the only thing that I can think of is that we need to get the fuck out of Dodge. Head as far south or north as we can before they put our heads on spikes and hang them on the Brooklyn Bridge. I'm getting the feeling that someone doesn't like us."

Robert and Kendra were the only ones to notice Cat's unintentional humor, but, oddly, Cat's tirade and then remorse gave Trent some comfort. Kendra's thoughts helped too. Not ten minutes ago, he had barricaded himself behind the rehearsal door, convinced that Cat was there to kill him. Paranoid thoughts consumed his mind since the concert ended. At one point, he convinced himself that one of the other band members had set them up. Cat's sarcastic rant had eased his worry. Trent figured that since Cat was acting like his normal self, he probably wasn't an assassin.

Trent agreed. "Yeah, we need to get out of New York. God knows what they have in mind for us."

"Look," Robert interrupted. "Everything you just said made perfect sense. No doubt that Richard's murder was a warning to you and anyone like you. You know that it's game over if we let them get away with it, right? We will lose everything. We need to fight them, and we need to do it now."

Robert spoke from the heart. He experienced oppression and humiliation in his time and believed in his soul that this was pure intimidation. Whenever someone tried to force him into doing something, his immediate reaction was to resist. Robert reacted the same way when phony woke people implied he was helpless because of his skin color. He confronted anyone who disguised their racism with false platitudes of concern. Low expectation bigots were still bigots. He could stand on his own two feet. Anyone who thought he couldn't just because of his complexion was a racist. They had to face this. The stakes were immense.

Robert continued. "You understand that murdering Richard was a sign that you're winning, right? Think about it, the only reason they took a step like that, to be that drastic, was because you got under their skin, and they didn't like it."

"He's right," Kendra interjected. "You guys got a lot of attention with your shows. There were thousands of anti-censorship posts tagged to your band online. I'm not sure how they got through the firewall, but I'm sure the government didn't like it."

Cat cut her off. "Well, I don't give a flying fuck how many 'dislikes' the mob gave the Speech Codes. It's all a bunch of bullshit. The bots, the likes, the AI, it's all manipulation. It's meaningless until someone else puts their ass on the line just to perform a show."

Kendra let Cat finish. She felt horrible for him. She briefly thought about trying to influence his anatomical voice and decided not to. This was not the time.

"I get it. The Gestapo murdered your friends, not mine. You and Trent suffered the worst, and Richard and Simon paid the ultimate price. Their lives meant something. But don't you want payback? Don't you want them to be remembered rather than erased when they manufacture the next crisis?"

"What the hell could we do about that?" Trent answered for Cat. "It's not a perfect world, and no one lives happily ever after. Let someone else do the dirty work while we get as far away from here as possible."

"Trent's right and by the way, what's stopping you from forming your own band and doing this yourself? Why do you need us?" Cat asked.

Kendra didn't have a brilliant answer for that, but she tried her best.

"It's very hard to put into words, but the only way I can describe it is that you guys have something. And not just that, it's the symbolism of you two continuing to do what you do despite what they did to Richard. I think that if you gave them the middle finger and kept going, you would really hit them where it hurts, their pride."

Cat shot back, "I don't think you really know what it's like dodging bullets while you are fighting your way out of a concert. I really don't think you get it."

Robert jumped back into the conversation. "I completely understand, Cat, but remember, we were there, too. We were there to see you and your band and were even going to discuss a collaboration with Richard. We took a chance too. Honestly, all this scares the shit out of me, but now everything has changed. To tell you the truth, I don't think you have a choice. I'm guessing you don't have a lot of money and have nowhere to go. Don't you think they'll find you if you take off?"

It was true. Both Cat and Trent knew it, but Robert hammered the point home. These people had killed Richard and recorded it. What would they do to the two of them if they tracked them down? Probably worse if they embarrassed them more. And what if they ran? What then? What jobs could they get, exactly? There aren't that many lucrative jobs for people trying to disappear. Menial labor paid in cash by a boss that didn't ask questions. Is that how they wanted to live the rest of their lives?

While Kendra refused to use her other assets for the moment, she wasn't above appealing to their egos. "At least if you stay, you can show them what you're made of and that you won't back down. Plus, we can help you get even with the motherfuckers."

Kendra read their body language and knew that she needed to take this in a different direction. They hadn't left the room. That was a good sign. But, the discussion had reached its limit, so she called an audible.

"Anyone want to go out and get a bite and more than a few drinks? I know I could use a lot of alcohol. I'm just guessing, but looking at the number of empties you both left, I'm thinking that both of you would at least be interested in getting some beers. Do I have that right? In fact, there's an outstanding sports bar over here somewhere. I'm trying to think of the name..."

"O'Hara's?" both Cat and Trent asked in unison.

"Yeah, that's it. They have every kind of bar food and draft imaginable. I want to get away from this shit for a little while. How about it?"

Trent asked the obvious question, "Uh, don't you think we really ought to lie low right now? Do you really think it's a good idea to go out in public?"

"Believe it or not, I think it will be okay. You guys know that O'Hara's is your typical biker bar, and we all look like we could fit in, and no one will notice us. If they're watching us, then I doubt they'll try to take us out in a public place. For now, I'm guessing they think they made their point with Richard, so my guess is that we are okay. Different story in the future, but for right now I think we'll be alright."

"Actually, I could really use something to eat and a few drinks. I'm in." Cat was extremely hungry and quite thirsty.

"Yeah, I'll do that." Trent joined in.

"Okay, let's go."

Chapter Six

"Why did I order the Cajun Death Sauce?"

Although Cat intended to keep his thoughts to himself about the wings being too hot, he voiced his pain to the entire group. Flames engulfed his mouth and eyes. He tried to prevent the rising magma with a long swig of his beer. Without thinking, he rubbed his eyes. That was a big mistake. This was going to be bad.

Kendra watched him struggle and shook her head. "Why the hell do you guys do that?" She directed her question to Cat but was curious about how Trent and Robert felt about such Y chromosomal stupidity.

"Why do we do what?" Cat answered her question with a question as he wiped both tears and ghost pepper infused sauce from his eyes with a paper towel. Ghost peppers had no flavor or any real purpose on earth. Their sole function was to make things as unbearably spicy as possible. Those who said they enjoyed ghost peppers for their taste were clearly lying and had to be masochists. Had he put his finger directly in his eye, the hot sauce would have incapacitated him.

"Why do you order wings that are hot enough to peel the paint off the walls? You look like you're about to keel over, and it really doesn't look the least bit enjoyable." Kendra asked, even though she knew she would never receive a coherent answer.

"What do you mean, they aren't enjoyable? These are fantastic." Cat mumbled as ghost pepper-induced moisture engulfed his face.

"Yeah, right, why don't you just admit that it's a stupid male thing to eat those things? You never see women eat them unless they're trying to get someone's attention."

"That's not true," Trent chimed in through a mouthful of chili con queso dip. "I've seen women eat them. In fact, I've offered them to women, and they've loved them."

"Wait. You've eaten wings while you were out on a date?"

"Yeah, why not?" Trent responded.

Even Robert agreed. "I've eaten wings on a date. I probably wouldn't order them on the first or second date, but once you get past the initial bullshit, then sure I would get them. Wouldn't think twice."

"No wonder you're all single," Kendra retorted. She should have ended the conversation after that remark. Unfortunately for her, she didn't and things got much worse. Especially after she uttered her next two sentences.

"Don't you know what *usually* happens on the third date? You obviously have no respect for what it does to us."

"Huh?" Cat asked.

"What?" Kendra responded without thinking. She didn't realize she had said the last part out loud.

"You were saying what it does to us? What does it do to you?"

Kendra had downed a few vodka cranberries. Perhaps with just one drink in her, she could have found a clever line to redirect the conversation. Unfortunately, she was honest instead.

"You know, you look like some kind of caveman when you shovel those things into your mouth while we watch, right? Second, well, do you know how bad you smell after eating those things? Especially the real hot ones? Mix that with the beer that sweats out of your pores and spews from your breath. It's awful. I can tell you I've wanted to spray perfume on men when they're not looking to keep from throwing up."

"Oh, come on Kendra," Cat shot back. He also had several drinks in him and was far more honest than normal. Especially with someone he just met and wanted to impress. "Women may say that they don't like Neanderthals, but they actually do. Face it, you don't respect prissy men who eat salads. We know it and you know it. That's why we order a steak or some other primal meal on the first date."

"Look at the ego on you! For your information, men taking care of themselves *is* attractive to us. Your egos tell you we want knuckle draggers, and that's another thing you guys lie to yourselves about. Fact is, most men can't help themselves and we have little choice." Kendra took another long pull from the straw stirring her fourth vodka cranberry and steered the conversation in an unintended direction.

"And don't you know how much it hurts?" she murmured out of the side of her mouth.

"Shit," her inner monologue screamed. "Why in the world did you ask them that? That's the last thing you want to discuss..." Then she thought to herself that if she kept quiet, the men would lose interest. Unfortunately, they didn't.

"What hurts?" Cat asked. He was genuinely curious about what she was talking about.

"Ehhh," Kendra muttered as she tried to buy time to think. What she said next really didn't help matters.

"Can't we just end this conversation now?" Yeah, that was going nowhere.

"No, what hurts?" Trent repeated Cat's question. She could feel the men staring at her.

"Ehhh," she repeated. "Uh, God, uh..." she stalled and took yet another long swig of her drink and then it hit her. "Well, let me put it this way. Do you know sometimes, the next day, after you eat those wings, how you feel with the aftereffects? You know, maybe in your stomach, maybe elsewhere?" Kendra tried to make them uncomfortable, so they would talk about something else. Maybe if she talked about bodily functions, it would unnerve them? She knew she could clear a room of males with a stray remark about her menstrual cycle or breast feeding. It didn't work. Unfortunately, they were really loaded and just stared and waited for her to answer her own question.

Then a lightbulb over Cat's head lit up. "You mean in the bathroom?"

"Sure, in the bathroom." Kendra whispered back to Cat without looking at him.

Cat's face flushed. Now it was his turn to search for a subtle method to end this conversation. Robert and Trent were still clueless, but Trent, being more drunk, blurted out, "You're talking about the next day burn, right?"

Kendra shielded her eyes with her hand. She would have given anything to be anywhere else at the moment but mirrored his comment with, "Yes, the next day burn. It burns a sensitive part of you. Well, there's a part of me that is very sensitive..." as she trailed off, Robert snapped to attention. Finally, he figured out what she was talking about and shielded his eyes with his hand.

But the third amigo didn't get it. "And?" Trent urged her to finish her sentence.

"Oh, my God," Kendra mouthed under her breath. She really regretted opening this door.

Robert and Cat pleaded with Trent with their eyes, urging him to run away. Far, far away. The silent eye daggers didn't work, so Cat summoned all the verbal and non-verbal communication skills he could muster to help tunnel through the mud in Trent's skull.

Cat asked, "What part does she have that we don't have that might burn when exposed to hot sauce?"

Trent paused, and then his eyes widened, and his face turned beet red. He finally got it and wanted to join Cat and Robert at the exit.

Robert gestured toward the largest television in the bar. "I see the Mets are up by two runs."

"What inning is it?" Kendra had no interest in baseball, but was happy to talk about anything other than that last topic.

They all turned their attention to the television, but the game faded out. The words "Special Report" replaced the Mets.

"Ah shit," Cat exclaimed. He would much rather watch the rest of the Mets game.

A disembodied voice spoke through the bar's sound system, causing all the TVs to switch to the announcement.

"We interrupt this broadcast for a special announcement from the President of the United States."

"Good evening, my fellow Americans, and the rest of you." Annabelle Ramirez started with her usual divisive opening line. She wanted to remind her subjects that they were in her country, not the other way around.

A smattering of boos emanated from the crowd in the bar.

"Thanks for giving me the time to speak with you for a few minutes this evening. As you can see, I'm coming to you from my kitchen in my home, my actual home, the one I lived in before the White House. I'm here because I thought that this would be a perfect reminder of just how far we've come but, more importantly, where we are going. I talked with you on Zoom and other platforms during Covid and I wanted to remind you of that time. That was a time in our country where the good people of America pulled together to beat the virus. When we sacrificed, we helped each other realize that we all needed to do our part. We wore our masks with pride, two or three of them sometimes. The best of us social distanced and took our shots, all for the common good and to do our part to beat the enemy."

She gestured behind her to a Sub-Zero freezer. "You, see? I still have my ice cream and my wine collection down there in my cellar. I'm the same person I was when we started this journey together. We brought change to this magnificent land of ours, but in the end, we are all just human beings. Human beings with flaws. Human beings with feelings and rights that are graciously granted to us by our government."

"It's very important to keep our flaws in mind for our discussion tonight. I know the topic of the human condition is top of mind for a lot of us. No one is perfect, only those who strive to grow. We will get there my friends, someday, but tonight I want to discuss a video circulating on the internet. It shows some very flawed people. I know the content is disturbing. There are those who understand its context and others who may not fully comprehend it. And while I just don't understand the depravity of some people who are lucky enough to live in our United States, I hope our discussion tonight will at least give you some comfort that we, as your leaders, understand and will do all we can to help our country heal. We will endure these difficult times."

"First, for those of you who don't know, there is a video online that depicts the death of someone who had become somewhat famous, or infamous, really. The name he went by was Richard Uprising, although we assume that was not his real name. The name was a mask and not the kind he should have been wearing. He wore a mask that hid a deeply disturbed soul who thought it was perfectly acceptable to insult and degrade others. His mask concealed the truly hateful person he is or was."

"I'm sure it's very obvious to everyone, but, you see, Richard was a racist. He believed that the White race was superior to the rest of us. He would have fit in nicely in Hitler's Germany as an arm of the propaganda wing of the Nazi party."

"But at least he was honest to a point. He told you what he thought and how he felt. Richard unmasked his true feelings during those performances and, unfortunately, there was a segment of our population who attended his concerts. Can you believe that? Those people paid to see a racist oppress people."

"I'm sure this video disturbed you. Let me be clear, even the uninformed don't deserve to die like that. Even the undeserved among us shouldn't suffer. Those who put an end to Richard's persecution were wrong, and we will prosecute them. Of course, we may never find them."

"However," Annabelle paused for just about five seconds, but it felt much longer.

"There is another side to this story and there are some people who will not say what needs to be said. As you know, I am not one of those people." She stopped again to give her fans time to finish their purple Kool-Aid.

"If there is one thing that everyone knows about me, it's that I will always tell you the truth. And, unfortunately, there is not much we in the government can do to protect people like Richard. He profited off of the misery of others. He enjoyed making others feel bad and denigrating anyone who is different. These vermin are the modern-day version of the Ku Klux Klan. Only difference is they sell tickets to other racists who gladly pay to hear them spew their vile hatred. The biggest problem is not the Richard Uprisings of the world. There will always be those who are uninformed. No, the ultimate problem is those who listen to him. Think about it, would Richard Uprising exist if no one bought tickets to see him? What if the venues refused to allow him to perform? Just think what we could accomplish if others did their part?"

"But he exists. Well, he used to exist at least. There is very little I can do to protect you from people like him. Remember, once Congress finally votes to criminalize violations of the Speech Codes, then there will be no Richard Uprisings. They will be in jail. Unfortunately, until that day comes, we will have to suffer with people like him in the world."

"Next, I want to talk directly to those who stopped Richard Uprising from spewing his hate. I want to tell you that while I do not condone what you did, I understand your pain and why you felt it was necessary to take such drastic measures, even if they were improper. Your pain is my pain. I understand how harmful and how hurtful his actions were and dream of the day when you will not feel the need to remove a cancer like Richard Uprising. We all dream of the day when we can live our lives in peace, without the offense and humiliation he caused you. I dream of a day when we will have cleansed this country of racist ideals that fuel its uninformed and misguided factions. Why did he hate you? What was your sin that

Richard could use to justify the harm he inflicted on you? Your only sin was being different. You might have gone a bit too far with your actions this time, but some day such drastic measures will not be necessary. One day, we will all understand that kindness and compassion and the desire to accept all groups should be the true calling of this nation of ours."

"Before I close, I need to mention two things. First, I want to announce a small step, to help prevent future bloodshed. And second, and more importantly, I want to issue a warning."

"First the announcement. Tonight, I'm announcing that we will send undercover agents to attend random concerts and monitor content. We hope to prevent a repeat of such violence. Importantly, this team will have no law enforcement powers but will simply be there to monitor the content and make sure that everyone has a good time. If mayhem erupts, then any monitor who is at the show will report to law enforcement so that we can inflict justice. We granted these agents the power to identify and publicly condemn individuals who engage in behavior that Richard Uprising would have found acceptable. These agents will be available to testify in any civil lawsuits. Hopefully, these measures will stem the tide of violence. If not, then we will consider more drastic measures."

"Finally, I want all of you out there who think this is some kind of game to know that we will not tolerate your behavior. We will prosecute those that took this unfortunate action against that racist, if we ever find them. But that is a reactive fix. It's not the root cause. There is very little we can do to protect those that behave like Richard Uprising. We must uphold the law even though I understand your motivations. Richard and his band stuck their middle fingers at us and the Speech Codes. But he was really hurting the oppressed the most. Again, we will not tolerate revenge killings, but we can't prevent them either. If you spew hatred like Richard Uprising, you are on your own. Consider yourself warned."

"Thank you again for allowing me to speak from my home to yours. I speak from my heart when I say, may God bless those Americans that are with me, and may he have mercy on the souls of the rest of you."

Ramirez faded out, and the Mets resumed their game.

Cat, Kendra, Robert, and Trent stared at each other, shocked by what they witnessed. No one spoke for several minutes until Kendra broke the silence.

"Did she really just say what I think she said?"

No one immediately responded to her rhetorical question. The speech had jolted them into sobriety. Kendra threw the question out again.

"No really, did she just say that she understands the feelings of murderers? That it's okay to kill someone if they offend you?"

The questions hung over the four of them like the sword of Damocles. No one wanted to answer, since a response might cause the blade to fall.

"I think she did," Cat sighed. He couldn't believe what he just heard.

"We're dead." Trent said while looking at Cat, but Robert and Kendra took notice. They would likely suffer the same fate.

"Actually, Trent, I think you're right, we are dead."

Cat's anger surged inside of him. He thought about Richard and everything he stood for. Richard was no racist; he didn't have a prejudiced bone in his body. Cat knew Ramirez was involved in this somehow.

But Trent was right. They were living on borrowed time. Ramirez would never stop pursuing them, but that wasn't all. She wanted to destroy everything the country stood for. Orwell had predicted this, and Cat needed to make a choice. Run and hide or live his life on his own terms? If he chose the latter, was he willing to go down fighting in order to stop this train wreck? In a sober moment, the former path might have appealed to him. Right now, it didn't.

"I think what Kendra said was absolutely correct." Cat could tell he was close to losing control of his temper as he started speaking in halting, complete sentences, a sure sign he was about to blow his top.

"Richard hurt them. They feared him and what he stood for. They hunted him down and we're next, but we also might be the ones with the best chance of stopping this."

Kendra said nothing, but the nervous smile on her face communicated volumes. Robert nodded his head as he spoke. "I was thinking the same thing, Cat. We can really fuck with them."

Trent looked terrified. "Are you crazy? Are all of you really that far out of your fucking minds? You heard the same thing I did. The fucking president of the fucking United States just declared open season on anyone who says anything offensive, and you want to go through with it? Are you all really out of your goddamn minds?"

"Trent, I heard the same thing you did." Cat's rage was clear as he used Trent's name while he maintained eye contact.

"I don't like being threatened. I don't like being lied about. Who the fuck does she think she is? How in the world is it ok to shut down disagreement by calling the other side offensive? And you know what she wants? She wants the right to throw us in jail. That's totalitarianism. And how many wars did we fight to end tyranny in other countries?"

After pausing for a second, Cat picked up his beer and chugged the remaining half of the glass. He swiped the foam off of his mouth and continued. "There's a way forward here where we can stick it to them. She wants us to be afraid. We are, but we can't show it. We can't be the only ones that see this for what it is. Ramirez wants to end all dissent and we can't let her."

Trent erupted, "And what can we do about it? Play cover songs in bars? What the hell is that going to do other than get our asses killed?"

"Trent, we hit them where it hurts. We hurt their pride. They thought Speech Codes would make us all cower in fear. We didn't. And when they realized it didn't work, they overreacted and lashed out. But you know what? Kendra and Robert are right. They are the ones that are cowering, not us. They fear they lost their grip on us and thought that they could kill Richard and end the argument. The argument is not over. Just hear me out..."

*   *   *

Swamp was stunned. Did Ramirez genuinely believe that people were that stupid? Did she think she could condone killing her enemies and face no repercussions? Wasn't she worried about a backlash?

Regarding a backlash, Swamp hoped that it would come at some point. Ramirez was gunning for complete control. Didn't people know that a government that stifled all dissent was not a government at all? That was dictatorship. Even committed leftists knew that someday they could be the next target of a future tyrant, didn't they? A second civil war might be inevitable if America continued down this path.

Swamp braced himself and turned on the news networks to find out what the talking heads were saying about Ramirez's speech. Who knows, maybe a commentator or two would condemn her for inciting violence against her political enemies?

He first switched on WOLF. The network leaned conservative, but it was the only one that presented both sides. WOLF's commentators heavily criticized Ramirez, the Speech Codes, and the country's direction. However, it was pretty clear these pundits measured their reactions to comply with the Speech Codes. Most cautioned Ramirez about inspiring extremism and criticized her for not sufficiently calling out the murderers. They wanted to believe her when she said the police were investigating the killing, but implored her to denounce the violence.

He then turned on NSMBC. This network aired Ramirez's propaganda. They repeated every lie she told and every narrative that helped her cause. When the facts didn't add up, they either changed the subject or ignored the story all together. Their "balance" was to hire people that once held contrary views and had now realized the error of their ways. It had to be different this time, right? Even NSMBC couldn't support a call to violence, could they?

Yes, they could.

The NSMBC commentator congratulated Ramirez on her "balanced and nuanced" tone. She applauded Ramirez for "moving the needle" toward a more inclusive and just society. The woman actually commended Ramirez for her stance on the violence and applauded her for understanding the motivations of the killers. Didn't they have every right to be outraged by Richard's offensive behavior? She believed that Ramirez's speech set the stage for an appropriate dialog on offensive speech, leading to a better America.

Swamp switched off the TV, stunned by what he had seen. How could anyone justify murdering someone simply because their words offended them? How could they ignore America's descent into authoritarianism?

It was time for a whiskey. Straight up, no ice. It was that kind of night. He poured himself a glass and contemplated his next move.

It was time to respond in kind.

Chapter Seven

"You're really serious about this?" Despite his tone, Trent was not being sarcastic. The four of them had argued about Cat's plan nonstop over the past few days. Robert and Kendra were on board, but Trent was the last holdout. He thought this was a terrible idea. Even Richard had not gone this far.

"Trent, I really think this can work."

The four of them agreed to meet at the rehearsal studio to discuss it again. Reasonable minds could differ on whether Cat's plan could work. Actually, that was being kind. No sane person would consider this unless they knew they had just signed their own death warrant. Still, Cat thought Trent would eventually come around, so he tried again.

"Ok, let me go through it again, but I'll put it a different way. I want you to think about the story lines from the old pro-wrestling shows we used to watch. Remember when they wanted to turn a bad guy into a good guy or a good guy into a bad guy?"

Trent stared at Cat with a stunned look on his face. He said nothing, so Kendra jumped in.

"Really? Pro-wrestling? That's the best you can come up with, Cat?" Her knowledge of that form of entertainment was rather limited, except she thought that only teenage boys would be stupid enough to watch it. She realized she was dealing with three men who hadn't really matured much beyond that phase of their development. Of course, that was not atypical in her dealings with males.

"Would you please?" Cat shot back. He sounded like a bickering husband, even though he and Kendra just met.

"Okay, okay, by all means. If it helps to talk about pro-wrestling, then go ahead." Kendra could play the nagging wife, too.

"Anyway, yes, remember when they used to change the storyline and the narrative for the arc of a character? You remember, right? They always did that, especially when the bad guy turned good?"

Trent couldn't remember the last time he discussed, watched, or even thought of pro-wrestling. Was Cat really serious? He was really invoking pro-wrestling nonsense to convince him to take part in a plot against the federal government? Could this be the dumbest conversation he's ever had?

Cat continued, "They started the ruse the same way, with some kind of misunderstanding. Something would always go wrong, like the bad guy's tag team partner would inadvertently hit him with a chair or they would have a fight over a female manager? Then, the bad guy would form an alliance with the good guy, even though he was his sworn enemy?"

Kendra rolled her eyes and wondered to herself whether she could get the last twenty minutes of her life back.

"Then they would schedule a grudge match so the characters could fight it out, but really all they were doing was setting up the big reveal?"

"The big reveal?" Kendra couldn't help herself. "Really?"

"Yes, the big reveal. That was when you found out that the former bad guy was only pretending to be good so that all the other bad guys could ambush the good guy. Once they revealed the ruse, all the other bad guys would gang up and beat the hell out of the good guy. It was the old double cross."

"I can't believe this..." Kendra shook her head, "there was no other way you could have explained this? No other way? Did either of you ever get past the eighth grade? Did you both have parking spots in Junior High School?"

"Yes, yes, I know. You females are oh so much more sophisticated than us. I know it's not highbrow television like

86

when all of those women whore it up on a reality show to marry the rich dude. Or when those catty housewives fight it out for our entertainment? Women don't seem to think that type of trash is below them. And tell me, how are those shows different from pro-wrestling? The government is lying to us just like reality TV. In fact, pro-wrestling might be more truthful since the wrestlers didn't really expect us to believe it. How could two 300-pound guys beat the ever-living shit out, leave no marks, and then do it all again the next night? Now, the assholes in the government think we are so fucking stupid that we don't know they're full of shit. They actually think we believe them."

"I see your point." Kendra chuckled. "It's hard to believe, but you might be right. The government probably believes we are dumber than die-hard wrestling fans."

"Can I finish now?" The couple bickered again.

"Yes, please do."

"Thank you." Cat continued. "We are going to do the same thing as the pro wrestlers. We'll make people think that we've learned our lesson from what happened to Richard, but it's all a game. Then, when we've played it out, we'll do the big reveal and show them we duped them all along. Unlike the government, we'll tell them we lied to them."

Trent nodded his head. He couldn't believe it, but Cat may have somewhat convinced him that this plan could work. However, he spotted a problem.

"Okay, let's say we do this. Would anyone believe it? I mean, everyone knows that you and I were in MicroAggression. The videos are all online. We've played 'offensive' songs for many years and then poof, suddenly, we just reinvent ourselves? Would anyone buy that?"

Cat had expected this question.

"No, it's not as simple as doing the opposite of what we used to do. Our old fans would revolt and the woke crowd would call bullshit. We just have to be far more subtle about it."

Subtlety intrigued Trent. In the last ten minutes, Cat had just about changed his mind. And he did it by talking about pro-wrestling.

"We are still going to be offensive, but we need to do it differently. We can only offend those who are on the 'okay to offend' list."

Trent had a confused look on his face. Cat had just lost him, so he took a different approach.

"Think of it this way. From what I've gathered about our current state of affairs, there is a spectrum of offensive conduct. Society accepts some of it, but not all of it. In fact, upsetting the wrong people or the wrong institution can get you killed. We'll play offensive stuff and get away with it as long as it is not offensive to the wrong people."

"I still don't get it," Trent confessed.

"I think I get what he's saying." Robert said. He largely stayed silent during Cat and Trent's exchange. He thought it was best for the old friends to settle their differences by themselves. However, Robert had a hard time following Cat's word salad, so he helped him, "there are certain groups of people you may make fun of, and no one will call you out. We can stick it to those groups because they don't count. There's one in particular..."

"White men?" Trent asked.

"Bingo," Kendra chimed in.

But Trent saw another problem. "How are we going to do that? Would anybody think that it's plausible that former MicroAggression members would sing songs denigrating White men? It's the same problem. No one will believe us."

Cat smirked because he had an answer to Trent's logical question. Despite his best effort, Cat's grin morphed into a demented smile his favorite comic book villain would have been proud of. He was ready for his own big revelation. However, instead of telling them, he wanted to show them. So, he put his hands together and cracked his knuckles. He moved his arm in a grand sweeping motion and pointed his index finger right at Kendra.

"Oh, boy," Robert murmured.

"What? Why are you all looking at me?" Kendra maintained her poker face for just a moment, but she couldn't help herself and laughed. She understood Cat's idea and thought it was fantastic.

"We have Kendra, and she can get away with singing just about anything, since she has immunity for offending males. Now, she can't sing the other offensive stuff. She can't risk becoming a Karen, not yet anyway. But we can position this as 'Trent and Cat try to atone for their sins as oppressors' or some other such nonsense." Cat spoke the last sentence in a singsong manner, mocking the absurdities that the woke crowd embraced.

He continued: "Then, once we take the joke as far as we can, we'll do the big reveal. We've been playing offensive songs all along, and none of you had a problem. When we play stuff that offends the wrong people, *then* you have a problem. Total hypocrisy. Hell, we could even break out some of our old favorites when the end inevitably comes. You know, stuff like: A Day in Algiers, Japanese Radio, you know, the shit that got Richard killed."

Cat glossed over the last part of his sentence in his stream-of-consciousness, but the others took notice. He really referred to his friend's death as 'the shit that got Richard killed'? Cat must have lost himself in the idea. He wasn't an indifferent person, but that was cold.

"Think about it, we sucker them in with stuff that is actually offensive, and we do it under the guise that Trent and I have gone woke. No one cares because it only offends White males. Then, everyone who tolerates anti-male music defends us until we embarrass them and expose them as frauds by playing the songs they hate. We'll get them to support us and then we turn on them. It's classic!"

Finally, Robert tried to bring Cat back down to earth. "Cat, you can drive trucks through the holes in your plan. First, you assumed we would get big enough for people to care about us. Second, if that happens, you assume that there will be people that both hate and defend us. Third, the logical outcome of all of this is that we all end up dead. Do you think that might be a problem? Maybe even a small one?"

"Well, I didn't say that my plan was perfect. I'll give you that there may be some minor speed bumps, particularly surrounding the dying part." Cat deadpanned, although the others weren't sure if he was serious.

"Death is a minor speed bump?" Trent asked.

"I don't think that any of these problems are insurmountable. We can work them out with a little fine tuning."

"Fine tuning?" Trent repeated.

"Yes, fine tuning," Cat answered.

Cat, Kendra, and Robert burst out laughing. Trent joined them after he saw the irony of their discussion. Robert wiped away tears from the gallows humor. "So, let me get this straight. Murder and mayhem are speed bumps. We can make some minor modifications. All will be wonderful with a little 'fine tuning'?"

Cat tried to compose himself and persisted, "Look, let's start with the cover songs and the offensive male stuff. We'll be safe with that. I said it before. I think we are all dead anyway, but at least we can make a living and do what we enjoy while we whistle our way into the graveyard."

Kendra, Robert, and Trent nodded in agreement. Everyone knew Cat was right. The best-case scenario was cancelation, and that assumed everything worked perfectly. At worst, they would join Richard in the afterlife. But at least they could say they died with their boots on.

Then Kendra threw a wrench into everything.

"I'll sing the anti-male songs, but I don't want to be the full-time singer. Maybe we could just strategically add it to a few shows? I think it would be cool if we let the audience wonder whether we are going to play that stuff. It'll add a sense of mystery and besides, those other songs don't all really work with a female voice."

"Actually, that brings up a good question." Robert said, as he considered the logistics. "We need to figure out who's going to do what."

Trent took it a step further: "Well, are we going to only stick with four people? Do we want to get someone else in? Five is a little easier to make sure we cover all the sounds."

Cat shook his head. "No, we have to stick with just us. We can't let anyone else in on this. We'll need to do it as a four piece."

"Agreed," Kendra concurred. "Has to be a four piece. I can also play a second guitar and cover keyboards when I'm not singing."

Robert added, "I'm best on drums. I can handle it if you need me to play something else. But I'm a hell of a drummer. Definitely not much of a singer, though."

"Well, that leaves it to me and you, Trent. Lead guitar or bass?" Cat asked, but he already knew the answer.

So did Trent. "Do we even really need to discuss it?"

"No, not really. I've got the lead guitar, and I can program some keyboard sounds and control them with pedals. I'll do the singing too, but I'm really going to need to work on it though. You guys know I sang a few songs with MicroAggression, but I've never been the lead."

Kendra interjected, "We can also do a couple of duets, too. That would be fun as part of the anti-male part of the show."

Hello.

Cat's anatomical voice was pleased.

"Okay, so that settles it, I'll sing and play lead guitar. Trent will be on bass; Robert will be on drums and the lovely Kendra will be on keyboards and a second guitar. She will do the singing when we bust out the anti-male stuff. Are we all agreed?"

Everyone nodded as they formed the band. They still had to address plenty of other issues. Robert, the practical one, brought the first one up. "Okay, so how are we going to promote this venture?"

"That's a good question." Trent's wheels turned in his mind. "We can't just do it over the internet. No way we'll get through the Patriot Firewall."

"Well..." Cat started as he thought out loud. "We could do what they used to do before the internet. Hand out compact disks at shows and litter the bars with stickers and flyers. Doesn't seem like we'll get much from it, though. The stickers with the encrypted QR codes worked well for MicroAggression."

Kendra had a better idea. "I don't think anyone has a CD player anymore and besides, even if we can get the QR code through the firewall, they'll remove the link, just like they used to. Oh, I forgot what they call it..." She paused for a second and looked down while her mind ran through her mental dictionary. "Oh right, de-platformed. They called it de-platforming. They'll harass whatever company hosted our website. That's been around before the Speech Codes, even when the First Amendment meant something."

"Right, de-platforming." Robert remembered. "When the government pretended that it couldn't do its own dirty work."

Kendra continued. "I think I have a way around it, though. We talked about it before. Swamp Simmons wants to meet you and I'm sure he'll be interested in what we're doing. He can get through the firewall. I think he has some kind of..."

"I've got it!" An idea flashed through Cat's mind so quickly that he cut Kendra off. "We need to talk to him. I have a hell of an idea how Swamp can help us pull this off. There are a few things I want to think through, though. You guys keep thinking because I'm not sure he'll do it. We need alternatives. If we don't get this right, it's all going to fall apart."

"Sweet, let's table that. We've got another problem..." Robert was about to drop another stink bomb into the room.

"What are we going to name this band?"

They all groaned. Band members fought death matches over the one or two lousy words that would sum up what they were all about. Sometimes it erupted in violence, or ended in tears. Rarely was anyone spared hurt feelings. This discussion only went smoothly in two instances. The first one was if the founder used his or her last name. That only worked when everyone else was along for the ride. Second, if a corporation manufactured a boy band and workshopped a name like the Sophomore Surprise or the Clear Skin Gang or some other canned nonsense. Everyone else dreaded this conversation.

"Oh God, no..." Trent muttered what they were all thinking.

Cat spoke up. "I think we should do something that reminds people of where we came from; play off of our past. MicroAggression was perfect. It's such a stupid word for so many reasons. The name told people we were ironic before they showed up. Maybe something like that? Maybe 'Trigger Warning' or something equally moronic?"

"That's a good one." Kendra liked the name but had another suggestion. "I'm thinking something slightly different. If we are going to go to the anti-male stuff, why not do something that goes with that? Like Groin Kick or Crotch Shot or FME for 'Fragile Male Ego'?"

"We could go that route, but I think it might be too limiting," Cat responded, "but I like it."

Trent threw out another concept. "Well, if we really want to get some attention, we could call it Wuhan Kung Flu?"

The four of them laughed and liked Trent's idea, but they all responded with a resounding "No" or "Hell No".

"I've got one," Robert added. "In fact, I've got a few. How about 'Your Lives Don't Matter' or 'Mostly Peaceful Protests' or 'Make America Safe Again'? Even the acronyms would work. We could put 'YLDM' or 'MPP' or 'MASA' all over hats and tee shirts?"

The three White people stared at Robert. He sat expressionless for as long as he could. He stared into their eyes to maximize their discomfort. They all seemed more inclined towards visiting a proctologist than engaging in this exchange.

"What?" Robert asked, making them squirm a little while longer.

Finally, he let them off the hook. "Yeah, maybe those won't work for this group. But if I ever decide to do a side project..." Robert chuckled.

"I think I've got it." Trent knew he had a good one. He was especially happy that his idea would move the conversation away from Robert's suggestions.

"What if we called ourselves 'Safe Spaces'?" Trent scanned everyone's faces for feedback. He sensed from their facial expressions that he was on to something, so he continued.

"Safe Spaces you know, the places colleges set up so that the snowflakes could avoid being offended? Theoretically, you could say whatever you wanted. Well, as long as everyone agreed. It was the ultimate joke. They called it the exact opposite of what it was. It was a safe space to speak as long as you didn't offend anyone."

"Safe Spaces," Cat repeated.

"Perfect." Kendra loved the idea. "It's perfect. It meshes with the whole storyline and the angle we're playing. The woke will think that we actually mean it and the MicroAggression fans will think we're being sarcastic. Brilliant."

"It really is," Robert concurred.

They waited for Cat to speak. He sat silently and mulled it over in his head. No one wanted to continue this discussion. Hopefully, this was the end. Finally, Cat spoke up.

"Safe Spaces, that's it."

And with that, Safe Spaces was born and began its journey to its predictable demise.

Chapter Eight

Cat's stomach churned as he heard the announcer introduce the band. Typically, he remained calm during performances. Playing guitar was second nature to him since he spent countless hours practicing in his early years. His hands seemed to have a mind of their own, consistently hitting the right notes and perfectly timing chords. He often operated on autopilot. But tonight was different. Tonight, he had to sing.

And not just sing. He had to take the lead. Cat swallowed hard and reminded himself that he had rehearsed repeatedly and knew exactly how he would handle his new role. Besides, who would know if he screwed it up? That thought calmed him a bit, and he started walking toward the entrance to the stage.

Cat wanted Safe Spaces' first ever concert intro to pay tribute to MicroAggression by opening the show with Damnatio Memoriae behind a semi-transparent curtain. Robert would start on drums while the house lights were on and the announcer was on stage. They would turn the house lights off after Robert drummed a few beats, leaving only the back light behind the curtain. The lighting sequence caused shadows to form on the sheet while the other band members entered the stage. It produced a simple yet striking effect of disembodied figures dancing across the screen. Cat would enter the stage last and then sing. The visual effects set the mood for the show and honored Richard perfectly.

Cat had a few moments before Robert started drumming. He stood by the stage, observing the audience. From his vantage point, he noticed how the crowd seemed exceptionally large for their inaugural show. How did they generate this much buzz so quickly? None of his earlier bands started with anything like this. They hadn't even fully implemented the marketing plan yet. He couldn't shake the feeling that something didn't seem right, and the fleeting thought caused his gut to flip even harder. No matter though. It was better than having no one there.

The announcer was halfway through his introduction. The volume on the PA system seemed abnormally low, and Cat could barely hear him. Perhaps it was the noisy crowd.

"Here they are, the locals that made good," the announcer screamed. "They stuck it to the fucking establishment, Ramirez, and her fascist thugs. You know them, you love them even if you hate them, here they are, Safe Spaces!"

Cat noticed the announcer had gone slightly off script. The "you hate them" line was not in the opening. The deviation struck him as odd, but he didn't have time to dwell on it. Robert was in his third repetition of the opening drumbeats. At least he was on cue. Probably just a hiccup.

BA DA BUMP, Robert hit the right beat again.

BA DA BUMP, he continued.

Robert's timing was flawless, but the drums seemed louder than they should be. Cat swore he made sure that the tech guys had set the drum volume at the correct level. Now it was clearly elevated. The drums would drown out his voice if the sound manager didn't fix it. Hopefully, he heard it too.

The house lights dimmed.

Cat was still off stage, so he motioned to the sound manager that the drum volume was wrong. He didn't respond. Then Cat motioned to the stage manager, who didn't acknowledge him either. He probably couldn't see Cat through the curtain and the darkness. Cat could see Robert, though, so he tried to get his attention. Unfortunately, Robert didn't respond. Of course, that really didn't matter, since there was nothing Robert could do about it, anyway. He just slowly shook his head back and forth while he drummed. That was normal for him. The music captivated him.

Trent strolled out onto the stage. He walked slower than usual, but he was still on time. The bass line in Damnatio Memoriae was very important. Trent hit his first few notes as he took his place behind his microphone stand on his side of the stage. Thankfully, Trent's bass meshed well with the drums. The sound guys must have fixed the drum level. They were still too loud, but at least they weren't overpowering.

Cat saw Trent standing behind his mic. He stood motionless but, oddly; he leaned almost halfway over toward the neck of his bass. How did he twist his back like that? Strange. Trent normally stood straight up and down, like a soldier at attention. Must be his nerves. He was always nervous before a show. Especially tonight. They needed to get their first show right.

Kendra scratched her pick over her strings and Cat heard the familiar screech of the Fender she played. He had somehow missed seeing her walk out on stage. Weird, she should have passed right in front of him. Everyone except Cat was on stage. Now it was time for him to join them.

However, a strange sensation came over him as he noticed that his back felt extremely hot. The best way he could describe it was as if someone held a huge hair dryer behind him and blew it at full blast. It wasn't painful, but it was definitely noticeable, and he hoped it would pass. There was nothing he could do anyway, as he had to get out on stage. He needed his microphone. Even if he sent a roadie out to get it for him, there would be a visible gap in the middle of the sheet. Great way to ruin Safe Spaces before it ever got started.

The heat on his back caused him to inhale heavier than normal, but he could only take in half a breath. This was a big problem. Cat needed as much air in his lungs as possible in order to sustain long notes. He tried taking smaller breaths to slow his breathing down, but it didn't help. He felt himself gasp.

Uh oh.

He considered stopping the song. But then he saw a red light shoot out from behind Trent. It was quick and ended just as rapidly as it appeared. He noticed it because it wasn't supposed to happen. Non-back lights would spoil the shadow effect on the stage curtain. Especially that red light. It would ruin the contrast. Cat's immediate reaction was to rip the lighting tech a new one. As he thought of the thousand curses he would unleash at him, an odd thing happened. The momentary distraction stabilized his breathing. It was as if someone startled him to cure hiccups. He wasn't gasping anymore. He composed himself and took a deep breath to finish the song.

Cat found himself at center stage. Odd, he didn't remember walking out there. He had planned to stop a few times and wave at the crowd from behind the curtain before he took his lead singer position. Cat knew he needed to ignore that anomaly, too. He needed to focus and lock in. He took a deep breath and sung the first line.

"These are the scrolls that bore his name."

He almost yelled. Cat had screwed up. He was much too loud. He was supposed to hold his voice low, nothing above a loud whisper. This wasn't a metal song. It was an intense boiler that grew in urgency and volume as the song progressed. Damn, he thought to himself. That's not like me.

"He was a minor pawn in the game."

Lower, but still not there. He needed to concentrate. Get ahold of yourself, Cat. Hit the right pitch and tone. No time for an inner shouting match. Something was wrong. A strange sensation came over him and he felt disconnected from his body. It was as if he floated above the stage, gazing at the crowd.

"With the stroke of a scribe, he's now erased."

He fell back onto the stage, looking at the crowd from behind the screen. That line prompted the stage crew to drop a small part of the curtain. It fell right on cue, but a red light shot out. It was supposed to be white. The light beam was also

98

much wider than it was supposed to be. It appeared fully formed, as if it had substance. Damn lighting tech screwed up again. Where did he find that red light? It was way too powerful for an indoor venue. Probably excessive for an airport show, too.

He shielded his eyes from the glare by looking down at his shirt and noticed a red dot.

"What the hell is that?" his brain both yelled and asked. Cat's mind was telling him he needed to get himself together. Nobody in the crowd knew they screwed up the lighting. But they'd definitely notice if he didn't sing or messed up the lyrics. "Ignore it and do better," he told himself.

He got to the point in the song where the full curtain was supposed to drop and reveal the whole band, and it did indeed fall. Right on time, no less. The stagehands followed instructions and shifted it sideways. Finally, things were going right.

Once the entire curtain fell, Cat caught his first glimpse of the full crowd. It was enormous. In fact, it looked like Woodstock. Where did the small club go? How did it turn into a vast field with an endless mass of humanity? It was bigger than any farm in upstate New York. What the hell had just happened?

Cat realized he had to be hallucinating. Did someone slip him LSD in a drink? If he didn't regain control of himself, this would be Safe Spaces' first and final show.

Right before he sang his next line, he heard a slightly off drumbeat. It was a small but noticeable error. Cat caught it because Robert never missed a fill. As he turned back to look at him, he observed Robert's head shaking violently, unlike its usual swaying to the music. His head convulsed, swiveling, as foam at first oozed and then shot from the corners of his mouth. He must have been choking. How could he keep playing? This had to be a drug-induced delusion.

Terror rushed through Cat as he tried to grasp what was going on. He tried to run back to help Robert, but he couldn't.

His feet remained firmly planted behind the mic stand. He just kept singing the lyrics despite every flight nerve firing in his body.

He needed to tell Trent that they had to stop the show. Few singers could lead a band while tripping on acid, and Cat was definitely not one of them. He turned toward Trent. Thankfully, Trent wasn't convulsing or foaming at the mouth. He looked perfectly normal. In fact, he returned to his old posture, standing straight up and down. Suddenly, Trent's body whirled toward Cat and stopped, and he stared ahead lifelessly. Then, he violently pivoted away and paused, leaving Cat to stare at his back. After a momentary hesitation, Trent spun like a top, as if a steel rod had impaled him through the length of his torso. At first, he spun quickly, and Cat thought Trent would screw himself into the floor. Then he slowed down and rotated at a snail's pace.

Cat still couldn't move but kept singing. As he stared at Trent, he looked down toward the lower part of his body and thought he saw some kind of fluid leak down onto the floor. He couldn't fathom any liquid suitable for a bass guitar, let alone one that would drip like that.

Cat's terror level had reached critical mass, but he couldn't move. He tried to stop the song, but the band played on. He fixated on the dripping fluid and then, out of nowhere, a raw piece of meat oozed down Trent's leg and fell down onto the floor. The mass of flesh slid slowly past another lump of mangled skin that clung to Trent's pants. How could that have stuck there? Trent's body had wildly rotated before it slowed. Shouldn't it have flown off? Cat guessed that someone had slashed Trent through his stomach. There was no other credible explanation for the carnage.

Even though Cat still couldn't move his feet, he felt his head turn autonomously.

"Oh God, don't make me look at Kendra," he thought to himself. He couldn't control this trip. Whatever drug this was, it had taken control, and he needed to ride it out. But his head stopped turning before getting to Kendra. Well, at least that was something. Maybe he had already peaked and the effects would wear off.

They didn't.

His head stopped and held in place. Cat couldn't move, and he focused his eyes on one specific person in the audience.

Oh, no. Couldn't be.

It was Richard.

It couldn't be him. Cat believed in God and the afterlife, but he had a hard time believing in ghosts. Richard had died a horrible death. If this was real rather than a drug-induced haze, then why would God force him to attend this concert? It made no sense. He should be in heaven, resting peacefully.

But he wasn't. Richard stood five rows back, illuminated by a spotlight that just focused on him. Darkness shrouded the rest of the crowd. The spotlight blazed piercing white light. Cat could see Richard's smirk clearly. He knew that look. Richard always got it when he had something up his sleeve. Cat knew not to bet on his hands when they played cards and Richard got that look. Unfortunately, they weren't playing cards, and Richard's grin looked demonic.

"How ya' doin', Cat?" Richard asked, but Cat didn't see him move his mouth. Nothing made sense. Why was his friend here?

Cat saw two more spotlights shoot down from the ceiling on opposite sides of the room. Each one illuminated a masked figure that was dressed all in black. The spotlights followed the ghouls as they walked toward the center of the room. Despite the packed crowd, they easily moved through the concert. They advanced slowly toward Richard.

Cat tried to scream a warning to his friend, but his voice went silent. Either his microphone had died, or he had lost his voice. Either way, Richard couldn't hear him as he just stared at Cat. His smirk remained, but his eyes were dead. Cat tried to look away, but he couldn't. It was as if he was in a trance and something compelled him to watch this madness.

The masked figures each grabbed one of Richard's arms and pulled them out to the sides. Richard didn't respond at all. His eyes stayed lifeless, and the grin remained frozen on his face. Cat heard Richard's voice.

"See ya real soon."

Richard's head tilted back, and a sword gashed through his neck. Blood exploded from the wound and splattered Cat in the face. Another black-clad figure, identical to the others, emerged behind Richard. He glanced at Cat and started cutting the blade downward toward the floor.

The first two ghouls pulled Richard's arms in opposite directions, causing his body to almost split in two. Only his head prevented his torso from ripping in half. Once the sword passed through Richard's crotch, he crumpled into a heap on the floor. The three figures stood at attention side by side, facing Cat.

Cat screamed and peeked behind him for an escape. He saw Robert, or what he thought was him. It was difficult to tell because his head was unnaturally twisted and his eye sockets were completely white. He had no pupils, and his jaw was slack and open, but his hands kept playing a perfect drumbeat.

Cat wanted to escape, but he still couldn't move. Worse, his head turned again. This time, his head turned away from Richard and toward Kendra. She stood in her normal position as she played her guitar. Cat noticed she had a slight cut running diagonally down from her shoulder. The wound appeared to be infected as yellow pus seeped out of it. It didn't seem to bother her as she stared straight forward and strummed her guitar.

As Cat opened his mouth to warn her about the mayhem, her head whipped around, and she stared straight at him. Her body didn't move with her head. Cat briefly closed his eyes, only to open them to Kendra standing right in front of him. She had a crater where her head used to be. Her skull appeared utterly destroyed, as if crushed by a sledgehammer. Her right eye hung out of its socket and dangled as it swung like a pendulum.

Cat screamed and noticed he could now move his feet. He picked up one of his guitars and threw it as hard as he could into the audience. The guitar smashed into two people in the front row, and they exploded into black ashes. A gap appeared, and Cat seized the chance to escape by sprinting through the mist where the fans once stood.

As he jumped off the stage, he felt a sharp pain in his right arm. He glanced down and saw a fine spray of blood spurting out of a horizontal gash. Cat guessed it was a bullet or a knife that had caused the laceration. Now, they targeted him. He had to leave as quickly as possible.

Cat put his head down and ran in whatever direction he faced. He pushed his way through the crowd, tossing aside anyone who got in his way. Believing he was near the exit, Cat turned around and found he had only moved six feet from the stage. How was that possible? He felt like he had been running for hours. He quickly turned and fled from the stage. After taking only a few steps, he hit a massive object and fell flat on his back.

Cat sat up and realized he had run into the ghoul that chopped up Richard. He didn't have many good options from the seated position, so he grabbed onto the creature's calf and pulled. It wouldn't move. Not a bit. The monster's leg remained anchored to the ground, making it impossible for Cat to knock him down.

He looked up. There was a dark void where the apparition's face should have been. He could see nothing. As a last-ditch effort, he tried to grab the creature's leg again, but this time, his arms would not move. Immobilized, Cat could only stare at the empty head.

A red laser shot out of the ghoul's head and temporarily blinded him. He tried to look away but still couldn't move anything on his body except his neck. Cat's head involuntarily pivoted down in a nod, and he noticed multiple red dots dancing on his chest. They converged together and stopped over his heart. He gazed upwards, then heard a gunshot.

Cat's eyes flew open as he sat straight up in bed. He struggled to breathe, as if submerged underwater. He grabbed his chest and his heart pounded. Was he having a heart attack? Maybe not, but whatever he was feeling was probably pretty similar to a massive coronary.

Sweat covered his face, and he looked at his clock. It was two thirty-seven A.M. Cat laughed nervously and struggled to breathe and suddenly realized what had just occurred. Safe Spaces hadn't even played its first concert yet, and he was already having nightmares. Perhaps his mind was trying to tell him something? Why did his brain subject him to a terrifying dream about zombie friends and Richard returning as a decaying corpse?

He fell flat on his back onto his sweat-soaked sheets and tried to get back to sleep.

Chapter Nine

"Pro-wrestling?" Swamp asked. Shockingly, he seemed skeptical.

"Yes, pro-wrestling..." Cat sounded more exasperated than he meant to. He understood Swamp's doubts. Hell, Cat had his own reservations about the plan. He just needed to convince him he had thought this through, and it was worth the considerable risk. Cat figured that he also needed to assure Swamp that he wasn't drunk.

"I had the same reaction too." Trent chuckled. "As crazy as it sounds, I think it can work."

"What about you two?" Swamp looked directly at Kendra and Robert. "Are you guys as nuts as they are?"

"Yeah, pretty much," Kendra admitted. "I thought he was nuts too until I realized we've got nothing to lose. Ramirez all but declared war on people like us. This will never end unless we stand up to her and the rest of the woke mob. If we're going down, we may as well stand for something meaningful. Besides, I can't imagine living the rest of my days playing insipid pop music. I would much rather go down standing for something."

Robert continued Kendra's line of reasoning. "Music has gone to shit just like everything else these days. Comedy used to challenge the establishment and ridicule the government and anyone in charge. Now, it's all about bodily functions and making the token white guy a stupid racist. When was the last time you heard anyone tell a political joke or make an anti-establishment movie? Remember those films about fraternities that stood up to the stuffy old dean who tried to kick them off campus? Music has the same problem. Punk bands used to tell anyone in charge to go fuck themselves?

Things are totally different now. The so-called artists toe the government's line. How many musicians take on cancel culture? It's like the artists are now in the club and want to make sure they get invited to all the right parties. It's pathetic."

Swamp didn't respond, so Cat asked him directly, "I know how you can help us with this Swamp."

Swamp wasn't ready to give them an answer. He needed more information. His initial reaction to Cat's idea was that it was a phony, nonsensical, scripted mess that would devolve into a circus. But then he reminded himself that the world had gone mad. Why couldn't they engage in a spectacle as ridiculous as pro-wrestling? Doesn't a ridiculous world deserve an absurd plot? Something so stupid had to work, right?

That's the question he kept asking himself. Could something like this really work? Was it really possible for them to transform into cartoon characters to prove a point about hypocrisy? Just to show the world's insanity?

Still, Swamp firmly believed that "woke culture" was inherently deceitful. It had nothing to do with protecting people's feelings. At its core, this orthodoxy was all about raw power and weaponized guilt employed to control thoughts and actions. Cancel culture was at its heart un-American. Well, at least un-American in the sense of what America used to be.

But Swamp had to give the woke mafia credit. They exploited America's guilt with the skill of a sociopath. In fact, they manipulated the country's conscience into thinking that slitting their own throats would atone for past sins. Their weapon was far more lethal than any assault rifle. Their plan was brilliant in its sheer ruthlessness. Making people feel ashamed of things they never did was the ultimate mind control. Jim Jones would have been proud.

"Well, what do you think?" Cat broke the silence.

Swamp was not ready to answer yet, so he deflected and asked another question.

"First, tell me how you think I can help you?"

Cat had a problem. He hadn't discussed his idea with the band and he truly wanted this venture to be democratic, where they all had a voice in major decisions. After all, a bad outcome wouldn't just result in a messy split over creative differences. No, a bad outcome meant death and destruction.

"Are you guys ok if we talk about this now?" Cat asked. "I mean it. I shouldn't have brought this up without talking to you guys first."

They all nodded in agreement

"All right then, here's my idea. We'll appear on your show to promote the new band. Trent and I will blindside you and talk about how we've seen the error of our ways and how the woke crowd may have a point. Then you'll tell us we're full of shit. This way, we can get the word out that the bad guys have turned good. We'll play the anti-male stuff at our concerts, and you'll rip us for being phonies. The drama will help publicize the shows. We all know controversy puts asses in the seats. After enough time passes, we'll let them in on the joke and how they are all a bunch of hypocrites."

Just after Cat said the word "joke" he had a flashback to his nightmare. He envisioned the ghouls sawing Richard into pieces. Then he saw Kendra's head caved in, Trent's disemboweled body, and Robert's arms drumming while his head was almost twisted off. He had a physical reaction to these thoughts, and he closed his eyes tight and balled his fist. The dream had really bothered him.

They all saw Cat's face contort and Kendra asked, "Everything ok?"

"Yeah." Cat's face softened a bit and transformed back to normal.

"What were you thinking about?" Trent asked. He knew Cat's face spasmed when something particularly awful passed through his mind.

"Sorry, it was that dream again." Cat didn't remember his dreams very often, but he couldn't forget that one.

"What dream?" Swamp asked.

"I dreamed about Safe Spaces' first concert. Nothing was as it seemed, and everything went wrong. Then these ghouls sliced up Richard and turned the band into gruesome zombies. Fun stuff. My guess is that my mind was trying to warn me that this is a terrible idea, but you know..." Cat trailed off.

"Oh man, that's awful," Swamp agreed. Cat was probably right. His mind was likely illustrating his fear about his plan to him. He continued, "I don't really remember any of my dreams, but when I first started this show, I used to have dreams where whatever I was doing, I just couldn't do it because something would always get in the way. Most of the time, it had to do with high school and graduation. Like I was on my way to the commencement ceremony and realized I had forgotten to take a particular class and I wouldn't be able to graduate. Someone once told me it was just my anxiety playing with me and that made sense. The worst dreams were where my father would just start berating me and he wouldn't stop. My dad was tough, but he was nowhere near what he was like in my dreams. Those nightmares were terrifying."

"Yeah, I think we can all agree that Freddy Kruger is after us, but I don't think that's really going to help much right now." They all laughed at Kendra's sarcasm and then she asked, "We're still back to the original question, Swamp, what do you think?"

Swamp nodded his head downward. Then he brought it back up slowly and made eye contact with each of them.

"I love it."

Wow, Cat thought to himself. Swamp Simmons thinks my batshit crazy cover band/pro-wrestling/political statement mash-up is a good idea. He was quite proud of himself.

"Look, there are some significant issues we're going to have to work through. But one thing the government doesn't like is when you taunt and humiliate them. Hell, I've been doing it for years and they've put a huge bullseye on my back. If this thing goes even halfway like you hope it does, then they're really going to hate you. They're going to hit you back hard. But at least you'll get Richard some payback."

Swamp's words resonated with all of them. They all knew the government didn't like to be embarrassed. When you fucked with them, they wouldn't take it lying down.

"So does that mean you'll help us?" Trent asked.

"Yes, absolutely, but I want to give your idea of staging an interview some more thought. Under any other circumstances, I would have responded with 'hell no.' I'll make an exception this time. I've kept this show real and if I'm going to do something like this, I've got to figure out how to manage the fallout once you do your big reveal. There's a way to do this and I just have to figure out what it is."

"Sweet." Cat was genuinely relieved that Swamp was in on it. Going into this meeting, he thought the odds were fifty/fifty at best. It wouldn't have worked without Swamp. His show was a goldmine for publicity.

"Okay guys, let's get started." Together, they outlined a plan. At best, they would all get canceled once they let the audience in on the joke. At worst, they would all die.

*   *   *

"Ladies and gentlemen, thanks as always for joining me on the Swamp Simmons Show and we have a really special program for you tonight." Swamp started with his typical introduction, but this would not be his normal show. He had previously made satire videos, but he made sure that it was obvious. He once made a video where he read government propaganda praising Ramirez while someone held a gun to his head. This time, he would play a fake version of himself. That made him uncomfortable, but it would be worth it if they pulled it off.

"We are going to do something different tonight. Don't worry, we are still speaking up for the little guy and making the powerful worry. Before we get to it, I want to give you some context and a warning as I introduce my next guests.

First the warning. We are going to present some unedited, disturbing images and those of you watching this with small children may want to stop now and stream it later. Particularly the beginning of this show, so please pause the video and get them out of the room. I'm about to show one of the most disgusting and brazen videos that has ever made it onto that wonderful thing we call the internet. Of course, your kids are going to suffer the consequences of these disturbing times, but they don't need to see this. Okay? Good."

"For those of you that didn't listen, consider yourselves warned. Recently, a video surfaced on the internet showing a senseless murder and I'm going to show it to you now. Most of you have probably already seen or heard about it, so I don't need to go into detail. I'm guessing you are all as outraged as I am. You know I'm talking about the Richard Uprising murder and here it is."

Swamp played the video and stopped it just before the terrorist was about to stab Richard in the stomach.

"I don't need to show you the rest. As outright horrendous as that video is, I'm not shocked by it at all. We've been heading in this direction for a long time. But there's something more appalling. Did you hear Ramirez's reaction to that atrocity? If you haven't had the displeasure of watching our wonderful president react to that video, please do so. For those who don't know, let me summarize it for you. Ramirez thinks what you just saw is okay. She thought this murderer had his reasons. Oh yes, she gave phony platitudes of not condoning killing, bringing people to justice, Yada, Yada, Yada. But let me ask you this: have you heard anything about the law enforcement efforts to find Richard's killer? Do you think our bastardized police force is turning over every rock, running down every lead in order to find these vermin? No? You don't? Neither do I."

"In fact, she all but declared war on anyone that disagrees with her and all I took from that speech was that she condones this type of violence as long as the victim is a person she doesn't like. Does anyone take anything else from what she said? God, I hope I'm not right because if I am, we're doomed. We have crossed over from merely dangerous times to a full-blown crisis of confidence in our system of government. I fear all of this. I truly do. If we don't turn things around soon, we'll lose everything."

"But we can take heart that there some people are fighting back. Of course, there's yours truly, along with others who publicly criticize the government. Tonight, I would like to introduce you to some familiar and not-so-familiar faces who are stepping up against tyranny. When I say familiar faces, I mean that Richard Uprising's band members won't back down. They've reformed MicroAggression with two new members and will continue Richard's work in standing up to Ramirez and her thugs. Please welcome their new band. It's called Safe Spaces." At that point, the camera panned over Cat, Kendra, Robert, and Trent, sitting in chairs in Swamp's studio.

"Now, before we discuss your new project, some of our viewers might not be familiar with you. First, we have Robert and I understand you are going to be the new drummer for the band." Robert nodded and replied, "that's right."

"Second, we have Trent who was the bassist for MicroAggression and will take on the same role for Safe Spaces." Trent looked into the camera and said, "Yep."

"Next, for a pleasant distraction from the others, we have the lovely Kendra. She's a new member as well and will handle guitar, keyboard, and some singing, is that right?" Kendra nodded to Swamp and the camera, but said nothing.

"Finally, we have Cat Chaotic. Cat and Trent were founding members of MicroAggression. He is going to take over singing from Richard and will play lead guitar. Do I have all of that correct?"

Cat smirked as the camera panned to him. "Yes, you got it. Swamp, I wanted to start off by thanking you for having us on your show. We are such devoted fans of yours and it's so great to meet you at last. I'm really excited to be here, even under these awful circumstances. Richard was a very dear friend of mine. I miss him every day. This is something that, oh, I told myself I wouldn't cry but, I, uh, just wanted to honor him. I, I, I, really miss him."

Cat was no longer smirking. He was genuinely on the verge of tears. It was a lot harder to talk about Richard than he thought it would be.

Swamp felt terrible for Cat, but, oddly, he also had conflicting thoughts. The showman in him knew that Cat's profound sadness at the loss of his friend would help the ruse appear genuine. But Swamp was also a human being. How could he not feel sorry for how badly Cat missed his friend?

Cat composed himself and stared directly into the camera. "I'm sorry. I didn't think this was going to be as hard as it is."

"Please don't apologize. Some sick person butchered your friend in cold blood. Who wouldn't tear up? Particularly the first time you talked about it publicly. Is that right?"

"Yes, it is, and it's hard. I don't think I can talk about him much more right now. It's just too much."

The camera turned back to Swamp, who said, "I totally understand. The last thing I'll say about Richard is that I'm really very sorry for your loss. I was a big fan of MicroAggression. I went to your concerts and just knew that you guys, well, what's the best way I can put it? You just got it. You understood what we're up against. In fact, Richard and I had plans to speak and maybe even collaborate on something. I can't fathom what you're going through."

"He was my best friend, almost like a brother to me. I think I can speak for Trent on this one point, as I think he felt the same way."

"Absolutely," Trent whispered into his microphone. "I miss him so much."

They all sat in silence for a long moment. The hush spoke volumes.

"Thank you." Cat continued. "I really appreciate you letting me speak about Richard, but I want to focus more on what we've got going on now. We're going to honor Richard's legacy by taking Safe Spaces in some new and interesting directions."

"Agreed," Swamp responded. "I would like that. So, let's start with you guys telling me what your plans are. You mentioned some 'new and interesting directions?' Safe Spaces isn't MicroAggression II?"

"Nope, not MicroAggression II. We've got some big plans, but let's start with what we won't change. We are definitely going to stick to our roots. You'll hear lots of covers from seventies, eighties, and nineties bands. We particularly like to focus on the new wave and punk groups. We'll even play some industrial too. The four of us absolutely love all that music as much or more than our fans do and we can't wait to get out there and play it."

"I love those groups from that era," Swamp agreed. "You guys were off the hook in those shows." Swamp wasn't lying about going to MicroAggression concerts. He was a huge fan of their original music and their covers and loved the band's energy when they played on stage. He liked how they weren't a tribute band. They honored the look and mannerisms of the earlier groups, but didn't copy them. They simply played their favorite music, allowing the audience to interpret it as they wished.

"But we've got some fresh stuff, too. As we mentioned earlier, Kendra is going to do a lot of singing. That opens up a world of possibilities. We are even thinking of some duets, but I'm most excited about Kendra's solo stuff. Kendra, you want to take it from here?"

"Sure Cat, thanks, yeah I've got a few songs in mind that are out of the norm, but we probably won't play them every time, just when the mood strikes me."

"When the mood strikes you, Kendra? Hmmm, intriguing. Can you give us a taste, so people know what to expect?"

"Well, I was hoping to keep this a surprise, but I guess I can give you a hint so you might know what you're in store for. One song I'm thinking about singing is 'Fragile Male Ego.' I think it's time we brought that one back."

"Really?" Swamp maintained a straight face, even though he was lying. "So, I see you're going to take Richard's lead and hit the offensive stuff hard?"

"In some respects." Trent chimed in; it was time to start the con.

"Well, yeah you are," Swamp retorted. He was setting this up nicely. "I know that song. The lyrics are rough. It goes something like: 'Men are from Mars; we are from Venus. You think you have balls but it's a half inch penis. You couldn't be dumber if you had a hole in your head. The only thing worse is how you disappoint me in bed.' That's not offensive?" Swamp posed the question with just a hint of outrage to sell it.

Kendra chuckled. "Oh, come on. Who are we talking about here? We're just having fun with it."

"I know." Swamp responded. "I'm the last one to tell you what you're allowed to say, but aren't you afraid of running up against the Speech Codes? I mean, this is exactly what they were supposed to prevent, right? Offensive speech?"

"We'll take our chances." Kendra raised her eyebrows as she played along with Swamp.

"Okay, I never heard Richard play that one. I don't think he could pull it off. But how do you think the wokesters will respond when you play some of the other stuff he used to play? I mean, what will happen if you play Got Called Racist?"

Trent jumped in. "Oh, we've dropped that one from the set list. I doubt we'll ever play it again."

The camera shifted to Swamp, who stayed quiet for a moment to enhance the dramatic effect.

"Why won't you play that one? It was a staple for MicroAggression."

"Yeah, I know." Cat inserted himself back into the discussion. "I don't think that song aged well. It's kind of dated."

"It's dated?" Swamp asked, and then he answered his own question. "Yeah, it is, but isn't that the whole point of MicroAggression? You played dated songs that people loved, even though they might be offensive to the modern audience. It was entertaining. What's the problem now?" This was going really, really well.

"Well, we're not MicroAggression anymore. We're Safe Spaces." Cat timed his response perfectly. "Besides, you know, some of that stuff really showed how privileged those people were. I mean the nerve of some of those people to say things like that."

"Wait, what did you just say?" Swamp shook his head. "You actually referred to a group as privileged?"

Swamp continued before any of them answered, "You know you have a real problem here?"

"How so?" Robert asked. This was the perfect time for him to jump in since they were discussing the word 'privileged.' It was an ad lib, but it meshed seamlessly with the plan.

"Well, you have no problem playing something like Fragile Male Ego, which any rational person would admit can be offensive to fifty percent of the population. You know, those with XY chromosomes. But you have a problem playing Got Called Racist? An anti-cancel culture song? How do you justify that?"

Robert then threw a haymaker. "That's really an oppressive way of looking at this Swamp. I don't think you have any right to question us. Me in particular." His tone was perfectly flat and Robert stopped talking to let the punch land.

Swamp momentarily forgot this was a hoax and genuinely became angry. He had immersed himself in an existential argument over woke culture's internal contradictions. He devoted his life to fighting the cancel culture mob and media propaganda and forgot that he was in an improv argument with four people who actually agreed with him.

"Look, people are going to have a good time at our shows," Cat interjected. He felt they had said too much. Better to hold some of this back for the next 'argument.' "It's just that, you know, we've evolved beyond our roots. We love entertaining, but we want to do it inclusively."

"Inclusively? Did you really just say that too? Did Richard ever say a word like inclusive? Ever in his lifetime? What you're really saying is that you've gone 'woke'. Don't sugarcoat that shit. I think Richard would be ashamed." Swamp tried to avoid cursing in his videos, so clearly he had forgotten the point of this performance. His slipup worked flawlessly.

"That really hurts, Swamp," Trent leaped back in. "I think Richard would tell us to do what we think is best, try new things for a new time, a new understanding. I think he would want you to give us a chance."

"Well, you may be right," Swamp conceded. "But do you think he would agree with a hierarchy of who you can offend? Wouldn't Richard want you to either offend everyone or no one? You can rip liberals, conservatives, Blacks, Whites, males, females, trans, homosexuals, whatever. Just don't pick on the groups that can't fight back. I mean, isn't that the way it used to be? Before we quote unquote, 'evolved'?"

"We'll take our chances," Kendra repeated her earlier line.

Swamp just stared at her and let out an audible sigh.

"Good God, okay? I guess we'll leave it there. Jeez. This didn't go anywhere how I thought it would. I guess I want to thank Safe Spaces for coming on the show?" Swamp's last statement sounded more like a question than he had hoped it would.

"I suppose I wish you luck in your endeavor and I'll keep my eye on you. I'm really curious about where you're going to go with this. We'll have you back on the show, and we'll probably have this discussion all over again. Again, thanks for coming on and best of luck to you."

Swamp stopped the recording.

"Well, how was that?" Cat broke the silence. It was much easier for him to snap back to being himself since he didn't believe a word he just said.

"Man, I think we nailed it." Swamp smirked. "I actually got mad at you. Can you believe that? I'm spent so I'll look at it tomorrow rather than edit it tonight. If there's anything worrisome, I can fix it with my deep fake tech, but I seriously doubt it."

"Sweet," Cat finally exhaled. "Now we just have to play the shows."

Chapter Ten

This time, Cat knew he was really walking out on stage and not having a nightmare or tripping on LSD. No ghouls in the audience, no zombie band members, just good time rock and roll. Well, at least for opening night. The band had other ideas for the future.

Safe Spaces' first show began with Damnatio Memoriae in tribute to Richard and MicroAggression. They followed with a few eighties "new wave" songs. It was important that Safe Spaces stayed in character. Better to wait on the offensive songs since many skeptics believed the fight with Swamp was a hoax. Of course it was. But, no reason to give them any ammunition.

During one song, Cat took a moment to look at the crowd. It was small, which wasn't surprising for their first show. They had booked a standard theater that could accommodate up to 1000 people. It was clean and didn't smell like soot, unlike MicroAggressions' last show. There was one other major difference. Currently, there were no bloodstains or dead bodies on the floor, but the night wasn't over yet.

Cat loved the marketing plan, but it depended heavily on his performance as a lead singer. He needed to make sure that he wowed the crowd and they came back for future shows. A crucial part of that would be how Cat connected with them. He had to make sure he stayed in character. If he let anything slip, then the entire plan would fail.

"First, I really want to thank you all for coming tonight." That statement wasn't part of the ruse. Cat meant it. He was extremely grateful for the fans putting down their hard-earned money to watch him do what he loved to do.

"We've picked a good mix of songs for you tonight, and I hope you enjoy your evening as much as we enjoy playing for you."

Cat heard scattered applause and a few hoots and howls from the small crowd. It was quiet enough so he could also hear the murmur of a couple of conversations. Large shows or rowdy crowds made it hard to hear anything specific. He rarely understood what song the drunk slurred as he screamed his request. There was one exception, though. They could always hear it when someone yelled "you suck". Those words of encouragement came through loud and clear.

"Please let me take a moment to introduce the band. We've got some unfamiliar faces, one of which is obviously much more pleasant than the others. The name of our new endeavor is Safe Spaces. Some of you know Trent and me from our MicroAggression days, but you came anyway. Thanks for that. I have a vast collection of shoes, bottles, and other projectiles you've thrown at us throughout the years. You can pick up your items in the dumpster in the back labeled 'lost and thrown'."

Robert hit a rim shot to emphasize how lame Cat's "Dad" joke was.

"Oh, thank you Robert. That's a perfect segue to introduce our new members. First, on drums and other instruments that keep the beat, the wonderful and talented Robert!"

Robert acknowledged Cat's intro by playing a few beats on his drums, which received considerable applause.

"Next, a familiar face that you may know, on bass, the esteemed Trent, say hello Trent."

"I'm Trent", he deadpanned into his microphone.

"Trent, you just don't know when to shut up, do you? Sorry folks, he's monopolizing the conversation. If he keeps going like this, we'll only get to play one more song before curfew."

The joke didn't fall totally flat like the dumpster one. Cat heard a few laughs and some applause. The positive response wasn't enough for Cat to feel comfortable, but it was a start.

"And now, the one you have all been waiting for, on guitar, keyboards, and singing, we have the lovely Kendra."

Kendra leaned into her microphone. "Hello."

Unsurprisingly, Kendra garnered a much louder reaction, especially from the males in the audience.

"And my name is Cat. You'll be hearing quite enough from me tonight, but now it's time to hear from Kendra."

Kendra walked out from behind her keyboard and took center stage. Cat switched places with her so he could sing backup vocals and play guitar. She gave a brief nod to the other members of the band to show them she was ready.

"Give her a beat, Robert!" Cat yelled into his mic.

Robert obliged.

Bum Ba Bump Ba Bump.

Bum Ba Bump Ba Bump.

Cat wailed a power chord, and Trent filled in the rest with his bass.

Kendra grabbed the microphone from the stand and strutted to Cat's side of the stage. She locked eyes with him and sang.

"They say the wall is collapsing."

"They say the wall is collapsing."

"They say the wall is collapsing, and the center is imploding, the right and the left are causing this disgrace."

"We have no power, and the masses are oppressed."

"No right to speak in our Safe Space."

Kendra spat the lyrics out. Her tone was combative without being shrill. Cat kept Kendra's gaze, and it looked like she was serenading him. Cat watched the crowd to get a sense of how they reacted to their dynamic. It was hard to tell, but he sensed a mix of shock, bemusement, and approval.

Kendra broke eye contact with him and turned to face the crowd dead on. She looked confident without being overbearing. She effortlessly assumed control of the stage, displaying a natural stage presence. Even though Cat had only watched her perform for a couple of minutes, he knew she was special. It was a duet, but he knew to stay aside. Give Kendra the lead and let the crowd embrace her. No sense becoming a distraction.

"Violence results from coercion of thought,"

"You will see. You will reap what you sow."

"The masses will rip the masks off their faces and then you will be the ones locked in your own Safe Spaces."

Cat continued watching her in awe. She commanded the stage but didn't imitate Cat's combative dynamic with the crowd. Kendra sung with natural femininity without going overboard. She wore a black miniskirt, stockings, and the same heels from the day he met her. Kendra also rocked a white, long-sleeved top with the top buttons left open. Her outfit wasn't slutty. But she also felt comfortable in a sexy outfit. That was who she was. She initially thought about wearing garters under her skirt and letting the audience catch fleeting glimpses of them for shock value. Safe Spaces needed attention, but that would have been too much, too soon. It wasn't a lingerie show, but perhaps she'd consider it in the future? Maybe, but better to let the plan unfold first.

Cat then jumped into the song and responded to Kendra.

"They say the wall is collapsing and the freedom that you're seeking cannot function and does not exist."

"The left, they say, is trying to protect you. You're a child, a slave, to the falsity that persists."

Then Cat and Kendra sang in unison.

"We are Safe Spaces, and we are here to rock you. We'll show you a mirror reflecting the abyss."

Kendra took charge and completed the song.

"Yes, the wall is collapsing..."

"Yes, the wall is collapsing..."

Kendra allowed the words to trail off so that Cat could play the final guitar riffs and bring the song home.

As Cat finished the last part of the song, he surveyed the crowd again. They loved Kendra. She had them mesmerized while she danced to the conclusion of the song. Now, granted, she had the male contingent of the audience quite taken with her, but the females also cheered for her. This was going well.

Then Cat noticed something odd.

A small group of older individuals stood by Kendra's side of the stage. None of them wore black attire, unlike the rest of the audience. One of the older males was recording the show. That wasn't unusual, but his phone was quite old. He was talking to a female in the group who was writing notes on a legal pad. Who used pen and paper anymore? This was definitely out of the ordinary.

They didn't look like the press, but that term was outdated. Anyone with an internet connection could call themselves a reporter.

This group seemed different, though, and while Cat noted it, he didn't have time to examine it. He had to move on to additional songs.

Next, they played a few of their favorite crowd-pleasing but non-offensive rock songs. The reception was positive, as Cat expected. It was time to take some chances. It was also time to acknowledge the obvious issue.

"Thank you again for coming tonight. Also, special shout out to those of you that were with us during the MicroAggression days." The crowd roared its approval to Cat's reference to Richard's band, and it meant a lot to him. He turned and looked at Trent. It was clear from his expression that the response touched him, too. Hopefully, they wouldn't piss off their fans too much once they let them in on the plan.

"We wouldn't be here without you. I know that I would have to work some really shitty office job if you didn't reach into your pocket. Could you imagine me in a cubicle? God knows I owe you a lot."

The fans cheered again. Thanking the crowd and their supporters was the simple part. Now for the hard part.

"There's one person I can't thank enough for everything he did for me personally, and I know a lot of you feel strongly about him. I might have mentioned him in passing tonight, but that was deliberate. I didn't know if I was going to make it through this show without bursting into tears."

Silence fell as the crowd sensed Cat was going to talk about Richard.

"I'm surprised I made it this long and, oh, fuck it, if it happens, it happens..." Cat trailed off. He almost lost control of his emotions, but persevered and his voice cracked slightly as he continued.

"I wanted to say to my dear friend Richard..." he paused and there was an audible gasp from the crowd. Together, they felt the heaviness in the air.

"I miss you every day. You helped me through some of my worst times and we shared some of my best. I'm carrying this on in your honor and, well, since I really haven't been good at anything else, I really don't have a choice." Some in the audience chuckled while others cheered. Some shed tears while they laughed, but the overall mood was still sullen.

Cat struggled to find a suitable moment to honor Richard. The MicroAggression fans deserved it, but the last thing he wanted was to turn the concert into a funeral. He wanted to speak from his heart, but was worried. He surprised himself by keeping everything somewhat together.

"Trent, do you want to say a few words now?" He turned to look at Trent.

Trent responded. "You expressed it perfectly. Richard didn't deserve that. I'd do anything to have him here with us. I miss laughing with him and I miss those deep conversations we had after a night out drinking. Along with you, Cat, he was my best friend. I know we can only move forward and play for him and his legacy and everything he stood for."

"Thanks Trent, I know Richard is looking down on us and smiling, and I also know that he wants us to play on." The crowd murmured and Cat sensed they needed to move on in a more entertaining direction.

"Can I say something, Cat?" Kendra asked. This wasn't part of the script, but Cat knew that Kendra intuitively understood showmanship, so he said, "of course."

"I joined Cat and Trent in this because I really believed in Richard and what he stood for, and I think that plenty of you guys agree. Also, I only agreed to this because we all pledged to do it right. I didn't want to just copy MicroAggression and have Cat do his best Richard impression. I wanted to honor his memory, but in our own way. It had to be Safe Spaces, not MicroAggression the sequel. Things are going to change."

Kendra's word choice in her last sentence signaled the rest of the band that she wanted to take over the show. The crowd responded with a mixed reaction. Kendra knew Cat had talked too much. They had to return to the music.

"Well, I'm done talking about it for now, so maybe I'll just show you. Take it, Robert."

Robert started the beat, and the others joined in with their sounds. The music was jazzy but still had the signature sharply angled guitars that had predominated throughout the genre of the material they played.

Kendra appeared fully prepared to dominate the crowd. This time, she didn't serenade Cat. She sang directly to the audience. Taking control, she snatched the microphone off its stand and brought it close to her mouth. She had to nail this song, or the plan would fail.

Kendra stood at center stage with one of her legs positioned slightly forward of the other. She intentionally adopted a masculine stance to assert her ownership of the stage for her song. Kendra gazed at the crowd and synchronized her voice with the instruments and unleashed chaos.

"My choices are slim; my pickings are poor."

"My best-case option's a freak and a bore."

"His breath is not bad; has something of a brain,"

"But the only time he showers is when he walks in the rain."

Kendra's cadence was more rap than melodic. Cat noticed the crowd danced far less than normal for a song with such a jazzy sound. They seemed mesmerized and shocked by Kendra's lyrics. Cat thought she was nailing it, but how was the audience taking it? Hard to tell. At least nobody threw anything at them.

"I wish I liked girls and men all rot."

"If a turkey baster had a paycheck, I would give it a shot."

They were pushing all their chips in by playing a song with lesbian and reproductive angles. No one was dancing. They just stared at the stage.

Kendra repeated the chorus a few times during the next part of the song. Failure of the lyrics means failure of the plan. Some in the audience heard them during the phony Swamp interview. Some of them didn't. It was now time to hit it hard.

"Men are from Mars, we are from Venus,"

"You think you have balls but it's a half inch penis."

"You couldn't be dumber if you had a hole in your head,"

"Only thing worse is how fast you finish in bed."

Cat noted Kendra's ad-libbed lyrics. They worked better.

Cat looked at the crowd after the chorus. This was the moment of truth.

They were dancing, moving, and screaming. Especially the women. No surprise that they related to that bilge. Surprisingly, a fair number of men were dancing, too. Others found it ridiculous and laughed. This was exactly the reaction Cat was hoping for. Kendra was an amazing performer.

Cat couldn't have asked for a better start. He mused to himself about whether they would have gotten out of the theater alive if they had changed the lyrics to ripping females? Maybe he would have escaped, but likely without some of his really important parts. This was the whole point. Hopefully, when they completed this sociological experiment, the chronically offended would have to confront their hypocrisy.

However, there was one big question. How high a price would the band pay for revealing the truth?

*   *   *

Robert started the postmortem discussion with a pretty simple question. "So, what did you guys think?"

The show had ended an hour ago, and they went to O'Hara's bar for drinks. Playing for over three hours left them feeling drained. They prepared for this evening for months, rehearsing multiple times per week, but performing in front of a live audience was always more challenging. No rehearsal could simulate the energy of a live crowd. The lighting didn't help either. The lamps, lasers, and spotlights broiled the band no matter how hard they tried to lower the temperature on the stage. Despite feeling physically terrible, they were mentally relieved to have finished the first show.

The waitress delivered their first round. Perfect time for a productive discussion about the show. Better now than before the alcohol kicked in. No one had any interest in a discussion about the dangers of hot sauce. Well, maybe after they finished the business stuff.

"I thought it all went well." Trent said. Then he looked directly at Kendra. "You really killed it. You were amazing."

"Thanks, Trent." Kendra didn't make eye contact with him. This was her defense mechanism. She didn't want her expression to give away how she really felt. Kendra hid it well, but she was a nervous wreck before the show. She sang backing vocals before, but this was completely different. The edgy material added to her anxiety, and she was worried she would screw it up.

Cat turned to Robert. "What did you think?" Cat wanted to give his opinion last, so he asked him first. "You had a magnificent view of everything from the drums, well, except having to watch my fat ass for a good part of the evening." Kendra let out an audible sigh and an "Oh jeez" but she giggled along with the rest of them at Cat's self-deprecating humor.

Robert hesitated briefly, and Cat noticed the slight delay. This made him nervous. Cat knew Robert would tell him the truth and wouldn't sugarcoat anything. He could be pretty blunt when he had a firm opinion on something. The more Cat got to know him, the more he liked him.

"I honestly thought it went really well."

Whew, Cat was relieved to hear that. He knew all of them could improve. They would make changes after reviewing the footage, but no one wanted to hear that their first attempt sucked.

Robert continued, "I think we kept the MicroAggression crowd interested, and I think we made some inroads with newcomers. I want to watch the tape and see if I can get a better sense of the response and where we can get better, but nothing major."

Trent agreed. "I think we've got a lot to build on. Cat, you were a little stiff in the beginning and you need to get rid of a couple of those jokes you told, but I think you did a fantastic job. Especially for your first time. I also think that later, when we incorporate more of the offensive stuff, you may need to get more antagonistic towards the crowd so we can keep the deception going and really sell it more. But I really think we did the right thing tonight by just testing the waters with the anti-male stuff. I really liked their response. Especially for our first show."

After Trent finished his comments, a silence came over the four of them. Cat looked at Kendra and she said nothing. He could tell she was uncomfortable, but he couldn't figure out why.

Finally, he couldn't wait any longer. "Kendra, it's your turn now. Give us your opinion and please be honest. We want to make sure we get this right and this is our Safe Space to say whatever you feel."

Robert and Trent both rolled their eyes, and Robert saw his opportunity to drive a point home. "Yeah, don't say that on stage."

That broke the ice and Kendra finally let loose, speaking a million miles per minute. "Look, I was terrified out there and, honestly, I'm still trying to calm myself down, so I just can't put my thoughts into any kind of coherent critique at the moment. Of course, I'm the type of person who can tell you twenty-five mistakes I made, but I think it might help me give you a better idea once I watch the tape. But I really need to do better if this is going to work."

The other three sat stunned.

"Really?" Cat asked. Was this girl crazy?

"Yes, really." Kendra responded far more sharply than she intended to.

"Twenty-five mistakes?" Cat laughed. "I didn't see you make any that mattered one bit, and I think I can respond for the rest of the group. You're out of your mind.."

Empathy was not Cat's strong point, but he continued.

"You were sensational. You're a natural at this. Kendra, you need to watch that tape. Anyone who saw that tonight knows that you absolutely fucking nailed it. You were unbelievable."

Cat waited for Kendra to respond, but she sat quietly. He wasn't sure, but he thought he saw her blushing. Cat truly hoped that he was making her feel better. Hopefully, it was just nerves.

"Kendra, he's right." Robert told her in a tone that was in no uncertain terms truthful.

Cat continued, "You all gave them quite a show tonight. I'm the one that needs to get better. If you were feeling nervous or were thinking you were making mistakes, none of it showed. And I've got to be honest with you. If that's the show you put on when you're nervous, then I can't wait to see you perform when you realize your potential."

Kendra remained quiet, but she cracked a bit of a smile. She appreciated Cat's clumsy efforts to connect with her. She kept her guard up when men praised her. They had ulterior motives. This time, she believed Cat's sincerity. His last comment particularly touched her, and while she didn't totally believe him, she was feeling better about things. She wanted to see the tape so that she could tear herself apart. That was just her nature. However, she thought the guys were sincere with their compliments, so she calmed down a bit.

Trent then reminded her. "I told you that you absolutely nailed it out there and I meant it. You crushed it."

Kendra's smile widened more into a half-smirk.

Cat felt he could give his assessment now that everyone else had spoken. "As far as my two cents, I agree with you guys that it was a good show, and that we had a lot of positives to build on. I'm still developing a comfort level with the banter part, particularly because I have to make everyone think that I've gone woke. I'll work on it. We can play the tape with the crowd noise, and I'll try to come up with better lines. Also, it would really help if you guys could think about this and maybe give me some ideas for lines I can use to engage the crowd better. I think I need to practice more. I'll get the hang of it soon."

Trent didn't want Cat to get the wrong idea. "Cat, I thought you did a good job, and, unlike Kendra, I could tell that you were nervous and stiff in the beginning. But you really seemed to get more comfortable as the show went on and that tribute you gave to Richard was moving. That was not bullshit. That was real. If anyone in the crowd could even think you faked that, then this would all be over. You're a natural when you speak from the heart. It's hard because you're playing a part right now, but you'll get the hang of it."

Trent was more diplomatic than Robert, but not by much. He was also truthful, and that would be critical to the band's success. None of them wanted to embarrass themselves. They also didn't want to let each other down. That required brutal honesty.

"Okay, let's all watch the tape when we have a chance and then we can talk about what went right and what we can clean up. Sound good? Robert asked."

Everyone agreed, but Cat had one more thing to add.

"One last thing. Did any of you see that group of people over on Kendra's side of the stage? Kendra, did you see them?"

"I didn't see anything. I was trying not to throw up."

Cat chuckled and then continued.

"Well, it was weird. There was this group of older people, and they were recording the show and taking notes on a legal pad. Yeah, writing with a pen on an actual piece of paper. They didn't look like reporters and definitely didn't fit in with our typical fans. Why would someone do that at our show?"

There was silence from the other members. "Nobody? Okay, I'll see if I can pick up anything else when I watch the tape and if you guys can just keep an eye out when you get a moment later on."

"Who's hungry? Where's the waitress? I'm starving. Who's up for wings?" Cat asked.

"Not me." Trent surprisingly declined. "I'm actually heading home. I'm totally wiped out."

"Me too." Robert agreed. "Want to split an Uber?"

"Sure. I have to head to the studio, though. I've got to upload the demo to the server so I can work on the mix tomorrow. Would really like to sleep in and do it at home rather than come all the way back into the city."

"Perfect," Robert answered. "I have to upload the video footage too. I'll take care of that tonight instead."

"Care for some wings, Kendra?" Cat smirked as he asked her.

"No, not tonight, but I could really go for steak. Mark DelaSpark's Steakhouse is right around the corner. I've been dying to get back there."

"Steak..., yeah, that sounds good, haven't had one in a while." Cat found it hard to give up wings, but steak sounded delectable at the moment.

"Me either and if you had your heart set on something spicy, they've got a Cajun ribeye that will melt your eyeballs if you order it bloody rare."

Cat looked at her and tried to discern whether she was serious. She grinned, but wasn't joking.

"I swear I won't judge you if you order it."

*   *   *

Niko was also quite hungry, but there was no time to eat. He was still waiting to speak to the team he sent in to monitor the Safe Spaces show and Max was texting him nonstop, asking for an update. The concert should've ended an hour ago, and Niko was sitting at a bar right across the street from the venue. They should have been here by now. Where the hell were they?

Max didn't want Niko to do this job himself. He was paranoid that one of the band members might recognize him from the final MicroAggression show. Niko thought it was a real long shot that Cat or Trent would remember him, much less see him in the audience. Regardless, Max was pretty insistent that they handle it this way, so that's exactly what he did.

Niko ordered a single beer and nursed for quite a while. The bartender seemed annoyed by his small tab, but Niko didn't care. When he spotted his team, he quickly rose to greet them. He needed to move them over to the side so no one could hear them speak. He didn't think anyone would pay attention to their conversation but, again, orders were orders.

Niko motioned to them to follow him to an area along the wall that had a shelf sticking out where they could put their drinks. Blocking off the area with his beer, he waited for them to get drinks and join him.

"So how did it go?"

"Well, they started in the traditional way with Damnatio Memoriae..." Niko's team relayed the night's proceedings to him.

After they finished, Niko called Max, who picked up his phone before the first ring ended.

"Hey Max."

"Hey Niko, how did it go?" Max got right down to business. Ramirez was waiting for him to call. He didn't have time to waste with pleasantries. As they say in most corporate settings, shit rolls downhill and when your boss is leaning on you for something, it probably means that he has a deadline, too. Things were no different with governmental black operations.

"Well, I haven't looked at the tape yet, but from what I understand from my people, it was pretty difficult to get a read on what they are up to. They played a lot of the songs that they used to play in Richard's days, but they also played some new stuff that took some real shots at men. It was the song that Kendra mentioned on that Swamp Simmons show and, apparently, it was as advertised."

"That's interesting." Max didn't have a handle on this yet. He needed to see the tape.

Niko continued. "One of my guys thought Kendra's driving it. They said at one point it looked like she was singing to Cat, and they thought they picked up on a vibe between them, but that could have all been an act. Again, I'm telling you what they told me since I wasn't there. I want to see the tape before I give you my opinion."

"Yes, yes, I know. I didn't want to take any chances on this. I understand and we'll see on the next one whether you go yourself, okay?" Max wasn't chastising him. He just wanted to reassure him he understood what could happen with third-hand information.

"Oh, I know." Niko knew what Max referred to and appreciated it.

"Did they mention anything about Richard?" Max beat Niko to the next part of his report.

"Yeah, they did. Apparently, Cat gave a really moving speech about him and dedicated the show to his memory. At one point, they thought he might cry on stage. They also thought that he was furious. I mean, enraged, really. He never lashed out or anything, but there was definitely an undercurrent of anger."

"Hmmmmm," Max responded as he thought that was really important information to have. "Good to know."

"Yeah, I thought so too. That was really about it. I'll let you know more after I watch the tape. We need to watch these assholes. I don't trust them one bit."

Max agreed. "I can't put my finger on it, but I don't trust them either. We might have some issues with this. If I had to guess, I think they are up to something, but we definitely don't want it to turn into another Richard situation. We don't need another martyr. Let me run this up the chain and I'll get back to you with the next steps. Thanks for all of your help with this, Niko. Really appreciate it."

"No problem," Niko responded.

"Great, I'll talk to you in the morning. Good job on this one."

Max immediately called Annabelle after he hung up with Niko.

*   *   *

"So, he was just up on stage, stark naked?" Cat laughed through a mouthful of cold lump crab. He and Kendra splurged on the seafood tower as an appetizer before their steaks came out. They ordered immediately when they sat down, as both were famished. Their decision not to order wings at O'Hara's had good and bad consequences. The good was that they didn't eat wings. The bad was that they wanted everything on Mark DelaSpark's menu delivered to their table immediately and that would cost a fortune, but, hell, Safe Spaces only had its inaugural concert once, right?

"No, not naked. The crotch piece from the medieval-looking pants thing they dressed him in opened up and his, um, member just fell out." Kendra chuckled. "I saw it from the side. Too bad he was just singing. If only he had been playing his guitar. He could have, um, blocked the view."

"He didn't feel the breeze?" Cat didn't believe this story. She had to be making it up.

"Maybe he didn't, but then again, maybe he did and just, um, liked that sort of thing. It's not like Michael didn't have an ego on him. And besides, he, uh, had nothing to be ashamed of." Kendra giggled.

"You mean you didn't tell him? The two of you dated, didn't you?" Cat didn't believe that either. How could she just let her lead singer/boyfriend stand on stage with his unit exposed?

"Yes, we did and no, I didn't. I mean, the female fans would have killed me if I told him to cover himself up."

Both burst out in loud, uncontrollable laughter at that one.

"Why Miss Kendra, I didn't see that coming from you at all." Cat maintained an even expression as best he could after trying to get hold of himself.

She had downed a few vodka cranberries, so that loosened her up. Honestly, she would have shared this story with Cat, sober or not. It was one of her favorites. Of course, it was one of her more embarrassing concert stories too, but she had told it countless times to many people. Things didn't end well between her and Michael, and she was glad that Cat didn't get defensive about her mentioning him. Most guys weren't that secure.

Cat surprised her when he didn't flinch at the thought of her dating. That was a good thing. She had thought multiple times of how best to tell him this story. She had even rehearsed it in different ways. Kendra knew that positive comments on Michael's anatomy were a risk, but she had grown increasingly comfortable with Cat and was glad Trent and Robert bailed so she could get him out alone. Over the past six months, they had all worked closely while building the band's foundation. However, she desired a deeper connection with Cat. In fact, that was one of her first thoughts when she saw him on the floor after Robert socked him. That was a telltale sign for her she needed to screen him at some point. This was the perfect time.

Kendra's process resembled a major league pitcher throwing nasty pitches at a batter who was unaware he was at the plate. Her first pitch was a high heater that played off of Cat's comment about letting Michael hang out there.

"Oh, yeah? Why is that? You don't think I know that sex sells? Groupies are just as good for me as they are for you guys, you know. It's just different. You guys see them as a fix for your endless sexual appetites, but I see them as ticket and merch sales. Why do you think those horny teenagers come to our concerts, anyway? It's not just to see us. They're hoping they get laid too, you know."

"You're definitely right, groupies help. Trent's a big fan. I never really got involved with them that much, though."

That was a foul ball. Time to throw him a curve.

"Trent touched them, but you never did, huh, Cat?" Kendra loaded the last barb with heavy sarcasm and skepticism. She continued. "Robert had his girlfriends, but not from that shallow end of the pool. I think his parents put the fear of God in him. He came from a really strict military family. And by the way? I'm calling bullshit on you. Don't lie to me. You and Trent are the same. There's no way you turned down all those young, attractive women dressed in their sluttiest outfits just dying to get your attention. You're telling me you said no? Even when they told you that you could do whatever you wanted? How about when they offered themselves and their friends up all at the same time?"

Even though Cat didn't know Kendra was screening him, warning signs flashed he was in danger. Instinctively, he knew it was better not to swing immediately at that pitch. He needed to consider his answer, so he said nothing. Instead, he grabbed an oyster from the seafood tower, put some cocktail sauce and horseradish on it, picked it off the shell with the tiny fork and put it on to a cracker. He handed it to Kendra, who put her hand up and waved him off. She then picked up her own oyster and squirted a little lemon on it. Kendra kept it in the shell.

She raised it to him and said, "I'm a purist." And swallowed the mollusk directly out of its home.

Cat laughed and thought to himself, "this girl is impressive" and ate the one he had just put on the cracker. Like most men in this situation, he did not know he was "at bat" and he took a late swing at her last pitch.

"Okay, I'll admit it. I've dabbled in that. I mean, who goes into this business and doesn't want those types of things? But you want to know a secret? Mind you, my friends would shoot me if I told them this, but I had actually turned down many opportunities with beautiful women. Sometimes, I even turned them down even though they brought a friend or three. I didn't say no all the time, but I can't lie either. That was really hard to pass up and, like I said, not every time. Who could turn that down all the time? But I swear to you I turned them down more often than not. I mean that. Problem was, I was always worried."

"Worried about what?" Kendra tossed one right down the middle.

"Well, I always worried that, well, what if one of them pulled the goalie? How many times do you hear about people in our business with illegitimate kids?"

Cat whiffed badly at that pitch.

"You *didn't* use protection? With those women? Are you insane?" Cat had swung so poorly at the pitch that Kendra expressed more disdain in her tone than she had intended to. She felt tempted to end the at bat and call the game immediately but ultimately decided against it. Instead, Kendra called it a major strike rather than an out. Yet, it would be difficult for him to turn the count in his favor.

"No. No, I did. In fact, quite the opposite. I was fanatical about it. I would always check, even if, uh..." Cat trailed off as he had permanently sealed those records. Did she really need to know that?

"Check what?"

"Ugh." Now it was Cat's turn to feel uncomfortable. He opened the door and now there's no point in prolonging it. Might as well get it over with. "I would always go to the bathroom as soon as it was, um, polite to do so and I would run water through the condom. Just to make sure it didn't leak."

Kendra laughed. "Didn't want to pay the child support, huh?" That was a wicked slider loaded with scorn and multiple meanings. That was her strikeout pitch.

"No, it's not that, well, not '*just*' that."

"What then?"

"Well," Cat pulled a long swig from his vodka soda. "It's more that I just never thought it was fair. I mean, using a kid just to get their hooks into me or what they perceived as my money. That's bad enough, and I never wanted to be a sperm donor. If I was going to have a kid, I wanted to be a father. I wanted to raise a child right and be there for them. Not just a fucking monthly check. I mean, a kid deserves that, don't they? To be wanted?"

Solid contact. Cat had driven a high fly ball deep into center field. Maybe even into the gap. Cat effortlessly reached first base, then unknowingly attempted to take second.

"I always thought that when I finally had a kid that I would do everything I could to make sure that they knew they were the most important thing in the world to me. And not at a superficial level, like, 'look what *I* have.' No, I wanted them to know that as special as they thought I made them feel, I got it back more."

Cat rounded third, and the centerfielder ran deep onto the warning track...

Despite herself, Kendra's eyes also moistened, and Cat noticed.

"What? What did I say?" Cat figured he'd touched a nerve, and he did. But not the one he thought he triggered.

Kendra stared at Cat. Did this guy really knock a Home Run without realizing it? Was he genuine, or did the pod people replace Cat Chaotic with someone who truly cared about things besides wrestling and football? Was he just saying that to get her to hop into bed with him? If he was, she'd have to admit it worked, but she couldn't allow it now. Not with her past. The band was too important, but one day soon? Well, that was looking like more and more of a possibility.

Kendra needed more information.

"No, it's something you said. That you wanted your child to feel like he mattered and that you wanted him to know that you got as much out of him as he got out of you. It's just so..."

"What? I mean it. Who wouldn't get pissed if they got manipulated by a gold-digging bitch? But that's not the kid's fault, right?"

That was enough. She needed to tell him.

"Can I tell you something that stays between us?" Kendra asked.

Cat thought for a moment and then responded, "Sure." Then he continued. "Of course, but just so I'm clear, you mean this in a 'doesn't leave this table' way or something the group knows?"

"No, I mean Robert knows this, but Trent doesn't. Not that it matters because I would tell him, it's just that I haven't gotten to know him well enough yet. Swamp knows, but he knows just because he knows everything."

Cat took another long pull from his drink.

"Of course, Kendra." Cat looked directly at her and raised his hand in a gesture like he was taking an oath. "Whatever you tell me will never leave this table and I'll never talk about it to anyone except you and when we're alone."

"Thanks. That means a lot. We touched on something before, about Michael and I dating?"

"Yes," Cat shook his head. "Look, I shouldn't have brought that up. I'm sorry, I should have..."

"No, not that." Kendra cut him off. "Well, it's not that we talked about it. It's that..."

Cat either ignored her or just continued interrupting her. "Everyone has a past, and yours is none of my business. I only mentioned it because I didn't expect that you would, you know, you allowed him to, um, hang out there. I mean, *literally* hang out there on stage."

Kendra chuckled. "Yeah, that's an interesting take on that. Hadn't thought of it that way. But that's not what I wanted to tell you. I wanted to tell you that when we broke up, we took the band with us. It didn't end well, and it ended any chance we had to make it."

Cat laughed. "Kendra, you're not telling me anything new here. That happens all the time. In fact..."

"I know Cat. I know. Everyone has that story. You're in the business long enough and it happens. Everyone knows that. What they don't know is why we broke up. That's something that only Michael and I know."

"I thought you said Robert and Swamp both know about this?" Cat asked.

"Yes, they know part of it. They don't know the whole thing. What they know is that I have an older brother named Douglas."

Kendra stared deeply at him as she spoke. Cat sensed from her expression there was more to this. Most people had a family. Why was that a big deal?

"He has a disability, and he lives in a facility back in Pennsylvania where I grew up. It's a wonderful place for him. He gets everything he needs, and the staff couldn't be more kind and helpful and loving toward him."

"Oh, you never mentioned him."

"No, I haven't. I only talk about him with people who understand. He means the world to me. I helped my parents with him when we were younger, and I go to see him every chance I get. At least once a month and I speak with him almost every day."

Cat felt touched that Kendra shared this with him. He took it as a sincere sign of trust between them and he understood what she meant.

"Family is everything and so many in this business treat them like shit. I don't really have one and I guess it's easy for me to say it, but I mean it. I wouldn't exactly call my ex-wife 'family' since we don't speak and had no kids, thank God, but..."

"Let's talk about her some other time." Kendra bristled when he mentioned his ex-wife. That was definitely a sign to her of their developing connection. She continued, "But you're right, and I always said that wouldn't be me. I wouldn't take him for granted." Kendra continued. "And I've paid a price for it, too."

"How so?" Cat asked.

"Well, again, Robert and Swamp don't know this part, but Michael and I were getting very close to marrying, and I told him that when we settled down, Douglas was going to be a large part of our life together. Not that I was going to have him move in or anything, but I wanted to have a house back in Pennsylvania so I could be closer to him. It didn't have to be all the time, mind you, but I just wanted to be there for him more than I was."

Cat knew what she was getting at. He hesitated but asked her, anyway. "I'm almost afraid to ask, but what did he say?"

"Look, I know I was asking a lot of him, but he was far from thrilled. He said that if things were going well with the band, we would be on tour for long periods of time, and he really didn't want to have to stay in rural Pennsylvania when he wasn't working. It was a deal breaker for both of us and that's why we ended it."

Cat paused in order to make sure he carefully worded what he thought.

"I hear what you're saying that you were asking a lot, but getting to spend time with your family is really, really important. It sounds like he just wanted different things in his life. There's nothing wrong with that, but I will say this. It seems like he missed an amazing opportunity to get to know someone who meant the world to you."

"I couldn't agree more, Cat. He missed out. Doug is such a great guy, and it's so important to me I get to spend as much time as I can with him. I haven't been able to do it now for obvious reasons. We're building Safe Spaces, but someday the 'building' part will be over and the 'enjoying' part will start. And that's when I want to bring him back into my life. Not my whole life, as I do plan on spending it with someone special. I just want him to be a part of it."

"I totally get it, Kendra, and if we make it out of this alive, I know you will have all of that and more."

Wrapped up in the moment, Kendra forgot the reality they faced, even if the plan worked. They stared at each other in silence. The ice only broke when a waiter placed two steaks on their table.

"Two Cajun ribeyes, bloody as hell."

Chapter Eleven

"Ladies and gentlemen, thanks as always for joining me on the Swamp Simmons Show. We've got a packed show for you, but I wanted to start off with an update on our favorite band, Safe Spaces. As some of you may know, they've really caught on over the past several months, and I understand that they have a tremendous show planned next week at the Palladium."

Everything was going according to plan.

The band had grown a following and even garnered positive press in the corporate media. Some of whom actually defended the band against Swamp's criticism of their hypocrisy. In fact, the online threats against him soared in both number and intensity, so he knew they were getting traction. But the viciousness of the current fury surprised him. He had really touched some nerves. To be fair, there were some supportive voices, but an avalanche of hate, vitriol, and threats of violence against him overshadowed everything positive. Ironically, the attacks against him made it through the Patriot Firewall. Were those invectives "non-offensive" speech? Welcome to America in 2044.

Funny enough, Swamp thought he had gone easy on the band.

The gloves would come off tonight.

"As a quick recap, Safe Spaces, the, um, successor to Richard Uprising's MicroAggression, has taken the concert scene by storm by playing offensive material. I wonder if anyone else thinks that these shows violate the Speech Codes? Better question is, does anyone really care? They were on my show last year when they first started their venture into the culture war, and I called them out on their hypocrisy. Here's a clip of our discussion."

Swamp played a four-minute montage clip of the earlier interview that centered mainly on the argument over whether playing anti-White male material was offensive.

The camera panned back to Swamp after the montage ended.

"Well, that was something. An update for those of you that don't follow the band. They played the 'half inch penis' song and plenty of other similar ones at multiple shows, and no one is investigating whether they've violated the Speech Codes. Shocking, isn't it? No one is calling them out except me, and no one is murdering their lead singer. My, how times have changed."

Swamp continued, "And to add insult to injury, their crowds are growing larger, and they seem to have unlimited potential because they've chosen targets that cannot defend themselves. This is the day and age we live in, and I don't see any of this changing, do you?"

Swamp paused and let that sink in. Then he started throwing haymakers.

"Let me ask you all a rhetorical question. If I parodied these songs by replacing the shots they take at White males with any other ethnic group or the myriad of supposed genders, do you think the speech police would come after me? Do you think someone would take my property? Burn my house to the ground? That's an unfair question because I get those threats all the time. Just because I present ideas that some people don't like. Does this remind you of any other time in history when a group punished those that they didn't like? Just because of who they were, not for anything they did? Do you understand the road we are going down? If you do, then I think you will see parallels."

Then he went for the jugular.

"After all, Kristallnacht, October Seventh, and other pogroms only happened because a majority hated a minority for who they were. Does that scare you? Particularly with what we are seeing today? Would it shock you if they changed the 'never again' phrase to 'well, okay, as long as it happens to a group I don't like'? I wish it shocked me, but it doesn't, and that may be the scariest part of all."

"We're in dangerous times, and it seems like Safe Spaces' popularity reveals the truth that the Speech Codes only apply to certain ideas. Are we so blinded by ideology that we can't even apply an unjust law equally to everyone? And that's the problem, isn't it? They designed the Speech Codes to be a weapon. You know it and I know it. But what's astonishing to me is that they didn't hide it. It's a blatant power grab." Swamp paused again and then continued.

"I mentioned earlier that I used to go to Richard Uprising's concerts and that I admired him. He warned us prior to the institution of the Speech Codes. Richard was the proverbial canary in the coal mine. He tried to tell anyone who would listen that we were on a very dangerous path. He paid for it with his life. It's my understanding that a lot of MicroAggression fans go to the Safe Spaces shows. I have to imagine that it's because they still play a lot of the classics from the earlier iteration of the group. I can understand that since it would be hard for me to enjoy any pop culture if I had a litmus test for the politics of those that are entertaining me. Hell, I might attend one of their shows since I would like to hear them play the classics too."

"And for those of you who would call me a hypocrite, I understand where you are coming from, but it's completely unrealistic. I cannot and will not hold people to an absolute purity standard. Of course, if someone crossed a line and I cannot support them anymore, I will just spend my entertainment dollars elsewhere. I don't have any problem with how people spend their money. No one should force you to spend your own hard-earned cash on anything other than what you enjoy. However, that's different from cancelation. Cancel culture doesn't allow you to just allocate your resources elsewhere. No, you must ostracize, erase, and ruin the ones you don't like. Get them fired if you can and forgive no offensive transgressions. Cancelation is like banishment and it's an old form of punishment. The Amish banished non-believers, so they are one predecessor to the cancel culture cult. Do liberals want to be like the Amish?"

"There was a time where you settled a disagreement by agreeing to disagree. You remained friends and went on with your lives. You tallied the votes, winners were happy, losers not so much. Not anymore. Now you call the person out online and tag their employer, so they lose their job. Companies used to ignore criticism. Not anymore. Now, they'll fire the person, and no one bats an eye. Either C-Suite really believes in it or they're cowards. Let's face facts folks, it's effective. If it didn't work, no one would do it. But it does, and it's scary."

"Let me end this segment on a positive note. Maybe I should attend the upcoming Safe Spaces show. I might be the person standing next to you, you never know. I really enjoy eighties music and their shows are very entertaining. Even if they offended me, I would never call for a boycott. They are saying words I don't like. Is that such a big deal? Does that deserve banishment? Wouldn't it be better if I engaged them? I'll debate anyone, anytime, anywhere. I won't run away from the fight."

"Now, onto some other news of the day..."

*   *   *

"Just how much did you guys rake in?" Swamp was backstage at the Palladium, chatting with the band after their soundcheck.

"Yeah, can you believe it, Swamp?" Robert beamed as he had reviewed the numbers before coming to the venue. "I knew that the merchandise sales were going well, but who knew there would be a thirty percent increase in tee shirt sales in just a year's time? It's unreal. And you know what's even better? A huge chunk of it is online. It's not just people attending the shows, it's people across the country buying the merch. It's really unbelievable how much traction we've gotten. I could see this two years from now, but, wow, this was quick."

"And that's not all," Robert continued. "The promoter called. He already sold the ticket allotments for an arena tour of the southeast. He said if this keeps up, we may do stadiums next year. Would have to be a split bill with a big name, but wow! Ticket prices are jumping too."

"Really?" Cat asked. "Even the secondary market?"

"Yeah, after we sold out, some are going to the ticket brokers. I hate those people, with the bots and all, but man, I never thought we would get to stadiums this quick. I hate to say it, but we might have made it." Robert chuckled.

Trent had been quiet for most of the discussion, but couldn't hold his tongue anymore. "Guys..." was all he said.

Here we go. It was time for Trent to be Trent.

"Does anyone else see the problem here?" He could suck the air out of the room with the best of them.

"I do," Swamp chimed in, but no one else spoke.

"Do I really have to be the one to say it? Again?" Trent said flatly. Still, no one responded.

"Ok then, I will. You all know what I'm about to say, but you're making me say it, anyway. Fine, I'll be the bad guy. There is another option here. We could keep doing what we're doing. Phase out the anti-male stuff, write some new songs. Grow this thing and live like rock stars, happily ever after, but..."

He trailed off. Trent wanted someone else, preferably Cat, to take up the voice of reason. None of them did, so he continued.

"I'm just saying that we have an opportunity, don't we? We could keep the big reveal to ourselves. Just go with it and, I don't know, enjoy this? Accept it all and get our kicks in before it all crashes and burns."

"I'm not selling out." Robert's tone was sharper than he intended, and Trent didn't like it.

"It's not selling out! We'll still play the MicroAggression stuff, and you know what? I'm just asking whether we could live with ourselves by just getting rich? Robert, I'm not married to this, but I'm just putting it out there for discussion because we are kind of at a crossroads."

"I really appreciate that you brought this up." Cat knew Trent was right. They needed to discuss the way forward. The band was already bigger than they ever imagined. If they scrapped the big reveal, they could make a lot of money and live the rock and roll lifestyle. Cat sensed he needed to jump in now rather than wait for anyone else. "Because I think..." he started.

"Can I say something before you do, Cat?" Swamp cut him off. He saw the direction this was going, and he wanted to give them his thoughts before Cat shaped the discussion. Swamp understood the dynamic between the four of them and while no one's opinion truly dominated, Cat was the most influential.

"Sure Swamp." Cat was a bit surprised he wanted to jump in, but he was also genuinely interested in what he thought.

"Thanks. Let me start off by saying that I'm really impressed with you guys. I've been to the shows and heard the commentary online. Your audience is really, really into you. I can't fully explain it, but your band connects on a deep level, and it isn't just because you are picking on White males. You're not a tribute band and you play your own music. You've forged a highly entertaining hybrid product that mixes nostalgia with a subtle comment on today's times and your fans love it."

Swamp continued. "But again, it is subtle. What I'm worried about is that most won't get it until you knock them over the head with a sledgehammer. You keep doing what you're doing, and you'll make a lot of money. No one would blame you for that."

Everyone in the band was silent. None of them had really considered abandoning the plan. Of course, none of them had focused on the end of the project either. They were too busy playing music and loving every minute. If they canceled the big reveal, then they would probably become rich and famous. If they didn't, they would likely end up dead.

Swamp finished his thoughts.

"But you know, there's an upside to finishing this. I told you guys that I quit a big tech job because I couldn't live with what I had done. I am directly responsible for designing the technology that became the Patriot Firewall. To be fair, I designed it for the military so we could jam the enemy's communications. I had no clue Ramirez and her thugs would use it to control American citizens. But I sleep better at night knowing I'm doing all I can to atone for what I did and pay my debt. The four of you have nothing to apologize for. You didn't give the government the tools to turn us into a police state."

"No, but I played a concert where they massacred people who paid to see me." Trent bowed his head as he spoke.

"That wasn't your fault, Trent." Cat's defensive tone hinted that Trent ripped open a wound that hadn't fully closed yet and he lashed back. "It wasn't my fault. It wasn't Richard's fault. That was all on the psychopaths that invaded our show. No one deserves to die like that. Especially just because we sang some songs that someone didn't like." Cat immediately pivoted to Robert. "What do you think?"

"Well, I completely understand Trent's thinking here. I mean, the numbers don't lie. We are already selling out arenas and stadiums are a real possibility. But I meant what I said: I'm not selling out but I'm okay with delaying the big reveal. Make some money on the arena tour and then blow this shit up? Maybe we could do the big reveal on the stage at whatever they've named that stadium in New Jersey now? If anything needs to be blown up, it's that place."

Cat trusted Robert's opinion. He was the most analytical of all of them. Sometimes, he could be even more incisive than Swamp. Where Cat often snapped on emotion, Robert was much more measured and circumspect. He offered Trent a delay in the big reveal, which was a great way to give him some breathing room.

All of them fell silent as everyone had spoken their mind. Well, not quite all of them. Kendra had said nothing, and they could not make this decision without hearing from her. Those were the rules of the group. Cat frequently had to nudge Kendra to talk.

Not this time.

"Burn the motherfucker down."

They all simply stared at her. It wasn't just what she said, but also her conviction. She was sometimes hesitant and deliberative before critical decisions. Not this one. This time, she shocked them.

The only word that Trent uttered was "Whoa."

Robert smirked and half laughed and nodded his head and said, "well that about says it all, doesn't it?"

"Yeah, it does," Cat laughed. "I'm glad we're going with the sex, drugs, and rock and roll routine for a while." Cat looked at Kendra when he dropped that loaded phrase. Their eyes met, lingered, and she smiled briefly before turning away.

Kendra sensed the others had also caught Cat's not-so-subtle signal, so she changed direction.

"What? What did you think I would say?" she asked with a bit more enthusiasm than she intended. "No way I'm letting them get away with this shit. And who the hell knows, maybe we'll get people to see that we're already in Orwell territory? Or maybe we'll all end up dead. If nothing else, we can say we tried to stop it."

"It sounds like we all agree that we should hold off for a while and, for the record, I'm not saying we should abandon everything." Trent said as he stepped in again. "I'm just saying that we ought to slow down and ride this wave a bit, make some money, and then think about the timing of when we unleash it. Please, just think about whether we really want to do this. Once it's out, then that's it. There's no putting the genie back in the bottle."

"But don't forget you have me in your corner." Swamp reminded them. "I'll be there to fight back when you blow this all up. I told you before, the drama we created touched a lot of nerves out there. More and more people understand the point you're making. There's an opportunity to do something amazing, more than just make money and live like rock stars. You have the chance to help me lead a movement."

The room fell silent again. The idea of changing the world was pretty serious.

"Okay, so we all agree we're going to keep thinking about this, right?" Robert needed to wind it up and move on to other business, including the night's set list. "My gut tells me we'll see through and we'll know when the time is right. Is that okay, Trent?"

"Fine, Robert." Trent responded flatly to Robert's jab at him. "And just so everyone is crystal clear, I do want to get payback. Richard was my friend, too. I'm disgusted by everything. What happened to him was so wrong on so many levels. This can't continue, and I'm happy to play my part in 'burning the motherfucker down.'"

All of them laughed. Kendra had a way with words. Trent finished the discussion with, "Let's kick some ass out there tonight."

*   *   *

Safe Spaces was finishing up the first hour of the show at the Palladium. They had played some of the most rocking songs by their favorite eighties and early nineties new wave and industrial groups. They also loved playing punk music from the seventies and the "hardcore" bands that grew out of it in the later years.

Richard loved punk music, and the fans loved the energy and raw power. Cat thought about adding one of his favorite punk songs to their catalog. It was a sarcastic take on one-night stands with plenty of profanity. They were thinking of having Kendra sing it in a grand twist of irony. That wasn't a typical punk song, though. Mostly, the artists took aim at politicians from the era. Things were really different now. No one took on the establishment if they wanted to make money or stay alive.

They had one more song to play before they took their first break. The plan was to start the second set with a goth song from the eighties and then turn it over to Kendra for the anti-male set. That part of the show had become very popular. So much so that they even considered closing with it.

The Palladium was their largest venue yet, and they nearly filled it to capacity. If it wasn't a sellout, then it was really close. They kept the first one hundred feet in front of the stage open as a general admission area for the fans that wanted to dance. Some "moshed" or "slam danced" which Cat despised. He particularly hated it when someone fell on the floor. He didn't want to see anyone get trampled. Cat had stopped shows when someone fell and didn't immediately get up. The last thing he wanted was for anyone to get hurt.

Thankfully, there wasn't a lot of moshing during the first set. That didn't mean the crowd was bored. They were really into this show and the band fed off their energy.

"Are you having a good time?" Cat asked the crowd, and they responded with a loud roar. A low energy crowd could be a big problem in a huge venue like the Palladium. Not tonight, though. The band's presence and the crowd's enthusiasm made the Palladium feel as intimate as a show at a dive bar. Better enjoy it now. At the rate things were going, their days of playing small shows were likely over.

"Good, glad to hear it. We're thrilled to be here. As some of you know, we like to change the set list and tonight's no exception. We've got a good one for you."

At that very moment, the crowd fell silent, probably gearing up for one of Cat's speeches. At prior shows, you could hear a pin drop when he spoke about Richard. Other times, they were raucous when he ranted about the government. When he was in a better mood, he talked about the local football or baseball team. Cat was a huge sports fan and never missed an opportunity to praise his favorites and rail against the ones he hated. He particularly had fun with fans in cities like Buffalo and Philadelphia, who took their sports way too seriously. Sometimes, when he was in a combative mood, he would come out wearing a rival team's jersey. His favorite pro-football team was from Texas, and he loved their home white jerseys. Cat wore one with the number "88" on it during a show in Philadelphia and was lucky to make it out of the venue alive.

Tonight, he was wearing a long-sleeved shirt over a tee shirt, so he was relatively safe. However, he planned to lash out against the government regarding the Speech Codes. Just as he was getting ready to let loose, a voice pierced through quiet and yelled,

"DEAD ALGERIAN."

The shout was loud, interrupting the silence of the crowd. Everyone in the audience heard it. There was no mistaking it, and the band couldn't ignore it. A large contingent applauded, yelled, and whistled in approval of the request. Others repeated the phrase and called out as they tried to goad the band into playing it.

"Dead Algerian?" Cat repeated into the microphone, his voice blaring through all corners of the arena. Repeating the phrase was a big mistake. If he could redo it, he would simply play the next song on the list. However, the crowd roared in approval once he said it.

Cat turned around and looked at the band to gauge their response. He glanced behind him and saw Robert nodding in approval. He then looked at Kendra, and she was laughing away from her microphone. Then he turned to Trent.

Oh boy.

Trent glared at him, but he didn't look angry. He looked scared. Trent walked toward center stage and motioned for Cat

152

to get out of earshot of the microphone. They met halfway between their positions. Somehow, the crowd had already begun clapping in unison. This audience wouldn't take no for an answer.

"It's too soon," Trent whispered loud enough so only Cat could hear him.

"Yeah, maybe it is, but let's just see how it goes, okay? They want to hear it and who knows, maybe this will sell more tickets?"

"Oh, you've got to be fucking kidding me?" Trent shot back, but he knew he had lost. "Go ahead, it's all our funerals this time."

"Maybe not. Let's do this." Cat motioned over to Kendra and to Robert that it was a go, but he also signaled for them to hold off for a moment.

He walked back over to the center stage microphone and grabbed it off its stand.

"So, you want to hear that one, do you?" The crowd roared even louder with a noisy mess of screams, whistles, shouts.

Cat continued, "You know that the name of that one is 'A Day in Algiers,' right? It's not the Dead Algerian." Screams and laughter echoed from the audience as Cat hesitated longer than necessary.

"I guess we could do that one, just for tonight, but let's just keep this between us, okay?" The crowd laughed as Cat continued. "Before we do, I hope you know that some people really misunderstand this song."

He paused and smirked at the crowd, making it seem like he was actually looking to engage in a discussion about the lyrics.

"Just as long as we understand each other." More laughter erupted from the crowd. Even Trent chuckled. And he was probably right. It was too soon. But it could also be a perfect addition to the show. Might as well give them what they want.

"Well, if that's how you feel, okay then, kick it, Kendra."

She hit the riff and a Sitar sounding melody erupted from her guitar. Robert and Trent completed the remaining part of the beat that blended rock and Arabic sounds. After she finished the intro, Cat leaned forward, picked a random girl in the crowd to stare at and sang one of his favorite songs that was previously buried in the ashes of MicroAggression.

"I spent a lifetime running on a day in Algiers,"
"I tried to flee my mind, but couldn't dismiss my fears,"
"The slaughter I committed and the Muslim I remitted,"
"Burned an image in my eye that I justified,"
"With a homicide."
"One day in Algiers."

He paused as the band filled in the measures between the first and second verses. He looked into the crowd. They were in a frenzy. Dancing, yelling, and clapping. He heard the crowd echo the lyrics along with him. This was going well.

"I live far away from my time in Algiers,"
"My body may be here, but my mind is in tears,"
"I've wasted time repenting, and the Muslim now is nothing,"
"Now I'm petrified."
"I want to be purified."
"Of a day in Algiers."

Cat believed that most of their fans understood the meaning behind this song. It was an homage to the controversy over early existential writing that used violent imagery to show the absurdity of the times. Extremes on both ends falsely portrayed it as racist. MicroAggression played the song because they refused to give in to those factions. Besides, had anyone ever committed a racist crime and blamed early existential writing for what they did? Would anyone believe such an excuse?

Cat continued to examine the crowd and noticed a similar group to the one he saw at an earlier show. They took notes and filmed using old phones. An older male and female were having a heated argument. He couldn't hear what they were saying to each other, but the male waved his arms frantically and shouted something at the group. Who were these people? Why were they here?

Cat didn't have time to investigate. The song neared its end, and he had one more verse to sing. It had a very noisy ending, and he needed to concentrate on what he was doing.

After the song ended, Cat wanted to engage the crowd again, but they were too busy screaming, yelling, and clapping. It was pretty clear they had nailed it. As they calmed down, Cat sensed his opportunity.

"So, what did you think?" The crowd responded to Cat with an even louder roar than the one that moved them to play the song.

"Glad to hear it. We love playing that one and if you ever want us to play it again, please avoid going to Algeria and killing people." That brought a mixed reaction of laughter, boos, and cheers.

"Boos? Really?" Now Cat was playing with them. "Man, we'll have to think about this. Anyway, I don't want to wear out my welcome here, so we are going to take a quick break..."

Chapter Twelve

"Why did we play that?" Yes, it was Trent again. Three days had passed since the Palladium show, and this was what? The hundredth time he had brought it up? Well, at least Trent wasn't cursing this time. That was a positive sign he was coming to terms with the band playing A Day in Algiers.

"Here we go again..." Kendra was losing patience with Trent. She snatched one of her guitars off its stand much harder than she intended to. The stand fell over and knocked over her acoustic guitar. The thud sound reverberated through the hollow body and Kendra sighed. Now she needed to tune it again for the show. Then she kicked one of her effect pedals that littered her corner of the rehearsal studio and let out an audible grunt as she wheeled to face Trent.

"Did you see how the crowd reacted? They loved it." She muttered through clenched teeth. Her tone made it clear she didn't want to talk about it anymore. One hundred times was enough.

"Yeah, it was tremendous." Cat intervened between them. He didn't want them to come to blows over it. They were waiting for Robert to arrive for rehearsal and hopefully, they wouldn't have to rehash it. Cat wasn't sure if he could protect Trent from Kendra if he bitched again. She had reached her limit with him. Cat continued to try to de-escalate.

"For what it's worth, I don't think we've done anything irrevocable here. It was just one song, one time, and who knows? Maybe more people will want to come out to the shows?" Cat wasn't bullshitting Trent. He thought that the crowd's reaction was so positive that he was going to talk to the band about making it a permanent addition to the set list.

Maybe even the closer. But given Trent's mood, it was best to wait to bring that up.

"I know," Trent responded flatly to Cat. "I'm not talking about the fans we are going to get; I'm talking about what's going to happen now. You know those oh-so-tolerant people who killed Richard? Do you think they're the type who will say, 'oh, don't worry about it, it's only a reference to existential literature?' No, I think they're more the type that will cut us to pieces."

Trent had a point. Cults don't forgive.

"Yes, but isn't that what we got into this for?" Cat asked in the most un-sarcastic tone he could summon. "We could have been a fucking boy band or played dance music and made a shitload of money. We didn't. All of us wanted to do something meaningful, not just overproduced pop drivel."

"Yeah, I know, but we all agreed to wait. Couldn't you have just said something like we haven't practiced that one yet, but keep coming to our shows and we'll get around to it? Or just ignored it?" Trent made another good point.

Kendra responded, "Of course we could have ignored it, but didn't you see that crowd? I'm sure they're tired of the Speech Codes too. They need us to be us right now." Trent thought she sounded just like Cat.

"Yeah, again, I know, but don't you think that the people that killed Richard are going to notice that? Aren't you worried that they'll get more angry at our fans and take it out on them, too?" Tough to argue with that one.

Robert walked in and immediately noticed the tension in the room. "What's up?" he asked.

"Guess what we are talking about?" Kendra asked him. She didn't mute her sarcasm.

"Oh, that again. I'm not really worried right now," Robert chuckled a bit. "Let's all calm down, and really, it's done now. The only thing to do is figure out how we want to play this. There's no point in fighting about it. It's time to move on."

Just at that moment, Robert's phone pinged. That type of notification only happened when he received an important message about the band's business, and he immediately looked down at it.

Robert furrowed his brow and raised his eyebrows. He leaned his head back and looked at the industrial ceiling of the studio. Kendra thought Robert should have spoken by now, and she broke the silence.

"What is it?"

Robert looked back down at the message and let out a muted "Holy Shit."

"What?" Trent urged him to get on with it.

"You will not believe this, but our tee shirt sales went up another twenty-five percent, and it's the same thing as last time. It's not just the people at the shows, it's the online orders. Also, other merchandise is up ten percent. Even stuff like sew-on patches and hats. Nobody ever buys that shit, but now they are. The videos of the Palladium show are going viral, with plenty of 'likes' and 'dislikes', but who cares? These numbers mean the views are turning into actual money."

"Wow," was all that Cat could muster in response. He tried again but just repeated himself, "Wow."

"And that's not all..."

Now Robert intentionally paused for dramatic effect and let them stay on the hook for a bit. Finally, Cat couldn't help himself and looked at him and said, "Robert?"

"Well..." Robert trailed off and waited for a bit to finish.

"Oh, come on!" Trent finally interjected and looked at Robert like he was going to kill him if he didn't speak.

"Not only has the arena tour almost sold out, but you know what else sold out? VIP tickets, can you believe that? They are going for close to double what we priced them through that stupid dynamic pricing thing! This is unbelievable."

"Double? Didn't we price those at $300? My God..." Trent trailed off and shook his head.

"This is unbelievable." Cat tripled his word production from his last two comments.

"Yeah, this is something. Guys, I think we can actually say that we made it now." Robert was not the type for false optimism. Clearly, this was big.

"Hell, I'll take becoming a bigger target for that kind of money. I can buy a lot more shoes." Kendra laughed and then asked, "Who's up for a seafood tower and bloody Cajun ribeyes? They're on me..."

All agreed. It was a great night to celebrate at the steakhouse, but Cat had to get in one last dig.

"And we owe it all to playing the Dead Algerian."

*   *   *

"Would you mind repeating that?" Annabelle asked.

Max knew that this call was going to be horrible. However, he didn't realize just how awful until Ramirez asked him to repeat himself. Sometimes she used it as a delay tactic to organize her thoughts. Not this time. This time, Max knew it was pure rage.

"Yeah, I know. I couldn't believe it either." Regardless of how Max really felt, he needed to say he agreed with her. If she got the sense that he didn't, well, she wasn't the type to hold back her wrath. Others had paid the price for crossing her. Max didn't want to be one of them. He continued.

"I figured that there would be some fans that would like them playing that old racist Dead Algerian shit, but I didn't ever once think it would be all of them. Apparently, Cat tried to explain it away by telling them that people misunderstood the song, but we all know that was all bullshit. They just like insulting Muslims."

Ramirez seethed as she processed this situation. She truly enjoyed intimidating people into compliance. But that could only go so far. She believed that controlling offensive speech would not only change behavior, but eventually change hearts and minds. Not only was the fact that the audience enjoyed it infuriating, it also called into question her premise. Did people only adhere to the Speech Codes and self-censor out of fear of social isolation and financial ruin? If so, then that masked the problem. Ultimately, she knew that if they changed the language, they could control the population. It was the only way for long-term success. Unfortunately, what Max was telling her was not a good sign.

"There's something else too..." Max knew the next bit of news was going to send her through the roof.

"What?" Ramirez spat out as if she had just had an insect fly into her mouth.

"Well, it wasn't just that concert. We've had our financial surveillance team look into their merchandise and ticket sales, and they are skyrocketing. They were doing well before that concert, but now it looks like, um, they're doing even better."

Ramirez didn't respond and just stared at him and that's when Max knew she was boiling. Nothing he said today could calm her down, so Max figured it was best to tell her everything now and get it over with as soon as possible.

"And that's not all. I hoped that there was no correlation between the concert and the increased sales, but we pulled the data off the SUNSHINE system. You know, the one that monitors every audio, video, and internet transmission. It looks like the band is knowingly or unknowingly leading a growing movement against the Speech Codes. An increasing number of people see them positively and are also complaining about the restrictions. It's not a huge percentage yet, but it's growing, and I don't like the trend line."

Max braced himself, but her silence continued. He waited for her to lash out at him.

Finally, she broke her silence. "Motherfucker," was all she said.

Max had never seen her so angry. Her normal response to bad news was to let loose with a storm of expletives and degrading comments about those who opposed her. As she calmed down, she would make broad statements containing parts of plans to deal with a situation. Sometimes she followed through on her rants. Other times, she was just blowing off steam. This time, all she could say was one word, or maybe two, depending on how you spelled that insult.

Max tried to wait her out, but the silence was deafening, so he finally broke it. "I guess it's time to take them out."

Still no response.

Uh oh. Max knew she couldn't hold back her fury for long.

"Yes, yes, it's time to take them out." Max expected screaming from her, but her voice was a little above a whisper.

"Okay, I'll talk to Niko. I'll tell him to put an operational plan together and..."

"No." She cut him off. Her voice was slightly louder than before.

"No?" Max responded with a question because he definitely didn't expect this response.

"No," she repeated.

"Okay." Max was a little surprised. This was not typical Ramirez. "What are you thinking, then?"

"Not now, no, we can't take them out that way, maybe later, but not now. We need to do something different; we can't just put a Band-Aid on it this time. This time, we need to remove the cancer completely."

Max sensed Ramirez was thinking through her next steps as she spoke.

"We can't turn them into martyrs this time. The people who love Safe Spaces need to realize that they are bitter clingers who pray to a false God. They're a cancer and we don't want it to spread and infect the rest of society. No, people need to see them for who they are. We need to turn them back into the bad guys and we need them to help us do it."

Max understood, but his initial reaction was that she was delusional. He didn't believe for a second that Cat and Trent had switched sides. The data they had on Kendra and Robert showed they were far more aligned with Richard. They were stubborn. They had to be playing some kind of game. Max thought Ramirez was going down a rabbit hole, but might as well indulge her.

"Umm, okay, but, um, just a thought. I really don't think Cat or any of them will go along with anything. We can try to threaten them, but I think another 'Richard' solution would terrify just about anyone who would think to join them, so why don't we..."

"Everyone has a price." Ramirez cut him off. "And I think that by the time we are done with them, Cat will beg us to pay whatever price we charge."

"Really?"

"Yes, really." Max hoped Ramirez didn't take his question as a challenge. Her tone suggested she did.

"I have an idea. It's risky but it will bring everything to a head. We can't let Safe Spaces control the narrative. It's time to end this nonsense. We've talked about the broad strokes before, and I'll fill you in on the details soon. First things first, though, I need to call a press conference, so let me take care of that and I'll call you back."

"Okay," Max answered, but didn't know where she was going with this. However, he noticed Ramirez had re-directed her anger in a practical direction.

"But I need you to do one thing immediately. I need you to..."

When Ramirez filled Max in on his first task, he remembered their prior discussions on the broad strokes of this plan. He had largely forgotten about it, but now that she reminded him, he marveled at her thought process. She was right; it was risky, but you know what? They needed to do something different. Taking them out, as they did with Richard, wasn't sufficient. The plan could easily blow up in their faces. But if it worked, it would put an end to everything.

"Okay, got it. I'll get Niko started on this. No doubt he's going to be all in, but I think it's best if we just keep the bigger picture between us for now, if that's okay with you."

"Agree totally," Ramirez responded. "Call you in a few hours."

"Great, thanks, and I know we'll make this work. We'll end this once and for all."

"Oh, it will end Max. One way or another, this will end."

*   *   *

"Every time I think they've gone as low as they can, they keep digging." Swamp was on a roll as he was streaming Annabelle Ramirez's press conference and jumping in to counter her statements in real time.

"But let's get back to her own words. Is there any better evidence of just how vicious the regime is?"

Swamp turned back to Ramirez's press conference.

"Thank you again for joining me tonight as I outline my plan to combat the seditious and racist poison that certain individuals in the music industry have spewed into our country. As you will see, our actions will allow the government to do its part to uphold the law and enforce the Speech Codes, as we believe that only the light of truth can disinfect the virus that is offensive speech. Our tactics are not heavy-handed. They are not overly restrictive. They are common sense measures directed to uphold our shared values and ensure that everyone, regardless of race, creed, color, national origin, gender, or sexual orientation, can have a good time while they attend any form of entertainment."

"Oh, puh-lease," Swamp jumped in. "Is this woman for real? Would you trust her on anything having to do with 'truth' or 'common sense'? Would you ever even associate those words with Annabelle Ramirez? How about words like 'lies,' 'oppression,' or 'despotism'? Those seem much more accurate."

Ramirez continued.

"Some of you may ask yourselves why my upcoming announcement is necessary, and I do have an answer for you. You can see for yourself. Just go online and search for videos of concerts where the 'artists' or who I like to call 'racists' play Islamophobic music. They have absolutely no shame in dredging up this bile from our past, and no respect for anyone who just came to their show to have a good time."

"Oh, that's a good one." Swamp interrupted. "She's obviously referring to Safe Spaces, and she's conveniently left out all the times they offended White males. Of course, those people don't count. Why bring logic or consistency into a discussion about something as ridiculous as the Speech Codes?"

"And I want everyone to have a good time, too."

"Ha." Swamp left his commentary at that.

"So that's why earlier today I issued an Executive Order consistent with my powers to enforce the Speech Codes to appoint the new 'Concert Freedom Commission'. The CFC will be the vehicle by which the government will do its part to ensure that everyone can enjoy live music."

"What?" Swamp asked.

"Yes, my little darlings, the CFC will be a new administrative agency in my government. Its first task is to conduct a study of just what steps we can take to ensure that concerts are non-discriminatory. Everyone should be able to enjoy them, not just the privileged few. And what good would a commission be without an effective leader? So, tonight, I want to introduce the new head of the Concert Freedom Commission. A wonderful friend of mine, Peter LeFleur, but everyone calls him 'Topper'. Pete, I mean Topper, I'm going to turn the Zoom feed over to you, so you can introduce yourself."

"Thanks Madame President."

"This should be good." Swamp giggled.

"I appreciate the kind words and want to first thank you for putting your faith in me to help with one of the biggest challenges of our time. In fact, and I can say this without hyperbole, this is the country's biggest challenge since the Civil War. Even bigger than January Sixth."

"Regulating concerts is one of the biggest challenges of our time?" Swamp snorted. "Since the Civil War? Only a mindless government bureaucrat could think like that, much less say it."

"I think Madame President correctly identified the problem. My job and the job of our team is to carry out her vision. We need to move forward and ensure that we don't return to the days where entertainment marginalized and oppressed the most vulnerable segments of our population."

"In order for us to complete this most important task, we will first do a thorough analysis of the 'root causes' of the issue. To do this, we will draft members of our team from other governmental agencies, such as the Federal Communications Commission, the Consumer Financial Protection Board, and the Internal Revenue Service."

"The IRS?" Swamp asked. "What in the world would they have to do with concerts?"

"We will collaborate with the government's best and brightest. Our team will drill down to the granular level, compile a workable list of common sense options, and present them directly to Madame President."

"Gee, what do you think those options will look like? Do you think any of them will give the government *less* power over you? Do you think the IRS might just financially ruin any of the bands the government doesn't like? No, can't imagine that." Sarcasm was one of Swamp's most effective verbal tools.

Topper continued. "Let me say a bit more about our list of options. Nothing will be off the table. Madame President assured me she will consider any legal option we propose. However, given the divide in Congress, the ultimate plan will probably not result in legislation. We will need an Executive Order or administrative remedy."

"How strange, a government bureaucrat giving lip service to our Constitution? You don't see that every day."

"We have a list of working ideas, including a robust concert permitting system. That will help us regulate the time, place, and manner of these shows. We are also looking at a consumer oversight rating committee as a parents' resource so that they can protect their kids from hearing unapproved ideas. Third, we may partner with the private sector to establish a clearinghouse where businesses can go to make sure that they are working with groups that align with their values before they partner with them."

Swamp could only manage an "Oh, dear God" in response to what essentially was a government blacklist.

"And remember, we are here to help you. We just want to make sure that the fun you are having is in line with the Speech Codes and our values as collective American citizens. Thank you for your time tonight and let me turn this back over to Madame President."

"Here to help you? I think we've seen enough of the government trying to help people."

"Thank you, Topper, and I really look forward to working with you. You covered everything, but I have some final thoughts."

"She can't help herself, can she?"

"Tonight, I want to close by saying that I sincerely hope that one day we can disband the Concert Freedom Commission. I know in my heart of hearts that American citizens would rather hear inclusive music so that we can all enjoy entertainment together. I hope that one day, regulation, permitting, and ratings will not be necessary because everyone will finally get it. We're all in this together and once we all agree that offensive concerts and entertainment have no place in our society, then we will all live together as one undivided country."

"Thank you again for allowing me to speak from my heart to yours and may God bless my fellow Americans and may God have mercy on the souls of the rest of you."

"What a load of bullshit." Swamp got straight to the point.

"You understand, ladies and gentlemen, that what we actually heard tonight was the beginning of the downward spiral into authoritarianism. This is not an innocuous administrative agency. None of them are, but at least some of them are supposed to meet some common purpose, like ensuring that we manage our land appropriately or that fisheries abide by certain regulations. Not this one. They designed this one for outright warfare on our individual rights."

Swamp paused and allowed his audience to digest what he just said. He was not exaggerating for dramatic effect. He knew Ramirez had planned for the long game. Protecting only non-offensive speech was a Trojan Horse. If she had her way, she would criminalize thoughts and statements, and the republic wouldn't survive.

"Don't think so? Did you listen to her? This is a textbook power grab and if you don't see that coming, then you haven't been paying attention to how these people operate. They start with something that sounds benign, like granting permits to concerts under the power of regulating the 'time, place, or manner' of speech and then guess what? You know who suddenly finds it hard to get a permit? The people they don't like. They have to go through endless red tape, never ending 'government reviews' and suddenly they find themselves subject to an IRS audit. What you have seen tonight is weaponization of government and you should all be really afraid of the consequences of this."

"We've seen it before. Administrations have unleashed the power of the government on their enemies. Don't believe me? Remember McCarthyism? Internment? The Tea Party? Operation Crossfire Hurricane? And now, I fear that this time there may be no going back."

"You think I'm going over the top with this? I hope you're right, but I fear you're wrong. We gave them the opening when we tolerated the change to the First Amendment. That was just the beginning. There's no telling what the fallout from this will be. I believe, though, that sometimes things have a way of backfiring. I pray that this is one of those times. Who knows what's going to happen now that we have the 'Concert Freedom Commission.' One thing's for sure: the government is going to regulate our speech even more. Things are going to get really ugly for many people."

"Hold on tight everyone, consider yourselves warned."

Chapter Thirteen

"If you thought you'd lead a peaceful life, now you know you were misled."

Cat belted out the lyrics to one of his favorite songs in their catalog. 'Peaceful Life' was a crowd pleaser. It had a rocking tune with a funky beat and a catchy keyboard melody. The audience loved to sing along, and that always fed the band's energy. The lyrics were pretty dark, though. They recalled a challenging and cruel time for the working poor. Of course, the problems described in the song seemed simple to modern listeners by comparison. But that was only in hindsight. Going through life is far from simple. Only the passage of time can romanticize it.

"The gold you thought that you'd found... was really all just lead."

"Times are different now... than you'd ever thought they'd be."

"You keep on bangin' your head, and if your head hurts now..."

"You just wait until the world knocks back and kicks you in your teeth."

The chorus was always the crowd's favorite part where they screamed:

"Bang bang bang ba bang bang bang ba bang bang."

The fans were full of energy and enthusiasm, which kept the music flowing.

Peaceful Life was their first song of their second set. Cat took his normal approach and minimized his audience banter during the first hour. No rants, no diatribes, no jokes, just ass-kicking rock and roll. He thanked the crowd for the applause, but nothing more. That was about to change.

"THANK YOU, THANK YOU, thank you very much. Wow, we always love playing that song and thank you for helping me sing it. It's one of my favorites. I always love it when we've got a fun group to help blow the roof off!"

The audience roared again. They were all feeling it tonight.

"So, before I turn you over to the lovely Miss Kendra, I wanted to thank you for the online feedback you've given us. Well, particularly to me. Man, you guys, oops, sorry, I mean you audience members can really throw some shit so tonight, I thought we can have some fun. I was thinking I would read some of the, um, constructive criticism you gave me. What do you think?"

There was audible laughter from the crowd that drowned out a few gasps. Cat was going to enjoy this.

"Let's start with something light, um, let me see, here's a good one, 'Cat, you suck. I hope your racist ass gets stomach cancer and that your wife gets raped by your Klansmen buddies. Die asshole.'"

"Lovely sentiment, don't you think? I'm not sure I could get stomach cancer in my racist ass, but that's just a technicality. Wife raped by Klansmen? Hmmm, I'm not married, but I figure anyone who's demented enough to marry me might not mind a gang rape by the Klan. Now if you said that she was going to be subjected to suffering a romantic evening with me, then she might take offense."

"Raped by Klansmen?" Kendra interrupted with an unrehearsed comment. "An evening out with you? I don't know, Cat; I could see if you asked to combine the two into some kind of sick role play, maybe there would be a problem. This is sex, drugs, and rock and roll, in 2044, right? Is anything off limits? If you asked every woman in here, someone has asked her for worse. Or does that only happen to me?"

Cat and Kendra shared a chuckle as their eyes met. He loved her unscripted banter and couldn't help but notice the not-so-subtle signal. He flashed her a crooked smile. She caught it and they both held each other's gaze for a second too long. Kendra dropped her eyes, knowing that they might just stay locked on one another if she didn't. Cat caught her hint and snapped back to the crowd.

"Do you want to hear another one?" Cat asked. It was a rhetorical question. He was going to read more mean messages, no matter how the fans reacted.

"How about this one? Cat, have you weighed yourself recently? I hope not, because you would destroy any scale not designed for farm animals. Eat a salad once a month so that maybe you can fit into a quadruple XL again."

That one caused a gasp from the crowd. Cat paused, adding a touch of drama.

"Whoa, man, that one hurt." Cat delivered that line with an obviously fake sense of sadness.

"I haven't been bigger than a double XL in quite some time. I know I'm no Elvis, but I don't think I have that much to be ashamed of, do I?"

The crowd laughed more, and women in the audience kindly catcalled and whistled.

"Do we have time for one more, Kendra?"

She purposely waited a bit and baited the crowd into a reaction. They gave her one when they screamed, laughed, and whistled.

"Well..." Kendra maintained an even tone, which caused the crowd to go into a frenzy.

"Oh, alright, how can I say no to that?" She really knew how to entertain them.

"Well, okay then, one more, 'Cat, you inbred, unvaccinated, piece of shit, MAGA voter. You need to take your stupid, uneducated White ass to the Kevorkian center and kill yourself. Do the world a favor and die before you procreate.'"

The crowd fell silent, which suited Cat's next move perfectly.

"There's a lot to unpack here, folks." Some muted laughs from the crowd.

"First, I got vaccinated. Knocked me out for days, but I did it."

That one provoked more laughs from the crowd, along with some cheers and applause.

"Second..." He paused again for theatrical effect. "I have a college degree, but it's not in gender intersectional race theory, so I guess I'm uneducated compared to all of those fry cooks."

That line drew more laughter, along with a smattering of boos.

"And one other thing, whoever tweeted this probably can't do a damn thing that's useful to anyone else in the world. And let me ask you, do you think useless left-wing professors who've contributed nothing worthwhile to society brainwashed this idiot?" The crowd responded with a mixture of boos, laughter, and applause.

"Don't misunderstand. I learned from some superb teachers who taught me how the real world works and challenged me with critical thinking skills. Most of the others, however, fed me a line of complete and utter bullshit that had no relevance to anything other than Marxist theories that have failed everywhere. I'll take the wisdom of your average truck driver, plumber, mechanic, firefighter, or pilot any day of the week over those useless people." There were some audible gasps from the crowd, so he doubled down.

"And to the author of those words of wisdom, yes, I'm talking to you, Tim, from the People's Republic of San Francisco. I'll bet you put your gender studies degree to good use. Better not waste daddy's trust fund too quickly or you'll have to go back to cleaning up dog poop."

Louder boos, mixed with laughs and applause. Cat loved offending the over-educated, common sense challenged part of the crowd.

"And finally, Timmy, my parents were at worst second cousins, so that's technically not inbreeding in most states."

The crowd roared in approval and applause at that line. He waited for it to die down so that he could start the intro to Kendra.

"I'll let you figure out who I voted for way back when. So, with that, I would like to..." but just at that moment a loud artificially amplified voice came out of nowhere and yelled, "DEAD ALGERIAN!"

Cat was stunned by how loud it was and laughed in response. How could he have heard that? Was it a bullhorn? How could someone get something like that past the metal detectors? He glanced at Kendra, Trent, and Robert, and they all shared a shocked expression. None of them had a clue how that happened and, besides, they hadn't planned to play that one at this show. However, this amplified heckler had his own ideas for the set list.

"Well, the song is actually called 'A Day in Algiers,'" Cat deadpanned, and the crowd went wild. "Here we go again..." Cat thought to himself. This time, he took Trent's advice.

"That one wasn't on the set list tonight, but maybe we'll get to it later in the show." As soon as he uttered the words, he knew he had made a mistake and wished he hadn't left an opening. Intuitively, Cat knew something wasn't right.

The crowd showered the stage with boos, but instantly, about fifty people on the front left began clapping in unison. How did that happen? It usually takes time to develop. Why did it originate from one side of the audience? Cat looked in their direction, and none of them looked happy. They just glared at the stage. What the hell was going on?

Cat motioned over to Trent, who was closest to that section of the audience. He walked over to talk to him, making sure that he was out of the microphone's range.

"Do you see that?" He whispered to Trent.

"Yeah, this is bizarre. What do you think?" Trent replied. He was worried. This time, Cat was too. Now, the rest of the crowd had joined in the clapping. Saying no was going to be difficult.

"Well, I think we should just play it and move on." Cat said, but he was nowhere near confident that doing so was the right decision.

To his surprise, Trent agreed. "Yeah, I think you're right. Let's just do it. Tell Kendra and Robert." Neither of them wanted to play the song, but they both sensed that not playing it may be worse.

Cat walked to the drums and informed Robert about the set list change. Then he walked over toward Kendra, and she signaled back to him she knew what was happening. Kendra walked back behind her keyboard and picked up her guitar and played a couple of warmup chords. The crowd erupted as soon as they heard the familiar riff. Whatever the outcome, it was pretty clear that a sizable part of this crowd really wanted to hear A Day in Algiers.

Cat walked to the stage front and grabbed the microphone.

"Well, that was interesting." He looked straight out at the audience while he addressed them. "This is a first for me. I've never been onstage at a show where someone in the audience was louder than me. Most of the time, you guys just have to listen. I guess times have changed in oh so many ways."

More laughter and applause from the crowd.

"Since this is a first, we are going to play one more before Miss Kendra takes over and, well, I don't have to tell you what it is. Kendra, would you be so kind as to get us started with that guitar of yours?" Kendra took her cue and strummed the opening chords of the intro to A Day in Algiers. Robert and Trent seamlessly joined in with their parts. The audience thundered its response. It was louder than normal. Loud enough that Cat might have a hard time getting the band's attention if he needed it. Cat guessed the crowd would calm down after this song, so he wasn't that concerned. Unfortunately, Cat was mistaken.

The song started with a musical intro before Cat began singing. He used the time to survey the crowd. He looked closely at the section that started the clapping, and he noticed something really strange.

None of them were paying attention to the band. They weren't dancing or singing. Instead, several men walked toward the center of the floor. Why did they bring a bullhorn in and demand this song and not pay attention?

Cat noticed other people in that section weren't paying attention either. They were rooting through bags. Others were recording the show with their phones. That wasn't unusual. The strange thing was that some of them pointed their phones in different directions, even toward the back of the venue and at the upper decks. What the hell were they doing? Cat's stomach dropped. Something was going down.

As Cat started singing, he noticed the men that made their way to the middle of the crowd had stopped and were looking directly at him. The ones digging in their bags also stopped and stared at the stage. They still weren't cheering or singing along. They just glared at him.

Cat didn't stop the song despite the crowd's strange movements. The rest of the audience was in a frenzy and sang along. Except for those odd fans, they still hadn't moved. None of them. They just scowled at him. What the fuck was going on?

Just as Cat started the third verse, all hell broke loose.

People in the center of the audience grabbed random people next to them and started beating them. Guards stationed in front of the stage saw the melee and ran into the crowd to break it up. But before they reached the chaos, other fans intercepted them and wrestled them to the ground. When the other security guards at the sides of the show witnessed the crowd attacking their colleagues, they ran to help them. Cat had witnessed fights while he was on stage, but nothing like this. He also realized that now there weren't any security guards left to protect the band.

BOOM!

An explosion detonated in the air over the crowd, and Cat jerked his body. This was not part of the show. Someone had snuck in fireworks. Flashes of light and sounds of screaming rockets pierced through the audience and drowned out the music as the show devolved into madness. The fans fought back against the agitators, but the fireworks, coordinated explosions, and beatings overwhelmed them.

Cat was stunned as he witnessed the mayhem. Trent and Kendra had stopped playing. Robert wore earpieces which prevented him from immediately hearing the explosions. He kept drumming for a moment, but then noticed the havoc and stood up from his drum set.

Cat got a hold of himself and yelled "STOP THIS NOW" into the microphone as loud as he could, but no one heard him over the explosives and the commotion. He immediately thought about Kendra and ran over to her. She didn't see him at first as the bedlam mesmerized her. He clutched her arm and dragged her back to Robert, who was standing in front of his drum kit. Cat screamed at him, "GET HER THE FUCK OUT OF HERE." Robert nodded his head and pulled Kendra over to Trent's side of the stage. Trent was waiting for them and looked at Cat. Cat motioned for him to leave with Robert and Kendra, and then he sprinted back to center stage.

Cat stood behind his microphone and looked at the disaster. The fighting had ended, and most of the audience had departed. However, there were still several fans in the general admission area who were trying to get out through the doors flanking the stage. Others tried to leave through the back of the hall.

The few that remained tended to their wounds. Unlike last time, no one appeared to be seriously hurt. Thankfully, there were no dead bodies on the floor. No doubt this was a coordinated attack.

Amidst the turmoil, Cat noticed a lone person standing on the floor, seemingly out of place. He didn't look bloodied or injured, but stood several feet back from the buffer between the stage and the crowd. He didn't move, but just gawked at Cat. The stranger smiled when their eyes met. Then he burst into laughter.

Cat looked around and didn't see any security guards nearby. He wasn't sure what this guy's intentions were, but he was on his own if they got into it. Still, his blood boiled at what had just happened and Cat stared him down. The stranger just continued to glare and laugh. Finally, Cat had had enough and yelled, "What the fuck?"

In response, the guy snickered and smiled and said, "you don't know who you are messing with, do you?"

Although Cat had heard him clearly, he asked the stranger to repeat himself, "what did you just say to me?"

The guy responded with more laughter and that pushed Cat over the edge. He jumped off the stage into the security guard area and tried to hurdle over the barrier to get onto the floor. Upon landing, a security guard grabbed Cat and bear hugged him. The stranger used that time to escape through the back of the hall.

Cat screamed obscenities as he tried to twist away from the security guard. Fortunately, or unfortunately, he had him in a death grip. Cat had completely lost it. He probably would have killed the guy if he had gotten his hands on him. Instead, he took his rage out on the security guard and yelled, "DON'T TOUCH ME, DON'T FUCKING TOUCH ME." Finally, he wrestled himself away from the guard and fell to the floor.

After he regained a bit of his composure, Cat got up on one knee and stopped for a second. He stood and brushed off debris from the floor. Looking up, Cat saw Kendra, Robert, and Trent approaching him. They had witnessed the entire altercation with the stranger. Cat made eye contact with the rest of his band and just shook his head.

Cat tried to walk toward them. As he staggered a few steps, he stopped and fell down to the ground. He was now sitting on the floor. Cat felt like hours had passed since he fell, but it was less than a minute. He had lost his concept of time along with his temper. He was so fixated on pummeling the stranger that he failed to notice someone wearing a security guard jacket off to the side of the stage. Whoever it was, put his phone back in his pocket. He had recorded the whole thing.

*   *   *

Trent drove everyone back to the rehearsal space from the concert. No one said a word during the thirty-minute ride. The radio was on and tuned to one of the band's favorite nineties stations, but no one was listening. They weren't interested in music at the moment. Trent parked in front of the rehearsal space, and still no one spoke. They all got out of the car and silently went their separate ways. Robert stopped them.

"What the fuck?" That's all Robert said, but it sufficed. If he remained silent, it may have been the last time they saw each other. Looking back, they might have been better off.

No one replied to him, yet they all paused and exchanged glances. Without saying a word, they all changed direction and walked into the rehearsal studio. Perhaps this would be their final meeting.

The four of them gravitated toward the round table and sat down in their usual chairs. They avoided eye contact, even though they were sitting in a circle. The shock became a heaviness as they all quietly processed the evening's events.

Finally, Cat couldn't take the silence anymore. He got up to leave. Without uttering a word, Kendra rose and locked eyes with him, which stopped him dead in his tracks. She turned around and walked back to where she kept her equipment and eased her way past her guitars and keyboards. Kendra squatted down and opened up one cabinet and reached in. She stood up and turned around slowly. In one hand was a large bottle of whiskey. She paused and then spoke.

"Cat, go get four glasses and put some ice in three of them."

Cat smirked and said, "now you're talking," and did as he was told. He returned from the kitchen with four of the largest glasses he could find. Two of them had ice. "I'm going neat too."

He passed the glasses with ice to Robert and Trent and handed the last empty glass to Kendra. She poured at least three shots of booze into each one and picked up her glass. Then she raised a toast to each of the others separately before putting her drink in the middle of the table as she said, "this one is for Richard" and took a long swig. The other three raised their glasses, and all repeated "for Richard" and took long pulls from their drinks.

Kendra held her hand up and said, "Hold on, I'm not done." She picked up her glass again and motioned to the others and said, "this one is for the fans. They spent their hard-earned money to see us tonight. No one deserved that."

They all downed more whiskey, far more than a polite sip. All four of them held their relationship with their fans sacred. They weren't just paying customers to them. They considered them family and loved them beyond their understanding.

"One more," she said, even though the other three knew she wasn't done.

"This one is to us. We've come a long way, and we've got a lot more to do, a lot more. This will not stop us. We are going to finish what we fucking started because we need to and, you know what? The world needs it, too. I haven't fully processed this yet, but there is one thing I know. I'm not ready to stop now. Not by a longshot."

Kendra's words lingered, but no one spoke. All felt the brown liquid burn and waited for the whiskey to kick in.

"Did you see what happened out there?" Trent whispered. He asked everyone, but he really meant it for Kendra, and she knew it.

"Yes, I did," she responded evenly. "But I don't think any of us really saw what happened. We saw a riot, but it was much more than that."

"What do you mean?" Robert asked, mainly because he was the one who had the hardest time seeing the crowd from behind the drum set.

"I mean that there is much more to this than what we know." Kendra continued. "What happened tonight made no sense. I've seen fights before, but nothing like this."

"Yeah, it was really bizarre." Cat added. "It looked like it was all coordinated. Tell them, Trent. You saw it better than I did."

"I saw it, but I couldn't believe it."

Robert was still confused. "You guys have to be more specific. The first time I noticed anything was when the fireworks exploded. What do you mean, 'coordinated?'"

Cat responded, "I mean, it looked like a group of people started the fucking riot, rather than a fight devolving into one. That happens, things spiral out of control. No, it was as if they all started the fight all at the same time with random people for no reason. Richard and I talked about it once. We talked about what used to happen back in the seventies and eighties where groups of, like, neo-Nazi skinheads, would just show up at shows just to brawl. In fact, there were songs about it. Some of the punk bands played songs that told those assholes to fuck off. They didn't want them at their concerts. Some of those songs were great. I wish I could remember the titles. It'll come to me. We should add them to the set list." They all chuckled slightly, but no one found it amusing.

"But those Nazis were never that smart, or that coordinated. They would pay money to buy a ticket, show up and fight for the hell of it. This looked different. As if someone planned it."

Cat picked up his glass and held it close to his lips. "Had to be. Now that I think about it..." He paused and took another long drink of his whiskey, which finished the glass. He grabbed the bottle and poured himself another stiff one and returned it to the center.

"They filmed it."

"What?" Kendra gasped. "You mean someone just recorded the show on their phone, like normal, right?"

"No," Cat grunted and picked up his drink. "There was a group of them recording in all different directions right before the shit broke out. It was as if they needed to get multiple shots and angles. They filmed us, the audience, and the top levels. Why the hell would they do that?"

"What the fuck?" This time it was Trent who uttered the now universal phrase of disbelief.

"Yeah, what the fuck?" Cat repeated and tipped his glass to deliver some more brown medicine.

"Robert, we had our cameras running, right?" Kendra begged and wished for Robert to give the right answer. "We need to retrieve our footage and get it to Swamp. We need to show this was a coordinated attack. That's the only way we survive this."

"Yeah, I know our cameras were running but..." Robert trailed off and then continued. "But if you're right and this was a coordinated attack on us, then who knows whether we have anything on tape that will help?"

"He's right," Cat added. "But I'm almost positive someone set us up. Did you hear what that guy said to me? The one I was literally going to kill if that guard hadn't tackled me."

"No," Robert responded, and he was the closest one to Cat. "I didn't hear it."

"He said we didn't know who we were messing with, or something like that."

"Oh, jeez." Kendra sighed.

Cat continued, "Yeah, not what you would expect to hear from a skinhead or someone who just showed up to fight for no reason. You would have thought he would have said something like, fuck off motherfucker or some such nonsense."

"Yeah, those guys don't exactly have a reputation for an expansive vocabulary," Robert chuckled. "Boy, I must be getting lit from the whiskey, but God knows I needed it. Let me start by securing the footage. Swamp helped me encrypt it, so it's probably safe. We're going to need it to defend ourselves when all this breaks. Then, I need time to decompress. You should all do the same."

"I think you're right." Trent responded. "I'm also feeling the whiskey and I can't believe it, but I'm kind of hungry. Why don't we head out and try to find some place down in Chinatown or somewhere we won't get recognized and get something to eat? In fact, there's this place on Mott Street that has soup dumplings..."

Suddenly, there was a knock at the door.

The four of them sat in stone cold silence as adrenaline shot through their bodies.

"Oh, shit," Kendra muttered under her breath.

Cat got up to answer the door. This was his idea and his mess, and he needed to confront whoever was on the other side.

"Cat wait..." Kendra whispered. He heard her and glanced back at her. Cat nodded, but stayed silent. Then he continued walking to the door.

Trent stood and followed, but Cat reached the door first. He peered through the peephole and let out a hissing noise. Cat turned back to the group and sighed, "It's the police."

A second knock at the door.

"Well, if it's the police, you guys don't want me answering the door." Robert laughed as he gave the others a smile with his gallows humor.

A voice from outside said. "It's the police. You need to open up. You're not in trouble. We just need to talk to you."

"Did you hear that, guys? We're not in trouble." Cat could match Robert's morbid humor.

That caused the group to laugh even harder and louder for reasons none of them could explain. Tears streamed down Kendra's face. Trent thought he might wet himself and Robert's sides hurt. Cat doubled over, feeling even more pain in his body. "Oh, God" was all said as he tried to get control of himself.

Thirty seconds later, Cat had somewhat regained his composure and tried to speak coherently. "Oh, God, please, please." He motioned for Trent to walk back toward the table. Trent moved back a few steps, but was still closer to Cat than to Robert and Kendra.

"Not in trouble..." Cat mimicked as he unlocked the door.

Chapter Fourteen

Cat laughed uncontrollably as he wiped away the tear streaks on his face. The policeman had to be joking when he said they're not in trouble. No one could be that stupid. Cat tried to gather himself to face the cop and whatever reality awaited him on the other side.

As soon as Cat cracked the door open, a detective's shield and accompanying ID burst through. Both objects hovered about one foot from his face. He had a fleeting impulse to grab the cop's arm and twist it. Apparently, the owner of the arm wasn't concerned about losing it. The hand disappeared quickly. Perhaps he realized his mistake and had second thoughts about keeping his arm.

"Oh wow, guys, look, the cops are here! Aren't you happy that they cracked the case of 'who staged the riot' so quickly? I sure am!" Cat's sarcastic words set the tone for a terrible start to the upcoming conversation.

The detective grinned at Cat's mockery, but admitted to himself that this guy had balls. He usually dealt with a mix of fear and indignation, not laughter and sarcasm. Especially after he announced who he was. He had witnessed many strange things in his twelve years on the job. Laughter was a first for him.

"Yeah, well, I'm not the riot police. They're kind of bored now since they say that protests are mostly peaceful." The detective had his own sarcastic streak. "My name is Detective George Jenkins, and I'm with the homicide unit. We need you to come down to the station to answer a few questions."

Jenkins was a shorter man, balding, with a wiry, toned build. He wasn't outwardly intimidating, but he was deceptively strong and could take care of himself in a fight if necessary. Jenkins didn't expect any trouble from Cat. He thought Cat would either refuse to come down to the station or come down quietly. George brought three uniformed cops with him just to be safe. He motioned for one of them to come to the door.

"Homicide?" Cat didn't expect to hear that. A surge of adrenaline rocketed through his body, which immediately ended whatever lingering effect the whiskey had on him.

"Yes, homicide, you need to come with me. You aren't under arrest, but I need to talk to you."

Kendra was now about ten feet behind Cat, so she heard every word and yelled, "Homicide? What the hell?"

"Why do you want to talk to me about a homicide?" Cat posed the obvious question that any innocent person would ask when hearing such a statement. Unfortunately, it's the same question most guilty people asked too.

"I'll explain it all when we get down to the station. You just need to come with me now so we can clear some things up. If you say what I think you will, then this won't take long at all." Jenkins employed a clever strategy to disarm an individual he believed to be innocent and had information he needed. Often, a regular citizen was terrified to talk to him, and statements like these eased their minds. The ruse worked equally well when he needed to talk to someone who he was sure murdered somebody. He played on their ego. He allowed someone to think he knew less than he did or gave them the false impression they could talk their way out of a charge. This time, George was being honest. Cat wasn't under arrest, so legally, he couldn't force him to come. Keeping him calm and persuading him to talk voluntarily was the key.

And it worked.

"You said I'm not under arrest, right?"

Cat knew full well that he had absolutely nothing to do with a murder. But he was rightfully suspicious. The sole reason he contemplated joining him was for more information, even if it meant playing a dangerous game.

"That's right. You're not under arrest," George responded.

"And if I come down, it will be on a completely voluntary basis, right? You're not forcing me to go with you, correct?"

"Yes, it will be voluntary."

"Okay, here's what I'll do. I'll come down under one..." Just as Cat offered his terms, Kendra squeezed his arm. He hadn't noticed that she had walked up behind him. She tried to turn him around so that she could look him in the eye. Her touch slightly startled Cat, but he faced her. She locked her eyes on his and squeezed his hand gently. "Cat don't trust him. Don't, I'm telling you...don't."

Cat knew she was right, but he also knew he had no choice. He closed his eyes slightly and nodded his head down a bit. Immediately, Kendra knew what he was going to do, so she clenched her teeth and clutched his hand harder. She threw daggers at him with her eyes, trying every non-verbal way she knew to convince him this was a bad idea. Cat kept his gaze on Kendra while he spoke to Jenkins.

"Tell me who died, and I'll come down quietly. Otherwise, I'm calling my lawyer, and you'll never hear a word from me ever again."

Cat mouthed "I'm sorry" to Kendra. She nodded her head down and all but closed her eyes. She kept hold of his hand but eased off on her grip. Her touch was urgent, but Cat felt it was more like she was saying goodbye. Her mind screamed that she would never see him again. Yet she had no choice but to let him go.

Cat appreciated her gesture so much, but he felt he had little choice but to go with Jenkins. How else was he going to get more information? Besides, he knew he could invoke his rights, so was it really that dangerous? Cat also worried about the potential public relations nightmare the band had on its hands. They wouldn't see it as his constitutional right. They would think he was guilty. The news coverage was going to be unfavorable either way, but at least he could say he cooperated.

"Okay, I'll tell you. Someone murdered Topper LeFleur outside your show tonight."

"Topper LeFleur? What on earth?" Trent said from behind Cat.

"Yeah, we found him strung up and disemboweled at your concert. Look, we know you were on stage, but it was at your show. I want to get as much information about what went on so we can piece this together. I'll fill you in on everything at the precinct." George was being honest. Well, mostly honest, anyway. Someone had, in fact, murdered Topper LeFleur and crucified him outside the show. However, that last sentence where he told Cat he would tell him everything was a complete lie. No detective would ever tell anyone everything he knew when he investigated a crime.

"Don't go Cat." It was Kendra again. She was giving him sound advice. He should have listened.

"Kendra, I know. I don't trust him, but what choice do I have right now? Call the lawyer and tell him I'm going down to the precinct. Try to get a hold of him tonight if you can. If you can't, please call him tomorrow morning. There's one other person you need to call about this and I think you all know who that is." Cat signaled to her he wanted her to call Swamp, but he had to choose his words carefully. One misstep and he could end up in jail or dead.

Cat turned away from Kendra and trudged toward the detective. As he passed, Jenkins said, "Thanks. My guess is you'll be back here in a few hours."

Kendra, Trent, and Robert stood by the door. As Cat got into the back seat of the squad car, he turned and nodded to them and mouthed, "It's okay."

The officer closed the door, and the car departed. Kendra tried to stop the detective and the last remaining cop from leaving.

"Detective Jenkins?" she said politely, but loud enough so that George could hear her. He didn't respond and kept walking. She repeated herself, but louder this time. "Detective!"

Jenkins turned back to her and waited for her to speak. As he looked into her eyes, he sensed both icy coldness and a burning rage. He waited for her to scream at him. But when she spoke, her voice was calm, cold, and even. She didn't shout or whisper but communicated in a flat but declarative tone.

"You and I both know that Cat had nothing whatsoever to do with any murder, and it's clear to me you are here to intimidate us. If that's your purpose, I can assure you it won't work. But touch one hair on his head and there will be hell to pay."

Jenkins didn't immediately respond. He just watched her glare at him, and she withstood the urge to speak further and fill the void of silence. Finally, the detective blinked.

"Why little Miss Kendra, what year do you think this is?" The detective demeaned her, like a teacher belittling a student asserting herself.

Jenkins continued his condescending tone. "This isn't 1984 when we beat perps into talking. This is 2044, and we've progressed. You think I'm one of those barbarians that uses my fists to get results? I'm offended and you should be ashamed of yourself, missy."

Now Kendra's expression changed to a smirk, but she kept staring at him and waiting for him to continue. He didn't. He remained silent, and this time Kendra broke first in the contest of wills. She licked her lips, raised her eyebrows, and spat out at him, "don't say we didn't warn you."

A broad smile appeared on the detective's face. He looked directly at her as he sat down in the passenger side of a second squad car. With a wave of his hands, he closed the door and dismissed the band. Jenkins kept a shit-eating grin on his face as the cop car vanished into the night.

*   *   *

Jenkins walked Cat up to the front desk in the precinct to check him in with the desk sergeant. George guessed it was a slow night. The desk sergeant paid more attention to his fantasy football team's stats on his phone than to any police work. Finally, Jenkins said, "hello sergeant" and that got his attention. He glanced up from his phone and looked at Jenkins, but remained silent.

Cat and the remaining uniformed cops stood behind a red line that was about five feet from the desk. No one without a badge could walk past it without permission from the desk sergeant. George turned to Cat and said, "I'm sorry, but I'm going to have to search you for weapons. I'll also have to cuff you for the walk through the precinct, but I'm assuming everything will go well and we can take them off once we sit down to talk."

Cat shook his head. This day did not turn out anything like he thought it would.

A police officer instructed him to place his hands against the wall, spread his legs, and then frisked him. After he finished, he bound Cat's wrists with handcuffs. "He's clean, just a wallet and a phone."

"Fuck, I forgot my keys." Cat wasn't joking, but the rest of them found his statement amusing considering they were questioning him about a murder.

"Full name?" the sergeant asked him.

"Carl John McKnight."

"Thanks," the desk sergeant wrote Cat's real name on a plastic bin. He took his phone and wallet and placed them in the container and put it on the shelf behind him. Then he looked at his computer. "Hold on, let me see what's open? Oh, okay, you can take him to Interview Room Six."

The cops exchanged nods, and then a buzzer rang. One of the uniformed cops opened the door and held it for the rest of them. Cat followed him and George trailed at the back of their line.

They walked through winding curves which passed desks and offices filled with both uniformed and non-uniformed police and civilian staff. All the offices and cubes were gray. The walls were all painted an ugly shade of green that seemed fifty years old. They walked for several minutes until they reached a long hallway which had several rooms with signs warning, "AUTHORIZED PERSONNEL ONLY. QUESTIONING IN PROGRESS."

They turned down the hallway and entered the last room on the left. Jenkins opened the door and motioned for Cat to enter. Cat did what he was told.

The room had bright white walls. It was empty except for some chairs and a lone desk in the middle of the room. The desk had a metal bar attached to it, but was otherwise unremarkable. Cat presumed the large mirror on the side wall was a one-way mirror. Cameras were visible in two corners. He loved watching reality cop shows on television, but never thought that he would sit in an interrogation room. Maybe he should have listened to Kendra.

Cat sat down at the desk and glanced at Jenkins. He waited a moment and neither of the cops moved. Finally, Cat held his shackled hands up and waved them at the detective. "Can we take these off now? I'm not saying that I don't occasionally like these, but I'm really not in the mood right now."

Jenkins had heard a version of that joke a few times, but Cat's slightly entertained him. He motioned to the uniformed cop, who removed them from Cat's wrists.

"Would you like something to drink, a water or a soda or something?" Jenkins always asked that question and would put a bottle of water in front of whoever he was talking to even if they said no. He would also offer the subject something to eat if he interrogated him for more than a couple of hours. Those cameras were recording him too and these simple steps helped in the evidentiary hearings when the defense lawyer inevitably argued that George had coerced the defendant into confessing.

"Well, I'm assuming you already have my DNA on something so sure, why not? I'll have some water." No sense risking dehydration from the whiskey.

Jenkins smiled at Cat's DNA reference. He knew he was dealing with someone who watched a lot of television. He also knew that Cat would be very careful when he answered questions. George was no amateur. He figured Cat would invoke his right to remain silent early because of the coded message he sent to the band as they left. Jenkins needed to get everything he could from him as fast as possible. He also knew that Cat's only purpose in coming to the station was to get information out of him. This would be an interesting dance. Especially since George had to play by a restrictive set of rules. He didn't have enough to detain him. Other cops would have beaten information out of him, but not Jenkins. He was a good cop and there were certain lines he refused to cross.

"I'll be right back." Jenkins and the cop left the room, leaving Cat alone at the desk.

George planned to be out of the room for about fifteen minutes so he could observe Cat's body language while he waited. Smart detectives learned a lot during this time. If Jenkins questioned a suspect he knew was guilty, he would let them sit and watch them for a minimum of thirty minutes and wait for specific cues. For instance, the old police adage that guilty people sleep while awaiting questioning had proven true more often than not. George knew Cat didn't murder Topper. However, he also believed that Cat knew more than he let on at the rehearsal studio. George didn't believe in coincidences, and there were just too many similarities between the two killings.

George watched as Cat sat quietly in his chair. He swayed a bit, probably because he had a tough time sitting still. Cat was fidgety, but the main thing Jenkins noticed was that Cat reached into his pocket every few minutes, like he was looking to pull out his phone. He looked exasperated when he realized it wasn't in his pocket. This was pretty common. These days, it's rare to find someone who can sit and do nothing. Minutes of undistracted thinking were taxing on electronically addicted brains. Of course, Cat was nervous, but that was also normal. Unfortunately, George could not glean much from his fifteen-minute observation, except that it seemed less likely to him that Cat was involved in the murder. Jenkins grabbed a bottle of water and walked into the interrogation room.

"Well, I'm glad you didn't make me wait too long. It's fucking boring without a phone."

George passed him the bottle of water and said, "You should see my kids without theirs."

"Okay, so can we just get to it? I would really like to get home soon and forget this day ever happened."

"Yes, but let me remind you that you are free to go at any time. You are not under arrest, and you can stop answering my questions and consult with an attorney any time you wish. Do you understand?"

Cat looked up at one camera and addressed it. "Yes, I understand."

"Alright, thanks. Let's begin this interview differently than usual. Most of the time, I would ask you a series of questions to establish a timeline of your whereabouts. Then I would ask you more questions so that I can catch you in lies. This time, I know where you were and what you were doing so, I'm going to lay my cards out on the table and tell you what we are looking at. We are not sure if you were involved in Topper's murder and if we can clear you, then you'll be home soon. If we can't, then this interview is going to go off in a completely different direction. Do you understand where I'm coming from?"

Jenkins was actually being straight with Cat during this part of the interview. He was attempting to ease the tension and lay the groundwork for being the "good cop". One of his partners would play the "bad cop" if George caught any hint that Cat was actually involved in the murder.

"I understand." Cat appreciated George's honesty, but he knew he needed to keep his guard up. He also knew that Jenkins was, for now, playing the good cop. He had no intention of speaking to the bad cop, but didn't want Jenkins to realize he was aware of the situation. Cat needed to walk a fine line. He had to be careful. Thankfully, he had nearly sobered up and was now running on pure adrenaline. He knew that a headache would follow as his body cleared the alcohol, but, oddly, that pain might help him since it would make him even more irritable and less inclined to fall for any tricks.

"Here's what I know. We found Topper strung up to a railing on the second floor of the parking structure outside your concert. Whoever did this slashed his abdomen in an 'X' pattern, cut his throat, and removed his tongue. We are still waiting for the autopsy results, but we think he bled out during the first hour of your show. Unless the coroner establishes a completely different timeline, then we know that no one in your band committed the actual murder."

Jenkins took a risk by disclosing all of this information to Cat. He felt he had no choice with so little evidence to go on. Of course, he didn't tell Cat everything and left out several crucial bits of information. He failed to mention that there were surveillance cameras pointed directly at the murder scene. Unfortunately, they 'malfunctioned' during the exact time that they crucified Topper. There was no evidence of a struggle. Therefore, it was highly likely that whoever did this killed Topper at another location and then brought him there to hang and bleed out. There had to be multiple perpetrators, too. No single person could have strung Topper up from the second deck without help. He would have been much too heavy for one person to stage the scene. Whoever did this wasn't afraid of getting caught, either. Hanging him up that high would have taken some time, and they risked being seen by someone, particularly at an event that thousands of people attended. Finally, Jenkins withheld the fact Topper had an "Anarchy" symbol carved into his back. He also omitted that fact from his case file. This was intentional and ensured that only a few people, including the actual killer, knew about the mutilation. Overall, it was a pretty gruesome scene, and that was saying a lot, given Jenkins's long experience in the homicide unit.

"So, if you know I didn't do it, then why the fuck am I here talking to you then?"

George was prepared for Cat's entirely logical question. "Well, I think you know why you're here. It doesn't take a rocket scientist to figure out that Topper was a problem for you and your band and, drum roll please, there are a lot of similarities to the Richard Uprising murder."

"Yeah, how's *that* investigation going?" Cat hissed through his teeth. "Funny that happened well over a year ago, and nobody's looking that hard to find his killer and yet you show up at my door immediately. Did you check any cameras near the warehouse? I'm sure they will help you catch the goddamn killer. Or maybe they won't. They filmed Richard's murder and you guys haven't solved it."

Jenkins ignored the sarcasm. "Well, just because you were on stage doesn't mean that you weren't in on it. I've done a lot of these investigations, and pure coincidences don't happen very often. There's usually some connection and until we rule it out, we talk to the people who have a motive and, clearly, you have that."

"Well, fuck you and fuck your motive. I have every reason in the world to be angry. Mainly because someone killed one of my best friends, someone who I was close enough to be a brother, and nobody seems to care. Not your police, not your government, and not even our goddamn president. Who, might I add, had the balls to go on national television and say that she understands the motives of those who killed him? Really? She understands the 'pure' motivation of murderers? How fucked up is that? I play guitar for a living and I'm the one who is at fault here? Fuck you."

Jenkins let Cat rant. Rule number one of a homicide investigation is to let the perps talk. Particularly when they've lost control. The more they spoke, the less guarded they were. Sometimes, they gave you a piece of information they were trying to hide and the more they talked, the more you could get. The trick was to guide them in the direction you needed them to go. Ask questions that would lead to a provably false lie or maybe get them to slip up and say something true. Since he had sufficiently agitated Cat, it was the perfect time to use one of his zingers.

"Are you done?"

It worked. Cat's blood boiled in full rage. He tried to keep himself under control, but it was getting harder to maintain his composure.

"Yes, I'm done, and I think there's no reason for us to continue talking."

Cat was a skilled agitator, too.

Jenkins lost his poker face and he let his frustration show. He had worked hard to rattle Cat and failed. He had nowhere near enough evidence to even get a search warrant. Not even their standby 'I'll rubber stamp anything' judges would sign off on this one. George had nothing but a flimsy motive. Cat had an alibi supported by thousands of people at the concert. The motive probably wasn't even enough to get his unit chief to sign off on paying the overtime for a surveillance detail. Jenkins had to let him go. Maybe the coroner's report and DNA evidence would justify bringing him back for additional questioning later, but that was it.

So, George played the last card he had.

"Since you've ended the interview, I'm required to advise you we cannot clear you as a suspect. Our investigation will continue, and you will be free to go in a few minutes. I just need to get some paperwork and your phone and your wallet and I will be back in shortly." Jenkins rose from his chair and turned to leave the room.

"Look," Cat stopped Jenkins and continued to talk, even though he had just invoked his right to remain silent. "You know I had nothing to do with this and you know I don't know anyone who would do such a thing, so I can't figure out why you brought me here. To be honest, I'm kind of shocked that you kept your word and are not beating the shit out of me or locking me up in some closet somewhere. Hell, I figured I would have been waterboarded by now. That's more than I expected, but I want to ask you one question before you go. Have you given any thought to just what might happen if someone indeed killed Topper in some twisted revenge plot for Richard's murder?"

Cat's question was rhetorical, and Jenkins didn't answer. Cat didn't expect him to, so he finished his thought. "If that's the case, Detective Jenkins, we've got much bigger problems than a dead bureaucrat. This country is about to tear itself apart."

Jenkins didn't respond, but he understood Cat's point. The thought hadn't occurred to him, but he couldn't discount the sentiment. He was worried about the country, too. His face contorted into a joyless smile. He left the room, shutting the door.

Cat watched him leave and tried to calm himself down. He spent the following minutes fixated on the one-way mirror, attempting to get a glimpse of what was behind it by sharply angling his view. Then he heard the door open. As soon as the door creaked, his anger resurfaced, but then he remembered Jenkins had to retrieve his paperwork and belongings. Wasn't his stuff on the opposite side of the station? How did he return so fast?

The door opened.

In walked a rather large, mostly bald, muscular man that was at least six inches taller than Jenkins. Cat didn't recognize him from this evening's events. He wore a black short-sleeved shirt and a pair of jeans instead of a police uniform. Cat didn't think he was a plainclothes detective because this behemoth couldn't hide in plain sight. He closed the door behind him, and Cat heard the lock engage. Then he turned back to face Cat.

"Who the hell are you?" Cat said incredulously. "I told Jenkins I'm done. Why is he sending in the bad cop? Get me a supervisor. I'm not talking anymore."

The monster stared at him in silence for a few seconds and then said, "Oh, I'm not a cop."

Cat's anger morphed into panic. Things had deteriorated in an instant. Bad meet worse.

The mountain continued, "You don't remember me? We've met before. Yeah, we met at a concert over a year ago. You were busy with your guitar and had plenty of other things on your mind, though. I was pretty busy with what I was doing, too."

Cat heard his words but wasn't really listening. His mind raced as he tried to process the situation. He rose to his feet, and the stranger stared at him straight in the eyes and motioned for him to sit back down. Cat had no such intentions, and his brain transitioned into flight or fight mode. He chose the latter.

His hastily designed plan was to move sideways away from the desk and run straight at Frankenstein, since he was only a few feet from him. Hopefully, he could knock him over and escape through the door. If he couldn't get past him or if he couldn't open the door, then he would battle until the end. Two men entered, but only one would leave.

Cat tried to push past the desk and balled his fists as he ran at the intruder. The room wasn't big enough for him to get enough momentum to tackle him. He needed to force him into the wall and wrestle him to the ground. Instead, Cat launched himself into his midsection and grabbed hold of him around the waist. That pushed the guy back, and he stumbled. Despite being shorter and lighter than his opponent, Cat was still big enough to hold his own.

Since Cat hadn't knocked him over, he ended up kneeling in front of him with his hands wrapped around his waist. Despite limited leverage, adrenaline gave him the strength to push him into the corner, away from the door.

After disengaging from the beast, Cat quickly ran to the door. He twisted the door handle with as much force as he could muster, but it wouldn't budge. He pounded on the door and screamed for help. Cat remembered that there were cameras near the ceiling, so he flailed his arms in front of them, begging whoever was watching to rescue him from this steel-cage match.

Unfortunately, as Cat tried to get help, he wasn't paying attention to his combatant, who had gathered himself together. He snuck up next to Cat and reared back and threw a punch that had almost all of his massive strength behind it. He landed his right fist square against Cat's temple. The force from Frankenstein's blow threw Cat against the wall, where he hit his head and passed out.

*   *   *

Jenkins asked the desk sergeant to give him Cat's wallet and phone and signed the paperwork to release his items. He grabbed the property release form for Cat's signature and made his way back to the interrogation room. A uniformed cop stopped him just as he turned the corner.

"You're Jenkins, right?" George didn't recognize him, so he read his name tag, which said his last name was Wainwright.

"Yeah, what's up?"

"You brought the rock guy in, right? Cat Chaotic?" Wainwright asked.

"Yeah, Carl McKnight. I did. He invoked. I don't have enough to keep him, so I'm going to release him. What's up?" Jenkins sensed that something was wrong.

"Well, we've got Department of Defense guys in there and they are talking to him. Three of them, one of them is in there now. The other guy said that they don't want us going in."

"What? Where are they?" Jenkins asked, but didn't wait for the answer.

He ran back to the interrogation room, where two men now stood guard. One blocked the interview room, the other guarded the surveillance room. Officers observed interrogations from the surveillance room, using either the mirror or camera. This was the only entrance to room six, as it was the last one at the end of the hall.

As Jenkins strode up to them, the first one showed a government ID and said, "Detective Jenkins, I'm Max Rodgers and this is my partner, Agent Johnson. We've got our partner in the interview room talking to McKnight now. We shouldn't need much time with him and hopefully, we'll be out of your hair soon."

Jenkins paid particular attention to Max's badge and ID. They both looked like legitimate DOD credentials. Still, Cat had invoked his rights so legally they couldn't keep him.

"What the hell is this about? You can't keep him. He invoked. I need to let him go."

Max smiled. "Well, that's classified, so I can't get into it right now, but don't worry that he invoked. This is a national security issue, so it doesn't matter."

"What the fuck are you saying? Why doesn't it matter?" Who did this guy think he was? George knew the rules were different for unlawful combatants under the Patriot Act, but Cat was still an American citizen. Something was wrong.

"Well, it doesn't, and we need to finish talking to him. I told you this is all classified, so back off and let us do our job," Max responded.

George just stared at him. None of this made sense.

Max continued. "I don't think we'll have to take him, but we might. If you need to call my chief, I'm happy to give you his number, but you've seen my badge and you know who I am, so do you need anything else? Otherwise, there's nothing else to discuss. Just give me his stuff and we'll finish what we're doing and be on our way."

Max immediately rubbed George the wrong way. His tone was extremely disrespectful, even for a fed. George especially didn't like Max talking down to him. He was a cop, too. There should have been some level of mutual respect. George had dealt with feds before, and those entanglements never ended well. Better to get this one over with. He gritted his teeth and handed over the property form and Cat's phone and wallet to Max. "You need to get him to sign that form, and you need to drop it off with the desk sergeant. Please give me your supervisor's name and number. I'm going to have to fill my captain in on this, so I'll need that info."

Max wrote a name and number on a business card, then gave it to George. "I already spoke to him, but here you go."

George took the card and turned his back to Max. As he walked away, he tried to ignore the warning sirens wailing in his head that something had just gone really wrong.

*   *   *

Cat shook his head as he tried to clear the cobwebs. It took him a moment to remember he was in the interrogation room. He had a headache similar to the one Robert gave him when he belted him. Cat tried to rub his head and found that he couldn't move his right hand. He tugged on it again and he heard a handcuff jangle. As the haze cleared, Cat realized the situation had gotten much, much worse.

Panicked, he scanned the room and froze upon seeing his reflection in the mirror. Cat had a swollen right eye and dried blood on its face. He looked as bad as he felt. He checked the cameras and noticed they all had covers over the lenses. Worse yet, Frankenstein sat in the chair across from the desk.

He stared at the beast and tried to tell him to go fuck himself, but he could only manage a grunt. His head still

200

throbbed, and his ears rang. Any more noise would worsen his headache, so he kept quiet.

Finally, Frankenstein broke the silence. "Hello Cat, I didn't get to introduce myself before. It's nice to meet you again. My name's Niko."

"Niko?" Cat repeated the name as a question because he didn't recognize him.

"Yes, Niko. You and I have quite the history, although I'm guessing you don't remember it right now." Niko's voice during the last sentence was high-pitched, different from how he sounded beforehand. That was his natural voice, and he was extremely self-conscious about it and tried to hide it. He had learned to control it, but that required him to always monitor himself when he spoke. He let his guard down for a moment and had forgotten to modulate it. If he wasn't careful, he would sound like a cartoon character, which was really a big problem because his primary job was menacing people.

Cat picked up on it and made one of his dumber decisions. He summoned the highest cartoonish voice he could and screeched, "Hi, I'm Cat. Wanna come play with me?"

Niko was stunned. The balls on this guy. He had just kicked his ass and had him locked him in a chair in the bowels of a police station and yet he ridiculed his voice? Niko was also a sadistic son of a bitch. He had plans for interrogating this asshole, and he couldn't wait to get started.

"I think you're going to change your tune really soon." This time, Niko controlled his voice. Even though he sounded threatening, Cat let him have it.

"Did you say change my tone? Interesting choice of words..."

That did it for Niko. He got up in a rage and landed another punch to Cat's left eye. Cat did his best to soften the blow by turning his head when he saw it coming. It helped a little.

Niko walked back around the desk and sat down. Cat watched him, and he could tell by the look on Niko's face that he enjoyed himself. But Cat knew better than to give him the satisfaction of letting him know how much that punch hurt, so he didn't react to it and sat quietly. Eventually, Niko broke the silence.

"Cat, I hope you keep talking shit, because I really enjoyed kicking your ass. I wish I had more time for it, I really do, but, unfortunately, I need to get down to it. I really need just one thing from you."

"Oh yeah? What's that?"

"I need you to make a video."

"Well, you might have had a better chance of me doing that with you when I was in college and really needed the money, but since I'm not into ugly psychopaths, you can fucking forget it." Cat just couldn't help himself.

"No, not that kind of video, and if you ever made one, we would know about it. No, we want you to make a video confessing you've seen the error of your ways and are sorry for the shitty offensive music you've made."

"Fuck you." Cat got right down to it, too.

"Didn't you hear me? I told you we don't want that kind of video." Niko tried his best with sarcasm.

"You're out of your fucking mind if you think I'm going to do that." Cat said flatly, even though his inner rage boiled. He hadn't yet lost his composure and figured he better keep his temper under control as long as he could.

"Oh, I think you will." Niko then waved his hand in the air and shouted, "Johnson!" Cat heard the door unlock and creak open.

A second individual walked in. He was slightly shorter than Niko and not as muscular, but still built. He moved over to Cat and grabbed his right leg and pulled it up so that it was resting on the table. Then he removed Cat's shoe and sock and held his leg in place. Niko reached into his pocket and pulled out a box. He smiled as he opened it and lingered his gaze on the contents for just a moment. He pulled out a large medical scalpel.

"Remember this?" Niko didn't sound like a cartoon. Instead, his tone was deep and intimidating. Some deep part of his sadistic brain took over and buried his natural voice.

Cat gaped at the scalpel as the video of Richard's murder flashed through his brain. "You sick, son of a bitch."

"Yeah, that's me, and now it's your turn."

Niko strolled slowly over to Cat's exposed foot. Johnson held it steady so Cat couldn't move. No matter how hard Cat fought against his restraints, the weighty desk kept him immobile. He tried to kick the desk with his other leg, but couldn't get any momentum.

Niko pressed the point of the scalpel into the ball of Cat's foot and cut a deep incision. Cat screamed in agony from the deepening wound. Niko laughed and continued his work. He dug the blade in deeper and wiggled it so it would inflict the most pain. The monster cut a diagonal line across the ball of his foot and then withdrew the scalpel. With a grin, Niko raised the blade, allowing both him and Cat to see it. Their reactions were quite different.

"Hmmm," Niko intoned as he raised his eyebrows and looked at Cat and then glanced back at the scalpel. "Ready for more?"

Cat screamed in response.

"Okay then," Niko answered for him and drove the scalpel back into his foot and drew it down in a diagonal which carved an all too familiar "X".

Cat howled in agony as he noticed the blood draining down his foot. He was terrified and let loose a string of profanity.

"What was that?" Niko asked him as his high-pitched tone returned. "You said you thought it over and you want to do the video?"

"Fuck off."

Niko laughed, but it sounded odd, almost a gurgling sound.

Johnson heard that laugh before and he knew he had to step in. Niko only made that sound when he lost his composure. If that happened, he would kill Cat and that would ruin everything. Johnson glared at Niko and mouthed, "Don't kill him."

Niko saw Johnson's silent warning, and he stopped himself from plunging the scalpel into Cat's chest. But he hadn't finished with him. Not by a longshot.

"Well, Johnson, it looks like Carl John McKnight enjoys this, so let's give him what he wants."

Johnson took a pair of handcuffs off his belt and attached one side to Cat's left ankle. He intentionally clamped it down tight, which caused him to scream again. He secured the other cuff to the desk so Cat couldn't move his left leg at all. Now Cat had his right wrist cuffed to the chair, his right leg up on the table throbbing in pain, and his left ankle cuffed to the desk. Leaving only his left arm unsecured.

Johnson unbuttoned Cat's shirt as Niko grabbed his left wrist. With his body paralyzed, Cat lacked the strength to move, but he tried to swing his left arm at Niko, but nothing happened. Johnson pulled the left side of Cat's shirt off and then grabbed his left wrist away from Niko and held it tight. He pulled Cat's left arm high above his head, which exposed his armpit.

"What the fuck are you doing?" Cat screamed and spat out saliva and blood. He shouldn't have expected an answer to that question.

Niko laughed and said, "We are honoring Richard Uprising."

Niko grabbed the scalpel again and waved it in front of Cat's face and then lowered it down toward his armpit. He drove it slowly into the exposed soft skin. Cat shrieked in pain. The slash on his foot felt like a mosquito bite compared to his armpit. Niko carved his flesh like he was a Thanksgiving turkey. He took out the scalpel and examined it.

"Oh, wait a second. I didn't finish the job. You need to match. I was supposed to carve another X into you. Let me start over."

Cat wailed as Niko drove the scalpel back into his armpit. The pain was excruciating. Blood gushed from the wound and Niko continued to laugh. This was Niko's life's purpose, and he truly enjoyed it.

After Niko finished the second X, he pulled the scalpel out and wiped it on Cat's shirt. Niko no longer smiled as he figured his favorite part of his job was over for the day. Cat had to comply after that.

"Now, where were we? Oh right, this is the part where you tell us you'll make the video."

Cat's body had gone into shock, but he was still conscious and surprisingly aware of his faculties. The excruciating pain from the cuts was unbearable. He had a high pain tolerance, but he also had no illusions that Niko was done with him. He was one sick individual. There was no telling how awful he was going to make the rest of his life. As short as that might be.

Like his previous decisions, Cat chose a terrible option.

"I'm not doing it. You're going to have to kill me."

Johnson cringed after Cat refused. He knew things were about to get medieval.

A clear look of dejection crossed Niko's face. He couldn't help but feel a little disappointed that his tactics hadn't broken Cat's will. But then he thought about it. What's stopping me from really carving him up? As he realized he now had the green light to cut Cat to pieces.

Niko's face changed to an expression of pure joy. He nodded his head, and a grin appeared. Niko stood up and walked around the desk. He laughed as he advanced on Cat and pointed the scalpel directly at his eye.

Chapter Fifteen

"I'm really worried about him," Kendra repeated for at least the fourth time. Over the past few weeks, she repeatedly started this conversation with Swamp and the band members. Still, she didn't feel any better. None of them did.

"I know, we all are," Swamp responded. They all felt the same way, but Kendra was glad that Swamp empathized with her. But his words only helped a little. She needed to see Cat in person and hug him. Then she would punch him in the face for being so stupid as to go down to the police station.

They all sat quietly for several minutes until Robert switched to the analytical part of his brain. He stood up and grunted as he straightened his back. Robert's knees and back told him they had been sitting in Swamp's office for a while.

"We've been talking about this for weeks and I'm just as sick about this as everyone else, but I think it's time that we look at this differently."

They were all lost in their own thoughts, and Robert's words barely registered, but Trent responded first, "What do you mean by that?"

"I mean, maybe we need to focus on what we can do, rather than how bad we feel? We've had this conversation a thousand times and gotten nowhere close to finding him. We've all let our emotions get the better of us, including me. Please don't misunderstand, I'm not passing judgment on anyone, I just think that we've worried ourselves sick. Not without good reason, but we need to switch gears."

"Switch gears? Really? What the fuck, Robert?" Trent's confusion turned to anger. He knew Robert could be cold, but even he didn't expect this. Robert didn't reply immediately, so Trent continued.

"The police took Cat away and we haven't seen him for weeks and it's time to switch gears? We don't even know if he's still alive. You saw that text message that Kendra got two weeks ago. Did that seem like it was him? If it was him, then someone's gotten to him because that didn't sound like him. He doesn't talk like that."

"I know Trent, really, I get it. I'm worried too, but I'm also concerned that we are letting our fear paralyze us. We all want to know where he is, what's happened to him, and whether he needs help. I'm not saying that we need to shut that part of us off, hell that would be impossible. I just think we need to channel our emotions better."

"Robert's right, and I have a suggestion." Swamp was concerned about the group's current dynamic. Cat was a born leader, which made up for his impulsivity and lack of empathy. Without him, this group descended into inertia. Robert was analytical, Trent was emotional, and Kendra was extremely smart. They complemented each other very well. What they lacked now was leadership, so Swamp tried to fill the void.

"Well, let me try that again. Robert is right, but you all are. You need to use these emotions but move them in a new direction, and I think I can help you."

None of them said anything. They just looked at him.

"Ok ... not the roaring approval I was hoping for, but I'll take what I can get. You need to work through a process to come up with a game plan."

"Cat's not a piece of software Swamp." This time, it was Kendra who brought some much-needed humanity into the discussion.

"No, no, he's not, and I wasn't implying that he was and really, I'm sorry if I did. I just want to try something, a process, to see if we can come up with a way to find him and help him, which, I think we all know, is what we want."

Crickets.

"Indulge me for a moment. Let's start by going back and laying out what we know was going on when the trouble started, maybe right before the riot?"

Robert responded, "Well, there wasn't much going on then. Things were pretty quiet. We played a few shows, not a tour or anything. But the main thing we were doing was planning the fall tour. That took up most of our time."

"Was Cat doing anything specific that you can think of? Anything out of the ordinary?"

"No, not really." Trent answered. "He was pretty stoked about the merchandise sales and working on some new stuff to sell. The tee shirts and the hoodies had almost sold out. He was working with the vendor to come up with some new designs. He wanted something really retro looking like the late seventies and early eighties. That shit has been making us a fortune."

"He mentioned that to me, too," Kendra added. "Nothing out of the ordinary, though."

"I talked with him about that too because I was knee deep in fall tour planning," Robert said. "The sales vendor wanted a big spread of redesigned shirts, some long sleeve ones, and some other new stuff. He even wanted us to skew the set lists toward the new designs of the tee shirts. Cat told him to go fuck himself, but not in a bad way."

They all chuckled at Robert's last sentence. They knew exactly what he meant, but it was hard to explain. Cat had this way about him. He could tell someone to perform that act on themselves and they would laugh about it rather than get angry. Most of the time, he got his way.

Swamp laughed too. He was also familiar with Cat's effect on people. "Okay, so I doubt the vendor had anything to do with it since he stood to make a butt-load of money off of your tour. It sounds like things were going very well."

"Yeah, they were." Robert answered. "We were planning on taking a few weeks off once we put the finishing touches on everything for the fall. We just had a few last shows to play to fulfill some commitments and then some downtime and maybe work on some new songs."

"Alright then, let's talk about the riot again. We've all watched the video and talked a lot about it over the last few weeks, but what really stands out to you about it?"

"It was something Cat said," Kendra offered. "I know it was hard to see from the videos, but he said that it was all so coordinated. It was on Trent's side of the stage, so I didn't have a good view. He said that it was almost like it was on cue. They immediately started fighting as soon as we started the third verse. He also said that there were some people taking video, but that their phones were facing different directions prior to the fights. It was almost like they were setting up their shots. Like they knew it was coming."

"This was definitely a setup," Trent agreed. "I didn't see any of the pre-fight staging he mentioned, but I noticed that it all started at once. That's never happened before. Nothing that big, anyway. And what about the fight Cat almost had afterwards? When the guy told him, 'You don't know who you're messing with?' It's like that guy was trying to provoke him. Then throw in Topper's murder and stringing him up outside? It's all too coincidental."

Robert concurred and asked, "The funny part about this to me is that is why haven't we heard much? I mean, there have been news reports, but Ramirez and her underlings have said nothing and that's strange. You would think that they would have made political hay out of this by now and they haven't. Isn't that weird?"

"It is definitely odd," Swamp added. "I checked with my police sources, and they talked directly to Detective Jenkins about it. He said Cat wouldn't talk, and he was about to let him go, but then the feds took him. He said that Jenkins is still on the case and running down leads, but he had nothing on Cat since then."

"Well, what do we know about Jenkins?" Kendra asked. "I can't say I got a good read on him when we met him, other than he was an obnoxious prick. Maybe he's in on it?"

"Yeah, I thought about that. It's possible, but my guys don't think so. From what they know about him, Jenkins is good police. He's not a hack and they haven't compromised him. In fact, my guys say he's a standup guy. He stays on the job because he's got a family to feed. I doubt he's in on it based on what they told me."

"Now that's interesting." Robert posed a pointed question. "Why would they send someone who, by all reports, is a good cop to take Cat away? Why didn't they send a dirty cop? I mean, if they wanted a hit job, wouldn't you send collaborators? Apparently, there are plenty of those."

"Good question." Swamp never considered that. Robert's ability to think in multiple dimensions genuinely impressed him. "Maybe they just needed to keep up appearances?"

"Maybe, I don't know," Robert continued. "But when Trent and Kendra went down to the precinct to talk to them, all they would say is that he wasn't there. Wouldn't tell us anything about the supposed federal agents that took him away. Not even the lawyer could get anything out of them. They gave us the blue middle finger."

The four of them continued to debate whether this was a police conspiracy or just some kind of ruse designed to destroy the band. They talked in circles and didn't notice a quiet voice that spoke from outside Swamp's office door.

"Uh guys..."

It was Swamp's assistant, Denise, and none of them heard her, so she repeated herself. "Guys," this time her voice was louder, but she still couldn't get them to notice her. "GUYS?" finally she all but screamed. That got their attention.

"What?" Swamp asked. He was more surprised than angry at her for interrupting them. Denise had worked with Swamp for the last ten years. She was fantastic at her job. He knew that if she interrupted one of his meetings, then it had to be important. And it turned out that it was.

"You need to turn on the television."

"What? What's going on?"

"Just turn it on," Denise implored. "Ramirez is about to make another speech and the commentators on NSMBC said it's going to be about Cat."

Chapter Sixteen

"Stop it Niko."

In all the commotion, neither Cat nor Niko noticed Max had entered the interrogation room.

"Just go outside. I might need you later, but right now, I need you and Johnson to guard the door. I'm going to need a few minutes alone with our good friend, Cat."

Niko frowned at Cat and then turned his attention to Max and scowled at him. "Just give me a few more minutes, Max."

"No, not right now. I'll let you know if I need you, and believe me, I might."

While Niko snarled at Cat, he was furious with Max. Why did Max stop him? He was so close to breaking him. Sure, he was about to gouge out one of Cat's eyes, but was that so bad? He had two of them.

Niko shot another quick glance at Max to let him know he wasn't happy. He turned back to Cat and whispered, "You know we'll see each other again, right?"

Cat stared back at Niko and returned the favor when he screeched in a high-pitched voice, "I'm counting on it, Niko."

Johnson heard Cat mock Niko's voice, and he grabbed Niko by the shoulders and ushered him out the door. He was lucky Niko complied. Otherwise, Cat probably would have had only five seconds to live. Ten at the most. Johnson figured he had no better than a five percent chance to save Cat's life if Niko went after him. Fifteen percent if Max helped him. Johnson knew the bosses had much bigger plans for Cat. He also knew that if he let Niko kill him, he would soon follow Cat into the afterlife.

Johnson closed the door, and Max sat facing Cat, looking at him. Cat was a complete mess, but Max was confident that his video guys could clean up most of his injuries with their deep fake technology. They couldn't give him an eye back, though. Max really enjoyed watching Niko do his work sometimes. Particularly on a piece of shit like Cat. However, there was also a more practical reason Max didn't want to intervene. He wanted to save the cards he was about to play so that he could use them later. Unfortunately, Cat's ability to withstand Niko's enhanced interrogation techniques forced his hand.

"Well Cat, I'll give you credit. You're one of only a few people I have ever met that could survive a round with Niko. Hell, most give up when they get a look at him, but I have to say you're one tough son of a bitch. That was a hell of a beating he threw at you."

"Gee, thanks. That means a lot to me. You want to do me a favor? Could you take my leg off this table? I don't think I've ever had it up for this long and it's falling asleep." Cat wasn't going anywhere since he had one leg and one wrist shackled. He also knew that Niko's pounding and surgical work had probably drained Cat of any energy to fight, so further combat was unlikely. Also, it was an easy way to engender some goodwill.

"Well, I guess I can do that. I doubt we'll have any more problems today. I'm sure we'll come to an understanding. And besides, Niko and Johnson are right outside that door and the only reason you have both of your eyes is that I called off Niko for the moment."

Max walked over to the other side of desk and helped Cat bring his leg down. "Tell you what, I'll also unshackle your other leg from the desk. I'm leaving your wrist right where it is, though, because I saw what you did to Niko. He's one of my best psychopaths."

Cat recognized Max's obvious ploy but was relieved to have his limbs free. The cuffs restricted blood flow and his body was just now repairing itself from the beating and cutting. He kept his arm down to stop the bleeding from his armpit and the cuts on his foot had somewhat clotted. Niko really did a number on him, and he needed medical attention. That was if he survived the next few minutes of his life.

"So, Cat, let's talk about why you're here, shall we?"

"You mean you don't want to fake being nice to me anymore?"

Cat never missed an opportunity to needle people he didn't like, even when they held his life in their hands.

"No, I don't plan on being nice to you anymore. You're the exact type of person I despise and the less I have to talk to you, the better. That's why I let Niko have a run at you first."

"The feeling's mutual, asshole. Well, except for the Niko part. He's one sadistic monster."

Max chuckled. "Oh yes, he is. He definitely has his uses. His heart is in the right place, though. He believes in the cause just as much as I do. Unfortunately, his methods have their limitations, but they sure are fun. Funny enough, that's exactly what I want to talk to you about."

"I already told Frankenstein that I'm not making the video and that you're going to have to kill me. It's pretty clear that I've been a dead man walking ever since I refused to bend over to the Speech Codes. I've made my peace, and I know I'm not getting out of here alive, so cut the bullshit and just get on with it."

"Wow, how very noble of you, Cat!" Max's voice dripped with contempt. What made this asshole think he was benefiting society? He offended the oppressed for a living and his ego told him he was some kind of martyr? He had a lot of nerve.

"You honestly think that you're on the right side of history, Cat? Someone who plays offensive songs and feeds on hate? If I let Niko kill you now, do you think anyone would even remember you at all, much less revere you as the leader of a just cause? I think you have an inflated view of yourself and your part in all of this."

"I don't think of myself as anything more than a musician. It's you that would make me into something more. You showed the world when you murdered Richard that you are all about control. You are the ones who won't tolerate dissent and side with the real tyrants. All my music does is expose you for who you are."

"Tyrants?" Max giggled. "Tyrants? What kind of tyrant wants to spare people's feelings? All we want is equity for oppressed groups and people like you think you can undermine that and get away with it? Things have changed and you'll get what's coming to you. You're an anachronism, a dinosaur, a relic of how we used to be."

"You're mistaken." Cat groaned. "You and the rest of your brown shirts don't see the backlash that's coming."

"Well, I will say this to put an end to the philosophical part of our discussion. There may be a backlash coming, but we are prepared for it. We've already put the pieces in place to deal with people like you and, ironically enough, you're going to help us finish the job."

"I fucking told you I'm not making the video, so find another stooge. I told you, and I told Niko that I'm prepared to die. Remember when that animal tortured me, and I told him to go fuck himself? You don't really seem like a stupid person, Max, but now I'm having my doubts."

Max smiled. "But you haven't even heard my offer yet. Sure, we've exchanged pleasantries and a few superficial theoretical thoughts on man's ability to express himself, but have you asked yourself what you're up against? Well, let me get more specific. Have you asked yourself what you and your friends are up against?"

Now Max had Cat's attention. "My friends?"

"Yes, your friends, you know, Trent, Robert, and, of course, Miss Kendra. But actually, they will only play a small part in all of this. There are many more people who will pay for this before it's all said and done."

"What the fuck are you talking about?" Pulses of cold energy ran down Cat's spine. He wasn't lying when he told them he was prepared to die rather than help with their demented cause. Max implying that he would target the others was a horrible twist, and Cat wasn't able to maintain his poker face and Max caught it.

"Well, there we go. I'm glad I finally got your attention. I was concerned for a moment there that we didn't understand each other, but now it seems like we've got some common ground. So let me cut through it and tell you what I mean. Let's start small and work our way up, shall we? Let's first talk about your oldest and best buddy, Trent."

"Trent's not afraid of you."

"No, you're probably right. He's got some secrets that are going to come out. I heard the comment you made to Jenkins about the handcuffs and it's funny you mentioned that since Trent has quite an affinity for those, too. He's also into some pretty kinky shit that I'm sure he'd rather bury. Hopefully, he'll stay off the smack once the pictures and videos of his fetishes come out, but you're right, that's probably not enough to threaten him. Hell, he may even get some dates out of it. But he has no family to speak of, unlike the people we are going to talk about next."

Cat's heart sank. Other people? He thought to himself. Who did he mean?

"So, let's talk about someone a little more substantial, shall we? Let's talk about your friend Robert and, more importantly, his family. Robert has some skeletons in his closet, which I'm sure he wouldn't want to see the light of day, but boy oh boy, his family is going to have a big, big problem."

"You sick son of a bitch," Cat hissed.

"You think so? I just think of myself as disinfectant. I eradicate invasive bacteria like you. Or better yet, I'm kind of like sunlight, illuminating the world so everyone can see what it is and revealing people for what they are. But enough with the fun stuff, let's continue."

"Now Robert is, well, he's kind of a boring guy. He's had a few sexually transmitted diseases, but any discussion about that in today's world would get us nowhere. I mean, who hasn't had something like that, right? He's also had some financial issues in the past, but it looks like he's cleaned up his act on that front. Not much available to go after him personally, but did you know his father was in the military during the wars in the Middle East?"

Cat didn't answer and instead just glared at Max, who continued. "Why yes, he was. He was one of America's finest and he served with distinction and is now drawing a pension from Uncle Sam that his family depends on. And you know what? I might have misspoken when I said he's one of America's finest. Well, unless you mean by finest that he committed war crimes. Yeah, go figure? After all these years, we've just now learned that his father might or might not have been involved in a massacre in a village in Syria that no one has ever heard of or may not have ever existed. It doesn't really matter whether that place exists or whether anything happened at all. But once we figure out the details, Robert's dad could be on his way to Leavenworth, but at a minimum, he'll lose his pension that he depends on."

Max paused and waited for Cat to respond, but he was silent.

"Isn't this the part where you tell me to go fuck myself, Cat? I've been paying pretty close attention to your interactions with everyone all day today and I'm kind of offended that you haven't told me to commit that act on myself yet."

Cat had nothing to say. He was powerless to do anything about it, so he just glowered at Max.

"I take it by your silence that we are now getting closer to the mutual understanding we were talking about earlier. Now, let's complete the process, shall we? You know what's coming, right? One more person in your life. Do I have that right?"

Cat braced himself.

"Priscilla, well, you know her better by her middle name, Kendra. Priscilla? Yecch! No shock that she goes by Kendra. What were her parents thinking when they named her after her great aunt? Maybe we could just disclose her real name to her fans, but really, would that be enough? Probably not. But has she ever mentioned her brother?"

Cat couldn't believe Max went there, but why was he surprised? He was dealing with evil people who didn't care one bit about anyone they hurt. In fact, they probably enjoyed it. No point in lying now.

"Yes, she mentioned him."

"Oh, she did? We've talked to many people in her life and only a few of them know about him. You two must be getting rather close."

"Whatever," Cat outwardly dismissed Max's insinuation, but that stung. How could he threaten Douglas?

"So, you know then that he receives significant government benefits for his issues, right?"

Cat couldn't help himself and started laughing. "You would seriously threaten someone with special needs? God, you people are even worse than I thought."

"Well, it's how our world works. You have to give a little to get a little. The government is always willing to assist those in need, but we won't help those who refuse to cooperate, if you will."

"Don't cooperate? What does Kendra's brother know about cooperating?"

"It has nothing to do with him. He's a number to us, a simple entry on a spreadsheet. He's not a person or anything. Think of him as a bargaining chip we needed to call in to help us address a problematic situation. And low and behold, you, and of course she, caused a problematic situation. He doesn't have to suffer, none of them will, if you do the right thing."

"Why should I believe you? What if I do what you want and you take it out on them, anyway?" It was a fair question, but one Cat shouldn't have asked. It's not like he had any say in any of this.

"Well, I thought about that too, and believe it or not, you have value. Not that we care about you or anything. But it's what you can do for our movement. We want you to make your video and then we want you to keep playing music, except you'll play songs that show that you've changed. Oddly enough, you have become something of a hero to the deplorables in this country. If we can show them you've turned a corner and come over to the correct side, your movement will be over, and we can all move forward together."

"You people are really sick. You can't just present your ideas to the public and let them decide, can you? It's far more important for you to squash their spirit. Your movement isn't a movement at all. It's the Fourth Reich."

"You say tomato, I say tom-a-to. Using such a term is meaningless. We are not interested in exterminating a race of people. We only want to protect the oppressed and ensure that everyone gets along. Breaking some eggs along the way is always necessary. But enough of the history lesson. Will you make the video? Before you answer, you ought to know that I may have one last card to play, but I'm not sure about it yet."

"One more? Oh, this should be good. You've threatened everyone I know and their families. I can't think of anyone else, and I've already told you I don't care about myself. I don't have any family, so what the hell else is there?"

Max laughed again. "You sure about that last part? That you don't have any family?"

"No, I don't. My ex-wife hates me and she's probably in the other room watching this and enjoying it. The rest of my family has passed on."

"You might actually be right. But you may also be wrong. You spent some time in Phoenix, right?"

"Yes." The question caught Cat off guard. "Why?"

"Well, I'm sure you've seen those DNA ancestry commercials where you can send in your spit for testing? We ran your DNA through all of those databases and our own, and guess what Cat? Congratulations, you just might be the father of a 16-year-old girl."

"Holy shit, that can't be?" Cat thought to himself. He had been so careful. How could that possibly happen? Max had to be lying...

"Don't plan the gender reveal party just yet, as we are still running tests. But if you are indeed expecting, then we will do everything in our considerable power to make sure that we use any leverage we have over you against her. Now, back to my question. Can we get you some medical attention so you'll look your best for your closeup?"

"Doesn't seem like I have much of a choice, do I?"

"No, you don't. You never had one."

"That certainly appears to be the case."

"I'm glad we finally understand each other. Now, let's head over to my office. We've got the finest IT guys and doctors that taxpayer money can buy. We'll fix you up real nice and pretty for your coming out party."

Chapter Seventeen

Swamp grabbed the remote and turned on the television. No surprise the WOLF Network was on. Swamp hated all the others.

Ramirez was at her desk in the Oval Office.

"Good evening, my fellow Americans, and the rest of you." Kind words from the so-called uniter in chief.

"Tonight, I come to you with a message of hope. A hope for a better future, for a more just tomorrow. I come to with a vision of a new day dawning. A day we've all been waiting for. It's not here yet, but we feel it coming in our collective core. Ladies, gentlemen, all genders, and non-binaries of the rainbow, the tomorrow we've worked for is almost here."

She paused a few seconds longer than usual and then continued.

"Now I know I surprised many of you out there by talking about hope in my opening. There has been little to be hopeful about these days. After all, I'm sure the riot at the concert a few weeks ago triggered many of you, as it likely brought back memories of January Sixth. A day none of us will ever forget."

"Oh, dear God," Kendra breathed out. "How many times are they going to milk that? We're in this mess because of how they manipulated that to get what they wanted. This is more like the Reichstag fire."

"And let us not forget, a good man lost his life that fateful night. Peter LeFleur, my friend Topper. They murdered him and strung him up outside that concert in a shocking act of brutality. Not only was it heinous, but it was also seditious. We will enforce the rule of law. I have mobilized all the federal resources necessary to find and bring his killers to justice. You can run, but you cannot hide."

For a moment, Ramirez lowered her gaze and shut her eyes. As she lifted her head, an unintended smile appeared on her face. She had tried to show empathy, but her smirk betrayed her deceit and revealed who she truly was. She continued, "Let's address the elephant in the room..."

"Holy shit. She can't do this, can she?" Kendra couldn't believe what she was hearing.

"You know me. I'm the one that will say what others leave unsaid and I want answers to many questions." She trailed off and paused again for a half second and then unleashed hell.

"Do any of you seriously think it was a coincidence that they murdered and crucified Topper at a Safe Spaces show? Would it shock you if I said that all signs point to someone who was involved in that form of 'entertainment'? After all, as everyone knows, you lay down with pigs, you get dirty. I, for one, think America could use a good cleansing. So, I am announcing tonight that I will make it my life's mission to make sure that I'm still around to sign off on the death warrant for whoever did this to him. Topper died too soon. He had only started his crucial work, but I swear to you now that his death will not go unavenged."

Ramirez paused and took a deep breath and looked down at her desk again. This time, she did her best to appear like she was composing herself. She slowly raised her head, and this time, she didn't smirk. Her warm smile concealed her forked tongue.

"I'm here to tell you tonight that things have changed for the better. We've made progress since 2021. We've leaned forward and maybe, just maybe, Topper's sacrifice will benefit us all. You don't have to take my word for it. This time, I have evidence. That's right, I have incontrovertible proof of just how far we've come, and I'm going to share it with you in just a few minutes. But I don't feel like I can do it justice without first showing you why we are here."

"Here we go..." Swamp knew what was coming.

"Now I know most of you have seen these videos on the internet, but I only think it's fair that I give a trigger warning. These images could cause flashbacks to January Sixth and other troubling times. So, if any of you prefer not to be exposed to such vile images, please take this opportunity to leave the room for a few minutes."

Her image faded out, but she narrated a video of the concert.

"As you can see here, we have footage of a so-called concert where bigots got together and denigrated the people they don't like. In fact, this segment shows when they played a song that celebrated killing someone solely because of their race. Not only can we hear the four racists spewing hate, but we can also hear Nazis in training singing along."

"I guess I'm a racist too," Robert muttered.

"I wish I didn't have to show you this, my little darlings, but, unfortunately, you need to understand the context of where we were just a short few weeks ago. But, like I told you in my first words to you tonight, there is hope. Believe it or not, I'm going to share with you tonight how far we've come just in those weeks since this concert. While our journey is not over yet, there is light at the end of the tunnel despite what we are seeing here. Look what happens next? To no one's surprise, riots break out."

That was the last straw for Trent. "These fuckers set this whole thing up and now they are blaming us? It's fucking evil."

Ramirez continued. "I don't think I need to say anything at this point. The video speaks for itself, so I'm just going to let it play for a minute."

She played what was clearly a highly edited version of the concert footage. They removed anything that might have shown they staged the riot. The video faded out, and Ramirez's face appeared again.

"Thank you for enduring that with me. I want to let everyone know it is safe to watch now. In fact, we just received some additional video. It's crucial that you all see this, even if you feel triggered. It's that important."

"What the hell..." Swamp trailed off. "What now?"

"There are two new videos we want you to watch. Both will show you why I am so filled with hope. Let me start with the first one, which was taken shortly after the insurrection. In it, you will see just what type of person Cat Chaotic is or, actually, was, but I'm getting ahead of myself."

They sat motionless, stunned by what they just heard. Kendra tried to speak, but all she uttered was "Cat" and "was"? Why did she talk about him in the past tense?

Ramirez's image faded again and then a video showed Cat standing on the stage after the show. The camera panned out, revealing someone standing near the stage, staring up at Cat. It was the person who Cat argued with after the show. But this time, Ramirez let the video and sound play without narration.

The fan stated in a weepy sounding voice, "That song really hurt my feelings" and then the shot cut immediately to Cat jumping off the stage, running toward the stranger, screaming obscenities before the security guard wrestled him down.

It was a total fabrication.

"Wait, that's not what happened," Trent murmured. "I was standing right there. That's not what he said."

"Holy shit," Robert whispered. "They doctored it."

"They really are evil." Kendra shook her head.

Ramirez reappeared on the television. This time, she couldn't hide her smile. "Now you see what kind of person we are dealing with here, don't you? He sings his racist songs and then goes after someone who dared to speak truth to power. His songs hurt people's feelings. They cause pain and suffering. You would think that there wouldn't be any hope for society when bigots are free to act like that. But as I told you earlier, today is a new day."

"We are all going to die." Trent was prone to exaggeration, but this time he wasn't far off and might have understated the extent of their problems.

"I have one more video to show you, and then I have an announcement. The only thing I want to say about what you are about to see is that there is hope. There is justice. We will progress and I hope that today is a major milestone in our march toward equity. I won't hide the ball from you anymore, so here it is."

An image of Cat replaced Ramirez. He sat at a desk, possibly in a library or office. Cat wore a suit and tie and had his glasses on instead of his contacts. The video was low resolution, so there was no evidence of Niko's beating. In fact, he looked healthy.

"Hi, my name is Carl. Many of you know me by my stage name, Cat, Cat Chaotic."

Kendra gasped. Otherwise, you could hear a pin drop in Swamp's office. The four of them stared at the television and their collective jaws dropped to the floor. Their utter disbelief at seeing him on Ramirez's broadcast undermined the relief they found in knowing he was alive. None of them believed this was real, but their eyes were telling them otherwise. They sat silently as they listened and tried to process what was unfolding before them.

"I want to take a few minutes tonight to talk to you about my behavior and how I made a living. And most of all, I want to apologize to the many people out there that I've hurt through the years. I take full responsibility for my words and actions and want to underscore that the fault for this lies with me, no one else."

Despite his disbelief, Swamp shifted his focus and began dissecting the video. He immediately noticed that Cat was reading off a teleprompter but was trying to sound as genuine as he could. He looked for subtle signs that the video was a deep fake, but none were apparent. Swamp made a mental reminder to review every frame in the video. He prayed that this video wasn't real. If it was bogus, it definitely wasn't a "cheap fake" whatever that was. In fact, it might have been the highest quality phony video he had ever seen.

"Many of you have suffered pain and anguish because of my behavior during my performances. I know I look different now. You don't see the rock tee shirt, the ripped jeans, and a sneer on my face. Right now, I'm not spewing racist, homophobic, misogynistic, and hurtful words. But I did and I own those words. Even if I could take them back, I could never atone for the anguish I caused."

"No way," Kendra exclaimed. "There is no way that's fucking him. It can't be."

"I don't think it's a fake Kendra," Swamp said. "I'm looking at it and I just don't see it. It has none of the signs."

"But now you are seeing the real me. You're seeing Carl, the genuine person behind the Cat Chaotic persona. I'm revealing my vulnerabilities, and I'm hopeful now that I can make amends to those I've hurt with my words and actions."

"Oh, hell no, that's not him, no fucking way." Trent had reached his limit. "I've known him for what? Twenty-five years? He doesn't talk like that, no fucking way."

"He's definitely reading it, no doubt about that." Robert looked directly at Swamp and Swamp nodded his head. "Yes, he is."

"Words matter and mine were terrible. I will do better and will try to make things right. A man should show what's in his heart by his actions, so I will dedicate myself to making sure that I have a better understanding of others and sensitivity to the situations they have lived through. I believe I can now be a part of the solution and no longer be the problem."

"Oh, please..." Kendra gave a voice to their collective thoughts.

"Finally, please know I will still play music that hopefully entertains you, but my shows will be more inclusive and equitable. If you forgive me and come to my shows, you will have nothing to fear. I'm on a journey. Please join me so that I can make this right. Thank you for joining me tonight and may you all find comfort in a world that is better than it was just a few weeks ago."

"What a load of bullshit," Denise chimed in from the doorway.

The camera cut back to Ramirez as she wiped tears away from her eyes.

Kendra couldn't take it anymore. "No way. She's actually crying on camera. She's the President of the United States and she's crying? Doesn't she know every woman in America is going to call bullshit? How many men does she think she needs to manipulate?"

"Wasn't that beautiful? Can't you just feel we've turned a corner? I mean, if someone who once sang a song like the Dead Algerian can change and come over to the side of goodness, there's hope for all of us."

"It's a Day in Algiers, you bitch," Kendra said to the television.

Ramirez continued, "There now, don't you all feel better? A new day is coming and I, for one, will be the first one to buy a ticket for his next show." She again went through the fake ritual of composing herself. "Okay, this is hard for me, but I told you I had an announcement and I do want to close with it."

"I believe that Cat's, I'm sorry. I mean, Carl's transformation has shown all of us that a more just and equitable world is indeed possible. But it isn't inevitable. We have to do our part and the only way to do that is to finish the job and criminalize the Speech Codes. For too long, people like Cat have undermined the plain meaning of the proper version of our First Amendment. We've all choked on Richard Uprising's toxicity, and that needs to stop. It is now time for those like him to pay for their offensive actions. Our jails and prisons will now have room for the bigots, racists, and homophobes who should have been there all along instead of those who have suffered oppression. The oppressors will now suffer the consequences of the evil they have wrought upon the rest of us."

Swamp looked at the others and quietly asked, "They've finally done it, haven't they? They were waiting for an opportunity to use the legal system to throw us in jail, and now they've found it. I can't believe it. This isn't the United States of America anymore."

Ramirez continued, "Our country is still a nation of laws, so I am announcing today that I will work with Congress to enact statutes that will punish offensive conduct. This will be a just system of laws that will provide due process but also swift penalties for those that continue to engage in such behavior. This is the singular solution we can implement to make sure that we rid the world of Richard Uprisings and Cat Chaotics. I will have much more to say on these topics in the coming weeks, but I want to close for this evening by letting you know that we have your back. You will not feel intimidated anymore. There is a light coming over the horizon and a new day dawning. And as always, may God bless those Americans that are with me, and may God have mercy on the souls of the rest of you."

Ramirez's image faded from the television. A WOLF commentator replaced her but said nothing. He stared at the camera blankly in stunned silence. Normally, he recapped the president's speech, but this time he said nothing. Finally, WOLF cut to a commercial rather than forcing their audience to endure dead air.

He wasn't alone. No one in the room spoke. None of them uttered a witty response. They all sat quietly and attempted to process or suppress their feelings. Anger, rage, sadness, and despair were all swimming around in their heads and in their hearts, along with a great sense of loss. Loss of their belief in ideals and pride in their country. Loss of a feeling that America was special. Tyrants could rule other places, but not the United States. No more. None of them wanted to believe that America was becoming a totalitarian government right before their eyes.

But none of them would take it lying down either.

Chapter Eighteen

Max winced as his burner phone buzzed a second time, reminding him he had received a text.

No need to look at the phone to read the message. Max knew who it was from. He hadn't spoken with Annabelle over the last three days and their last conversation did not go well. And calling it a conversation was generous. A more accurate description was that Annabelle screamed at him for twenty minutes. Unfortunately, things had only gotten worse. He remembered an old saying someone once told him: things may not be your fault, but they are your problem. And yes, recent uncontrollable events had become his problem. But she wanted to talk now, so the next few moments of his existence were going to be very unpleasant.

It was only eight A.M., and he had already looked at the overnight SUNSHINE data at least six times. Max reviewed the reports every morning after he cleared the crud out of his eyes. Today, he refreshed the data every five minutes, each time hoping for a different result. Unfortunately, it never changed. In fact, it had gotten worse. The crud felt more pleasant than what he was seeing on his screen.

His phone buzzed again. She sent another text?

Uh oh.

For a fleeting moment of self-delusion, he hoped that ignoring the phone would make her texts disappear. No such luck. He picked up the phone and braced himself.

The first text was "SUNSHINE?"

The second was "FIVE MINUTES".

Annabelle rarely sent texts, but when she did, they were short and cryptic, but these were crystal clear. She wanted to speak to him in five minutes about the SUNSHINE data. Her all caps left no doubt about her mood.

Maybe he could tell her he was busy and ask to reschedule? This was another bad idea because he needed a cover story. As angry as Annabelle was, she might send someone to find him. She was just that type of person, and it wasn't worth the risk of infuriating her further. Better to take it on the chin now, so he responded with a "thumbs up" emoji and prepared himself for her wrath.

Against his better judgment, he refreshed the SUNSHINE data one last time, praying for something positive.

Nope, nothing positive. It was a shitstorm that he couldn't control. What he could control was preparing himself to discuss the details in the unlikely event she let him speak. Most likely she wouldn't and would be content to unleash a deluge of insults and unanswerable questions at him.

And what a shitstorm it was. Despite all their efforts, the SUNSHINE reports strongly showed that they lost more support than they gained, especially regarding criminalizing the Speech Codes. In fact, there was a significant backlash growing against all restrictions on speech. The hardcore leftists were all for it since they supported governmental oppression against people they hated, which was pretty much everyone except their fellow Marxists.

Yet, SUNSHINE screamed that the rest of the country was turning against the Speech Codes. Despite the coordinated narrative from the government and media on the riot videos and Topper's murder, the trend was in the wrong direction. Even Cat's confessional video backfired, particularly among the center-right. Although not typically politically active, these individuals were skeptical of government action but didn't fear the administration as much as the hard right. The center-right mostly wanted to be left alone but was generally passive. Not anymore. In fact, SUNSHINE showed that the center-right was now actively opposing the Speech Codes. This was not good.

But as bad as that was, they had bigger problems. The center-left trend lines were particularly troubling. This demographic was mostly supportive of government control and action. This was the group they counted on to join their cause in droves, but that was not happening. How could these people not support criminalizing the Speech Codes considering the riot and Topper's murder? If those events didn't convince them, what would?

Still, there was worse news. The underlying reasons for these trends would send Annabelle through the roof.

Max's video link on his desk terminal rang exactly five minutes after he received the text.

"Morning Annabelle."

Silence.

Maybe she wanted him to use her code name. "Sandy?" he asked, "Are you there?"

Again, silence.

The display on his terminal showed an active call, so she was still on the line. Was she muted? He could only hope. Couldn't be a technical issue, could it? The Department of Defense heavily encrypted these links, so maybe it malfunctioned?

"Annabelle?"

Still no response, and panic set in. His mind wandered. Did someone steal her phone and bypass the security? Seemed impossible.

"Yes, I'm here Max." her voice was quiet but clear. There were no phone issues. She was furious.

He swallowed hard. There was no positive way to return her greeting. Anything he said was going to further infuriate her. So, he answered with the worst possible phrase. "What's up?"

"What's up?" she murmured.

Oh boy.

"I know. It doesn't look good."

"Doesn't look good?" she half laughed. Annabelle repeated words back when she was on the verge of losing her composure.

"No, Max, you're absolutely right. It's doesn't look good." Her voice dripped with sarcasm. "In fact, we are losing support, Max. Losing it and that's not what this was all about, was it? They were supposed to agree with us so we could throw the oppressors in jail."

Max detected more than rage in her voice during the last part of her rant. She genuinely sounded upset that the propaganda that they unleashed wasn't working.

"And do you know why we're losing? It's him, Max. Swamp is killing us. Why are they listening to that fascist bigot?"

Max tried to de-escalate her anger. "Well, the numbers really haven't moved, but maybe we haven't given it enough time yet?"

It didn't work.

"You know, I told you we needed to take him out earlier." And there it was. Max knew that was coming, but he didn't expect her to lob that grenade so soon. She needed to blame someone for what was going wrong. He was there, so by definition, he was wrong. Time to fall on the sword.

"I know you did, and I agree he has to be our focus now. And we are taking steps to stop him."

"Oh, you are, are you? Stopping him now when he's already got a hold of these idiots. He's killing us, Max. I told you. I fucking told you he was dangerous. We needed to take him out before, and you didn't listen."

At best, she misremembered because the fact was Max wanted to take him out early, but she was against it. No reason to bring that up. The truth was irrelevant now. Better just to apologize and offer ideas to fix the situation. He had to be careful, though. If he gave her any hint that he blamed her, then it was game over. He wondered how many corpses' last words were 'I told you so?'

"Look, you were right. I totally agree we need to go after Swamp and get after him hard. SUNSHINE shows that he's been killing us with those videos. We need to figure out a way to take him down. In fact, our guys intercepted his last video and buried it on the internet as deeply as they could. But that will only slow it down from going viral. Once it's trending, then there's not much we can do until we figure out how he gets through the Patriot Firewall." Max cringed as he uttered the last part of that sentence. He immediately wished he could take it back, but there was no getting around it, so Max stiffened himself for Ramirez's wrath.

More awkward silence.

Max didn't like silence. He would often break it just to fill the void. This time, he didn't. Instead, Annabelle spoke, but barely above a whisper.

"But you see, everything Swamp is doing is undermining what we did to Cat, right? He's ruining it. He's convinced his bitter clingers that Cat's confession wasn't real. They think we coerced him. If more people believe that, we've got enormous problems. You thought things were bad back in 2016? They are about to get so much worse. What if he exposes what you guys did?"

"Come on, Annabelle, he doesn't know. No one knows. Topper was a deep fake. We created him. We covered our tracks way too well. For all they know, Topper really existed. Niko only killed and strung up some bum who nobody will ever miss. Our Psychological-Ops guys did the rest. And that group that started the rampage at the concert? All our guys did was encourage some true believers to riot while Niko's guys filmed it. Besides, anyone we were even slightly worried about talking won't be able to anymore."

Max knew everything depended on public support to criminalize the Speech Codes. Enough people needed to truly believe that throwing people in jail for offensive speech was in their best interests. Unfortunately, the SUNSHINE data showed that simply wasn't happening. The riot and Topper propaganda weren't working. Without all that, this wouldn't work. Everything depended on it.

"Have you watched Swamp's new video yet?" Annabelle asked. Max sensed more concern than fury in her question. She hated the fact that Swamp evaded their AI algorithms and wanted to take him out by any means necessary.

"No, I haven't. I just sent it to you. Let's watch it."

Max started the video, and Swamp appeared.

"Ladies and gentlemen, thanks as always for joining me on the Swamp Simmons Show, and we have a really special hour for you tonight. I have some special guests with me. In fact, I have all four members of the rock group Safe Spaces. They've been here before, and I thought tonight would be the perfect time to bring them back."

"All four members?" Annabelle asked Max, who just looked at her and shrugged his shoulders.

The camera captured a tight shot of Swamp, showing him from his chest and above while an American flag waved in the background. He was looking directly into the camera. Swamp opened his mouth to speak and then closed it. He paused and rolled his eyes up sideways toward his forehead and ear.

"What's that, Mr. Producer?" Swamp spoke to someone off camera who communicated through his earpiece. "You say there are only three members of the band here tonight? That can't be true. I was told all four would be here?"

Annabelle and Max exchanged another confused glance.

The camera zoomed out and panned the set, slowly sweeping from left to right. As the shot changed, Swamp narrated. "Here they are, Mr. Producer. Here's Robert and Trent and right next to me I have Kendra..." His voice trailed off as the camera stopped moving and stayed fixed on Kendra.

"Yes, I know that's Kendra, Mr. Producer, and I know she's the one that you would rather look at, but just stop the nonsense and please ask the cameraman to keep panning."

The camera didn't move.

Swamp continued his discussion with his producer. "Yes, I know the audience would also much rather look at her than anyone else up here, but just indulge me for a moment and show the entire set."

The camera shot moved again and finally stopped on a cardboard cutout of Cat.

"Now Mr. Producer, Cat Chaotic is sitting right there in that chair."

The cutout was life-size. In the picture, Cat's head tilted slightly to the right but looking straight ahead. Cardboard Cat had a closed black eye and scars on his face. He had a goofy smile and one index finger pointed directly out at the camera, like he was giving a signal of approval to whoever he was looking at. He resembled a deceitful car salesman who had conned a customer into thinking they got an incredible deal.

The producer divided the screen, placing Swamp on one side and Cardboard Cat on the other. Swamp continued his voiceover discussion with the producer.

"What do you mean, he's only a cardboard cutout? Mr. Producer, did you bust out that bottle of Old Uncle Crow that you keep in your desk?" Swamp feigned perfect indignation. "That's the real Cat Chaotic, well, as real as he gets these days. In fact, Cat, say hi to the audience." An animated mouth appeared on Cardboard Cat and said, "Hi Everybody," in a high-pitched voice that sounded like a cartoon character.

"Oh God," Ramirez muttered. The prior videos were bad, but Swamp took this one to a new level. This would be a train wreck.

"Great to see you, Cat. You're looking well."

Cardboard Cat's cartoon voice continued. "Well thanks Swamp, I'm feeling a little flat today, but overall, everything is going as good as gumdrops for me these days. It's all sunshine and rainbows for good old Cat. I want to let everyone know that I've found my voice and now I'm ready to sing super pleasant songs to all the boys and girls!"

"Oh God," Ramirez repeated.

"A little flat Cat? That's the best you could come up with? Horrible. You need to work on your jokes. I saw you on that video and wondered, was that really you? Kind of strange you told everyone how you screwed up and how you were going to make everything better by playing wonderfully cheerful songs. So, I wanted to have you on the show tonight to discuss. And, to begin, let's talk about the obvious issue regarding your recent television appearance. For the record, I, for one, thought that it didn't look forced at all." Swamp deadpanned the line perfectly and then continued.

"No, siree, it looked like you were just happy as hell to be there, and no, you didn't look threatened or forced to say things that were totally against everything you've ever stood for. Unfortunately, though you know Cat, there are some negative Nancy's out there, so maybe you can reassure everyone tonight that you had an epiphany all on your own? And please tell everyone that you really believe that the best way to entertain people is to make sure that you sing songs that don't use no-no words."

Cardboard Cat responded. "Well Swamp, let's just say that I spent a lovely evening in a police station a little while ago. While I was there, I said to myself, Cat, maybe you are looking at this all wrong? Maybe that cop's fist in your face was a blessing rather than some thug beating you senseless? Maybe it was a sign from God almighty himself telling me in no uncertain terms that I've been saying naughty things and that I've hurt some poor snowflake's feelings? And maybe that second fist that landed in my stomach was really a bolt from above? Maybe that crack in my ribs really was symbolic of how I fractured our society. Shouldn't I just do what our benevolent leaders tell me to do and say what they want me to say?"

"Well, that's very enlightened of you, Cat. I can see how repeated blows to the face can help you realize you need to change. Maybe electrodes on your balls helped, too? I would think those messages would get through loud and clear. And maybe, just maybe, you can help us better understand your change of heart so that you may inspire others to see the errors in their ways?"

"All I can tell you, Swamp, is that for some inexplicable reason, I felt this pounding on the side of my head and heard an odd ringing in my ears. It was hard to tell, really hard to tell, because I was kind of in this fog and I wasn't sure where I was. But one thing I knew for sure was that those police officers who surrounded me were there to help."

"Really? Well, how did you know that, Cat? I mean, some might misinterpret a fist to the face as malicious, but you didn't see it that way? You saw it as God illuminating a new righteous path for you? Can you please explain?"

"Well, shucks Swamp, that's the simple part. They told me they were there to help me realize God wanted me to change, and that was good enough for me. And who was I to say no?"

"That's really powerful stuff, Cat. So, if I'm hearing you correctly, God told the police to beat the hell out of you in order to show you that you needed to change course?"

"It had to be Swamp. Who else could have given me this black eye and these scars?"

"I think you're onto something, Cat; the elites only have our best interests at heart, so maybe I've been all wrong on this? Maybe the solution here is for us all to be honest and open and to reflect on what we've learned throughout this experience."

"Words of wisdom Swamp, words of wisdom."

"Well Cat, I wanted to thank you for coming on, but before we let you go, maybe we can do an encore, if you will. I know your band members are really worried about you, and I know that they have some questions." The camera panned out and showed the entire set.

"Please let me go first, Swamp," Kendra said.

"Of course, Kendra. Go right ahead."

The split screen now displayed Kendra and Cardboard Cat.

"Cat, can you please tell everyone why we are here today and what got us into this mess?"

"I'm glad you asked Kendra; you see, it all started when a good friend of mine started a band and he said some bad words. Some people told him he shouldn't, but he didn't listen. He thought that all those people who listened to him sing were just going out for a night of entertainment. They didn't like that he didn't do what they told him to do, and then the strangest thing happened. His guts fell out all by themselves. Never saw that one coming."

"All by themselves? Cat, you saw the video, right?"

"Well, sure I did! But that had to be fake news. How would the cops ever let someone get away with murder? Must have been another one of God's messages that he delivered to Richard, just like he delivered those fists to my face."

"Yes, God works in mysterious ways, Cat, but the question I have for you is how did you respond? What did you do with God's message?"

"Kendra, let me explain it like this. I had this idea, and I wanted to figure out a way that I could say naughty words but keep my guts inside my body. You see, I like my innards right where they are. I had grown attached to them. So, I thought that maybe, just maybe, the key was to say certain no-no words and avoid others. If I was really careful I could, um, how do you say it? Avoid cancelation?"

"That's right, Cat, now you've got it." Kendra laid on the sarcasm thick. "You avoided cancelation by only saying approved bad words. We all know that calling White men icky names is A-Okay. I even helped you by singing the Mars and Venus song, but there's more to it, isn't there?"

"Um, yeah, there is, but I don't know. I don't know if I should say it." Cartoonish Cat's voice trailed off.

"You might as well say it. What's the difference now Cat, we're all screwed, anyway."

"You got that right." Swamp interjected into Kendra and Cat's conversation.

"Well..." the cartoon voice drew out the word for dramatic effect. "Okay, I wasn't exactly honest. See, I had this idea that I would make people think we had, um, what do they call it now, awoken or became woke? Is that right? I wanted to convince everyone that we had turned against who we are, but I only wanted everyone to think that and then I was going to give them a big surprise."

"A big surprise?" Kendra's deadpan was perfect. "What do you mean?"

"I wanted to do a big reveal. Like when you find out that the bad guy was really the hero's father. Our big reveal was going to be that we had played everyone, and that we were double crossing those idiots who thought we had gone woke. You see, on pro-wrestling..."

Ramirez couldn't take it anymore. "Pro-wrestling?" she spat. "Pro-wrestling? He's really talking about pro-wrestling, and we are losing to this guy? What the fuck?"

"Holy shit," Max said.

"I think people get the idea Cat, no need to go into the intricacies of pro-wrestling." Kendra cut him off. "This doesn't seem to be the most thoughtful plan you've ever had."

"No, it wasn't, but you know what? I learned that there are plenty of people who are perfectly happy to, um, cancel someone they don't like. Even if all they did was say bad words. But you know what I also learned? You can also get away with an awful lot if they like you. Play for the right team and pick the right target and you're good. You can pretty much say anything you want about someone that the government doesn't like."

"That certainly seems to be the case, doesn't it, Cat?"

"It sure does, and I learned something. Cancel culture is fine, as long as it's directed towards someone you consider an enemy; it's part of what has led us to our present utopia."

"Utopia is an interesting word choice." Robert jumped into the conversation, so the camera widened to show the entire stage.

"I can't think of a better one, Robert, can you?" Cardboard Cat responded. "I mean, what other time in history would you want to live in? You now have the power to use your smartphone to get even with someone who says something you don't like. You just have to be on the right team, but that's not a problem for me anymore! I'm in the club now and as long as I do what they tell me, I can live my life as they choose. I know that I've got things to do, words to say, and places to go. As long as the elites and the loud minority are on board, I'm all set."

"And just where is that, Cat? Where are you now, and what do you have planned?" Trent asked.

"I can't really tell you all of that, but don't you worry. I will be out there singing those joyous songs soon. But I need to address a tiny misunderstanding with some wonderful folks in the government, Trent."

"Oh, what's that?"

"I'm sure it's just a well-intentioned mistake rather than some plot to frame me, but some of our betters implied I was involved in Topper's murder. I know, I know, you could have knocked me over with a feather, but it's true. The good people in the police and the government will get this cleared up real soon, but until that happens, I don't think you'll be seeing much of me. In fact, I might have stayed too long already, so if someone could please give me a hand, I'll need to get on my way."

Kendra responded to Cardboard Cat, "I don't blame you for wanting to leave, Cat, but I wanted you to know that we really miss you. I mean, we miss the real you and we want you home safe, so please take care."

"I sure will, Kendra, and once this all blows over, we can go back to making music fun again!"

The camera remained fixed in a wide shot as a stagehand walked behind the group and picked up Cardboard Cat and took him off stage. Then it panned back to Swamp and zoomed in on him as he began his closing monologue.

"Thanks Cat. I echo Kendra's sentiments. We just want you home safe. We haven't seen or heard from you in weeks, and we hope you are still alive and well. But I wanted to start my closing tonight with a confession."

"I was in on the entire scheme to make everyone think Safe Spaces had gone woke. If you remember our first show with the band, we had an 'argument' about what they were doing. Well, now you know those arguments we had were largely staged and what we presented to you was more of a debate about the Speech Codes. The main reason I thought that this was the right thing to do was that the whole thing was satire. It was kind of like the time I did the show with a gun to my head and spouted the governmental lines about why the Speech Codes were necessary. That was an obvious parody, but this was very subtle. I always planned to let you in on it and, after all, what we do here is to help America see the truth. But I sincerely apologize if you feel misled. Just understand that these are desperate times, and they call for desperate measures. I won't insult your intelligence and promise you I will never do something like that again. I would if I thought it would help. But I swear that if I ever do something similar, I will always let you in on it when the time is right. I do not take my audience lightly or for granted. In fact, you are the reason I do this. I truly respect your intelligence, but you have to entertain someone to inform them. I know, I know, that sounds like a 'narrative' and most of you know that's a word I disdain because it's a euphemism for the lies the government and media feed you. But I felt that all of this was necessary, and I hope this helps you understand why."

"There's one other thing I want to mention before we move on. Just so you know, if I ever do anything like that again, you will eventually know the truth. I will never leave you hanging. What I mean by that is I had previously recorded a video where I disclosed everything you needed to know about Safe Spaces. You would have seen that video if anything ever happened to me. If they threw me in jail or killed me or God knows what else they did to me, an algorithm would have automatically uploaded it to the internet. And you know what? That's not the only video I have ready to launch. I have hundreds of hours of tape ready to go that will tell you everything I know about the government, the media, the Patriot Firewall, and many other things. And some of it is new information. If my heart stops beating or if I cannot enter a code into my system, then my servers will release everything onto the internet."

Ramirez looked at Max. Her eyes blazed and her lip curled. This was about to get ugly.

"He had that fucking implant, and we didn't know about it? How the hell did he get away with that?" Ramirez referred to a pacemaker-like device which would signal a server to unleash data if the heart stopped beating. The government collected the codes used by these devices so that they could disable them. Nothing in his file showed he had the implant, or for that matter, his code. They still couldn't find him, anyway.

"He must have done it on the black market," Max responded, even though he knew Annabelle didn't want to hear it. It wasn't like she was listening to him anyway since she focused her anger on Swamp.

"The last thing I want to say tonight about the Safe Spaces storyline and our interview with Cat is that I know him well. More importantly, Kendra, Robert, and Trent know him better than I do. It's pretty clear to us that his confessional video was a deep fake or coerced. You saw a far more authentic version of Cat tonight than anything that has come out from the disinformation governance board and Ramirez's mouth."

Annabelle murmured audibly as she bristled at Swamp's last comment. Swamp was among the few who could mock her without consequences. Most wouldn't dare violate the Speech Codes, and the firewall prevented almost everyone who tried. The problem he posed grew worse with every video he released.

"Make no mistake, we are in dangerous times, ladies and gentlemen, but I'm optimistic that the tide is turning. As most of you know, I have sources deep inside the government who abhor what is going on, but still work there. These people have their reasons, but they also act as moles. They've seen the government's surveillance data and there is nowhere near the support for the Speech Codes that they have led you to believe. I have it on good authority that there has been a significant backlash against the idea of criminalizing the Speech Codes. In fact, now more people than ever are souring on the idea of the Speech Codes themselves. They've gone too far, and people have had enough. They know it, we know it, and the short answer is, we are winning."

"We've got a rat in the house," Max said to Ramirez, as if she didn't know.

"No shit." Ramirez tolerated minor leaks, but this was a big one. Some of the SUNSHINE numbers were accessible to certain members of congress and other high-level officials. They had to have a security clearance and agree with the cause. However, even those trusted team members couldn't get the aggregate numbers without a significant security breach. Ramirez wished Swamp was bluffing. But deep down, she knew that he probably wasn't.

"But let me tell you, ladies and gentlemen, the progress we've made is fragile. The elites will not let this go easily. They will fight to preserve their power over you and dangle the insidious idea that cancelation only gives bad people what they deserve. They'll tell you that you have the power to stop ideas you don't like by doxing someone and shaming those whose thoughts you detest. Cancelation powers are seductive to someone who may feel they have no other purpose in life. But there are two very important things you need to know if you are going to go down that path."

"First, you need to make damn sure that you are on the correct side of every issue. If you step out of line and have an independent thought, they could also cancel you. You're not safe unless you are useful. Think of some of our previous presidents. They could get away with anything so long as they did the elite's bidding. They were untouchable until they were expendable. If the feelings of the moment 'evolve' into something different, they'll use everything you say or do against you later. They will offer you up as a sacrifice if the purity of the moment demands it."

"Second, please understand that as bad as things are now, criminalization of speech will make things much worse. There will be no going back. If our government can legally throw you in jail for the words you say, then we are no longer a democracy. We will become a dictatorship. That would be the end of the free United States of America, and that's why we need to stop it at all costs. But remember, there is hope. Tell your congressman that you are absolutely against the Speech Codes and that you want them repealed. Tell them how worried you are about America. Make sure they hear your voices. What you think is just as important as what they think. Thank you for listening tonight and God bless you and may God bless the United States of America."

And with that, the video ended.

Max and Annabelle didn't speak, but both realized that they had reached a tipping point. Swamp had not only ridiculed the Cat confessional, but he had harpooned the underpinning of the Speech Codes. His audience was too big and they could no longer tolerate his insults. He eviscerated their propaganda, and the SUNSHINE data left no doubt. Swamp was changing the narrative.

Max broke through the heaviness with an audible breath that flapped his lips so that he made sure Annabelle heard him. His reaction was a blend of a sigh and symbolic derision. He didn't want to start their next conversation. He wanted Annabelle to initiate it so that she wouldn't misconstrue anything he said. The noise worked.

"Yeah, my thoughts exactly."

Max detected a change in her voice. She sounded defeated. This was the first time Max ever heard her sound like that, and it was a terrible sign.

"Annabelle," he paused for effect, "We have to take them out. I'm sure we can have our ops guys at the CIA and the FBI track Swamp and the rest of them down. Let's make an example of them. We can do it in an even more, um, showy way than how we took out Richard, and we can make everyone fear crossing us. I think if we..."

"No, it's too late for that." Annabelle cut him off and stared at him. Her gaze could shoot icicles. Max had been nervous around her before, but this one was one of her scariest moments. Despite her rage, or maybe because of it, she continued.

"Well, what I mean is that it's not really too late. It's just not the right time. There are way too many people who suspect we were involved in Richard's murder. More who believe we coerced Cat into the video. We need to reset the narrative. We need to convince them that Swamp is lying. If we just kill him and the rest of the band, we only reinforce that he's right and we really can't have that."

"Yeah, I guess you're right. Swamp just pissed me off so much that my emotions got the best of me. I'm sorry, but sometimes I can't just help myself." Max embellished a bit, but he was angry. He firmly believed in the cause and knew, deep inside, that his side was correct. Max found she liked it when he was overly dramatic, but he had to be genuine. Laying it on too thick might get him killed. Thankfully, it seemed to have worked.

"I know, I feel the same way, believe me, if we could cut Swamp to pieces on live television and change this, I would, but, huh..."

Annabelle stopped mid thought. She sat and stared straight ahead, saying nothing.

"Annabelle?" Max asked after giving her a few moments to work through it.

"Yeah, I'm still here, but something just occurred to me..." she trailed off without finishing her sentence.

"What?" Max asked. This one might be something big.

"Well, I realized something when I was talking about slaughtering Swamp on live television because people believe what they see when it's live. I know they don't always believe it, but most of the time they do."

"Yeah, that's true. Where are you going with this?" Max asked a genuine question. He didn't know what her angle was.

"Well, one thing that Swamp keeps harping on is that we coerced Cat into confessing, which undermines our story that he changed, right?" Max detected heightened excitement in her voice. She had turned on a dime. This told Max she was really buying into whatever she was thinking. The despair was gone. She had a plan.

"Yeah, that's a huge part of what he's been hitting us with. What are you thinking?"

"Well, why don't we make Cat our mouthpiece? We can make him tell the world on live television that what Swamp is saying is bullshit. Hell, we can make him go out in front of a crowd and force him to contradict everything Swamp says? And why limit it to a onetime thing? We could make him go on a tour giving speeches all over the country and say whatever we need him to say?"

Max liked where she was going, but he was worried. "Do you think that would work? I mean, people already think we coerced him. If they see him as compromised and think we are pulling the strings, won't that be worse?"

"Not if we make him say it every night, in front of a different crowd. Remember, the key to changing the narrative is to keep repeating the lie, no matter what anyone says. They need to believe what we tell them rather than what they see and hear. Sounds stupid, but it works."

"Yeah..." Max was still processing her idea, but he liked what he heard. Unfortunately, something was nagging at him.

"Yeah, what?" This time, Annabelle noticed Max might not like her idea. She wanted to know now if Max saw a hole in it.

Max picked up that she wanted him to be honest, so he told her what he actually thought. "Do you think he'll go along with it? He's a stubborn son of a bitch. I told you what we had to do to him at that police station. I honestly thought that he might not make the video despite the beating Niko gave him and how I threatened his friends. Do you think he will actually agree to go on an apology tour?"

Ramirez chuckled at the thought of naming it the 'apology tour' and was glad that Max was honest. She wasn't fully on board yet, but she definitely believed her idea had potential.

"I think he'll do it. He's worried about what we have over him and his friends. Cat will do anything we say. Don't we also have something on him about a daughter or something? Did we figure that one out yet?"

"We're pretty close. Still not sure though. If he has one, she's in Arizona somewhere. When we told him, he was genuinely shocked. I honestly think he didn't know. If she's there, we'll find her. Unfortunately, we've had to rely on public databases. Much slower than our usual methods. Problem is that we think she's a minor with really screwed up ancestry. Forced us to work through all this nonsense. We'll know soon."

"Well, there you go. I didn't think Cat Chaotic would care that he had a kid out there, but whatever works. Hell, pull his fingernails off if you have to. Anything is fine by me."

"Yeah, I think the daughter thing will work if she exists. We also have it over the other band members and their families, so there's that, but I would feel better if we had something more concrete over him. There's something about him that really worries me, but I think you're right. We need to play the cards we have in our hand."

"Yes, we do." Annabelle's voice, quiet yet defiant, showed no trace of the defeatism Max had heard earlier. She continued.

"Max, interesting. You bring up a card game. I've been thinking about it like that too. And this fucking game we are playing is about to go into the final rounds. It's no time to blink and bet the minimum or fold and hope to survive one more hand. Nope, not at all. It's time to go all in and finish this, once and for all."

Chapter Nineteen

"You've been a hard man to get a hold of."

Kendra spoke the words into the speaker on her phone, but she was under no illusions that Cat heard them. The last time she saw him was when he got into the police car and mouthed "it's okay" to the three of them. Obviously, he wasn't okay, far from it. She called, texted, emailed, and asked others to contact him and he ignored just about everything. The only communications she received were a couple of cryptic texts from his phone that said how well he was doing right after his television appearance. She didn't believe he sent those texts. None of them did. Everyone still thought that his confessional was fake or coerced, however, the longer he ignored them, the more they doubted him.

Could Cat have really gone woke?

Kendra hadn't fully come to terms with that possibility, but the more he avoided her, the more she worried. Swamp and the band intended for the cardboard cutout stunt to both humiliate Ramirez and goad Cat into talking to them. Apparently, it worked because Cat returned her text shortly after that show went viral. He even agreed to talk. While she was relieved that they would finally speak; she was nowhere near confident that he would actually accept her call. He did, and hopefully, it was a positive development.

Still, he hadn't actually responded to her greeting, so she tried again.

"Cat? Are you there?"

Silence on the other end. Her blood boiled. Why the hell had he agreed to a call? She drifted her hand toward the red disconnect button and muttered, "You know, you really suck.

How many messages have we left you? How many texts have you ignored?"

No response. Her rage grew into an uproar, and she wanted to hang up. But she didn't. Deep down, she knew they would never speak again if she hung up on him. She waited. Finally, she reached her limit and yelled, "what the fuck Cat?" He responded just before she pressed the red disconnect button.

"Well, I've been busy."

Not her desired response, but still something. Cat's tone was flat and lacked any remorse or emotion. His voice clearly conveyed he would rather not have this conversation. Message received loud and clear. Kendra responded in kind.

"That's the best you could do? You've been busy? You haven't spoken to us in months, and we've been worried sick about you and all you tell me is that you've been busy? Like you're ghosting me after a one-night stand? Who the fuck do you think you are?"

Kendra wasn't sure whether it was his callous attitude or the universal "blow off" words that infuriated her more. Like everyone, she hated feeling rejected. It wasn't a perfect comparison, but this felt like a breakup call. But it was worse than that. Her feelings for him were more complicated than a romantic entanglement gone wrong. This wound felt deeper and cut closer to the bone. It felt more like he was letting her down.

Then Cat spoke again.

"It's really not like that at all." Cat lied and delivered that trite missive in the same flat tone. He didn't like lying, especially to Kendra. Cat didn't like to lie, and that was one of the most disingenuous statements he ever uttered. Her retort that he was ghosting her after a one-night stand wasn't completely accurate, but not that far off, either. In fairness, he had his share of meaningless sexual encounters. Cat had told more than a few women that he had to get up early the next morning after a night of heavy, alcohol induced, sloppy, animalistic relations. He usually told some version of this lie as the booze secreted out of his body. Like clockwork, as his BAC dropped, regret and fear rose. He worried he had drunkenly made a half commitment to someone he barely knew. He almost felt like this phone call was a metaphorical walk of shame.

Kendra knew he was lying. "What do you mean 'it's really not like that at all?'" She half laughed and half spit as she threw his words back in his face. Kendra rarely went 'psycho bitch' on someone who had treated her wrong. Her typical response was to withdraw and direct anger inward, but not this time. This time, she was going to let him have it.

"Well then, 'Mr. Cat Chaotic, Mr. Let's stick it in everyone's face and go down swinging.' Just what it is 'it' like then?"

"Well..." Cat tried to respond, but no more words came out. He only agreed to speak to her because he figured he couldn't ignore her forever. He cared deeply for everyone, but everything had changed. Cat thought he could protect them if they only understood his Safe Spaces experiment was over. They needed to move on. He couldn't tell her what happened to him at the police station. Cat worried they would want to go ahead with it anyway, despite how the government threatened not just the band but their families. How could he live with himself? This was all his fault.

"Things have changed, Kendra. I can't do what you are asking me to do and, honestly, I think you should reconsider the whole thing."

Kendra mentally prepared for this, but the words had a deeper impact than expected. She lashed out in kind.

"Reconsider the whole thing? What are you an asshole? Do you know how close we were to breaking them before you made your video? And you want to stop now?"

Cat's anger was about to boil over. He became even more enraged when he realized how mad she was.

"Breaking them? Are you serious?" Cat hissed. "Do you know what these people are capable of? You think for one moment that I would have humiliated myself on television for no reason? Have you been paying attention this whole time, or do you think this is just one big sick joke? Really, Kendra, I thought you were smarter than that."

Even in his fury, Cat realized he had come dangerously close to revealing too much. He should have hung up, but he didn't.

"What do you mean, what they are capable of? We knew what we were in for from the very beginning. For fuck's sake, Cat, they killed Richard for political reasons. They disemboweled him on video and put it on the internet as a warning to everyone else. Of course, I know what they are capable of. I've been a dead woman walking since the beginning of this whole thing. We all have, but we all knew that was the price we were going to have to pay. Now you are turning your back on us and everything we stand for just because they did something to you? Are you listening to yourself? You can't be. This is not the same guy as the one I saw in that bar, scarfing chicken wings and unleashing venom at Ramirez because they used Richard as a pawn in their sick game. A game, mind you, where the outcome will be governmental control and power over everyone who doesn't agree with them. I know it seems like a long time ago, but Cat but you were the guy that was ready to fight, ready to save this country. You're not dead yet Cat, you're alive, so start fucking acting like it."

"What the fuck do you know, Kendra? You're not the one who was down there ..."

"And I told you not to go." Kendra all but screamed into the phone. "But no, you wouldn't listen. You knew better. I said call the lawyer, but you knew you could find out what they were up to. You tried to beat them at their own game and now look what happened? After all the good we did, after all we sacrificed, you went on fucking television and gave it all up. Everything we stood for, even when we were winning. And now look where we are, Cat. Here I am, begging you to stop what you are about to do so we can beat them. I mean, really, we could end this, and you're throwing it all away after I told you not to go."

"Yes, I know you said that, but I had to go and, as sick as this sounds right now, I'm glad I did. I learned things. Things I wish I didn't know, but I still learned them and, Kendra, I'm telling you, you don't know what we're up against. You think things are bad now? Just wait. You just wait until they unleash everything they have against us. I wanted to warn you, Swamp, Trent, and Robert that believe it or not, it can get worse, much, much worse."

"Yes, we all know it can get worse. In fact, we all expected it to get worse when we started this fucking thing. But there's obviously something you're not telling me, and I need you to be honest. I'm sure Swamp and the rest of us can help, but you've got to be specific. We can't help and we can't fight if we don't know what we're fighting against. Cat, you've got to tell me."

"I can't Kendra. If I do, many people I care about are going to get hurt. I just can't let that happen to any of you." Cat choked over his last words and tried to compose himself because he didn't want to let Kendra know his emotions had gotten the best of him. He was still furious with her, but he also knew she was right, so he switched gears.

"You know Safe Spaces couldn't have worked, anyway. It was a stupid idea and I'm really, really, sorry that I got you guys to go along with it. I put your lives in danger for what? A rock band that emulated pro-wrestling? I mean, as I say it now, I can't believe how ridiculous it sounds. We actually tried to go through with this, and I almost brought you all down with me. I'm so sorry, so really, very sorry."

Cat choked over his last words, and he knew Kendra could tell he was on the verge of tears. He truly felt sorry that his science experiment blew up in their faces. Cat couldn't bring himself to tell her that the government was using their families to blackmail him. He had to take that secret to the grave. The fact was that he had endangered all of their lives and regretted it. He still believed in free speech principles, but now realized what a fool he was.

Hearing Cat sob, Kendra felt her own tears welling up, but, for now, she stayed composed. She knew she would have to let her emotions out at some point, but not now. Not during this argument. Still, Kendra couldn't help but soften her tone after Cat let his true feelings slip out.

"We all went into this with our eyes wide open, Cat. Trent was the most vocal, but we all knew how crazy this was. We did it anyway, knowing full well we were all in mortal danger. But you know what? We did it because we believed that the country was worth saving and the fact is that we can't see it through without you. Especially with you turning on us and going on your public apology tour."

That last sentence stung. Pangs of electricity shot through Cat's nerves and up and down his spine. He felt cold and physically shuddered from the sensations. Cat felt extremely guilty about the confessional video and couldn't bring himself to watch it afterward. Deep inside, he understood that delivering humiliating speeches before live audiences would only worsen matters. His current plan to deal with it was to use vodka to manage the guilt.

"But you don't know the danger you're in, Kendra. I swear, the things I heard in that police station were some of the coldest, cruelest, most sadistic tools that they could use to bring us down. They mean it Kendra. They really do, and I just couldn't let that happen. I just couldn't."

"How are you going to live with yourself, Cat?" Kendra whispered. She sensed defeat in Cat's voice. That was a bad sign that she wasn't changing his mind about the apology tour.

"I was thinking vodka."

Despite her anger, she chuckled at Cat's response. He could always make her laugh, which meant things could easily get really complicated between them. The closest she came to hopping into bed with him was during their dinner at the steakhouse. She stopped herself because that could complicate the band dynamics at a critical moment. What they were doing was too important. Now matters were worse. She was prepared to use any means necessary to get him to change his mind. Hopefully, she wouldn't have to do that. Now was not the time for more complications.

Thankfully, Kendra only let out a small laugh, so she ignored it and continued, "I mean, you truly believed in all of this. I know that. And now, you're tossing it all away, thinking that you are saving us when all you are doing is just delaying the inevitable. There won't be much to save if we don't finish this. If you make those speeches, you'll help hammer the final nails in the coffin of what this country is all about. Vodka may help you get through it, Cat, but it will only enable you to lie to yourself."

Cat recoiled, balled his fists, and released his fingers to open them. This tic usually accompanied flashbacks to things he had done wrong. It also happened when something shook him to his core. He was going to respond to her vodka comment with a zinger about her own drinking, but then he stopped himself as his mind wandered in a different direction. He engaged in an inner debate about whether he wanted to venture into a topic that would skate on even thinner ice. The silence became awkward as Cat finished his internal discussion. Despite his doubts, he went there anyway.

"Kendra..." He said her name in a mournful tone, which caused his voice to trail off. The uncomfortable silence affected Kendra as well, and she stiffened herself for a heartfelt response. She had maintained her composure but didn't know how long she could keep it up.

"Yes Carl." Kendra never used his real name before, and that got his attention.

"I..." Cat tried again to express his thoughts, but he couldn't.

Kendra waited a moment to let him finish, but she realized he couldn't, so she tried to help him.

"Carl, please just tell me what you want to say. I have a bad feeling that this might be the last time we speak. I hope that isn't the case, but if it is, we both need to lay it all out, right? We owe each other honesty, don't we?"

Again, silence. Kendra decided not to break it this time. She had to let him figure it out for himself. Kendra could tell his emotions were taking over, and he needed to reconcile his feelings on his own. She didn't expect him to hang up, but if he did, it would be better if they parted on honest terms.

Cat's head was swimming. He knew Kendra was right. This might be their last conversation since he realized the speeches could end their relationship. Summoning all his strength, he spoke once more, hoping it wasn't the end.

"Kendra, I care so much about you and the rest of the guys. Trent has been one of the best friends I've ever had, and I don't know where I would be without him. He's someone who worries all the time, but it's because he cares. He cares deeply about people and would do anything for anyone. Jeez, I should have listened to him. And Robert, I know I haven't known him for that long, but he's the type of guy that someone like me needs in his life. He's dependable, he's smart, he's funny, and he's a damn good businessman and he's been the driving engine behind everything we put together. But Kendra, even with all of that, you matter more because I feel like..."

His voice trailed off again. He didn't have to finish his sentence because Kendra knew what he was going to say. She wanted to have to have that conversation at some point, but not now. There was definitely something between them. But this was not the time.

"Carl, please don't..."

"No Kendra, I have to. You said it before. You were right, this might be the last time we speak, so I have to ..."

"Please Carl." Kendra cut him off. "Please, *please*, let's not talk about that right now. Let's have that conversation later, okay? Let's stay focused on the band; there's no going back once we go there. Things could get messy. We're at a real crossroads right now and we don't need a truck driving right through the middle of it."

"Okay," Cat conceded. She was smarter than he was, so it was clear she knew his intentions. But maybe she was right. Maybe this was not the right time. This could be their last conversation, and the last opportunity to share his emotions with her. He tried one last time. "Can I just say one thing about that, then?"

It was now Kendra's turn to impose an uneasy silence. She needed time to process what she heard and figure out just what to say. Kendra knew they had to discuss their feelings for each other, but this really wasn't the time. She really didn't want the traditional male/female relationship issues to affect this decision. Kendra realized she had one card left to play, and it was honesty, so she laid it down.

"Okay, but before you do, I need to say one thing, okay?"

That caught Cat's attention. Either Kendra would reject him or state that it wasn't the right time. Neither possibility was pleasant. With no good options, he uttered one word.

"Okay." The universal male response to when a female imposed her will.

Kendra smiled to herself. The first time she saw him onstage, she immediately felt attracted to him. Oddly, seeing him on the floor after Robert clocked him only increased her interest in him. Kendra would have slept with him after the steakhouse, but she stopped herself. She realized that the only way to avoid the inevitable conversation was to play a mind game on him.

"Look, you and I need to discuss that, but if we do it right now, you won't like my response, and neither would I. I'm sure you can understand that my feelings about you are extremely complicated right now. I know you have your reasons, even though I don't understand them. But you are about to do something that goes against everything you stood for. From my perspective, you are undermining everything we are about, and our sacrifice will have been for nothing. You are throwing it all away. In all honesty, if you go on the apology tour, then I just don't know if things could ever work out between us. But I owe it to you, to be honest. That's how I feel right now."

Kendra flinched as she knew she just used the nuclear option and turned his feelings for her against him. She knew it was a pretty dirty trick when she implied that there was a connection between him doing the apology tour and the two of them being together. Kendra hated doing it, but there was too much at stake. She was also being honest. These next few moments would determine whether their relationship would now go in an unpredictable direction. She tried to prevent the genie from escaping the bottle, but she knew she was definitely rubbing the glass.

And it worked.

Cat's mind processed what she said and the inherent "carrot and stick" approach she used against him. Kendra made it clear she had feelings for him, but the apology tour could complicate things. She was clever enough to avoid directly tying the two together, but strongly implied it instead. Kendra was also crafty enough to not shut the door completely. That gave him hope they could be together regardless of the path he took. He was glad she stopped him from going there.

Kendra couldn't resist rubbing it in a bit more.

"So, what was it you wanted to say, Cat?"

They were not on video chat, so she couldn't see his facial expressions, but she had a pretty good idea that she had made her point. She was glad she didn't have to resort to the 'any means necessary' approach to stop him from going on the tour, but she had been prepared to if she had to. And by any means necessary, she meant Any. Means. Necessary.

"Okay, um, let's table that discussion for another time."

Checkmate.

"Yes, I think that's best. I know in my heart that this won't be our last conversation and I think, deep down, you know it, too." Kendra was confident that she had reeled him in, but he wasn't in the boat. This wasn't over.

"Cat, I think that..."

"But..." Cat interrupted her.

She wasn't expecting that, and she responded with, "huh?"

"No, you go ahead," Cat responded.

"No, you go," Kendra countered. "I cut you off. Sorry about that."

"No, it's okay," Cat continued. "I know that this is not what you wanted to hear, but I am going to go ahead with the speeches."

"What?" Kendra was stunned. Five seconds before, she was certain that she had gotten him to stop this madness and maybe laid the groundwork for a future together. Instead, the conversation took a one-eighty, leaving her dumbfounded.

"I told you; I just can't let them hurt everyone. Kendra, I know how you feel, but you just don't understand yet. You're not the only one I've endangered. Many people are in serious trouble because of me. I can't let that happen."

"Cat, please. Please don't do this. I can't. I can't just let you throw this all away. It's very important. You're very important. We can fix whatever it is. You can't just go that way. You just can't."

Kendra pleaded with him. She was grief stricken at the thought of him humiliating himself, but her anguish morphed back into anger.

"Kendra, you're in danger. Everyone you care about is in grave danger if I don't go through with this. I can't emphasize it enough. You need protection."

Kendra seethed. He was really going through with it. This was the end of everything. Safe Spaces and the movement were all done. Inhaling deeply, she spoke what felt like her last words to him.

"Cat, you couldn't be more wrong about this. I can't believe you really think that you're helping us. You're not stupid, and I know that deep down you don't want things to go this way. You don't want to ruin everything we worked for. Whatever they did to you or whatever they are threatening you with pales compared to what's coming next after they have publicly broken you. This is our last stand. If you think you are protecting us, this is not the way to do it. We don't need that kind of protection. What we really need is you. You're our leader and you've failed us."

Kendra hung up the call.

Cat sat dazed in his car. He couldn't believe what she said to him. Failed them? She had some nerve saying that he had failed them. Didn't she trust him enough to know that this was necessary? Why did she think he would roll over for no good reason? She didn't take the beating. Niko didn't carve her up like a jack-o'-lantern. She had no clue what had happened to him. The funny part was that they didn't break him with the beating. They broke him when they threatened her and all the band members' families and, of course, that daughter he knew nothing about.

Oh yes, that. He had almost forgotten about that threat. Cat had spoken to Max several times. He never said whether they found his supposed daughter in Arizona. They had only discussed the government's 'request' that he go on the apology tour. He assumed that if they had found her, they would keep that fact hidden from him until they needed to use it. Pawns are only useful until they fulfilled their purpose. He was dealing with sick, amoral savages who had absolutely no issue with using every bit of control they had over him.

Cat hadn't tried to find her because he was worried that the government was watching him, and he didn't want to do their dirty work for them. He did plan on tracking her down if she existed when the apology tour stopped in Arizona. Unfortunately, he had a good idea of who her mother was. He cringed at the thought of having to deal with her. That was one of the worst breakups he ever had. He hadn't spoken with her since and, as bad as it was, Cat didn't want to lead Max to her.

Besides, he doubted she would take his calls, anyway. Yeah, it was that bad of an ending.

His mind wandered back to Kendra, hanging up on him. She had some nerve to lecture him. He really had feelings for her, which made it hurt more. It was his fault, and it was worse because he couldn't explain the consequences to her. Cat had to bear that part of this mess himself.

Still, Kendra should have realized he had a valid reason for making the video. Perhaps that was a sign that their relationship wasn't meant to be? He hoped not. Cat truly believed they had a future together, but he was glad he didn't tell her how he felt. She probably knew anyway, but at least he never said it. There would be no turning back if he told her he loved her.

His mind then shifted gears again and told him he needed to start his car and start driving home. He had a lot to do to prepare for the apology tour. Humiliation caused him to avoid thinking about it. Then Cat remembered he needed to stop by the liquor store on his way home because he was running low on vodka. Ironic.

He let out a defeated "Oh fuck it" and put his car in gear.

*   *   *

"I'm pretty sure he's going to go through with it." Kendra shook her head as she told the others about her conversation with Cat.

"Well, what did he say?" Trent asked in a tone that sounded like he was grasping at straws.

Kendra shook her head again and audibly breathed in and out. She didn't believe it herself, but she had to tell them.

"Well, he didn't exactly come out and say it, but it's pretty clear that the government is threatening someone or something very important to him and he thinks he has no choice. The only good news I can tell you is that there's no way he's actually gone woke. He doesn't agree with them, that's for sure. Obviously, something horrible happened or is going to happen and he doesn't seem to think that there is any way out except to do what they say."

"What did you say to him?" Trent continued. "Did you tell him what we talked about, how we are all dead anyway and that if he goes through with it, it was all a fucking waste of time?"

"Trent, I tried, I did. I even did something that I told myself I wouldn't do, and it didn't work. As much as I don't want to believe it, I think he made his final decision. I think it's all over."

"What was that?" Robert asked.

"What was what?" Kendra replied.

"What was the thing you said you wouldn't do?"

"Ugh," Kendra immediately regretted opening the door to that part of the conversation.

She breathed in heavily again and just started talking again.

"We almost had that discussion. You know, the one that is coming between us."

"No, what?" Trent wasn't being facetious; he truly didn't know what she was talking about.

"Alright, I don't have time to beat around the bush like I did with the chicken wings. We started the discussion about what's going on between us. It's pretty clear that there is something there, and, yes, I think it's mutual." Kendra sighed audibly as she uttered the last sentence, and then continued. "I'm being pretty blunt here with you guys because we don't have time."

"Oh, boy," Swamp said. He sensed the chemistry, but understood it wasn't the right moment. It might get messy if Cat and Kendra acknowledged the elephant in the room.

Kendra closed her eyes, as she couldn't look at them when she told them the next part. "I even tried to use it against him."

"What?" Swamp was now sizing up the elephant.

"Yeah, I know." Kendra opened her eyes but looked away. She was really uncomfortable telling them this, but felt she had no choice.

"What did you do?" Swamp asked.

Kendra took another deep breath and closed her eyes again. Her next words would elicit a similar reaction to that elephant taking a dump in the center of the room.

"I all but told him I felt the same way about him, but that it wouldn't work out if he went on the apology tour."

No one responded as the last sentence hung in the air, similar to the stench from the elephant's business.

"Yeah, I know," Kendra repeated, trying to break the ice that formed like a glacier over the room.

"Well, what did you want me to do? It's over if he does it, right? You all know that."

Robert was the first to respond. "Man, that's cold."

"Oh, really Robert? You want him to do it?" Kendra sounded exasperated, but she knew she had crossed the line.

Robert stared at her and responded. "Look Kendra, it's pretty obvious what's going on between the two of you. Any idiot could see that, but going there? Wow, I would think ..."

Trent stopped Robert mid-sentence, "Whoa, wait, Kendra? You and Cat? Really?"

They all looked at Trent and tried to read his expression. Was he serious? None of them spoke out loud, but the collective unspoken consensus among them was Trent really had no clue. He wasn't drunk this time and there was a sense of 'here we go again', but this time Kendra tried to use this to her advantage.

"Okay, that isn't the most important thing right now, right? Don't we have a bigger problem with Cat going on his apology tour and what we're going to do about it?"

She had a point, but Trent wasn't letting it go. "You mean to tell me you knew Cat liked you and that you told him that the two of you could be together if he didn't go through with the speech tour? And he said no?"

She wasn't oblivious to the blow to her ego. She also had no interest in dwelling on that aspect of the issue. However, Trent couldn't help but inadvertently rub it in.

"Look, I don't think that I have to tell you that men will ignore just about every principle they have if there is even the potential for sex with a woman they're attracted to. They'll sell their soul in order to get two and a half minutes access to the holiest of holies, but you actually played that card with him, and he still said no? I mean I've heard that sometimes men will say no but that only happens when..."

"Okay, Trent." Kendra tried to cut him off, but either he didn't hear her, or he didn't care.

"... they really think a woman is completely unattractive and that can't be the case with you, can it? I mean, even at last call at the bar..."

"*Okay, Trent!*"

That one got Trent's attention, and he stopped himself from finishing his thoughts on the subject.

Kendra continued, "Now, if we could please forget about Cat rejecting me for the moment and get back to dealing with the immensely more important issue of trying to save the world from Marxism."

Swamp tried to hold it in, but he couldn't. He laughed out loud when Kendra said that they were saving the world. He agreed with her and found this whole discussion amusing, but also knew that they needed to move on.

"Guys, Kendra's right." Swamp was still laughing, but continued anyway. "As funny as that was, we need to focus. We're running out of time. His first stop on his national apology tour is in two weeks in Washington, D.C. It's all over if he goes through with it."

Kendra agreed. "No one will stand up if they break someone like him."

"Kendra, something you said, I want to make sure I heard it right." Swamp asked. "You don't think he's gone woke? I mean, we're fucked if he has, but if he doesn't really believe what he said, then, well, we might have a shot. Are you sure?"

"I really don't think he's gone over. They scared him. He kept saying that we had no idea what the government was capable of and how he needed to protect us. If he had truly turned into one of them, then he wouldn't be talking like that. Shit, he probably wouldn't have even spoken to me. He was really emotional, too. I've never seen him like that. I know he's doing this under duress. He even said he needed to protect us, and I told him we didn't need that. We needed our leader."

"And you told him you would fuck him, too." Trent couldn't resist throwing that one in.

"Yeah, and he said no," Kendra answered, which caused them all to burst out laughing again. Swamp made another attempt to refocus the discussion after a few minutes of laughter.

"Oh, okay, oh, we can't go there again, okay, not until we figure this out." Swamp's laughter was trailing off, and he was almost back under control.

"Do you think he would talk to me, Kendra?" Robert asked. "I mean, I have a good relationship with him, and he has seemed to listen to me in the past. Maybe I can talk some sense into him?"

"Look, I don't want to set myself up for another 'Kendra gets rejected' joke, but I honestly think that if I couldn't change his mind, then none of us can. He seemed to be embarrassed by the confessional video, though. He got emotional, and I asked him how he was going to live with himself after doing it."

"What did he say to that?" Trent asked.

"He said he was going to use vodka." This time, the ensuing laughter was more of a knowing chortle among them. That was a quintessential Cat response.

Robert continued with his idea. "What if I could record him, the real him, saying that he was only doing this under duress? Swamp could post the recording online to show he hasn't really gone woke. Maybe that would do it and he wouldn't go through with it?"

"Hmmm," Swamp responded to Robert. "That's not a bad idea. I think you might have something with the embarrassment angle. But it would have to be something big. Something the government couldn't deny. I wonder if ..." he trailed off as his thoughts coalesced around the beginnings of a plan.

"What?" Kendra asked. "Wonder what?"

"Look, I've got something in mind, but I'm going to need some help. It's not something any of us could do by ourselves, but there may be someone I know who can pull it off. If I can get him to..." Swamp paused for a moment. "Look, I have an idea that would either work spectacularly or fail miserably and blow up in our face."

"Where have I heard that before?" This time, it was Kendra's turn to inject a bit of humor and sarcasm into the conversation.

Swamp smiled and replied, "You mean a rock band that co-opts a pro-wrestling plotline in order to stop governmental oppression? You mean something that sounds so stupid and has to boomerang back but actually, sort of, kind of, worked?" Swamp gently matched Kendra's sarcasm with his own.

"Yeah, I mean something like that," Kendra continued with a smile.

"Well, I don't think that this idea reaches that level of stupidity, but it definitely has the potential to fail spectacularly. Unfortunately, it's likely to expose me, but that's going to happen, eventually. Let me make a couple of calls. If I can get the guys that I have in mind onboard, here's what I'm thinking we can do..."

Swamp gave them the broad strokes of his plan, and at the end, they all agreed it was all or nothing, or worse than nothing really. But this was likely their last shot. Failure meant the game was over.

Chapter Twenty

"Hit that power chord hard, really hard, and give it more of a rrrrrr sound. It's got to really stand out from the keyboard overlay. I think it's getting lost in the wash between the..." Richard's voice faded away, as it always did when he labored through the monotonous task of transforming a demo into a finished song. Cat likened the process to preparing gumbo or some other complicated stew. They started with a base, built a complex roux, added spices, boiled it, and brought it all together. If they rushed on any of those steps, then the end product would suck. Nobody was interested in a lousy song. Much less subpar gumbo.

Cat waited for Richard to finish his thought. He didn't, so Cat offered another suggestion, "Well, I could bend the chord a lot more so that it stands out?"

Still no response. Clearly, Richard was still tinkering with the spices. The boil would have to wait.

"Rich?"

"Huh?" Finally, some daylight.

"Sorry, I said, that I could bend the chord some. Give it some oomph, you know, something like this." As Cat spoke, he pushed his two fingers so that the string moved side to side across the neck of the guitar. By manipulating the strings, Cat made the pitch vary, rising and falling with each motion.

Richard heard the fluctuating noise from Cat's fingers. That was the rrrrrr sound he wanted. "Yeah, do that again."

Cat smiled. Hit the chord again and really bent the strings hard.

"Oh man, that's close to what I was thinking, but it's not quite it. It needs something..." Richard trailed off again, but not for long this time. He raised his hand and poked out his index finger and pointed directly at Cat. "The flanger pedal. Bend it like you did and run it through the flanger pedal. It needs that bend, but the pedal will give it that waaah sound."

An outsider hearing these nonsensical words might assume they were tripping on mushrooms, but they were mostly sober. They had worked together so long they understood each other's gibberish and Cat knew immediately that Richard had hit on it.

"Shiiiiit," Cat drew the expletive out because it was the absolutely perfect sound effect to mix with this chord progression. The effect drove the angular reverberation of the chord, so it shredded through the keyboards and minimized them without replacing them. The outcome resembled a siren interrupting a church service, the perfect sound for this song.

"I disconnected the flange earlier, but give me a few minutes to hook it up. I only had the clean pedals set up today, but holy shit, that would sound on point. It's like a punch in the face and it'll rock. What a riff. I think we can repeat it several times. What do you think, Rich?"

"I think you're right." Richard agreed. He nodded his head and scratched at his three-day-old beard. He rarely shaved while they were working on new music. "I was thinking a B Minor progression, but what you just hit sounds awesome. Maybe I'll save that other one for the one we're working on next week. Do me a favor and just record the riff itself so we don't lose it, okay?"

"Yeah, I already saved it on the third track. I wanted to make sure I kept it exactly as we had it. We don't want to lose this. Also, I think we can use the lines from that song 'Skinner Cage' that we never finished. We'll have to change it a bit and it's nowhere near done, but I think it has a lot of lines that'll fit. It's furious stuff, but that riff is angry. Perfect flange material. Trent will love it."

"Yeah, it's angry, and I was thinking the same thing about Skinner Cage. The title won't work, but some of those lines will." Richard smirked. "Too bad. I was really looking forward to a go around tonight."

The two of them loved writing new music, but Richard was referring to the fights they sometimes had when they couldn't agree on something. This discussion was more pleasant than others. When they really got into it, they would call Trent in to mediate, even though he was barely involved in the writing process. His specialty was postproduction and mixing. They collaborated on just about everything, but Cat wrote most of the lyrics and Richard usually composed the music. Most of their conflicts erupted when Richard felt that Cat's words didn't 'marry up' to the emotions of the music. And 'marry up' was the perfect description. Their bickering resembled a couple that was married way too long. And sometimes they got heated. Anyone who heard them during a major argument would ask themselves why on God's green earth did these two people ever work together. However, they were both highly skilled musicians and intense conflicts sometimes arose during their collaborative efforts. They recognized that their best work arose out of these arguments, so there were no lingering hard feelings. They usually went out together immediately after the brawl ended and got drunk.

This time, it wasn't necessary for them to let it go.

"Yeah, it's funny. I hate when that happens," Cat laughed. "We should probably call Trent to mediate more, but sometimes I hear the recordings the next day and I'm like, 'why the hell did we fight over it?' Remember when we almost came to blows over that guitar part in 'Quicksand'? It was two in the morning, and we had to finish the last bridge. I swear I almost smashed my old Jazzmaster over your head, but we gave it one last go and that fucking nailed it. That was the only night I can think of where we didn't go out together afterwards. I went out myself and got shit-faced at O'Hara's. I listened to the rough cut the next day, and it was amazing. Trent did nothing to it. I think it was the final mix."

"Yeah, you just have to be less of an asshole and more reasonable like me," Richard maintained a straight face, but he could only keep it for a moment. Cat caught it when Richard smiled and burst into laughter. Both of them roared, nearly in tears.

Cat composed himself first. "I know, I know. I can be a real jerk sometimes. Like the time I told you I would rather stand six inches in front of a PA system blasting Yoko Ono singing that Merry Christmas song rather than listen to the lyrics you wrote for that song 'Pile up'? Oh wait, no, you said that."

Cat's zinger brought on another round of laughter.

This time, Richard regained his composure first. "Pile up?" he asked through giggles that he still couldn't quite control. "You mean that song about a blind guy driving a car? *That one*?" Cat couldn't believe Richard had dusted off that gem.

"Yeah, that one. I thought it would be funny if he took the family car out for a spin. And don't give me any of your shit. You thought it was funny, too."

Richard had to admit Cat was right. It was hysterical. But the problem was that the sound and lyrics didn't mesh in the initial song cut. He couldn't stand it when the feelings of the two components were completely different. The guitar riffs had an automotive vibe, but it wasn't a playful melody. The sound was too serious for a song like that. Cat's lyrics were a novelty, and it just didn't work.

"Well, you were all but making a Stevie Wonder joke with it," Richard retorted. "Besides, you liked the final version, anyway. It worked much better when you changed it into a disappointed teenager who had his parents' car for the first time. He took the girl out and didn't get laid. We kept the title. It worked flawlessly."

Richard was right. The final version was much better, and it was a hit during the shows. The fans loved the double entendre of the title and the lyrics. However, that song was atypical in their catalog. It was lighter than most of their songs, but still had dark undertones that clashed perfectly with the pop sensibilities in the guitar sounds. It had a heavier keyboard component than most of their other stuff, too. But the crowd loved it, and they would usually play it during one of the final encores.

"I know. I can't say it fits in, but it balances the shows. It's one of my favorite songs to play at the end of a gig. Besides, I'm sure we would get killed online if we didn't play it." Cat was only half kidding about the set list.

Richard opened his mouth to respond, but something in Cat's line of reasoning piqued his interest and he stopped short. He closed his mouth and remained silent, but his eyes lit up like he had an idea. Cat had seen that look before. It meant that he had a superb idea. Cat knew better than to interrupt him when he entered this state.

"What if ... hmmm," Richard began, but abruptly halted. Cat waited, but Richard's eyes told him it was something big.

Richard waited too long, so finally Cat said, "What? What if 'what?'"

"What if, what if," Richard repeated.

Cat sensed he was close and finally, Richard got there.

"What if we played it live, and it was just how you wrote it? We played a song about how a blind guy crashed a car? Can you imagine what the audience would do? I mean, the regulars would get it. Well, at least I hope they would, but what about everyone else? What do you think they would do?"

Cat paused and pondered Richard's questions. "Well, I might be the wrong guy to ask. I mean, I wrote the damn thing and hell, I thought it was funny, so maybe you ought to ask Trent? At least he didn't write it, but he might be afraid to play it."

Richard laughed at Cat's dig at Trent. "Point taken, but try to step back for a moment and think about this. Think about what it would be like to antagonize a crowd, but if it was, you know, just part of the show. I mean like a character on a television show that everyone hates because he's awful because he says offensive things. You've seen them. You know, the guy who insults the others, but he's endearing somehow? Back when people used to laugh at themselves?"

"I don't think we have too many blind audience members that want to laugh at themselves," Cat quipped with a completely straight face. He wasn't trying to be funny, but they both stopped and realized the unintentional humor in his response. Cat continued.

"Maybe, but maybe it's not humor that will drive that. Could it be something else? Maybe it's..." Cat processed his thoughts as he tried to come up with the right description of what he was thinking.

Now Richard felt intrigued. "What?" he asked.

"Well, have you noticed how things have changed? I mean, people have become more and more uptight and offended by things? Like what happened when we were in college, when we had those 'See Dick' shirts for rushing the fraternity? We made a joke about those anti-drunk driving ads from the eighties where they said not to be a dick and don't drive drunk? We put the same stick figures on the rush shirts and said, 'See Dick, See Dick rush, See all the girls love Dick.'"

Richard snickered. The shirts were funny, but he didn't understand Cat's direction. Maybe he was just going off on a tangent. Maybe he was bringing it back to something relevant. "Yeah?" Richard still didn't follow. "They also used the same schtick on those sex education posters. 'Don't be a Dick, use a condom' or something like that. They tried to use humor as they scared the shit out of you, so? What made you think of that now?"

"I was getting to that. Remember how one sorority got offended by the shirts and we had to go to that sexual harassment seminar?"

"Yeah, kinda?"

Cat continued. "We all thought that was funny, but then the Greek council forced us to go to those seminars. I mean, you would have thought that they would have just laughed at it or ignored us. But no. We offended them, so they forced us to go to sexual harassment re-education training."

Richard nodded his head. "Yeah, God, that was awful. What a waste. But wasn't it just those Omega Eta hags? I mean, weren't they the ones that forced us to go? Really, talk about a group that should be happy that we were making sexual jokes. Good God, most of them really needed to get laid."

"No doubt they did. Ugh, come to think of it, I might have been with a couple of them at last call." Cat laughed.

"Oh, man, you did? I hope I didn't, but I might have..." Richard thought out loud about memories he was trying to bury.

"Anyway," Cat tried to bring the conversation back to the main point. "I don't think it was just them. The real problem was not that they complained. The bigger problem was the council listened to them and made us go through that bullshit seminar. Makes you wonder, doesn't it? I mean, why didn't they just ignore us? Why did they go along with it and give us the attention we wanted? I mean, we had done a lot more offensive shit than that."

Richard nodded his head and looked away. "Yeah, we did. Thank God smart phones really weren't much of a thing back then. If there had been pictures or God help us video of some of the stuff our guys pulled, then I think we would all be in jail. And I get it, the always offended crowd always complained. I wonder if we could play offensive songs to get the crowd going? Remember when the metal bands used to use that satanism nonsense to infuriate the church? All that did was get them noticed. What if we did the same thing, but with politically incorrect songs?"

"Hmmm, I wonder..." Cat thought to himself as he thought Richard might have really hit on something. "Okay, I'm not married to this and I'm kind of thinking out loud, but I think it's worth a try. There are some really interesting songs from the seventies and eighties that are really cool, but definitely politically incorrect. No one is really playing that stuff at the moment and it's certainly something different. Maybe it's worth testing it out at some point, but I was getting at a problem."

"What's that?"

"Well, going back to that sexual harassment seminar, remember when that guy who led it corrected me when I talked about my 'girlfriend' and said that using such a term is demeaning because it could imply that I am relegating a woman to a 'girl' status?"

"Yeah, vaguely."

Cat continued, "Remember how we all laughed at that asshole later? I even changed my words to nonsensical ones like 'person friend' and 'birthing person'? I embarrassed the guy because I showed him just how absurd he sounded. But there was something sinister in what he was doing. He insisted I change my language in order to force me to speak how he wanted me to."

"Yeah, that was pretty funny, but what does that have to do with this?"

"He was trying to control me, but when I exposed him, I embarrassed him. He didn't even buy his own bullshit. And that was in a college setting."

Cat sensed Richard somewhat understood his concept, but wasn't fully there yet.

"What I mean is, if someone at a college didn't even believe politically correct nonsense when I confronted him, then how will we get any traction with the non-college crowd? This stuff hasn't spread to corporate America or anywhere else in society. Not yet, anyway. So why would anyone outside campus care if we sing offensive songs? People outside of college can still say what they want, right?"

Richard nodded his head. Now he got it. "Okay, I get it. You're saying that the satanism stuff that the metal bands played was truly offensive to the church. Parents were genuinely worried about their kids hearing it. So, if the politically correct people today don't really believe what they're saying, then playing those songs won't really gain any attention? No one else will care if we make Stevie Wonder jokes?"

Cat laughed. "Maybe they won't, but maybe they will. Couldn't you just see some stupid politician using us as a scapegoat? Or rather, as a cudgel? Politicians are just like that guy in the seminar. He wanted to control me so badly. Part of me thinks that he really thought that the stupid seminar would change my mind. He got so mad when it didn't work."

Richard cringed. "Yeah, he did, and he's the type that would scream about us online now. I've got another idea, too."

"Oh yeah, what's that?" Cat asked.

"What if we went on a college tour and we played those songs? Just imagine those snowflakes protesting us and yelling 'Free Palestine' or some other bullshit like that? That would draw a lot of attention to us. Attention sells tickets and tee shirts. Besides, I would love to play more of the dark music from the eighties in our shows. A lot of our stuff sounds like that anyway and I think that there'll be some nostalgia for it that will bring out the older crowd. I was listening on..."

While Richard continued on about potential additions to the set list, Cat heard white noise coming from the speakers in the studio.

"Do you hear that?" he asked Richard.

"Hear what?"

"That, it sounds like white noise. Don't you hear it?" Cat asked.

"Nope, nothing, but like I was saying, there was a real cult following of the dark alternative music. All those British bands that came after punk died..." Just as Richard continued, the white noise got louder.

"Come on, you've got to hear it now, right?"

Cat looked directly at Richard as he spoke, but Richard ignored him and kept going on about dark eighties music. The white noise grew louder, to the point Cat couldn't hear Richard's voice.

"Richard?"

Still no response. He kept talking without acknowledging Cat had said anything.

"Richard, RICHARD?" Cat almost screamed, but Richard kept speaking as if nothing was out of the ordinary. Had Richard forgotten he was in the room? Panicked, Cat jumped from the chair and twisted the volume dials on the soundboard. It had no effect, and the white noise grew even louder, to where it sounded like a hurricane.

Suddenly, a deafening explosion filled the room, engulfing it in blinding light. Cat's ears rang and his own screams sounded muffled.

He called out to Richard, and this time his voice was clearly audible.

He also heard a response.

"Who?"

"What?" Cat responded to the voice.

"No, who's Richard?" The blazing white light faded, and Cat turned to his right toward whomever spoke to him. It was one of Max's men who had met him backstage at the park in Washington, D.C. The first stop on his apology tour.

"Richard?" Cat asked. He didn't know whether he directed his question to Richard in his flashback or to this thug.

"You said Richard, who is Richard?" the thug repeated. Was this guy serious?

"Oh, sorry." Cat composed himself. His heart sank as he realized where he was. His situation flooded back to him, and he sighed and answered, "Richard is... he's..."

"Who?" the thug insisted.

"He's no one."

Cat cringed when he uttered that last statement. That was so far from the truth. MicroAggression was gone, but he thought about Richard every day. It felt like a million years had passed since they had that conversation about taking the band in a new direction. The truth of his situation nearly made him cry, but there was no turning back.

The thug continued, "Alright, you're on in ten minutes and, since you zoned out there, I'll go over it again. We'll play an intro video over those monitors that flank the stage." The thug pointed to two massive video boards, each around 50 feet in height and width. "See them?"

Of course, Cat saw them. How could he not?

"You need to be standing at that podium so that the president can introduce you. We are broadcasting this live, so just wait for her to finish her opening remarks and then read your speech off the teleprompter. That's it, are we good?"

"Yes." Cat muttered.

"Good. Oh, and Max wanted me to remind you we're watching you. Just because you can't see us doesn't mean we're not there. His exact words were 'remind that piece of shit of what will happen if he crosses us.' So, I don't need to say anything else, right?"

"No, you don't," Cat whispered back.

"Good, then when you get your cue, you walk out there and stand there and smile, but not too much. Act contrite and show them you're glad to be here. Remember, you're showing them you've turned your life around, but there's no need to cry or do anything like that. You want to act more like you're celebrating that you're finally on the right track. Got it? Are we clear?"

"Yes, we are."

"Outstanding. Now go over there where that woman with the headset is waiting. She'll give you your cue. I'll be waiting right here watching everything you do. Just remember, fuck around and see what happens. I have my orders and oh man, I so hope I get to follow through on them. Personally, I think this apology tour is bullshit. I hope I'm the one that takes you out. Killing you would make the world a better place."

That last line ignited Cat's anger, which engaged the sarcastic part of his brain. "Gee, I hope you don't kill me so I can nominate you for the next Nobel Peace Prize."

"Yeah, that's pretty funny, asshole. But you just wait, I'm going on the tour with you. We are going to become great friends. We've got plans for you."

"I can imagine you do." Cat sighed and decided against making a homosexual joke at the thug's expense. Better not to antagonize this despicable individual.

Cat turned and walked toward the girl in the headset, but he was really oblivious to where he was going. After taking a few steps, he collided with something. He looked up and exclaimed, "What the hell?!?" and realized he had bumped into a man who was slightly taller than he was. The individual didn't budge and blocked his way and just stared at him. Finally, Cat had enough, and started yelling.

"Look, I told fucking Father Flanagan over there that I'll do it, okay? Really, what the hell do you..."

"I'm not with them," the man responded evenly. Cat immediately noticed a very soft expression on his face. He seemed different from Max's other henchmen. Could this guy be a friend?

"You're not?"

"No, my name's Jack and Swamp sent me."

"Swamp?" Cat lowered his voice, knowing that he was being watched. He immediately turned to look for Father Flanagan and he was gone.

"Him?" Jack asked. "I had a friend of mine take him for a walk. He's gone. You'll probably never see him again."

"Oh, man," Cat breathed.

"Yeah, I'm here for you. Well, not just me. You've got some friends here now. I've got fifteen of my best men dispersed around the stage, most are in the front. A few more in the crowd. They'll take out anyone who tries to hurt you. We're all here to protect you."

"Protect me?"

"Yes, protect you." Jack continued and glanced around to see if anyone was listening.

"We know they've done something to you, and we know they're threatening you. At first, we thought they doctored the video, but Kendra confirmed it was real. I know what you're going through because the same people threatened me. They threatened all of us. We're ex-police and some are ex-military. They forced us out because we aren't corrupt. We lost everything, just like you. Happy to tell you everything over a few beers one day, but I've about one more minute before someone gets suspicious. I need you to shut up and listen to me for one minute." Jack's voice was quiet, but urgent.

"Swamp sent me here to protect you, no matter what you say out there. You might not think you have a choice, but you do."

Cat locked eyes with Jack and he lifted his head slightly, urging him to go on. Jack obliged. "I won't sugarcoat anything. You're in deep shit, no matter what you say at that podium. They're probably threatening you or someone you love, and they *are* the type that will follow through. But I can guarantee if you do what they tell you to do and you lie for them, things will be much worse for you and whomever you are protecting. You might not know it, but you have an immense opportunity today. You can make it right, but you have to do it now. This is your one and only chance."

Cat stared silently at Jack.

"You are not alone right now. No matter what you do, I will make sure you get out of this puppet show alive. But if you go through with it, this will be the end of you. You have value for them, so you'll survive this mess if you do what they tell you. You'll probably spare whoever it is they are threatening. But make no mistake, being alive and actually living are two different things. Carl John Cat Chaotic McKnight will no longer exist. Replaced by a minion for the state. You help them, you're part of the problem."

Cat's heart sank. Of course, Jack was correct. Didn't he know that Cat already ruminated on those exact thoughts?

Cat tried to respond, but Jack stopped him.

"Let me finish, as I have about thirty more seconds before I have to go. Just to be clear, I will get you out of here alive, regardless of what you do up there. But if you apologize, then you'll never see me again. Cat, I'm not threatening you in the slightest. Your friends all love you and understand that you have to do whatever you think is best. But if you do the right thing and fix this mess, then we'll be with you. There are more of us than you think. They know we are growing stronger and that's why they're doing this to you. If you join the government, they will be your master. If you come back to us, we'll be your friends. I've been there, so I understand. No one can make this choice for you. It's yours and yours alone. Now make it and live with it."

After the warning, Jack turned and walked backstage.

Cat stood and stared as he watched Jack disappear into the background. His body trembled, struggling to accept what he had just heard. Heat tingled on his feet, reminding him of Max's consequences. His stomach churned in knots, warning him there were no good options.

He thought about that conversation he had with Richard during his flashback. He remembered how naïve he sounded when he asked Richard a rhetorical question of whether people can say what they want. Cat retched at the thought. Maybe it was the vodka? No, he knew better than that. He shook his head and his mind swirled. His heart raced. Despite Jack's words and every thought in his head telling him not to, he marched toward the woman in the headset.

As he trudged toward her, he heard the drum intro to Damnatio Memoriae. The bass kicked, and the guitar screeched. These were familiar sounds. He had heard them hundreds of times, even in his nightmares. Unfortunately, this wasn't a dream. No waking from the night terror today.

He looked out into the crowd. The scene reminded him of the last concert they played when the riot broke out. People screamed at each other through fences while the police tried to separate the warring factions. Some prayed, while others squared up to fight. Several held up signs calling him a sellout or a racist. America in 2044 was truly depressing. It was also an enormous moment that Cat found himself in. He asked himself how he ended up here?

Cat glanced at the podium. It was about five feet high and there was another large screen hanging thirty feet behind it, high above center stage. The woman Father Flanagan directed him to was nearby, but Cat felt like he had walked for an hour to reach her.

"Cat, good, you're on in three minutes. I'll signal you to walk over to the podium. We have another few songs to play, but the last ones will be a medley, and that's what you'll walk out to. Then, once you get to the podium, we want you to stand out there for a few minutes while we finish playing your music. After that, President Ramirez will appear on the video screens to introduce you and then you say what's on the teleprompter. Easy enough?"

"Yes" was all Cat said.

He closed his eyes and heard the beginning of "Pile up" over the loudspeakers. They picked a good one, didn't they? Instead of feeling chills, he now felt the burning heat of embarrassment. He never expected his own songs to humiliate him, but this time, they did. However, he wasn't ashamed of the words he wrote or the music he played. He was ashamed of who he was.

Halfway through 'Pile up,' the woman ordered him to go out onto the stage. "You're on now," was all she said as she pushed him on his shoulder.

Cat shook his head and obeyed. He plodded to the podium as a mix of cheers, boos, and screams rained down on him from the crowd. This was what they had waited for. He felt like he was the grand finale of a freak show and his sense of humiliation soaked deeper into his soul. Still, for reasons he couldn't explain, he kept walking to the podium and took his place behind the microphone and teleprompter and flashed a strained smile.

The music continued, and he swallowed hard and steeled himself for what he needed to do. He took a deep breath and waited. His eyes turned toward the screen beside him. He saw footage of the previous concerts and the ensuing riots. They looped a segment of him yelling at the plant in the crowd at the end of the melee. Subtitles repeated the lie that the plant said Cat had hurt his feelings. Next, they showed an image of Topper strung up and disemboweled. They cast the depiction of the corpse in stark red and black colors, and it flashed in and out for dramatic effect.

Abruptly, the music and videos stopped, leaving silence. Cat stood alone at the podium. He felt all eyes staring at him, since there was no video or sound. The crowd was briefly stunned by the sudden silence and hushed. The calm didn't last. They started screaming and chanting, some of it almost sounded tribal, as if they had prepared a script of what invectives they wanted to hurl at him.

Finally, the video screens resumed and displayed the symbol of the President of the United States. The crowd fell silent again. Cat could still feel the weight of all of their eyes on him. He felt naked and mortified, but he didn't move. He stood motionless and gazed back at the crowd and waited for Ramirez to continue the degradation.

"Good evening, my fellow Americans, and the rest of you." It was Ramirez's voice, but not her image. She spoke while the symbol of the President remained on the screens.

The crowd responded to Ramirez's voice with more boos, screams, expletives, and incoherent shouts. A fight erupted in the back of the field, prompting security to intervene. Cat didn't notice, but different security guards returned to the stage after the original ones left to break up the fight.

The presidential seal faded out, and Ramirez replaced it, which intensified the screams, jeers, and curses.

"I want to welcome you to the end of the beginning of one man's journey on his road to redemption. You should not admire this man, but you should see him as an example. An example of hope and the reality of our struggle. He's an example of just what's possible when a movement like ours takes hold."

More yells, taunts, and applause from the crowd. Security tried to separate the various combatants, but they made little progress. They couldn't control the mob.

"Thank you for coming today, because Carl needs our support. When he approached me about doing this tour, I asked him why? Why do you think that's necessary? You made that wonderful video and bared your soul. But Cat, sorry, I meant Carl said that wasn't enough. He asked me if he could do more. Do you believe that? Cat Chaotic of MicroAggression and Safe Spaces wanted to make sure that everyone understood he was wrong. He wanted to testify to you, my little darlings. He wanted to tell you the truth. When he asked, I listened."

Curiously, the crowd laughed at Ramirez's last statement. Regardless of their tribal allegiance, everyone in the audience recognized her blatant lies. Nobody believed her, not even her supporters. Everyone saw she had no clothes.

She continued lying to everyone. "Carl said he had heard that some people questioned just how sincere his awakening was, and I told him he had come to the right place. We, the government of the United States of America, stick by our friends and Carl McKnight, formerly known as Cat Chaotic, was now our friend. Of course, we would help him assure the people of our country that he had changed."

Cat resisted the urge to roll his eyes into the back of his head. She could really shovel some shit, couldn't she?

Ramirez picked up another heaping load.

"Before I turn this over to Carl, I want to remind all of you..."

Suddenly Ramirez stopped, and her face froze right in the middle of her sentence. The audio went silent. Her mouth was open but didn't move. The sound started again, but in halting, choppy words rather than sentences.

"For... speech... racist... code... Topper."

Cat watched as her face contorted. He thought to himself, my God, why was she doing this on Zoom?

Next, the screen pixelated, and a sharp noise pierced through the speakers. The screeching ended, revealing a frozen image of Ramirez's partially obscured face.

The crowd roared with laughter. Even Cat smirked at the all-too-common problem of the post-Covid age.

The screen went blank, and Cat glanced at the girl who directed him to the stage. She looked back at him and stuck out her index finger and began rolling her hand, mimicking the cranking of an old film projector. He guessed she wanted him to start his speech. Cat tapped his mic, but no sound came from the system. He looked back at the girl and shrugged his shoulders.

Then, ear-piercing feedback shrieked through the speakers again and the screens flickered. He guessed Ramirez had fixed her Wi-Fi and would be back on the screen soon.

The screen sputtered, revealing a person's outline. It looked masculine, so it probably wasn't Ramirez. Maybe it was some IT guy who would announce that technical difficulties would delay his humiliation for a few moments.

Indeed, it was someone making an announcement, but it wasn't an IT guy or anyone else Cat expected.

He watched the screen, but he couldn't see who was coming on. The image was still mostly pixilated. Suddenly, a booming male voice echoed from the speakers.

"Our dearly beloved *El Presidente* is having some technical difficulties, so in her place, we bring you alternative programming."

The voice mocked the "El Presidente" reference in a faux Hispanic tone. Someone had a pair of steel balls to call her that.

The distorted image prevented Cat from recognizing the person, but the voice seemed vaguely familiar. Clearly, this wasn't an IT issue. Who was it?

"Good evening, and welcome to a special edition of the Swamp Simmons Show."

Oh no.

Couldn't be him.

This had to be a flashback or a delusion. Or maybe the aftereffects of too much booze? Maybe Ramirez still had IT problems and someone mistakenly uploaded a Swamp video onto the screens?

It just couldn't be him.

Yet Swamp's voice continued. "Today we are interrupting all broadcasts and drawing back the iron curtain to reveal the real regime running the United States of America in all of its tolerant and uncorrupted glory." Swamp paused and smirked, just begging the crowd to applaud.

"Just kidding. Well, half kidding, really. Today, we're going to give you a glimpse of what your government is doing to one of its citizens and how your so-called betters have used deceit, blackmail, lies and violence to control you and your thoughts. That's right folks, America has now become a real deal dictatorship, a good time banana republic. Our air quote elites have stolen your inalienable rights. Those that were given to you by God himself. And, unfortunately, I'm here to tell you that you let them do it."

Despite Cat's shock at seeing Swamp on the screens, his mind jumped into flight mode. He scanned the area for an escape route. Questions raced through his mind. Is the crowd looking at me? Will anyone notice I've left? Where will I go?

He looked into the crowd and immediately noticed that they were completely silent. They stopped booing, cheering, fighting, and screaming expletives about his mother. Most of the spectators stared at Swamp. No one was really paying attention to him. This might be his only opportunity to escape. His instincts told him to run. Oddly, he stayed right where he was.

"And speaking of real, we technically have the real Cat Chaotic here, live and in the flesh. But I know I'm not the only one asking myself just who is the real Cat Chaotic? Is he the guy on the podium who 'apologized' to you in that video? Or is he the guy on stage singing 'A Day in Algiers'? Today, we are going to find out."

"You son of a bitch," Cat's inner voice screamed at Swamp. And then another thought occurred to him, "He's going to make me do it, isn't he?"

Oh yes, he was.

Swamp continued, "Let me tell you all what most of you already know. Someone is blackmailing or threatening Cat or, more likely, threatening someone he loves and cares about. He's not the type to get intimidated, he doesn't back down from anyone. I know he didn't make that video willingly. In fact, I'll bet those same people forced him to come here today and disgrace himself. Ramirez and her cronies want you to think that he has joined their side, but my guess is that he's a puppet. They want to make him into a mouthpiece for the fascists in charge. In fact, I predict that if we removed Ramirez's hands from his ass, he would tell you what he really thinks. But you know what? I'm not really sure."

"That motherfucker," Cat's inner voice spat more venom at Swamp. He knew what was coming, and it roiled his stomach. He was worried he might vomit and thought again about just taking off running. Unfortunately, he had missed his window since now the crowd had their attention fixed on him, wondering what he was going to do. They were no longer quiet, either. The pro-Ramirez faction screamed in rage at Swamp and his mother, and how they engaged in illegal acts with each other. Pro-Swamp supporters cheered and ranted wildly about what Ramirez should do to herself as well.

Then Swamp revealed his plan.

"So, I'm going to do a little experiment right here, right now, on live TV. Reality television at its finest. I don't need to tell you that this could either be one of the greatest moments in our history, or it could turn into Al Capone's Vault. And ladies and gentlemen and others, I can let you in on a secret. I'm going to tell you the God's honest truth. This is no lie. I honestly don't know what he'll do. I'm taking the biggest risk of my broadcast career and probably my life when I turn this over to Cat. Hopefully, I'm not wrong about him, but if I am, this will all blow up in my face."

With a smile, Swamp stopped speaking momentarily, allowing the significance of the moment to resonate with the crowd and viewers around the world.

He continued, "In the spirit of openness and honesty, I need to tell you two other things. First, I've jammed the feed of this broadcast, and no one can stop it. You will hear whatever he says, as he says it. Second, just so he can really speak his mind, I have planted my men in the crowd, and they will protect him no matter what he says. All those security guards you see are only there to protect him. We've, um, escorted the jackbooted thugs off the premises. No matter what he does or what he says, he will survive today. This is the only way we can ensure that we are all going to hear what the real Cat Chaotic thinks."

Swamp paused again and smiled at the crowd. He raised his eyebrows up and began nodding his head and softened his voice. "If I'm wrong and Cat has in fact gone woke, then you people can join him on his apology tour. If I'm right and Ramirez coerced or threatened him, then he can set the record straight. Like I said before, this is the ultimate in reality television. No producers, no editing, no bullshit, just balls to the wall free speech. Something this country desperately needs right now."

"Are you fucking kidding me?" Cat said audibly rather than to himself and just as he mouthed the words, he heard them reverberate through the speakers and the screens. He jumped back, as he didn't know the microphone was on.

Swamp laughed. "Oh, good Cat, you're still there. I forgot to tell you I turned your mic back on. Sorry about that."

Half the crowd roared with laughter while the other half of the crowd screamed in anger.

"You fucking asshole."

Swamp giggled. "Now I know you knew the microphone was on for that one, but that's probably the first real thought that's come out of your mouth in months. My God, the real Cat Chaotic might speak today."

Cat stared at Swamp's image and seethed. He said, "I'm going to fucking kill you," and the entire world heard him.

"Now there's the Cat I know and love. Well buddy, I would love to chitchat with you some more, but my time is limited and now it's your turn. You're the star of this show and all you need to do is tell everyone how you really feel. What are you going to tell them, Cat? You've awoken and all the things you did before were wrong? Or are you going to tell them the truth?"

Swamp smiled, Cat didn't.

"Just what's it going to be, boy? The fate of your soul is now in your own hands and the floor is yours."

Swamp disappeared, and Cat's image replaced him. He looked at himself on the big screen. The first thing he noticed was his expression. He looked miserable. His eyes narrowed, his mouth drooped, and he noticed that the creases on his face and forehead were deeper than they had ever been. He had bags under his eyes and looked much older than he pictured himself.

He kept staring at his image, and just a moment later, the look on his face changed. His features blurred, and he wondered if the camera's zoom effect altered his appearance. He looked down, hoping and praying it was true.

But it wasn't.

When he glanced at the screen again, Richard's face had taken over his body. What the hell was this? Had Swamp messed with the feed again? If Swamp hadn't altered the video, then Cat knew he had either descended into insanity or was seeing a ghost.

No matter what the cause, seeing Richard's image caused a strange feeling to wash over him. For the first time in a long time, he felt calm. He ignored the crowd and Swamp and focused on the screen where Richard's gentle and knowing expression had replaced his own. Maybe this was, in fact, Richard speaking to him from heaven, trying to ease his mind. That thought comforted him, and he smiled.

"It's okay," Richard's apparition said to him through a grin. "Do what you need to do. Everything is okay, I promise. You've got this."

And just as suddenly as Richard's likeness appeared, it vanished, and Cat saw his own image again. However, this time, his face looked serene. His features were neutral, which seemed odd but welcome. Inner peace would be really nice at the moment.

He glanced back at the crowd. As he did, he glimpsed at the teleprompter. Cat immediately noticed the first few words of the speech they were forcing him to parrot.

"I come to you a broken man."

He silently read the words again.

"I come to you a broken man."

As he repeated the falsehoods in his head, he balled his right fist and began rubbing his thumb up against the bend in his index finger. It was that twitch again. The friction produced a grinding sound as his thumb vibrated against the joint. That sound. Every time he heard it, he lost his temper. He didn't do it when he was just annoyed. No, this tic warned him he was about to explode.

Memories came rushing back to him as the rubbing noise grew louder. The flashes were just bits and pieces of recollections he had about Richard, Kendra, Trent, Robert, and Swamp. They all wanted to help pull America back from the brink of tyranny. They all knew it was dangerous. All the plans backfired and now he felt degraded.

He read the words on the teleprompter again, but this time he read them out loud.

"I come to you a broken man?" The words echoed through the crowd, but Cat unintentionally voiced the sentence as a question.

Did they break him, though?

Maybe they did? Or maybe they didn't.

He looked up at the crowd and this time his thumb opened up from his index finger and his fist slowly opened. That motion released the tension in his hand, and his right arm gradually drifted away from his body. He lacked control over this extremity, and his head followed his arm's movement. His eyes followed the floating appendage, and he saw his fist ball again, but then suddenly flew open as he grabbed the side of the glass teleprompter.

His left hand followed his right. Together, his hands clasped both sides of the screen, and ripped the glass off of the stand.

Cat brought the pane above his head and smashed the screen down on the floor, where it shattered into thousands of jagged shards of glass. He glanced down and observed the light reflecting and dancing on the fragments. Then Cat swung and toppled the second teleprompter. He slowly picked his head up and looked back at the crowd. He clenched his teeth and narrowed his eyes.

Cat had had enough. They hadn't broken him yet.

"Enough of that. They didn't break me. Not by a longshot." Cat remained oblivious as his words boomed through the speakers and radiated out over the world. The spectators were in a frenzy, but Cat couldn't hear them. They were fighting and pushing each other, but he couldn't see them. He only focused on his rage.

Cat scowled at the crowd and grasped the sides of the podium. He dug his fingers into the wood so hard that he almost put holes in it. The cheap particle board was no match for the pressure he inflicted on it.

Some audience members pushed through the crowd and rushed towards the stage. They made their way to the fence, which buffered the audience from the podium. One of them waved his fist and they all then turned around and formed a protective barrier. These must have been Jack's men.

Cat glanced to his left and spotted Jack with two guards. They smiled and nodded at him. Jack signaled Cat to look across the stage. Two men approached the podium. They stopped about ten feet from him and grinned.

Cat nodded at them, then turned back to Jack, who waved his hand and urged him to get on with it. Cat obliged.

"If you haven't figured it out yet, Swamp was right. He's an asshole, but he's right. Everything I said in that video was a lie." He spoke clearly, despite the narrow opening of his mouth as he ground his teeth.

Half the crowd roared in approval. The other half jeered. Cat didn't notice. He no longer spoke on behalf of America, the crowd, the band, or Swamp. He spoke for his soul.

"Yes, they coerced me. They beat me, they cut me, but you know what? Once they figured out that I didn't give a shit about myself, they went for my jugular. They figured out who I really cared about and that's who they threatened. These are the people that rule over you. They are sick individuals and I only agreed to repeat their lies because they threatened people I love."

The crowd had gone mostly silent. Cat noticed the change despite his rage. There was a stark difference between the screaming and cursing audience and the one that now hung on to his every word. That fact frightened him a bit because now his words mattered. He almost completely forgot that Swamp had broadcasted this to the universe, but the crowd's silence reminded him he needed to choose his words carefully.

Patrick Silken

"And why did they do it? Is it because I said some bad words at a concert? No, it's because they fear they can't control me. If they can't control me, then they can't control you and that's unacceptable to them because that's what they really want. Absolute control over your thoughts and deeds."

"And why do they want control? It's because they're frightened of you. They know that if you ever fully realized that our government has become a machine that only serves itself, then their reign will be over. You are an obstacle to their perpetual power. And they don't like obstacles."

"And how did they control us? This was not some Soviet-style brutal dictatorship straight out of an action movie from the eighties. They didn't roll over us with tanks or unleash shielded stormtroopers to beat us with batons. They didn't need to do something so outdated. All they had to do was change the language. Tell you what you saw and heard was not true. They gaslit you. They unleashed guilt. Once they did that, we controlled ourselves out of fear of isolation and financial ruin. Fear of shunning and banishment from society. They called us racists, bigots, white supremacists, and homophobes and tried to get us to believe that shit was actually true. They unleashed us against ourselves."

"And after all, isn't that what cancel culture is all about? Get people to control themselves and make the price of speaking out so great that no one would dare step out of line. It's what the Amish did with banishment. It's what the Romans did with Damnatio Memoriae and it's why the Soviet Union airbrushed rogue government officials out of their history. They use these tactics because they work. History has shown that."

"And that's another thing. Why don't these assholes live by the rules that they force on you? Did you ever notice all the armed guards that surround those who want to take your right to protect yourself away from you? The ones that want you to pay for green energy fly around in private jets? Do any of them live in the neighborhoods most affected by defunding the police? How many of them attended fancy dinners mask-less while they forced the help to wear those useless chin diapers? You are being lied to and ruled by hypocrites, evil fucking frauds, and it's time now to tell these assholes who's boss."

The majority cheered at the last line. It seemed like even those that supported Ramirez agreed the elites were charlatans. Cat continued.

"Oh, and these elites had accomplices in their scheme to control you. They corrupted the schools, the media, and big tech and other institutions and used them to lie to you. How did they do it? Sometimes it was outright falsehoods. Other times, they just ignored anything that didn't fit their narrative. How many times have they told you that something you saw with your own two eyes didn't happen? Or that you and your children have to pay for institutional wrongs that occurred centuries ago? How often have we seen the government target its justice system against those they fear or dislike, while shielding the corrupt as long as they're on their side?"

"That's what they did to me. A police officer took me to the station and some thugs beat me and sliced me up. Just like they did to Richard. They couldn't break me, and I told them to go fuck themselves. But guess what? That's when they got medieval on my ass."

"You see, they quickly realized that I could take a beating, but they also figured out that I was vulnerable to threats against my friends and family. No one else should pay my debts, but that's how they intimidated me into making that video and going on this public humiliation tour. Just ask yourself what would you have done in that situation? Would you let your children or your family pay the price for you?"

"I don't think you would. Most of us would take the hit ourselves. I have only a couple of things left to say before Ramirez and her thugs take me out for good. For what it's worth, I never thought I would say this, but the battle for America's soul is far from over. If you asked me that question twenty minutes ago, I would have told you the United States of America was done. But what I've seen today has changed my mind. There are those that will risk everything to save the country they love. Swamp and the guys protecting me here today have laid it all on the line. Robert, Kendra, Trent, all of them could have just let it go and lived the life of a rockstar. But they didn't, none of them did. And my dear friend Richard gave everything. He lost it all. But what he valued meant so much more."

"This is going to sound really strange right now, but I truly believe that America's best days are ahead of her. I know I've been ranting and raving about corruption and what happened to me, and it's hard to see how I honestly believe that, but I do. I think that our country is going to change and grow. Yes, no doubt, we have drifted so far away from our founding principles. But when a new day dawns and we find our way again, we will have learned that cancel culture is a failed experiment and future generations will never repeat our mistakes. Our time will serve as a warning to all that a government that colludes with the media, big tech and the educational-industrial complex is totalitarian. A government that does not respect the rights of its citizens to think, speak, and assemble freely cannot stand for long. It will inevitably falter, and power will have to be returned to the people. Dictatorships never last."

Cat had lost all track of time. He didn't realize that he had spoken for far longer than he had intended. He felt a tap on his shoulder and Jack was standing behind him. Jack beamed with pride, but also had a look of urgency. Cat covered the microphone so Jack could speak without broadcasting it to the world.

"Uh Cat, we need to go. That was amazing. I couldn't have said it better myself and I have to tell you now. Thank you. Everything I heard about you was true. Thank you for all you did, but we need to get you out of here."

Cat looked at him. He wasn't sure what Jack was referring to since he couldn't quite remember anything he said. He felt like he had just started ranting before Jack tapped him on the shoulder. Obviously, that wasn't the case.

"Yeah, you're right. Let me wrap this up then."

"Ok, but please make it quick."

Cat looked back at the crowd. The audience, mostly quiet, simply stared at him. Cat drew a blank on the best way to end his speech. So, he just spoke from his heart.

"Uh, my friend here says it's time to go, so I'm going to make a better decision than most of my prior ones. I'm going to listen to him but I want to say one more thing, though. Look, even I know that there will be consequences for what I've done today and nothing I said will make a damn bit of difference to the government. I also know that the threats that they've made against the people I love are not idle. They are real and all I can say to them is, I'm sorry. I just couldn't go through with it."

Cat closed his eyes, nodded his head down, and drew in a deep breath. He exhaled and raised his head up. His eyes narrowed, and he opened his mouth just a sliver as he gritted his teeth again. He spoke through the slight opening and his voice came out strong as a steel girder.

"But I want to make something absolutely clear. If you haven't listed to one fucking word I've said so far, I want you all to hear this."

He paused before he spoke to the world one last time.

"The game is on and I'm playing to win."

The spectators went into a frenzy. More fights broke out. Someone rushed the stage and one of Jack's guards flattened him before he could get anywhere close to Cat. Some in the crowd applauded and cheered. Others screamed profanities. Cat raised his index finger up as if he had something else to say. Just as he did, Jack put his arm around him and whispered in his ear.

"I know you have plenty more to say, but we really should go. I'm pretty sure that this is not the last time you're going to be in front of a crowd. We stay here any longer, and it just might be."

Cat lowered his hand and nodded his head.

"Yeah, you're right, we have to get out of here and I need to get to Arizona," Cat responded.

"Why Arizona?" Jack asked.

"It's a long story and we'll have some time later, but I need to go there. I need to find out whether I just signed a death warrant for someone I've never met, but who means the world to me."

"Well, I can't say I understand anything you just said, but you can explain it to me in the car while we're getting the hell out of here."

"That's a good idea."

They exited the stage and Jack directed Cat into a black SUV waiting in the parking lot. A few seconds later, it sped off into the Washington, D.C., twilight.

Chapter Twenty-One

Cuh-crunch, cuh-crunch, cuh-crunch.

Kendra got a warm feeling from the sound her feet made in the snow. The noise evoked a sense of nostalgia, since winter had always been her favorite time of the year. She spent some of her happiest moments as a little girl ice skating and sledding or simply enjoying the look and feel of a snowy day. Those memories were more meaningful to her when they involved spending a winter day out with her brother Douglas. They wouldn't come home until dusk at the earliest, to warm up with a bowl of her mom's homemade soup. Doug was the only person she knew who shared her love for snow. Kendra called him every time it snowed to tell him she was thinking of him and that he should get out and enjoy it. As time went on, she realized the snow melted faster than it used to when she was younger. Snow's fleeting nature was part of its magic. It's important to cherish certain things before they're all gone.

Today was ideal weather for her, clear, bright, and cold. The sky was as deep blue and brilliant as she had ever seen. Kendra wore sunglasses to reduce the intense glare caused by the sun's reflection off the snow.

It was just perfect.

Cuh-crunch, cuh-crunch, cuh-crunch.

She realized the only reason she could hear the crunching sound was because it was so quiet in the park. The sound differed slightly from the sounds of her childhood steps because she had worn her black boots with the funky heel. She never wore heels in her younger days, which made sense as her childhood felt like a distant memory.

Today, she walked faster than she did during her youth. Back then, she would have stopped and admired Washington,

D.C.'s monuments to the founders of her homeland. Sadly, only a few monuments remained after the riots and protests. Kendra didn't have time to waste on them today, anyway. She needed to get to Swamp's meeting, which started in fifteen minutes, and she was at least twenty-five minutes away. Not a big deal. They could wait, but she hated to be late for anything, so her unconscious mind pushed her to walk faster.

Cuh-crunch, cuh-crunch, cuh-crunch.

As she continued on her pace, the warm feelings of her childhood fondness for winter intensified and she forgot about how late she was. Then something in the back of her mind told her to stop and look around.

It was almost like a sense of déjà vu.

Even after she paused and scanned the area, she couldn't quite identify what caught her attention. She walked on a concrete path. On her left, she noticed several snow-covered trees that were set back from the walkway by about fifty feet. There was a grass expanse between the path and those trees. Kendra still didn't know what she was looking for, but this wasn't it. So she turned to her right.

She noticed a couple of wooden posts. They were about one hundred feet ahead. She wasn't sure, but assumed it was a sign explaining the area's significance. Something like, "Here once stood a monument to Thomas Jefferson that was removed because he owned slaves." There were plenty of those signs in the park. Still, there was something special about this place, but what was it?

A memory suddenly rushed back to her as she approached the posts. She flashed back to a Safe Spaces concert, but not a memorable one. There were no riots, disturbances, or stabbings. A regular concert where she performed music with Trent, Robert, and Cat, and the audience enjoyed themselves. Nothing more, nothing less.

But in this memory, she sang "Peaceful Life" as a duet with Cat. Playing that song live was one of her favorites. The first few lines kept running through her head.

"If you thought you'd lead a peaceful life, now you know you were misled."

This piece of data wasn't especially remarkable, and she couldn't understand why she remembered it now. Cat and the band had been on her mind frequently in the last several months, even though Safe Spaces had been on an unwanted hiatus. That break started when Cat told the world what he really thought. And if she was being honest, it wasn't the band that occupied most of her thoughts. It was Cat. She was so proud of him. She had replayed the speech in her mind many times since he left. Unfortunately, she would have to sort out her feelings some other day. For now, she remembered when he said his last words.

"The game is on and I'm playing to win."

Cat's speech.

That was it. That was why she couldn't shake the memories.

"Holy shit," Kendra thought to herself as she quickened her speed up to the posts.

Right before she arrived, she glanced behind the wooden structure. It was another nondescript, snow-covered field with no markings or monuments. Yet, this was no ordinary place. Although the makeshift stage with flanking big screens, screaming crowds, and brawling police officers had disappeared, this area remained hallowed ground for her. This is where Cat made his stand.

"Holy shit," Kendra repeated to herself.

She stood and stared at the field, reliving that fateful day in her thoughts once more. She remembered Cat's words and how he told the world how he really felt despite the danger he was in.

Kendra had spoken with him several times during those intervening months, but she hadn't seen him. He could be in Arizona, but she wasn't certain. Her feelings for him became needlessly complicated when she found out he may have a daughter, so she distracted herself. She focused on her work with Swamp, but, again, if she was honest, none of it worked. Kendra reminded herself that she and Cat had a lot to discuss. Yet the thought of him made her smile. She looked forward to that conversation and hoped she could tell him how she really felt sometime soon.

"If you thought you'd lead a peaceful life, now you know you were misled."

She lost track of time, mused through her memories, and went down several rabbit holes. Her concentration was deep, and unfortunately, she ignored her surroundings.

Kendra didn't notice the "crunch crunch crunch" sound behind her. It had started off faint but was now getting louder. She also didn't notice that the sound was picking up speed.

Crunch crunch crunch.

Kendra sang the same verse to herself and paid no attention to the sounds and didn't notice that it was footsteps. And they were getting faster.

At the last moment, she heard them.

She gasped as soon as she realized someone was there. Kendra had dropped her guard and now someone was behind her. She jumped up, startled, and her mind immediately switched over to survival mode. Waves of adrenaline flooded her body as she recognized the imminent danger. Despite her terror, a fleeting thought crossed her mind. "How could I be so stupid?"

She wheeled around and faced her attacker. Her immediate instinct was to scratch his face to pieces with her nails. As she raised her hand to claw at him, she realized she had gloves on.

"Whoa," was all she heard.

Finally, she looked in front of her and realized there was no attacker. Instead, she saw a tall, skinny teenage boy whose eyes were as big as saucers. The kid wore an open black leather jacket despite the cold. He probably had nothing more than a tee shirt on underneath. He completed the outfit with ripped jeans and a beanie hat.

They both stared at each other. While she tried to process who he was and what kind of threat he may be, he tried to avoid Kendra gashing him with her gloved hand.

"Hey, sorry. I didn't mean to scare you."

Kendra had unwittingly held in a deep breath and exhaled deeply after she realized the danger had passed. An immense cloud formed as she blew it out and it hung in the frigid air between them.

"No, it's ok, sorry I didn't mean to scare you either."

"I just wanted to give you this," he said and handed her a half sheet of red paper.

Her heart continued to pound, yet she calmed down enough to take the piece of paper from him. The teenager tacked a few more of those same papers on the board between the two posts. As he turned to leave, he glanced over his shoulder and said, "hope you can make it," and then disappeared into the park.

She looked at the paper he had given her.

She first saw the words at the top of the page "A Tribute" emblazoned in bold, black lettering.

Just below that was a lowercase "to" and just underneath that were the words "Richard Uprising, Cat Chaotic, Safe Spaces". Further down the slip was "The MicroAggression Experience" in black outlined calligraphy. The rest of the handbill contained the names of the bands playing at the concert, along with a QR code that provided further details.

Kendra stared at the page, stunned.

She realized that while this piece of paper in her hand may be small; it was enormously important. She glanced at the board where the kid had placed the other copies. What she saw left her speechless. There were stickers and posters plastered all over it. Some handbills promoted other tribute bands that played concerts in the past few months. Multiple stickers displayed phrases such as "The Real Cat Chaotic Spoke" and "The Game is On" and "Damnatio Memoriae" in highly stylized fonts.

Kendra couldn't look away. She tried to read every shred of paper posted on the board. Taking it all in, she realized it was time to let the past go. This was no time to reminisce. Uncertainty loomed, but these paper scraps and stickers revealed a shifting tide. She knew things were painful now and would get worse before they got better. But the future was too important to let the past consume her. They had a very real shot at winning this. She was damn sure that she would do her part not to waste the opportunity.

It was time to act.

Time to go for their jugular.

The game is on, and I'm going to win.

She clenched her teeth and started running to her meeting with Swamp.

Cuh-crunch, Cuh-crunch, Cuh-crunch.

As her pace quickened, a final thought crossed her mind.

"If you thought you'd lead a peaceful life, now you know you were misled."

Acknowledgements

Thank you so much Scott, Jim, Scott, Brian, John, Derek, and Rachel. I couldn't have done this without your invaluable feedback and help.

Summary

It's 2044, and the United States is in a dark place. Elections have consequences and America has chosen unwisely. The protesters are now in charge, and they've unleashed the enormous power of the federal government against their enemies. America's new ruling class has eviscerated the First Amendment, eradicated free speech rights, and will stop at nothing to hold on to their power. The government has become a machine that will crush anyone or anything it cannot control.

The regime cannot control Richard Uprising. He leads a rock band that stands up against the elites and their unquenchable thirst for power. What they do to Richard is unspeakable, but what they unleash may be America's last best hope. Join the band on their journey to freedom and find out what they can accomplish when they have nothing left to lose.

This story is a work of fiction from the mind of Patrick Silken. None of the characters in this story are real and any similarity to any real person is purely coincidental. This story takes place in the future, so by definition it hasn't happened, but could it happen? Well, you be the judge of that...

Printed in Dunstable, United Kingdom